'Don't run now,

Mariah said breathless... ...that unfair. You had yo...

'You can't change my mind,' Adam bit out.

'I wouldn't presume to. I know you're not going to stay,' she went on, her voice shaking. 'But at least leave me some memories to keep when you're gone.'

'Haven't you heard a word I've said?' he growled.

'Yes,' she whispered. 'And a few you didn't. You don't want to hurt me. You're concerned because you can't live up to my morals. We shouldn't run around because you can't marry me.' She took a deep breath. 'And I'm saying I don't care.'

Dear Reader,

June is definitely a hot month! Our latest HEART-BREAKER title, *Prime Suspect*, comes from Maggie Price, a woman to watch—she's new but she's very special. Maggie herself once worked as a crime analyst for a police department so she really knows what she's talking about.

Fans of hers will be pleased to see Beverly Bird return with a new set of linked books and these are unique; set against the background of the traditional Amish community and centring on the hunt for missing children. Look out for *Loving Mariah*; we thought it was terrific!

Mind Over Marriage is a very moving and emotional tale of a marriage granted a second chance when a wife *forgets* that she's divorced her husband! And finally, don't miss the latest instalment in Maggie Shayne's novels featuring the Brand family, *Badlands Bad Boy*. Wes Brand is part Comanche and a real lone wolf.

Enjoy them and come back next month, when Nora Roberts is kicking off a brand-new mini-series!

The Editors

Loving Mariah

BEVERLY BIRD

*Silhouette, Silhouette Sensation and Colophon are
registered trademarks of Harlequin Books S.A., used under licence.*

*First published in Great Britain 1998
Silhouette Books, Eton House, 18-24 Paradise Road,
Richmond, Surrey TW9 1SR*

© Beverly Bird 1997

ISBN 0 373 07790 4

18-9806

*Printed and bound in Great Britain
by Mackays of Chatham PLC, Chatham*

BEVERLY BIRD

has lived in several places in the United States, but she is currently back where her roots began, on an island in New Jersey. Her time is devoted to her family and her writing. She is the author of numerous romances, both contemporary and historical. Beverly loves to hear from readers. You can write to her at P.O. Box 350, Brigantine, NJ 08203, USA.

Other novels by Beverly Bird

Silhouette Sensation®

*A Man Without Love
*A Man Without a Haven
*A Man Without a Wife
The Marrying Kind
Compromising Positions

Wounded Warriors

Silhouette Desire®

The Best Reasons
Fool's Gold
All the Marbles
To Love a Stranger

For Ho-Ho Bear and his very best friend.
I sure do love you!

Prologue

"You know, if this one doesn't pan out, maybe you ought to think about shelving it."

Adam Wallace's gaze swiveled around to his brother. He folded one more sweater and placed it neatly in the open suitcase on the bed.

"You want to run that by me one more time?" he said, his voice too quiet.

"You heard me," Jake Wallace answered neutrally.

"Just trying to convince myself that I didn't."

Adam slapped the suitcase closed and crossed his arms over his chest. He was the shorter of the two, but he was broader, more solid, and he looked stronger, though that was misleading. They had had more than enough skirmishes over the years to prove that they were evenly matched in any fight. Even now, in their thirties, they could go at it like junkyard dogs when the situation warranted it.

Adam was starting to think this might be one of those times.

"He's my kid." His voice dropped another notch with warning.

"He's been gone for four years."

"Was there a statute of limitations on this? Did I miss something?"

"Yeah. You've been missing whole chunks of life for a while now."

Adam's eyes narrowed. "It doesn't matter."

"It ought to."

Adam swung.

Jake had agility on his side. He danced out of the bedroom door with a quick step to the left. "You done now?" he asked.

"No." Adam grabbed the front of Jake's flannel shirt, fisting it in one big hand, cocking back with the other. It only irritated him more that Jake showed no reaction.

"Are you telling me to give *up?*" he demanded. "To *forget* him? Yeah, that's your style."

Jake ignored the personal slight. "Listen to me, bro. We can wrestle over it later if that's what you want, but just hear me out first. All I'm saying is you've been obsessed with finding Bo for a long time now. Hey, I would have done the same thing in your shoes. And I've been right there with you most steps of the way, haven't I? But it's one thing to devote yourself to a war you've got a prayer of winning, and it's something else again to keep on butting your head against *something you can't change.*" He let those words hang between them a moment. "Adam, he's gone. Maybe you can't find him. Maybe there's not a damned thing you can do about this any longer."

There was a sharp, sudden pain in the area of Adam's chest, quickly replaced by a dull ache. He no longer felt like fighting.

"I can't accept that," he said flatly. He dropped his fist.

Jake smoothed his shirt against his chest with a quick frown. "Man, sooner or later you've got to."

"No. I'll find him."

Stubbornness was a Wallace trait, Jake reasoned. "Maybe you won't," he repeated just as obstinately. "Maybe Jannel took him and left the country."

Adam rounded on him again. "He's out there, damn it. It's like misplacing something in your own home. There's only so many places it could be."

"The world's a hell of a lot bigger than a home, bro."

"If I keep throwing out bait, somebody's got to bite."

"Man, we've looked and looked. We've chased down every lead, every hint, every long shot, for four *years* now. What are you going to do? Spend the rest of your life dashing around the country every week, every two weeks, looking into some godfor-

saken town, finding nothing? You've put every dime you ever
had into this!''

''Not quite.''

Luckily, there had been some significant dimes to start with,
Adam thought. They'd both been athletic kids. Jake's love had
been football. Adam's had been baseball. Adam, at least, had
gone on to play professionally. He'd spent some twelve seasons
catching for the Houston Astros and loving every minute of it
before he'd come home from a road trip one August to find his
wife and son gone.

He'd never seen it coming, and that had turned him into a bitter
man with a painful awareness of just how much of a fool he could
be.

He'd retired from baseball with two years left on his contract.
He'd moved out of his home in Dallas, though that and his va-
cation home in Galveston remained empty with mortgages still in
his name because they were both places Bo might manage to find
his way back to. He'd moved into this three-room apartment
above a storefront on Story Road, between Dallas and Fort Worth.
It was cramped and it was old, but it was reasonably close to the
airport. And Adam spent a lot of time moving through the airport.
He'd finally established priorities, and he attacked them single-
mindedly.

The storefront housed the unimpressive offices of ChildSearch,
a national network of mostly unpaid computer buffs who could
hack their way into anything. There were a few investigators on
staff as well—Jake was one of them, though he had always do-
nated his time. But most of the company's queries and searches—
both legal and those that fell into a gray area—centered on the
mind-boggling network of data bases a minor child might fall
into. The legwork didn't start until the computer guys got a hit.

In the four years since the company's inception, ChildSearch
had found roughly twenty percent of the children they had looked
for, a pretty good record. But his son hadn't been among them.
The company hadn't yet turned a profit, either, and even Adam
admitted it probably never would. Those parents who couldn't
pay staggering sums to find their child were never charged.

He jerked the suitcase upright and placed it on the floor. Ready
to go again, he thought. He wouldn't eat and he'd barely sleep
and he wouldn't come home until he had long since exhausted
this latest lead.

''It hurts,'' Jake said quietly. ''Hell, it hurts me, too, Adam.

He's my nephew. He's a Wallace. But you've got to come up for air here, bro.''

Adam's blue-gray eyes slashed in his direction again.

"Look what it's doing to you. All I'm saying is, you're going to have to make a choice soon. You can go on tearing yourself up like this, day after day. Letting it drive you. If this lifetime's all we get, then that's going to make for one miserable existence. Or when—*when*—it becomes clear that there's no more hope, you can try to put it behind you. Like a death in the family. You can't bring somebody back who's died, either. You've got to start over, Adam.''

"You're treading on thin ice."

"Yeah, well, I'm going to keep up until I crash through."

"You're close."

"I'm finished." Jake finally crossed the room to stand beside him. In a symbolic gesture, he began packing stacks of Bo's pictures into a briefcase that sat on the small scarred desk. "So what did I miss?" he asked. "Where are you headed off to this time? Did Berry or Philip come up with something?"

Adam shook his head. Bill Berry worked the computers out of Los Angeles. Philip Rycroft was an investigator based in Manhattan. They were two of the best resources ChildSearch had, and they *were* on the payroll.

"Milk-carton call," he answered.

"Oh, man." Jake tried not to swear. The milk-carton tips were wrong a good ninety percent of the time. Maybe some kid looked a little like the picture, but it was usually someone else. In a few spare cases, someone was merely trying to play hell and havoc with an enemy, tipping off the authorities that the kid they claimed as their own was actually stolen.

The cartons and mailers were especially iffy in Bo's case. He'd been three when Jannel had taken him. He'd be seven now. That made for a lot of changes. Bo's milk carton was one of the deluxe models, with a photograph on one side as he'd looked when he'd been taken, and an artist's rendering on the other of what he might look like today. But still...

"Just Bo?" Jake asked, looking for a trace of hope. "Or did they see Jannel, too?"

"She's not on the carton." Adam rarely spoke her name.

"Yeah, well, I thought whoever took the call might have asked."

"It was Rebecca. Yeah, she asked. But this kid was alone."

"Anonymous?" Most tips that come in on the hotline were. "Or do you actually have someone to interview this time?"

"No. She wouldn't leave her name."

Jake swore again. "Where?" he asked finally. "Where did she spot him?"

"Pennsylvania," Adam answered neutrally. The tension between them was all under the surface now. "Lancaster."

Jake nodded. He had been through that area once long ago, in a memorable summer spent traveling coast to coast after college. He briefly remembered his traveling companion, a leggy redhead whose name escaped him at the moment.

"The city or the county?"

"County." Adam finally relented. The hell of it was, he really couldn't remain angry at Jake all that long. The two of them were all they had left. "The caller said she saw a kid who looked like the picture in a farmer's market in a place called Bird-in-Hand."

Jake sorted through his memory. "That's a village. They're sprinkled all through there. The county's mostly rural. Farms. Lots of cows, corn and horse manure."

"Yeah."

"Low population." That was good, Jake decided, thinking like a detective again. "Spread out over a whole lot of acres." That was bad. "I can fly up on Wednesday, if you need a hand circulating the pictures." It was grunt work, legwork, but it was mostly how things got done.

Adam shot him a look that was almost a smile. "I'll call, let you know."

Jake thought some more. "It's Amish country."

"That's what I hear."

"Those folks can be a tough nut to crack. They don't always talk. They don't care for outsiders. In fact, they make it a religious point to keep to themselves."

Adam picked up the briefcase. "You've been watching too many movies. Kids are common ground. Most people put aside their differences to help find kids."

"Do we know anybody up that way? Someone who might get you an in?"

"Nope."

"Well, hold on to that famous Wallace temper, bro. Something tells me it won't get you far in the Pennsylvania Dutch heartland. And you might want to try out a few manners, too." Jake picked up the suitcase. "Need a ride to the airport?"

"Yeah." It would save on parking fees, Adam thought. Jake had had one good point: his money wasn't gone, but was getting to the danger point of running low.

As always, Jake read his mind. "You already live like a pauper," he muttered. "Like a damned *monk.*"

They went downstairs, onto the street, and walked half a block to Jake's restored '56 Thunderbird. The canary-yellow paint gleamed in the Texas sunshine.

"A woman," Jake went on, popping the trunk. "*That's* what you need, bro. A woman. Someone to help get your mind off all this once in a while." He heaved the suitcase inside.

"Jake," Adam said, going back to the passenger door.

"Yeah?" He looked over the car at him.

"A woman got me into this nightmare. Now shut up and drive."

Chapter 1

Adam allowed himself to think about Jannel on the flight north. Maybe it was because of Jake's lecture. It had started a panic inside him, like a scurrying animal in his gut that had just woken up and realized it was trapped. Not that he believed Bo was forever gone—no, he would never accept that. But he considered the way he had searched for him to the exclusion of everything else these past four years, and he knew why he had.

The closed goal-oriented life he had fallen into allowed him no time to be so foolish, so unutterably stupid, again.

He didn't trust himself. He just didn't trust his perceptions anymore. He'd been caught up in a world that wasn't real when he'd married Jannel, but he hadn't *understood* that it wasn't real—that was the hell of it. He'd been a grown man earning millions of dollars to do what sandlot sluggers were doing the country over, and he had reveled in it, considering it no less than his due, because he could hit that ball farther, he could throw that ball harder than nearly anyone else. Jannel had just popped up in the middle of it, and it had seemed right that he should have her, too.

He'd met her at a black-tie dinner at the Astros' owner's country club. If there had been flaws and imperfections in that room, outside of a few busted knees and pulled hamstrings suffered by the players, they were hidden well. The women were the crème de la crème, and Jannel had stood out even among that competition. She'd caught his gaze across that crowded room, held it and lifted one corner of her mouth into a smile. He'd fallen for her hook, line and sinker, then and there.

She'd been the perfect baseball wife. Independent enough not to whine about all the road trips. Blond, trim, sexy, she was the kind of woman who wouldn't even go out to get the newspaper in the morning without makeup. She'd gained a perfectly acceptable twenty-seven and a half pounds when she'd been pregnant with Bo. She gave parties, worked the team's favored charities and spoke of nothing that was going on inside her.

Adam hadn't realized that until it was over, that he could not remember even one single conversation between them that had concerned what she felt, what she thought, what she wanted or liked. They spoke of Bo, of Adam's schedule. They gossiped of teammates and debated current events. But she'd never easily given up any glimpses into what was inside her. There'd always been a certain aloofness about her. He'd thought at the time that it was just an independent streak. In retrospect, he knew she'd been cold.

Still, he had never thought it was a bad marriage. He'd been stupid, complacent, the worst kind of a fool, until he had come home from California on that hot August night to find her gone.

There'd been no note. No explanation. Some thought it odd that Adam hadn't suspected something was amiss when she hadn't flown west with the other wives for the big series against the Padres. But she'd had the flu the week before and she'd said she was still tired. Adam really hadn't expected her to go.

For a couple of shell-shocked days, he had been convinced that her disappearance was a matter of foul play. It happened to men in the national spotlight—rarely, but it happened. Then Jake had pointed out that most of her clothing and all her jewelry were gone. Their bank accounts had been cleaned out, and Bo and his favorite toys were missing as well.

Pain clenched in Adam's chest again and receded. He took a quick swig of his beer and nodded wordlessly when the stewardess offered him another.

Jake had just gotten his promotion to detective that summer. It was Jake who had taken on Jannel's missing-persons case, over the protests of superiors who felt that he was too intimately involved. He'd dug and dug while Adam had been paralyzed with confusion and the loss of his son. Jake had searched while Adam struggled with the shaming fact that he barely felt the absence of his wife of five years; the loss of his child, his boy, was staggering, and he didn't know how he was going to pick up the pieces and go on.

Jake had learned that the wealthy family Jannel claimed to have had in Miami, the family Adam had never met, did not exist. He'd learned that Jannel had a fairly significant cocaine addiction, which Adam had never suspected. And finally, he'd learned that Jannel Payne Wallace herself was...no one. There was simply no bureaucratic record of such a woman, at least not until she'd taken Adam's name. And that made her damned hard to trace, to follow.

All in all, he and Jake had finally figured out that she had made off with the better part of two million dollars.

That was when the rage had set in. Adam's confusion had given way to a hot need for revenge, a burning desire to make everything right again, to get his kid back, to make her pay. And out of that need, ChildSearch had been born.

What tortured him still was that she had not just asked him for a divorce. What blew his mind yet was that she had not taken the easy, dignified way out. Legal avenues would have allowed him visitation, maybe even custody of his son. They would certainly have afforded her plenty of wealth. She would have come out handsomely in a divorce settlement. She had to have known that.

Why?

Why had she taken Bo? Her pregnancy had been a surprise, unplanned, he realized, looking back. He hadn't consciously wanted a child—he'd been having too much fun playing ball to consider playing daddy—but with that first ultrasound, he'd known Bo's life for the miracle it was. Jannel, on the other hand, had been an adequate mother, but not even with her own son had she ever revealed any true, strong emotion.

Why?

Had she been coerced? Had she gotten herself in trouble somehow with one of the characters who supplied her habit? Had she been forced to run? But then why take Bo? And how the hell could two people, a strikingly beautiful woman and a little boy, disappear without a trace?

She'd come out of nowhere and had disappeared into an abyss, taking the one thing that really mattered to him. There were no answers. But he would keep looking. He would look until he drew his last breath.

The stewardess came and took his half-finished beer. They were landing.

Maybe this time, he thought.

It was something he had thought enough times before that he winced.

The first thing that went wrong was the weather. When he'd left Dallas, it had been a relatively balmy fifty-odd degrees. When he stepped out of Philadelphia International it was into the remnants of the previous week's blizzard.

Jumbled and clumped mountains of snow lined the roadways and the lots. These were no pristine postcard drifts—they were the angry testimony of countless scores of impatient people battling nature to get where they thought they needed to go. The heaped masses looked gray tinged and mean with their patina of exhaust fumes and smears of brown.

An arctic wind blasted him from across the rental-car lot. Adam zipped his jacket—nowhere near warm enough, he realized—and found a pair of gloves in his pockets. He ducked his head into the wind to try to find the car he had reserved.

By the time he reached it, he was frozen to the bone. He threw his suitcase into the trunk, swung his briefcase into the passenger seat and sat for a moment with the engine idling, waiting for some semblance of heat to fill the car. He studied the map they'd given him at the rental-car desk.

His gaze coasted over the pinpoints marking villages Jake had mentioned. Intercourse—that raised a brow. Paradise. Churchtown and Christiana, Angel's Cross and Divinity. Names that spoke of hope and promise, he thought. Maybe it was an omen.

He put the car into gear and drove, believing that until he got off the turnpike and hit Route 10 heading south. It wasn't a highway. In fact, with the snow crunched and shoved to either side of the road, it was barely a single lane. And that lane was icy.

It was heading downhill and curving around sharply to the right when the milk truck in front of him didn't stay with it. The truck went into a skid, and top-heavy, crashed over onto its side. Traffic stopped. People spilled out of their cars, shouting. There were a spattering of small businesses and some homes on the cross streets, and humanity streamed from the buildings, rushing to the stricken vehicle. Others went in search of the nearest telephone. By the time Adam recovered from his surprise and scrambled out of his car—only seconds, really—there was nothing for him to do.

The bystanders had helped a dazed-looking man out of the passenger door of the cab, now facing the sky. Adam stomped his feet. Damn it, it was cold.

He got back into his car shivering. An hour and a half later, he was still there.

He sat and glared. Impatience throbbed inside him, though he knew it was a little irrational. But there had been too many close calls and near misses with too many cases over the years. His heart thudded harder and harder with a sort of learned desperation. He became convinced that during this time he was stuck in traffic, Bo and Jannel would somehow vanish from Bird-in-Hand. She would know he was coming. Again—dear God, *again*—he would get there only to find that his boy was just...gone.

Adam smacked his palm against the steering wheel hard enough for it to hurt, then he heard a thoroughly alien *clop-thud-clop* sound from directly behind him.

He looked up sharply into the rearview mirror. It was a horse-drawn Amish buggy. Not that he had no experience with horses, but he realized he'd rarely heard one trotting on asphalt before. Or snow and ice and asphalt, as the case was, which explained the alternating sharp clops and muffled thumps of the animal's hooves.

He couldn't see the driver. The buggy was enclosed. But the long reins jiggled, giving direction, and the horse—a beautiful bay steaming with exertion in the frigid air—neatly picked its way around and through the snarled traffic. The comparatively narrow buggy slipped along the shoulder of the road with no problem, its right wheels up on the drifts, the left on the cleared roadway.

The driver passed the accident and went on his way. Too late, Adam jerked to attention, shoving against the car door. By the time he thought of catching a ride with the buggy, it was a quarter of a mile ahead.

What the hell was he thinking? He couldn't just up and leave the damned rental car in the middle of a road.

Jake's words came back to him, unwelcome and troubling. *Obsessed. Consumed.* He shrugged them off deliberately.

He was stuck for another hour. With the truck blocking the road, with the traffic jammed in both directions and hemmed in by the snow, the tow truck had an impossible time getting through. The injured driver had to walk to the ambulance—parked six cars back—under his own power. Dusk began falling, and though Adam wouldn't have believed it possible, the temperature plummeted right along with it. He turned the car on periodically to keep warm.

When he finally reached the village of Bird-in-Hand, it was nearly five-thirty. He began looking for the farmers' market with absolutely no intention of cooling his heels until morning, but he drove past the place four times before he finally noticed it.

No airy, open outdoor stalls in this neck of the woods, he realized. This market was indoors, in a huge warehouse-shape building. "Good enough," he muttered, parking and getting out of the car. Presumably it would at least be warm inside.

He tried the door and found it locked. The place was closed for the day.

He swore angrily and went back to the car. Fresh snow was falling. He was getting a headache.

"Chill out," he muttered to himself." Just calm down. Look for the bright side."

He was here. At least he had gotten here. And Jake the Master Detective had a theory: he always swore it was a lot easier to nab bad guys in inclement weather. He said blizzards and hurricanes were a boon for law-enforcement agencies, because even crooks shared the very human trait of heading for shelter when the weather got bad. They settled in somewhere, usually with a friend or at home, and they stayed put for a while. If at no other time, the cops could usually find them then.

Jannel would do the same thing, Adam told himself. If she was here, she would close the doors and pull the blinds and stay put.

If she was here. If this wasn't another wild-goose chase.

He started the car again and drove to the first motel he noticed, listening to a voice on the radio bemoan the current cold snap, warning that it would get worse and that there would be more snow by morning. The motel was an inn with a central section that was shaped like a boat. He stared at it blankly for a moment, thinking it seemed out of place in this landlocked country. Then again, he had seen palm trees in Michigan, an igloo in Pasadena and a miserable excuse for Paul Bunyan outside Miami.

The artificial sound of gulls piped over loudspeakers in the parking lot annoyed him, but he was able to get a room and—wonder of wonders—found a refrigerator and a microwave within it. He battled the roads again to find a convenience store, and came back to shove a frozen dinner into the microwave. He ate at the desk, pouring over maps, scowling at the artist's composites of Bo. He tasted nothing.

Too much farmland, he thought. If the farmers' market didn't pan out, he'd spend half his days driving.

By nine o'clock, there was nothing left to do but wait for morning. He hated the waiting the most.

By three o'clock the following afternoon, he was still empty-handed. As always, it brought a near physical pain of frustration. A sensation of pressure leaned on his chest and there was a knot of tension behind his eyes. It made his voice harsh, his face hard, his motions abrupt. People stopped talking to him willingly, and he had to browbeat them into answering questions.

He had covered every single booth in the market. He would have been finished sooner, but the sky had dumped another few inches of snow on the county overnight. Some of the merchants had been late opening. None of them recognized the composite of Bo. None of them thought there was anything familiar about his picture taken four long years ago.

Adam stopped at the snack bar, more out of a need to regroup than to eat. He wolfed down a hot dog, not bothering with catsup or mustard or relish. He was eating purely for sustenance, because intellectually he knew it was time for a meal.

He didn't see the elaborate and finely stitched quilts hanging from rafters overhead. He didn't appreciate the prime steaks and beef in the display coolers, nor did his mouth water at the rows upon rows of canning jars filled with relishes and homegrown vegetables and fruits. He chewed and he thought, and he finally noticed that some of the shoppers passing by had a relaxed but competent air about them.

He sat up straighter on the stool, his eyes narrowing. They weren't browsing, he realized. They had come specifically for some item. So it was reasonable to assume that they had been here before, maybe even the previous Friday.

He got to his feet again abruptly and threw a bill on the counter. He started to move off without waiting for change, remembered his vow to pinch pennies a little and drummed his fingers on the counter while the man collected his money. Good thing, Adam realized. The bill had been a ten, and the hot dog had cost a dollar seventy-five.

He finally began moving up and down the aisles with new purpose. He stopped strangers and asked if they had been there on Friday, the day the anonymous woman had called Child-Search's number on the milk carton. He showed both the composite and Bo's old picture around once more. And got nothing, not even a nibble, not the slightest hesitation before the invariable volley of "Sorry's" and "No's."

It seemed impossible. *Someone* in this building on Friday afternoon had seen a boy who looked like Bo's composite. But even Adam was reasonable enough to know that he was not going to find that someone today.

Some of the merchants were beginning to close up. He folded the dog-eared pictures carefully, almost reverently, and tucked them into his jacket pocket. His mind kept going in all the directions Jake had taught him as he went back to his rental car. Where did people *have* to go? To post offices. To grocery stores. They needed remedies for their colds and to get their hair cut periodically. If that person was Jannel, she would need cosmetics and to get her nails painted as well. He would go back to his room, lay his hands on a phone book and make a list of all such places. He would begin visiting them tomorrow.

He drove back to the motor inn. At the traffic light on Route 30, he hit the brake and remained there long after the light had turned green again. Horns beeped behind him with surprising politeness, as though to remind him to move rather than to curse him for tying up traffic.

He made a sudden decision and put his turn signal on. He veered out of the left-turn lane, back into traffic and crossed the intersection.

Farmland.

He had started with the village of Bird-in-Hand because it was the orderly, practical way to begin a search. Bo had been seen there, and Jannel was a woman who liked civilization. But if she wanted to get lost like a needle in a haystack, well, then, it had always been his experience that haystacks were found on farms.

He didn't expect to find her crossing a road. He didn't anticipate a hand-painted arrow pointing in her direction, not even in a village called Divinity. He noticed the welcoming sign—a weathered plank of wood on the side of the road, bearing the name and a design of blue flowers. He passed through another quaint cluster of buildings, then the land opened up into rolling fields again and he cruised. And this time, almost in spite of himself, he noticed that the area was beautiful.

He had crossed a road and entered into another world. And it was a world where time had not so much stopped, he realized, as it had slowed down and stalled. The snow that had irritated and thwarted him since he'd gotten here now gleamed an almost ghostly blue. Streaks of orange from the dying sun flayed it in patterns cut by the slanting shade of the trees. He found himself hitting the brakes again and again, pausing, as he passed orchards. The trees were bare of leaves, but their naked limbs were alive with glittering diamonds.

A fairy land. He was a little embarrassed by his own fanciful thought.

He saw a windmill—a working windmill, for God's sake—turning slowly. Ice had fanned out from each of its paddles and winked in the sun. He drove on, feeling more curious than urgent now.

Some cows stood pressed against the leeward side of a huge barn. They turned bored, inquisitive eyes on the car as he passed.

There were silos and old two-story farmhouses. There were poultry buildings and carriage houses—not antiques, not restored but the real thing. The few horses he saw—he imagined most of them were in their barns at this hour—all looked healthy and sleek and strong. And land. There was a lot of land, enough to strike even a man from Texas. It rolled and undulated to form tree lines that rose over more hills and reached for the sky. And the virgin snow remained unblemished by anything other than foot- and hoofprints now and again.

A frozen creek curved around the next homestead. The road followed it for a while, and he drove through a covered bridge before he actually realized what it was. Then he came out and followed the ribbon of black road again as it snaked on through the whiteness.

Another world.

He realized that it had been a long time since he had seen another human being. He had just begun wondering about that when he spotted a boy trudging along the edge of cleared macadam. He was ten, maybe twelve, and because of that he didn't bring the immediate thump of hope to Adam's heart that he might have if he had been younger. He was dressed all in black, in a woolen jacket and broadfall trousers and boots. He wore a wide-brimmed hat. Given the scenery, he didn't seem out of place or odd at all.

Adam was well past him before it occurred to him to show him Bo's picture, and that amazed him, too. He stopped the car and looked back, but the boy had already turned up a drive and had nearly reached the house at the end of it.

Adam let out his breath and drove on. And then, as though God in the outskirts of a village called Divinity was giving him a second chance, he saw a woman.

She, too, wore black—stockings and shawl and shoes. But a flash of azure showed beneath her dark apron. It was startling enough in the monochromatic landscape to snag his attention right away. She drew the shawl protectively over her head as flurries began drifting down yet again.

She picked her way toward a mailbox. Adam coasted to a stop beside her and lowered the passenger-side window. She kept walking but her spine jerked straight, as though she knew she was being stared at.

He took his foot off the brake and coasted forward again. When he was abreast of her this time, he called out to her. She paused and looked at him.

"Can I help you?" Her voice was polite, neither warm nor cold. She was startlingly pretty. He noticed flyaway strands of golden hair; the cruel, relentless wind had dragged them free from the white bonnet she wore beneath the shawl.

"I need help," Adam said simply, as he always did. "I'm trying to find my son."

The woman's reaction was the same as he had gotten the world over. Mention a missing child, he thought, and nearly every human being softened to some extent. This woman's eyes widened and she took a half step closer to the car.

"Has he run away?" She looked out over the fields as though she thought to spot him there. "He'd be cold if he hasn't found shelter. Why did he come out this way?"

"No. That's not it. He's been kidnapped."

That had her retreating again, fast. Her expression closed down. "I doubt if you'll find him here, then."

"I have reason to believe he *is* here. Can I show you a picture?"

Her gaze veered away. "We don't steal children, mister. We have plenty of our own."

"My wife stole him."

It was the part that usually brought a flare of understanding to most people's eyes. This woman looked back at him, horrified, then frightened, then unsurprised.

"It's a cruel world you live in."

She came forward again. "The picture?"

He gave her both of them, the composite and the one as Bo had been four years ago. Unlike many people, this woman studied them thoroughly. Then she frowned as though worried or concerned.

Hope flared.

"Is he Amish, then?" she asked finally.

The hope ebbed, leaving his voice sharp. "No. I told you. He's my son."

"Katya!" came a masculine voice from the house.

The woman jumped visibly. For a brief moment, her eyes reminded him of a doe caught in headlights, panicked, trapped, believing deep in her heart that it was useless to try to move or run.

She thrust the pictures back at Adam. "I must go."

"Wait! Why did you ask me if he was Amish?"

She looked at him helplessly, torn between answering his question and responding to the bearded man who was still shouting from the porch. "You should ask the woman at the school," she blurted and turned away.

"A teacher? What school?" She was already walking away. Adam bit back on a curse. "What's her name?" he called out.

She looked back at him fast and kept walking. "She hasn't one."

"She doesn't have a *name?*"

"We don't recognize her," she called back.

"Katya, I want you in here *now!*" the man roared. Adam fought the urge to get out of the car and plant a fist in the guy's jaw.

"Give me a minute here, would you?" he shouted to him, then he remembered his brother's warning. With an effort, he added, "Please."

It didn't help. The man started down the porch, and Adam thought he heard the woman gasp in alarm.

"Look, I need something more to go on here...uh, Katya," he tried desperately. *Please, don't let her slip away.* But his thoughts were already rolling on ahead. He would remember this farm. He could come back, ask more questions, when the man wasn't around.

Katya looked back at him frantically, as though reading his mind. "I can't help you. Please don't return. You'll cause me trouble. Just ask the woman at the school!"

She began to run up the drive. Adam watched her. The man caught her elbow when she reached him and propelled her the rest of the way to the house. Something old and nearly forgotten twisted Adam's heart momentarily, then he put the scene out of his mind again.

He headed back to the motel. He'd call Berry, he decided, and have him dig into the school records in Lancaster County. But Katya's voice kept coming back to him and he realized Berry probably wasn't going to find anything. Not only because it was damned hard to do so through educational databases—it was a sure bet that Jannel had changed Bo's name and there were millions of seven-year-olds out there with blond hair and blue eyes. But because of the question the woman had asked him.

Is he Amish, then?

A staggering thought hit Adam. It carried enough impact to make him pull off the road again. Was *that* how Jannel had been hiding them? Was she pretending to be Amish?

No. Impossible. He simply couldn't believe that she had been so unhappy with him that she would hide from him in plain black stockings and serviceable shoes. Not Jannel. Not a woman with a cocaine habit, a woman who fairly kept her hairdresser on retainer.

You should ask the woman at the school. We don't recognize her.

Okay, he thought, driving again. Okay. There was a reason Katya had looked at Bo's pictures and had made that suggestion. His pulse quickened as he sorted through it. Did the Amish send their children to public schools? Maybe they didn't, and that was why Katya hadn't known what to call the teacher, because her own child or children did not go there. But, then, why suggest that he talk to her?

What's her name? She hasn't one. It was an odd way of putting it, but he thought it might equate.

He got back to the motel and stopped at the front desk. "Question," he said to the girl there. She was the same one who had taken care of him when he'd checked in the night before. She'd been irritatingly eager and friendly then, wanting to waste his time with chitchat, and she was no different now.

"Sure." She grinned, leaning over the counter toward him. "What can I help you with?"

He thought sourly that if she leaned any farther with that cleavage she was going to have an accident. Something about her eyes told him she probably wanted to.

"Do the Amish send their kids to public schools?"

"Oh, no. In fact, the Supreme Court exempted them from mandatory attendance beyond the eighth grade back in '72."

"So where do they go *until* the eighth grade?"

"They have their own little schoolhouses."

"Where?"

When her frown deepened, he realized he was shooting questions at her quickly and harshly. He didn't care.

"Well, they're all around," she answered finally. "On the farms."

"The *farms?*"

"That's right. The parents donate the land. You can usually tell them because they sit all by themselves, you know, without a lot of barns and other stuff around them. They're usually at the far end of some field. Sometimes there are baseball diamonds or a swing set or some such thing. And they're small. I mean, eight grades are all squeezed into one room. Can you believe it?"

He was startled. "In the nineties?"

"Well, they're not, like, in the nineties, you know."

He thought again that it wasn't a place for Jannel. And maybe that was why it was the perfect place to hide. He turned away.

Berry could check the public-school records, Adam decided. He'd get up in the morning and drive the back roads, looking for little buildings sitting by themselves at the edges of fields.

Chapter 2

Mariah knew who he was as soon as he stepped out of the automobile he parked in front of the school.

It was late and her students were gone. She'd spent an hour grading the papers her older children had turned in that morning, and she was just straightening the desks and sweeping the floor when she noticed the dark red car beyond the window. She put the broom aside with exquisite care and went to the glass to watch.

So, she thought, he had found her. That was a good sign, that he was astute enough to have gotten this far. It also made her heart skip a beat.

His appearance startled and intimidated her. She hadn't expected someone so...well, formidable. She hadn't anticipated that his face would be so hard. Then she understood her reaction. He was well into his thirties. The shaven faces she saw most often were all much younger than Adam Wallace's. It was the people's way for a man to grow a beard as soon as he was baptized and married, and most Amish men married by the age of twenty-five.

Not that she couldn't have encountered many clean-shaven faces of some age, if she had simply strolled through one of the villages or the city of Lancaster. But she didn't do that often. It was difficult enough to remain here, in the heart of the settlement.

In either place, she was different, set apart, painfully alone, but here, at least, she was alone among the dear and the familiar.

She scowled as Adam Wallace approached. He was aggressive, she decided. And very determined. It was in the way he moved. He had an athletic stride, a sort of unconscious confidence about him. He had golden hair and it was a tad long—not by Amish standards, of course, but by those of the *anner Satt Leit,* the other sort of people who lived in the villages and the city. It was wind-blown and unkempt, and he kept tunneling his fingers through it as though to tame it, when what he really needed to do was harness the wind that tussled with it.

As a boy he would have been almost pretty, she realized. He was very attractive, and the dimple on his chin made something squirm briefly inside her. But age and time and care had etched his features, bracketing his mouth with small furrows. His eyes were pale, and he wasn't really dressed for the cold.

Adam felt someone watching him, but he couldn't be sure where the gaze was coming from. He glanced around and saw no one. There was a barren field behind the school building. It had been plowed recently for some reason. Brown showed in neat rows through the snow. A white three-board fence separated it from the building—also white, with a gray shingled roof. He could tell because the warmth of the smoke had melted the snow near the chimney.

It looked like a plain but cozy house. A long eaves trough hung out over the front porch, shielding it from the elements, so that, too, was clear of snow. White posts supported the eaves. There were two windows, and a paper cutout of a snowman taped to the glass of the door.

He stepped up onto the porch, stomped the snow off his boots and knocked. Though he was cold and disgruntled and feeling a hell of a lot more pessimistic than he had two and a half days earlier, suddenly, out of nowhere, his heart began to pound.

This was it, came an unbidden thought, though he had no particular reason to believe it.

It had taken him a long time to work his way down to this particular schoolhouse. If things didn't work out here, he was back to square one. There were a whole lot of schools sprinkled over the Amish countryside, a circumstance he'd understood once he'd begun looking into them. The Amish were thriving. Through a healthy birthrate and a tendency to fiercely protect their way of life and keep people within the fold, they numbered over one hundred and thirty thousand strong. It was not uncommon for a family to have as many as ten children. Less than six was a rarity.

Lots of children, he thought. And one-room schoolhouses in which to teach them all from first through eighth grade. With families sending so many kids to a single school, it made sense that each one could serve only a dozen or so households.

Lots of children, his mind insisted again. And he had searched through every one of them for a single small boy, because Berry had come up with nothing on the computers. It was still possible that Bo was enrolled in one of the public schools, and Adam would turn his efforts to visiting them personally if and when he found nothing here.

He knocked again. "Hello!" he called, moving to peer in one of the windows. The door finally opened, even as he took a step.

"Yes, hello," came a soft, breathless voice. "Can I help you?"

Adam looked back over his shoulder. And stared.

He had learned about more than just the Amish school system in the past couple of days. He'd been told, too, that the reason the people all dressed alike, in plain clothing, was so that no one individual should stand out. The sin of arrogance and pride, he thought, and he knew immediately that this woman would stand out anywhere, no matter what she wore, even if it were sackcloth.

Her clothing was nearly identical to Katya's. Black tights, black shoes, a dress of deep purple beneath a black bibbed apron. Her hair was very dark and pulled back, parted severely in the middle. She wore a white bonnet and not a breath of makeup. Altogether, it should have made her look homely and plain, but it didn't even come close.

It was her eyes, he reflected. They were the most vivid shade of violet he had ever seen.

No, it was her face. Every feature fit perfectly and smoothly with the next.

Maybe it was just everything all together, he thought, that rich, dark hair and the exotic eyes and a porcelain complexion. She was trim and reasonably tall. Or maybe, he realized, maybe it wasn't anything *physical* about her at all.

Maybe it was her...peace.

He frowned when that struck him. She watched him steadily, without impatience, her hands clasped together in front of her, and he got the feeling that she would do it all day if need be.

"You're staring at me," she said finally, softly.

Adam jolted. For the first time in his life, he actually blushed. "I'm...uh, sorry."

"Was there something in particular you wanted here?"

"Yeah." He was rattled, he realized, and that alone was amazing. He began digging in his jacket pockets for Bo's pictures before he remembered that he had last slipped them into the back pocket of his jeans. He felt himself flush again and hardened his jaw.

"I'm looking for a boy."

"Then you've certainly come to the right place. I have many here to choose from."

He looked at her sharply, wondering if she was being sarcastic. But of course she wasn't. He doubted if she had the capacity for caustic wit. Something about her was just too...gentle. Too serene.

"My son," he clarified, finding his voice.

"I see." Her brows went up prettily. "And you think you'll find him in an Amish schoolhouse?"

"I have reason to think so, yes." He thrust the pictures at her. Mariah took them, but she didn't look at them. She didn't have to.

Her eyes stayed on his face. Adam had the uncanny feeling that she was searching for something.

"Come inside," she said finally. "It's cold. You're shivering."

She stepped back and disappeared through the door again. Adam followed her. It was true that he was cold. He'd been cold since he'd stepped off the plane on Sunday. What shook him now was that the woman had not appeared to be uncomfortable in the wind at all, and she had been standing on the porch without the benefit of coat or shawl.

His heart thudded oddly. There was something almost otherworldly about her, and that was yet another whimsical and thoroughly uncharacteristic thought.

"Tell me about your boy," she prompted, perching neatly on the edge of a desk. She still hadn't looked at the pictures, he noticed.

"My wife...my ex-wife took him." He had learned not to use the word "'stole'" around these people. They were simply too shocked by such a concept. "Four years ago, when he was three. He's seven now."

"That makes sense."

He felt another jolt. She *was* being sarcastic, he realized. But somehow she pulled it off with such mild gentleness that it didn't sting.

"I haven't seen him in a while," he went on. "I...don't know what he's like now. What he enjoys. What he hates. I just don't know anymore."

The pain in his eyes almost decided Mariah right then and there, and she wasn't a woman given to haste. She had to steel herself against it. She had to be sure.

"I see," she said quietly. "I'm sorry."

"I can tell you that he tried to climb an apple tree when he wasn't quite three. He fell out and landed on the fence underneath, and he's got a little scar right about here." He touched his chin.

Mariah swallowed carefully. She had been right, then. This man was the boy's father.

"He's seven," Adam said again, "and he's blond and he's got eyes like mine. I know there are a million kids out there like that, but this one has a scar right below his lip and he used to have this sly, kind of mischievous way of moving his eyes to the side and—"

He broke off abruptly, looking almost lost. Mariah watched him and her heart hurt for him all over again.

She finally looked down at the pictures. "Why are you looking for him here?" she asked, stalling.

"Someone called my company—we search for lost children— and said they saw a boy matching his description in a farmers' market in Bird-in-Hand. I checked there, but nobody recognized the pictures."

"And?"

"So I started asking anyone I saw. People on the roads. And a woman named Katya told me to ask a woman at a school."

"Katya Essler."

His pale eyes narrowed. "She lives up the road a way." He motioned with his thumb. "She has an impatient brute of a husband."

"Yes. Frank. That's the one." She smiled briefly, but it was not a happy look. She sighed. "They're not the norm. Please don't let them color your perceptions."

Adam frowned, wondering why his perceptions should matter.

Mariah handed the pictures back to him. "I'll keep my eyes open for him. I'll look around."

Adam made an ugly sound. "Don't bother. If he's not your student, then he's not here. He's not in an Amish school. I've been to all the others." He started to turn away, then he looked back at her sharply. "Do you have a name?" he demanded suddenly.

"Yes."

Adam scowled. He thought she'd hesitated for the briefest of moments. He thought he'd seen pain—something deep and profound—in those violet eyes.

He finally shook his head. He wasn't even sure exactly what he was asking.

"You're not the one, then," he muttered. "You're not the teacher Katya didn't know. The one without a name. She told me specifically to ask that one about my Bo." He raked his fingers through his hair again. "Hell, maybe she *did* mean a public school." To go through them, he would need Jake, but he'd start first thing in the morning without him, working on his own until his brother could get here.

Mariah's breath snagged. *My Bo.* There was something about the way he said it. She hesitated, then compromised with her caution. "It's me."

He looked at her vacantly. "I'm sorry?"

She took a deep, careful breath. "It's me. I'm the one without a name."

Adam was confused. She had just said she wasn't...and if she *was,* then why didn't she know Bo? Something hard and hot lodged in his throat and he crossed back to her quickly.

"Do you know something?" he growled. "Are you playing with me?"

"No." No, she definitely wasn't playing. Mariah felt her pulse scurry. Anger and frustration came off him in waves now. And they had another effect on her, too, one she was not quite willing to name. He was big, strong and in spite of all she had learned to deny over the years, he was so *male.* She had learned not to appreciate that which she could not have.

Even his scent was masculine and strong, she thought, and it hit her now because he was standing close to her. She had to look away from his eyes—as cold and gray as metal, though she had thought earlier that they were blue. She dropped her gaze to his hands, and they were big, too. They were fisted now.

She realized she was flustered. She had not bargained on this man, on this particular man.

"I didn't say that," she went on a little breathlessly. "I didn't say I know where your son is. I just said that I'm the woman without a name.''

"And a minute ago, you told me you *did* have one.''

She smiled thinly. "You don't understand.''

"So enlighten me.''

He was quick. She liked that. It made her want to smile. "I was born Mariah Fisher.''

"Okay,'' he answered, and his voice held a measure of waiting.

"They no longer call me that,'' she went on.

"So what do they call you?''

"Nothing.''

"Why?''

"They don't see me anymore.''

"They don't *see* you? What are you, a ghost?'' He remembered thinking earlier that she seemed otherworldly, and though he was a practical man with a good many worldly concerns, a man who didn't believe in such things, it shook him up a little.

"In a manner of speaking,'' she said quietly, with that pained small smile again. "It's called the *Meidung*.''

"Meidung,'' he repeated, echoing the German accent her voice had suddenly taken on.

"Yes.''

"In English?'' he prompted.

"I'm...I'm been...shunned.''

Adam cleared his throat carefully. "Shunned.''

She came off the desk and drew herself up, turning her back to him. "Our people have a certain way of doing things, a code of good and acceptable behavior. I acted differently. I...sinned. Now they don't see me anymore.''

He was flabbergasted. "That's archaic.''

"Not really.'' She finally looked at him. "Sin is a common Christian theme.''

"Yeah, and God accepts apologies,'' he snapped.

Her fleeting smile came back. "So He does. As do the Amish. I, however, will not apologize.''

His head was spinning. For the first time, there was a bit of a bite to her voice. "So they just shut you out?'' he asked. "Pretend you're not there?''

"More or less.''

"But you teach their children.''

"There is that.'' She went to a coat hook on the wall and plucked off a plain black jacket and a shawl. "There are several reasons for that, actually,'' she went on, shrugging into the short coat, pulling the shawl on over it. ''The first is that they have a somewhat limited choice. They needed a teacher for this house, and no one else volunteered. It's difficult for a woman to do this job if she has a family to care for, and most of the women in this *Gemeide* are married with little ones.'' She caught his look. ''This district,'' she clarified. ''A *Gemeide* is a church district. And the church is the utmost authority. It runs the schools.''

''So they're stuck with you, whether they like it or not.''

A short, quick sound escaped her, almost like laughter. ''Something like that. For the time being, anyway. Someone else will come along eventually, and then I'll be gone.''

''What are the other reasons? You said there were several.''

''Ah, well, I've vowed to teach nothing beyond what is acceptable to them. That was their biggest concern.''

Adam thought about it, frowned, then shrugged. ''That's a pretty common situation between employers and employees all over. You've got to do the job the way your boss wants it done.''

''Have you been all over?'' she asked suddenly, and she seemed intent on his answer.

''I've seen a lot.''

Looking for his Bo, no doubt. She realized suddenly that she was almost certain she would help him now. It was too soon to be absolutely sure, but she had a feeling she could trust his heart. She was sure there was one in there, underneath that gruff hustle-and-hurry exterior. And if she could just trust his heart, then perhaps *he* would help *her*.

It was what she had bargained on.

''Come back tomorrow,'' she said, moving toward the door. ''A little earlier than this, though. I'm usually gone by now. You got lucky today.'' She wondered if, subconsciously, she had been waiting for him.

Anger hardened in Adam's gut again as he watched her go. How had he allowed himself to get sidetracked by her pained smile and her deep violet eyes and strange stories? His gut clenched as he realized that that was exactly what he had done.

''Where is he, Mariah?'' he demanded, following her. His voice grated. ''You're transparent as glass. Damn it, you *know* something.''

''I'm going to look into it for you.''

He grabbed her arm. She spun back to him fast, gasping a little. Her mouth stayed open in a silent cry, though he couldn't be sure if it would have been one of outrage or fright, because she wouldn't let it out.

"You *know,*" he said again, angrily. "Something. This is my kid we're talking about, and I want answers."

"And I would like very much to be able to give them to you," she said evenly, her eyes huge, "assuming you stop manhandling me."

He felt shame, even as his fury burned. "I'm sorry," he bit out, dropping her elbow, stepping deliberately away from her again. Then he heard his own apology and wondered what in the hell this woman was doing to him. *Sorry?* For doing whatever it took to get answers about Bo?

"You should be," she chastised.

"Don't push it. What the hell do you want from me?"

"It might be a start if you'd stop swearing."

"What difference does it make? You're not...you're not devout. You just stood here and told me that you were *Mei*—" He couldn't quite remember the word she'd used. "Whatever."

"I committed one specific sin that I will not confess guilt over," she said, and he realized that her voice was hot now. Hot yet soft. Velvet and fire. It was, he realized, like the warning growl of a cat.

"I came back here in spite of that," she went on, "even though I knew what awaited me. And I did that because outside of my *one* transgression, the *one* area in which I strongly disagree with the church, I believe in the way in which I was raised." Her eyes narrowed. "That Amish way does not advocate coercion, physical or otherwise. There's no need to drag me about, and there's certainly no reason to swear at me."

"Yeah, well, old Frank seemed to drag Katya a bit," he muttered, at a loss.

"And I told you they're not the norm."

"Yeah, you did."

Her expression softened. "I'm going to try to help you, but I won't promise anything. You must give me time. Come back here tomorrow."

And he knew, instinctively, that he was going to get nothing more out of her than that.

His impatience tried to goad him into shaking her, that drive—*obsession,* came Jake's voice—that he'd lived with for so long now. She knew something. He was sure of it. He was close, and he needed to do something about it right now.

Maybe Jake's lecture had been prophetic. There wasn't anything he *could* do, he realized. Not here, not now, not with Mariah Fisher. He could shake her until her teeth rattled out of her head, and he knew that she would not reveal one single thought until she was ready.

He had known her less than half an hour, and he already knew he had never met a woman like her.

"Okay," he said gruffly.

She nodded slowly. "Good. Now, please, if you'll step out of the way? I need to lock up here."

He did so as obediently as if he were one of her schoolboys, and listened to the snick and jangle of her keys in the lock. He looked up and down the road, and around the fenced yard of the school.

There was no buggy.

"Where do you live?"

"In the village." She stepped around him and went down the single step into the snow, picking her way prettily.

"Divinity?" It was the closest one.

"Yes."

"How do you get there?"

"I walk. It's difficult to keep a horse in the village. Very little forage. And of course we've not allowed automobiles."

She was being sarcastic again, he thought, in that quiet, soft way that almost made you miss it. "That's got to be five miles," he called out in the direction of her back, finally following her.

"Seven," she corrected. She hit the road and turned down it. "But I don't stay on the roads. As soon as I'm able, I'll cut across the fields."

"Wait!"

She stopped and turned back to him. "I told you we'd finish this tomorrow."

"I wasn't thinking of Bo." And it stunned him to realize that, if only for the moment, that was true. "Uh...can I give you a lift? Or would that get you *Meidunged* or whatever, too?"

She gave him a full smile. "No, it will not get me *Meidunged*. I was hoping you'd ask."

Adam was startled. "Well, then...hop in."

"Thank you."

She went back to Adam's rental car and opened the passenger door, sliding inside. By the time he got behind the wheel, she'd

crossed her ankles neatly and sat with her hands folded in her lap
in that quiet way she had. He looked across at her, frowning.

"So if cars aren't taboo, why all the horses and buggies?" he
asked.

"Oh, we can ride in them. We mustn't own or drive them."

"That makes no sense." He'd been about to say "no damned
sense," and stopped himself.

She opened her mouth, nearly calling him by name, and caught
herself.

"What's the difference?" he demanded.

"Owning cars, driving them ourselves, might encourage us to
leave the settlement. We'd become like you people, competing
with each other, buying bigger and better and fancier ones to
outdo our neighbors." She smiled again, looking directly at him
this time, and it took his breath away. He forgot to turn the key
in the ignition.

"But?" he prompted.

"But we're hardly stupid. Any number of things—emergen-
cies, for instance, or visiting in other counties—might necessitate
traveling quickly or far. So in those cases we hire someone to
drive us. It's a compromise." She gave him that intent look again.
"We're basically a people of compromise—at least that was the
original idea. Some settlements get carried away. But most of us
compromise with life. That's important. That's what you must
remember."

He was struck again by her words, by her intimation that he
would need to understand. And he knew again that it would be
useless to ask her why.

He finally drove.

They reached the village, and she directed him down a narrow
side street to a small white house with a neat window on either
side of the door. There was an iron gate between hedges and a
path to the street that was neatly and narrowly shoveled free of
snow. In the spring, the small porch would be flanked by gardens.

Adam realized the place suited her. It was exactly what he had
anticipated. And then he realized, too, that they had never finished
their discussion about why she was permitted to teach the children
of people who had shunned her.

"What else?" he asked suddenly. "Why else do they let you
run the school?"

She had just reached for the door handle. She looked over at
him again, surprised; then she gave that quick smile, the one that

didn't quite find her eyes. "They're hoping that as long as I live among them, I might eventually come to my senses, confess and come back into the fold. They think that if I stay here long enough, the *Meidung* will become too hard on me. They think that deep down I want to embrace the church again, because I came back here." She looked away. "One out of three is a start, I suppose. They're marginally right."

Though he didn't know her, he had a strong feeling anyway that no *Meidung* could break her. If the others were right, it was in that she wanted to come back but couldn't find her way without compromising herself.

"They?" he asked carefully. "When you say they, do you mean the church?"

"And all the people."

"Your family, too? Are they here?"

She got out of the car and bent to look back in at him before closing the door. "Oh, yes."

"And your own *parents* don't have anything to do with you?"

"Parents and seven brothers and sisters. No, they really don't."

"Dear God." How could any parents harbor a belief so strong that it would make them willingly turn away from their own child? It seemed especially twisted and cruel to him because he wasn't so lucky as to have the option. He could not even fathom turning away from Bo. He could not understand a God who would want him to.

"What did you *do*, Mariah?" he asked finally, imagining the worst sort of horrors.

She gave that sad smile again and straightened. "I broke a life rule. I went to college. Thank you for the ride. I'll see you to-morrow."

Chapter 3

I went to college.

Adam kept hearing her voice, that soft almost-sarcastic, not-quite-bitter tone, as he tried to run Jake to ground in Dallas. He ate another frozen dinner—or rather, he heated it. The beans tasted like wax and the beef had the texture of rubber, and he finally pushed the plastic tray away to rub his eyes tiredly.

She'd be eating alone as well, he thought. She'd be sitting in a plain but somehow pretty kitchen. He imagined rose-colored curtains there. A hooked rug would cover the floor. She'd eat neatly, her eyes on her plate, shutting out the silence. A silence borne because she had dared to educate herself.

He was out of his mind to be dwelling on it. She wasn't his problem, not beyond digging out of her whatever it was that she knew about Bo.

He picked the phone up again. This time he tried a bar halfway out of Dallas called the Roadhouse. When Jake was between women, he could get down and dirty with the best of the bad guys he chased. And Jake was between women often enough.

The bartender called for him. His brother's hello came over the line simultaneously with a crashing sound in the background.

"Slumming again?" Adam asked.

"Hell, yeah. What's up?"

"I think I've got something this time." There was an incomplete silence filled with shouts, laughter and more crashing from the bar. "What's going on there?" Adam demanded.

"Huh? Oh. Dispute over a woman. Not mine. I don't care. The badge is at home. Now you want to give me that again? You've *got* something?"

"Could be."

Jake's silence was stunned.

Adam told him about Katya, who had sent him to Mariah Fisher. "I've got a gut feeling this woman knows something."

"You've had feelings before," Jake said cautiously.

"Turns out she's the woman with no name," he pointed out.

"So?"

"So she said she'd try to help me. That I should come back tomorrow."

"Where is she?"

"In a house in a village called Divinity. During the day, she's at the school."

"She's Amish?"

"Well, yeah. Sort of. She lives that way, but she's not with the church anymore." He didn't bother to go into the whole *Meidung* thing. He felt oddly protective of her pain, anyway.

"She has a phone? They didn't used to. Allow phones, that is."

"I have no idea if she has one or not." Adam frowned, impatient now. "What's your point, Jake?"

"Where are you calling from?"

"My motel room."

This time the silence was total.

"Let me get this straight," Jake said finally. "There's a woman named Mariah Fisher. You have reason to think she knows where Bo is. She's at home. You're in your room. You're going to wait until tomorrow to talk to her again. What in the name of God is going on up there?"

Adam didn't answer.

There were three possibilities, Jake decided. Adam was out of his mind. Or Jake was actually speaking to an impostor; this wasn't his brother at all. Or this woman was something else again. "She asked you to wait and you're *waiting?* You?"

"Knock it off," Adam finally growled. "I don't have any choice. She's the hottest lead I've had in a while, and I don't want to scare her off."

"Right." Adam had never done anything less than barge in like a bull in a china shop, Jake thought, and the damage be damned. *Especially* if he had a hot lead. "I'll see if I can get a flight out of here tonight."

"I don't need you yet. Stay put. Let me run this Mariah thing out, and if I fall short, then come on up. Then I'll need to do the public schools."

Jake scowled. "I think I'd better—"

"Don't waste the money. I'll call you when I need you. I just wanted to give you an update tonight."

"None of this makes a damned bit of sense," Jake muttered. "I don't like it. Jannel in an Amish settlement? And you're sitting back and thinking, sure, I'll wait? No way. This is all crazy. Unless..."

"Unless what?" Adam asked sharply. He knew that tone. Jake drew the word out as his mind caught up with his mouth. It was something that happened with some frequency.

"Chew on this one a minute," Jake said slowly. "What if she's not hiding from *you,* bro? What if she's hiding from, say, a drug dealer?"

"We've been through that. I was thinking the other day that she couldn't have been so miserable with me as to hide here," he answered, "that she'd have to be hiding from something worse than I ever was. But it still doesn't wash."

"Why not?"

"Same old thing we've been butting our heads up against all along. If she was in trouble, if she was running *from* trouble, then why the hell did she take Bo and put him at risk, too?"

"You're asking me to understand a woman who didn't exist, stole your money and your kid and took off?" Jake burst out. Then he heard himself. "Sorry."

"You've been in and out and through all her drug friends a hundred times over the years," Adam pointed out, ignoring the outburst. It was still too painful to consider anyway. "You've interviewed every one of them. And no one seems to think that her coke habit had anything to do with why she'd gone."

"So I'll go through everyone once more. One more time. Can't hurt, right?"

"Thanks, Jake."

"And *then* I'll fly up."

"I just told you—"

"Bro, I *gotta* meet the woman who can make you sit back and wait."

Mariah paced in her living room.

She was chilled to be bone, and it had very little to do with her not-quite-warm house. She had long since reconditioned herself to the cold. She had been back in the settlement for nearly two years now, and she could scarcely remember what central heating felt like. Still, every time her bare feet moved from the hooked rug and fell on the cool hardwood floor beyond its edges, she winced unconsciously and drew her shawl a little tighter over her full white nightgown.

She finally went to the wood stove in the hearth and yanked open the door. Her mahogany hair, free now and streaming to her waist, swung forward and nearly ignited. Angrily she swept it back again. She pushed some wood in and when the fire was going strongly, she slammed the door and resumed her pacing.

She didn't know what to do now.

She couldn't be sure what was right, and there was no one to talk to about it. It wasn't just that they didn't see her. It was more that they wouldn't understand her dilemma even if they did.

The deacons would simply put the boy they called Noah in Adam's path, she thought. They would do that much and no more, would let God's will prevail. She pressed her fingers to her temples. Maybe, she thought, just maybe, she was wrong and they were right.

She had no right to stand between this man and his child. Theirs was a sacred bond, and she could not interfere with it. She could not make the decision as to whether or not it was right to reunite them. One part of her—the part of her that was still staunchly Amish—strongly believed that God had already made the decision for her. He had allowed that milk carton to fall into her hands, had He not?

But then there was Noah.

No, not Noah, she corrected herself. Adam called him Bo. He was the same child. If nothing else, Mariah was certain of that. He had the scar Adam had spoken of. And he had that funny way of sliding his eyes, the way that always made her laugh. He looked so very much like Adam. Blue eyes? No, she thought, when Adam had described them that way, he had been generalizing. She had never met a man with eyes quite like Adam Wallace's or like his son's. They were not blue. They were not gray. They...changed.

She covered her face with her hands. What was she to do?

Someone had to protect Noah, she thought. He was an innocent, merely a child, with no real apparent memory of what had happened to him before. She had taught him for two years now and she was sure he did not realize he was adopted, though that was an *anner Satt Leit* word. The Lapp family had simply opened their arms and had drawn him in, giving him love and a home.

Noah had been then, and was still now, at the mercy of adults. If she told Adam who he was, would Adam pluck him out of the settlement, no matter that he was a flower that needed the nurturing earth to grow? Noah—*Bo*—had spent more than half his life among the Amish. These ways were all he knew anymore. It would be so cruel, so devastating, to snatch him abruptly away.

The church would not stop it from happening. They would not protect Noah—*Bo*—from such culture shock. The Amish way was one of nonresistance, of following God's will. And God had put Noah—*Bo,* she told herself yet again—on a milk carton.

She went to the kitchen and stood on tiptoe to reach it. She had cleaned it out and had stored it neatly on the top shelf of a cupboard. She had not seen Adam's Bo in the farmers' market. That had been a lie she could only hope God would forgive her for. She'd just needed to bring him here—had needed *anyone* from that ChildSearch place to come. That this man had turned out to be Noah's natural father was coincidental, and perhaps better. When they had told her on the phone that was the man who would be coming, she'd had mixed emotions.

But she wasn't yet sure of that, and from the beginning she'd needed to be able to retreat if it looked as though Noah would be hurt. She couldn't let Adam Wallace get too close to the truth until she was sure. That was why she had told that one small, misleading white lie.

She'd had the milk carton for nearly five weeks now, torturing herself over it, wondering night after night what was right. Perhaps she would have agonized over the decision indefinitely, but then the previous Friday little Lizzie Stoltzfus had disappeared.

That had finally decided her, at least to take the first step. To attempt *something*. And if the settlement hated her for it, if they punished her even more when they found out about it, well, then, they punished her.

Mariah laughed a little giddily. When she had called Child-

Search's number, she had been so sure she was ready for whatever came of her action. She had control of the situation. Though it went against everything she had been taught, she still and always would believe that knowledge was good. It lent power. And all the knowledge in this was on her side. *She* knew who Noah was. *She* knew where he was. And Adam Wallace was in the dark.

When had everything changed? With the first thump of his impatient fist on her schoolhouse door? Before that, when she had seen the way he carried himself, the way he walked? She had no control here, she realized, none at all. Perhaps there wasn't even a decision to make. He could probably find Noah now without her help. He was here in the settlement, and she knew he would keep looking until he found his boy. He would show those pictures around, and sooner or later someone like Katya would tell him just a little bit more, enough to lead him the rest of the way.

He was a strong man, so much stronger than she was, and so much more than she had bargained for. Despite the eight years she had spent away, first earning money for her schooling then going to college, despite her *Meidung,* she was still very much a part of the settlement. She was a woman sheltered in too many senses of the word. She was no match for Adam Wallace. How proud of her, how arrogant, to think that she might be.

He had held his temper in check today with an effort, and it had still nearly gotten away from him. She shivered and drew her shawl tighter.

He was so intense. So...powerful. But, she thought again, *but* there was something kinder there, too, underneath. It was just all tangled up with his pain and his impatience.

So she would believe in his kindness. She would trust it just a little, but she would have to trust herself more, no matter that she was a little frightened of him. She had to protect Noah, she decided finally. That was paramount. She would get beneath the hard, impatient surface of Adam Wallace to the kinder man she sensed beneath, because that was the only hope Noah had.

Adam was also the only hope Lizzie Stoltzfus had, and the three children who had disappeared from the settlement before her. *Nonresistance.* Curse it, she thought angrily. Someone was stealing their children, and the church wouldn't do a blessed thing about it. They wouldn't go to the law, because they had no use for the outsiders' government. They would let it happen, because it was God's will.

''The hell it is,'' she whispered aloud, and flushed beet red at her own blasphemous words. But if God had anything to do with the disappearances of those children at all, then it was in leading her to Adam Wallace, in leading her to a man who might find them.

She finally forced herself to go to bed, and tried desperately to believe that.

Adam came back to the schoolhouse at nine o'clock the next morning. Mariah hadn't expected that. She wasn't prepared for it.

She was just getting the children seated—they had arrived half an hour earlier, after the milking and morning chores were finished on their parents' farms. But they were still excited, chattering, milling, and she was just barely establishing some order when she heard Adam's boot heels on the porch outside.

Impossibly, she recognized the rhythm of his steps, though she had heard them only once before. Impossibly, she could *hear* the confidence, the surety in his stride. Her blood went rushing and wild.

For a horrible moment, she couldn't even think. *Noah.* She looked frantically for his blond head in the crowd. He was at the back of the room with the other second-graders. Someone had drawn an unkind picture of someone they shouldn't have, and they were all crowded around it, laughing.

Not like this. Dear God, he can't find him like this, she thought. He would just barge in, recognize the boy, and shatter his world with the truth. Though she thought Adam Wallace had some kindness underneath that gruff exterior, she also knew that emotion would not allow him to heed it when he saw his child again. Not unless she could somehow prepare him first.

She wasn't ready. She wasn't in control. Had she ever been, even once, since he had first set foot on her schoolhouse porch?

Mariah flew. She dropped a pile of books she had just gathered off the floor where someone had left them. They thumped and scattered all over again, pages fanning, and she ran to the door, wrenching it open even as Adam raised his hand to knock.

''What do you think you're doing?'' she cried.

Her vehemence startled Adam. Here, once again, was the fire he had noticed before, in that singular moment when she had discussed her *one* sin. He stepped back.

"I need to talk to you."

"Not *now,* for heaven's sake!"

"Why not? You said to come earlier."

"Don't you think you're overdoing it a little bit? I meant *after* school!"

"I can't wait that long, Mariah." His voice held a warning now. It was tense, and something hot flowed right beneath his words. Her heart exploded, because she knew it was a miracle that he had even waited overnight.

"You must," she managed.

Adam stared at her. He wondered again who she thought she was, that she should just ordain that he be patient and that he would blindly and meekly obey her. He was even more sure this morning, after sleeping on it, that she knew where Bo was. Or at least she knew *something.*

"What the holy hell am I supposed to do with myself until this afternoon?" he demanded.

"Hell is *not* holy!" Mariah stepped quickly out onto the porch and closed the door behind her, trying to get a grip on herself. "You might take a peek inside yourself," she answered finally.

"Huh?"

She closed her eyes a moment and took a breath. When she was steadier, she started over.

"You never gave me your name," she began. That was the first thing that had to be cleared up here and now, she decided. She was trying to hold too many reins at once. So many times she had almost slipped and called him by name, and that would be disastrous. She had to tell him the truth gently, carefully.

His eyes narrowed. "Adam Wallace."

"May I call you Adam?"

"I don't give a damn what you call me, as long as you start talking."

"I can't do that right now."

"Why not?"

"Because there are thirty-six children inside, waiting for me to teach them something. And if you think that's an easy task, instructing eight different groups all at the same time, all something different, think again."

Adam felt that bemused feeling coming on again.

She had done this to him yesterday, too. He had come here with a purpose, and somewhere along the line those violet eyes had searched his face, she'd gone off on a tangent and he'd ended up forgetting for a while what he had come for and why. She wouldn't do it again.

"Damn it—''

"Stop swearing at me, Adam! Stop it *now!* If not out of respect for me, then do it because it's in your own best interest. I can't think when you act angry.'' She pressed her fingers to her temples. "And if I can't think, I can't help you.''

Guilt and panic rolled over in his gut. "Okay, okay. All right,'' he said hoarsely. "Calm down.''

"I'm trying to.'' She choked back a wild laugh. She was about as calm as a windstorm at the moment.

"I'll come back,'' he said. "Don't get upset.''

"Thank you,'' she breathed.

"What time? Tell me exactly what time I should be here, then we won't have this misunderstanding again.'' Dear God, he thought, how did she do this to him? She'd turned everything around. He was holding on to his temper for all he was worth, and he didn't even know why.

"About three,'' she nearly whispered.

"Fine.'' He snapped the word out, cutting off the end of it. He had no idea whatsoever what he was going to do in the meantime. There was no orderly way to proceed with his search, until he had exhausted the avenue of Mariah Fisher first.

He went back to the car, angry and amazed at himself all over again. Her voice stopped him.

"Adam.''

"What?'' he snarled, looking around at her again.

"Think. While you're waiting, think.''

"About *what?*'' He just narrowly avoided swearing again.

"What troubles you?''

He stared at her in disbelief.

"You're angry,'' she went on. "You move too fast. Something has you all tangled up inside.''

He couldn't control himself any longer. "Well, what the hell do you expect of me, woman? What do you *think* has me tangled? I want my kid back!''

"Yes,'' she said quietly. "And perhaps now you will find him. The question is, what are you going to do with him?''

And with that she stepped neatly inside again. She shut the door in his face hard.

Chapter 4

A thousand times during the course of the day, Adam determined to go back to the school. He would force her to cough up whatever she knew. Hell, there were laws in this country. Her people might think they were above them—he considered the way they had gone to war with the Supreme Court for the right not to send their children to high school. But he'd show them that they were wrong. He'd get a judge to force Mariah Fisher to comply with him.

Which would take all day, if not several days. It would alienate her as well. He shouldn't have cared, not as long as he got the information he sought, but oddly, he did. So he waited.

At precisely 2:50, he drove from the motel back to the schoolhouse. When he stopped in front of it, the clock on the car's dashboard read 2:59. He measured his steps to the door to reach it at precisely 3:00, wondering if he had finally, completely lost his mind.

Once again, she opened it before he could knock. This time she held a mug in her hand.

"Coffee, Adam?" she asked politely. "I have pie as well, if you'd like a snack."

He stared at her. "You want some kind of coffee klatch now?"

"I'd like to talk. Would it hurt if we were comfortable while we did so?"

He was starting to hate that reasonable tone. It tied him in knots he never saw coming. It invariably had him doing things he would never have dreamed of otherwise.

"Yeah," he said shortly. "Fine."

Mariah told herself she was much more in control than she had been earlier. And she believed it, until he brushed against her to come inside. It was an inadvertent touch and she doubted very much if he was even aware of it. He was in a hurry. Again. But she felt the strength and the intent of him even through his jacket, and some sense of heat that she was sure she imagined. It startled her. It flustered her. It made something curl in her stomach and her skin pull into gooseflesh.

"Where is it?" he asked.

"I'm sorry?" She looked at him, her violet eyes huge, a faint blush coming to her skin.

"The coffee, Mariah. Where's this coffee?"

"Oh. Oh, right here. I'll...get you some."

She was nervous, she realized. Why? He watched her rush to a small table in the far corner of the room. Her hands were a flurry of motion as she poured a mug of coffee from a thermos there and cut carefully into a pie. She carried everything back to the desk and he thought she trembled.

"Please, sit down," she almost gasped.

"And where would you like me to do this?"

Mariah looked dumbly around the schoolroom. Where indeed? Suddenly she felt herself blushing even deeper as she tried to imagine his large, muscled body easing into one of the child-size chairs.

Muscled? She had no way of knowing whether he was muscled or not. Ah, but he would be, she thought.

"Take my...you can use my desk," she managed.

He watched her a moment longer. She thought his scowl was one of confusion now. At least it wasn't as fierce. He went to her chair and sat. After a long moment, his eyes left her and he took a bite of the pie she'd placed on the desk.

"This is cake," he said, chewing.

"No. No, it's not. It's shoofly pie." Her words rushed out. She was glad to have something innocuous to discuss, if only for the moment. He would get back to the subject of Bo soon enough, she knew.

"Whatever," he answered. "It's good."

"Thank you."

He looked up again. "You made it?"

"Last night." She had not been able to sleep after all. She'd tried briefly, then had gotten up to bake. Sometimes it helped, and the children loved it. "Coarse batter is easier to cook in a wood stove," she explained inanely. "It's far more difficult to do delicate pastries, to moderate the heat properly."

He looked at her with an unreadable expression. "That's very interesting." Even he realized his voice was too polite. Strained. "So what do you know, Mariah? I've got to tell you, I'm running all out of patience here, pie or cake or what have you."

"Yes," she said uncomfortably. "I know."

He pushed the plate away. "Well?"

"Adam, what is the most important thing to you?"

His jaw hardened. "Do you have to ask?"

"I need to be sure."

"Why?"

She took a breath, clasping her hands in front of her. "I just do."

"Fine. I'll say it. Bo." His words were like bullets. "Now where is he? What do you know?"

Mariah took a deep breath and steeled herself to ignore his questions. "And when he was with you?" she asked. "Was he the most important thing then?"

Adam opened his mouth and closed it again. Damn her, he thought. He didn't know if he was angry or amazed. "What are you doing, Mariah?" he snapped finally, disbelievingly. "Trying to ascertain if I *deserve* to have my son back?"

It was close enough to the truth to make her skin go pale.

Adam stood up from the desk. He planted his large palms on the top of it and leaned forward, toward her. He scared her more than a little this time.

"Let's clear something up here, lady. The law is on my side in this matter. Do you want me to drag the courts into this? I've already done it once, with my ex-wife in absentia, and managed to get custody. Married parents have joint rights to their child. When she disappeared with Bo and didn't respond to announcements of the hearing, she violated my rights and proved herself to be an unstable parent. The hell of it is, I don't have my boy to keep custody *of* because I can't find him. But I can tell you this. As soon as I—or the law—catch wind of where he is, they're going to turn him over to me. So if I take you to court, they'll *make* you tell me under oath. They'll hold you in contempt, if you don't. They'll make you tell me what you know, Mariah. And I don't really give a damn which way we go about it. I just want answers, and I don't care how I get them.''

He watched her, waiting for her reaction. Then he realized that he should have known that bullying her wouldn't work.

She drew herself up. ''It's not necessary to threaten me, Adam.''

He gritted his teeth. ''Don't you dare. Don't you dare start that.''

''What?'' She frowned, confused.

''That *voice*. 'Please, Adam would you go walk on the moon.' Next thing I know, I'm weightless.''

She didn't smile. ''You'll do whatever you're comfortable with,'' she said stiffly.

''Damned right.''

''As will I. And I'm not comfortable telling you anything, until I know what you're going to do with the information.''

''Damn you!'' he snarled.

Mariah jumped. ''I need to rationalize this in my own heart first. That's all.''

''You just don't get it, do you? *Your heart has no place in this!* Your heart doesn't matter! This isn't your concern. This is between me and my kid and my ex-wife!''

She steadied herself again with great effort. ''Of course it is,'' she answered reasonably. ''But you're wrong, too. It concerns my heart greatly.''

He stared at her a moment longer, then he finally raked both hands through his hair. He wasn't sure what was happening here, but he was torn between anger and frustration and shock.

In all his life, he had never met anyone he couldn't cow.

''Please, if you'll just answer my question,'' she went on. ''That's all I ask.''

''And what if my answer doesn't measure up?'' he snarled.

''I don't know,'' she answered helplessly.

''I don't even remember what your question *was!*''

''Your Bo,'' she whispered. ''Was his happiness the most important thing to you when you were with him?''

Because he sensed that it mattered more than he could possibly understand, Adam gave it true thought.

His head hurt.

"When I was with him, I was a very busy man," he said finally.

"You still are, Adam. You drive yourself."

"Yeah. But back then I was pursuing something that didn't end up mattering."

"What?"

He gave a self-deprecating snort. "A ball game. I played baseball."

She blinked. "For money?"

"Yeah. With the Astros."

From her eight years outside, she knew a little about the World Series and Super Bowls and the like. Mariah was impressed. "I see."

"Was Bo's happiness the most important thing then?" he repeated almost to himself. "No, Mariah. No, because you never really appreciate what you've got until it's gone."

Her heart squeezed. She realized, a little dazed, that he could not have given a better answer. It was so honest it hurt.

"The time he fell out of the apple tree," Adam went on. He moved away from her desk and began pacing, as she had done the previous night, and Mariah thought he was just as tortured as she had been. "We had some people over for a party. Steaks on the grill, that kind of thing. It was mostly guys from the team and their wives. I'd told Bo to stay away from that damned tree. And I turned my back to get a beer and up he went. Then there was this ungodly squeal and the crack of branches and he was crying, these great big hurt sobs. He broke his arm, too." He stopped to look at her. "Did I want to shake him? Sure. I could have killed him. And there was blood all over the place and his arm was crooked, and I threw him in my car and drove hell bent for leather to the nearest doctor. And I kept thinking, God, he's going to bleed to death. And I was too scared to think that it was just a cut on the chin. I thought that if he died, I'd die. And I blamed myself, too. Because I knew that kid, knew there was no way he was going to be able to turn away from what he thought was a nest up in those branches, and I turned my back anyway and gave him the chance to climb. So all I could do was yell, like it was his fault." He stared at her. "Is that what you wanted to hear, Mariah?"

"I...yes," she admitted baldly.

"I was on the road every summer through the three years I had him. Five games home in Houston, seven away, nine home, seven away. That was the way the season went. And when he was two, I tried to take him with me. Jannel stayed home. What a fiasco. Trying to get luggage off the carousel at the airport, the rest of the team halfway to the bus, and there goes my kid, racing down the concourse just as fast as his short, little legs could carry him. Was I ticked off? You bet I was.''

He came to stand close to her to look down into her face. Something shook inside her.

''What do you want me to tell you, Mariah?'' he went on more softly. ''That if I had him back today I wouldn't be mad if he did that again? I'd be mad. I'd be furious. Because I was famous, and any crazy fool could have grabbed that boy and taken off with him just for the sheer kick of it, just to kidnap Adam Wallace's son. And Bo had already gotten far enough away from me that I couldn't have stopped it from happening. And I hate myself, too, because I swore that day that I'd never take him with me again, not unless Jannel came too, and I never did—even though he begged me. It was too much trouble, and I had my priorities screwed up. It was always the game. Everything was the game. I didn't like distractions before I went out to home plate. But if I had taken Bo with me on that last August road trip, then Jannel wouldn't have been about to disappear with him, would she?''

His guilt, his sorrow and remorse, hurt her. Mariah didn't realize she was crying until Adam's eyes narrowed. He brought his hand up and caught a tear on his finger. Something shuddered deep inside her.

She stepped back quickly and scrubbed her hands over her cheeks herself. ''I...let's go.''

''Go,'' he repeated almost dazedly. He was still looking at his finger, frowning as though a million secrets were revealed in that single teardrop.

''We'll take your car.''

''Where?''

She didn't answer. She couldn't. All her words were wadded in her throat.

At least, she thought, at least there was no longer any doubt in her mind about doing the right thing. She knew what it was now. She would do it, then she would pray that Adam's heart, the heart he had just allowed her to glimpse, would prevail.

No man could be so honest and yet be cruel, she told herself. Surely not.

She grabbed her coat and her shawl and hurried outside. He followed her a heartbeat later.

Adam almost wished she could drive. Suddenly, he didn't feel capable of it. His pulse was like thunder. He heard the rush of blood in his ears and the dull, erratic thud of his heart underneath it. His legs felt filled with air and his palms sweated in the icy air.

She knew where Bo was, and she was going to take him to him.

Adam knew that as certainly as he knew his own name. She had known all along, from the start. And he didn't know whether to rage at her or hug her or cry.

She had reached the car and she slid into the passenger seat. He had to force himself to take another step to follow; then he was jogging.

"Where?" he asked again when he got behind the wheel, and they both understood that this time he wanted directions.

"Make a U-turn." Her voice was strangled. "Then go right at the next turn."

He turned the key in the ignition with fumbling fingers. He almost missed the turn. Without even realizing it, he pressed down harder and harder on the accelerator. If she hadn't cried out, he would have flown right past the road.

He hit the brakes hard and swerved. Neither of them spoke. Adam didn't trust himself to try.

"Left," she said quietly, finally. "You'll need to turn again in about five hundred feet." This time she warned him well ahead of time.

Adam felt light-headed. He took one hand from the steering wheel to drag his sleeve across his eyes. The drive was interminable. The scenery flew past them.

"Adam," she said in that near whisper.

"What?" he croaked.

"Be kind. Promise me you'll be *kind*."

He took his eyes off the road long enough to stare at her.

"Think of him, Adam. No matter what happens, put his happiness first. Please. I'm begging you. This is the only world he knows."

He was beginning to understand all her high-and-mighty questions. He hated her for them. Who the hell did she think she was? She had known. She had known all along.

"Yeah," he heard himself say. "I promise."

Then, suddenly, he slammed on the brakes. The back end of the car fishtailed on a patch of ice, and Mariah gasped and her hand went involuntarily to the dashboard. He didn't need her to tell him. He knew. Adam's heart roared now. In the distance, halfway across a field, small black figures zoomed this way and that. Playing...ice hockey.

His head swam. Black-clothed figures. Amish kids. *Bo?*

He stopped the car, pushing frantically and hard at the door. He got out to stand and stare.

Mariah finally breathed again after the wild, frightening ride. She picked her way over the snow to stand beside him. Adam seemed as frozen as the landscape. She put her hand on his arm and for his sake, for Bo's sake, steeled herself against whatever she might think she felt there this time.

"They call him Noah," she warned softly. "If you ask for Bo, he probably won't answer."

Adam looked at her—uncomprehendingly, she thought. He finally started walking again. She hurried to follow. She could only pray that the implications of what she had just said would dawn on him before it was too late.

And she knew that when they did, it would hurt him unconscionably.

Adam kept going until he was no more than fifteen paces from the ice. The boys swarmed, shouted, playing as hard and as competitively as boys the world over. In that moment, there was no difference between this crowd and a group of youths in the center of a city somewhere, jostling each other over a basketball. No difference, perhaps, except that these boys were all dressed alike.

He knew Bo immediately, anyway.

Adam's reaction was literally physical. It was a hand wrenching painfully at his heart. He felt tears burn at his eyes. So long, he thought. So damned long. He knew the straight bowl-cut blond hair, streaked with brown, the way his own got in the winter. Four years fell away. Bo was taller now, and more sure of his feet. He'd be able to run even faster down an airport concourse. The boy turned and shouted something to a teammate over his shoulder. Got his words down better, too, Adam thought.

He opened his mouth. And then Mariah's voice echoed somewhere in the back of his mind. *They call him Noah.*

That was when Adam understood what she had been trying to tell him.

Something unseen pounded him in the chest. The game

stopped, with a lot of skidding, sliding. Shavings of ice sprayed. A good half of the boys crowded the edge of the ice to look their way. Bo was among them. His blue-gray eyes bounced off Adam without recognition.

"No." He heard his own voice without even realizing he had spoken aloud. "Oh, Lord, no."

"Adam..." But there was nothing she could say, nothing she could do to soften the blow. She was stunned by how very deeply she wanted to.

She barely knew him. She had wanted to protect Bo. She had *meant* to do that, but now all her intentions veered and she would have done anything to take away this man's pain, instead.

"I'm sorry," she whispered. There was nothing she could do.

Adam didn't answer.

Four years, he thought. More than half Bo's life.

There would be no reunion. No matter how he had imagined this moment might be, Bo didn't even know him. He had lived for this, had waited for this, had worked toward it, for what seemed like a whole lifetime. And now it was wrenched away from him, even as he grappled to hold the dream back. He couldn't force himself on the boy, at least not now, not without causing him cruel confusion and panic, not without shaking his world.

Jannel hadn't kept his memory alive. She hadn't bothered to take any photographs with them. That choked him, though it shouldn't have, until he had an even more staggering thought.

They call him Noah. She had even changed his name. She had wiped out every trace of the boy he once had been.

It was too much to take in, to accept. Adam's brain felt swamped, incapable of clear thought. He made a strangled sound and turned away.

"Adam!" Mariah cried. But her voice didn't stop him. She watched helplessly as he jogged back to the red car and drove away, tires squealing.

Chapter 5

For three days, Adam prowled the county like a wounded animal looking for a place to die.

He had never seen it coming, and that made him feel like a fool. He cursed himself for never once waking up and smelling the coffee over the years, for harboring that ridiculous image through all of his search, of a toddler on chubby legs, with apple cheeks and mischievous eyes. He'd been aware of the clock ticking, and had never once considered the implications of those ticks. He'd known Jannel would probably change their names, but hadn't considered the ramifications of that on a three-year-old.

He ducked his brother's calls almost helplessly, knowing that if he didn't get in touch with him then, Jake would almost certainly turn up on the next flight. Adam didn't want to see him, but he felt incapable of doing anything to prevent it. The dogged hope he'd carried inside him for years was jagged and broken and dying, and he needed to be left alone to come to terms with it. Besides, what the hell could he say?

I found him. It's the most amazing thing. He's seven. They call him Noah. He's got friends, a life, and I'm not part of it. He doesn't even know me.

No, he thought, no.

A sense of aimlessness stole over him. He could not remember a time in his adult life when he had not had a purpose. Every time he'd gone to bat he'd been thinking World Series. Every day since he'd retired, he'd been looking for Bo. Now he had found him, but he couldn't touch him, couldn't reach out to him, and there was nothing left to do, no purpose to anything anymore, at all.

Finally on Monday night he began winding down. He still had no answers, but there was little ground left to cover. He'd driven blindly through every nook and cranny of the settlement, as though something about it all would tell him how to fix this mess. He finally stopped at the motel, found more frantic messages from Jake, and still couldn't face them. He stuffed them into his jacket pocket and took off again.

It was a little past ten. He found a tavern on Route 30, a neighborhood kind of place, small enough to be cozy, long and narrow, with a handful of booths along one wall. The bartender was perfect, friendly without being flirtatious, competent without hovering. Adam thought he'd get drunk. He ordered a double shot of bourbon.

The first mouthful of alcohol hit his stomach and went sour, and he knew it wasn't going to work.

He went back to the car and found himself in front of Mariah's house, without having any conscious intention of going there. He sat with the engine idling and considered why he had come. He couldn't talk to Jake because Jake hadn't *seen*, he realized. Jake could not possibly understand the enormity of this. But Mariah had been there. She knew.

He made a decision, turned the ignition off and went up the walk. Even at this hour, she answered his knock much more quickly than he might have expected. The house was dark behind her, and he realized that he had probably woken her, but he couldn't bring himself to care. He needed...something. And he knew instinctively that he'd find it here.

Still, when the door opened, he wasn't prepared for what greeted him.

For a moment, he barely recognized her. He thought she had a roommate, maybe, someone who wasn't Amish. She certainly didn't look Amish in that moment. Then his heart stalled. Words—whatever greeting he had been about to speak—caught midway in his throat. *Her hair.*

It was so incredibly long, so rich, wild and spilling, and he'd never had any idea, with it tucked neatly into that bonnet she always wore, just how much of it there was. He'd acknowledged from the start that she was beautiful. But all week he had thought of her as somehow untouchable, distant, even prim. And now a woman opened her door.

A woman in—God help him—a nightgown. Adam shoved his hands hard into his pockets, confused.

"What's happened to you?" she gasped.

"To *me?*" His eyes narrowed. "What do you mean?"

"You look...bad."

One brow went up. "Bad?"

Her mouth curled. "I guess I could put it in terms you'll understand. Just once. You look like hell."

He was surprised. Then he shocked himself with a hoarse bark of laughter. "Yeah. I imagine I do."

She stepped back from the door. "Come in."

"I don't want to cause you any trouble."

"I was up. Awake."

"No, I mean—" What *did* he mean? He broke off and looked around at the quiet, deserted street. The windows would have eyes.

"I don't want to bring the wrath of your church down on your head all over again."

"You won't." She shook her head, motioning him inside again. Still he didn't move.

"Letting a man into your house in the middle of the night wouldn't get a rise out of them? Your deacons or whatever?"

"Ah, Adam, you have so much to understand yet about my people. Please come inside. It's cold. I want to close the door."

He still thought going in was a bad idea, because although one long curl of hair had fallen forward over her shoulder, the rest of it streamed down her back when she turned around, a midnight waterfall tumbling clear to her hips. She was barefoot, and he couldn't decide if she still looked like some kind of otherworldly angel or if she had stepped out of the pages of time. But he knew that going inside her home, being alone with her while she looked like this, was perhaps the poorest choice he could make in a lifetime full of many. He was feeling too...raw. And a raw, vulnerable man would take solace where he could find it, right or wrong, and the repercussions be damned.

He stepped over the threshold anyway, into her home.

It was tiny, neat and country pretty. He was startled and a little shaken to see the hooked rug he had imagined on the floor. It was a hundred blended shades of mauve and violet, burgundy and rose. A lantern hung on the wall nearest the door. She went to it and lit it, and it threw off a golden glow. The heat from a wood stove in a corner hearth was barely adequate. There was a single sofa, an armchair for reading, and a rocker to one side of the stove.

"Have you eaten?" she asked, closing the door behind him.

"I'm not hungry."

"That's not what I asked." She disappeared through a door in the back of the room. He followed her into the kitchen and found rose-colored curtains there.

She was rummaging through a refrigerator.

"You don't have electricity." He was bemused all over again. "Do you?" He hadn't noticed any wires leading into any of the houses on this narrow street.

Mariah glanced over her shoulder at him. "No. That would bring the *Meidung* upon me for sure."

"So how does that run?" He motioned at the refrigerator.

"A hydraulic motor, just outside."

Adam shook his head slowly. "What's the difference? It's like the cars. What's the *point?* A refrigerator is a refrigerator, no matter what it runs on."

"You disapprove."

"I'm confused. I like consistency."

She finally straightened with a casserole dish in her hands. "It's not electricity we're against, so much as all the things that come with it," she explained, nudging the refrigerator closed with her elbow. "Televisions, radios, telephones—they all intrude upon family life. But…" She trailed off and began slicing at a brisket. "It would be very, very difficult and time-consuming to keep food cold any other way."

"Compromise," he muttered, forgetting that he had meant to tell her to put the food away.

"That's right. The biggest purpose of the *Ordnung*—"

"The what?"

"Our rules. Their purpose is to keep us insulated from the outside world, not to make it impossible for us to function." She smiled. "Family," she repeated. "The concept of family has to be protected at all costs. If you really think of it, that's our reason behind everything. The point is not to live in an outdated world, Adam, in the past. That's simply the result of the *Ordnung*. Its purpose is to preserve our values. We decry the modern world because it would threaten them. Look at your lives, and look at the simple peace of ours. We don't want to lose that.''

Adam made a sound in his throat that might have been agreement. She put a plate on the table. He didn't mean to sit, and did it absently. "I guess it would be hard to remain separate if you got hooked on the power companies."

"Yes." She beamed at him as she would a student who had just figured out a difficult lesson. "That's it exactly. So, you see, 12-volt current is perfectly acceptable because it comes from batteries. Whereas 110-volt electricity is tapped from public lines, from *your* companies, so that's unacceptable."

He shook his head, worried because it suddenly seemed to make sense to him.

"Eat," she urged.

"I don't—"

"Try."

He cut off a piece of the meat and put it in his mouth because he didn't want to offend her. He took a second bite because he had always loved corned beef and this was really good. With the third, he wondered just when he had last enjoyed a home-cooked meal, and he was shaken because he honestly couldn't remember.

Years, he thought uncomfortably. It really had been years.

Mariah hovered. She was unable to sit still. She had expected he would come back sooner or later, but she hadn't expected that he would come *here*. Now she was nervous and self-conscious because she wasn't dressed, and because she had been largely instrumental in bringing this hurt upon him.

She poured him a glass of milk and went to adjust another lantern hanging from the kitchen wall, keeping her back to him.

"What is it about women?" he muttered, "That so many of you think you can fix anything with food?"

"It's a nurturing instinct, I think."

"My mother used to do this." He helped himself to more cold potatoes. She had left the casserole dish on the table. "Before she...well, when I was young. Skinned knees, broken hearts, anything, and out came the leftovers."

"Used to?" Mariah asked. He wasn't ready to talk about Bo, so she would listen while he rambled.

"My mother's gone," he answered flatly.

Mariah felt her heart move. "Like your wife?"

"Ex-wife," he said shortly. "No, my mother died. Eight years ago. Her liver gave out. She had a drinking problem." She had never known Bo, he thought. He had always wondered if that might have made a difference, if Bo could have infused some sunshine into her miserable world. Probably not. And even if he had, when he disappeared it would have started her drinking all over again.

"I'm sorry."

Adam jolted a little at Mariah's voice, lost as he was in his own past. "Don't be," he answered shortly. "We weren't a close family." He and Jake had only bonded after everyone else had been gone.

"How many of you are there?"

"Counting my parents? Five to start. We're down to two now."

"Two siblings?" She wasn't sure she wanted to understand.

"I have a brother, a year younger than me. And a sister who'd be...twenty-seven now, I think."

Her breath stalled. "You think? Is she dead, too?"

"Hell if I know." She was staring at him, appalled. Adam tried to explain. As though there was any explaining the Wallaces. "Kim vanished ten years ago. We've never been able to find her, either."

"That's terrible."

"Lately I've been too busy looking for Bo to dwell on it. And my brother Jake seems to think she wants to stay lost." Then something else occurred to him. "What about you?" he asked suddenly.

She had brought the lantern back to the table, but now she was fussing at the sink. She glanced at him over her shoulder, scowling. "What about me?"

"No husband, no children?" A thunderbolt hit him. "Did they *Meidung* you, too?"

Mariah turned sharply. "No! Oh, no. I had the choice."

"What choice?" *Were* there kids who didn't speak to her? Was there a man who loved her, but who had actually turned his back on her? Adam realized that the possibility bothered him, immensely and absurdly so, on some deep level he didn't want to look at too closely.

He scowled at her, his eyes narrowing. For the first time he tried to guess her age, and he put her somewhere around thirty.

"I had the choice of marrying," she said quietly. "I was... supposed to marry. I left instead."

"Left."

"For State College. Penn State. To go to school. Eventually I went to school," she clarified. "It took me about four years to earn enough money to be able to enroll. Scholarships don't come easily when your high-school diploma comes from a correspondence course."

His eyes narrowed. "What did you do?"

"I don't understand."

"To earn the money. How did you do it?"

"Oh. I was a sort of governess for a while, for a wealthy family in Huntingdon. I lived in there, but I was free evenings, so I waited tables in town."

A simple education shouldn't have been so hard for her, he thought. It seemed unfair, and it bothered him deeply.

She gave him her back again. And he knew that that was all she was going to say on the matter, at least for now. He thought she'd probably tell him more, all the sordid details, when she knew him better.

That thought stunned him. He was not going to know her better. He was going to solve this nightmare, somehow, and go home.

Adam finally pushed his plate away. "Where's Jannel?" he asked finally.

Mariah finally came back to the table. She sat across from him, clasping her hands together in front of her, in that way she had. This time she put them on the table. "Who?"

"My ex-wife."

"I don't know."

The anger, the impatience, that was never far from the surface tightened his face again. And she wondered suddenly what he would do when he understood how deeply involved she had been in all this from the start. She shivered a little.

"Adam, I honestly don't," she rushed on. "Sarah and Sugar Joe have had Noah for four years now, or so I'm told. I've only been back from State College for two. I wasn't here then, when he came to us. I don't know what happened."

Sarah and Sugar Joe. Where they pretending to be Bo's parents now? Dear God, had Jannel just dropped him off and *left* him? He didn't know if he was relieved or horrified not to have found her, too.

"What the hell kind of name is that?" Adam snarled, because he had to strike out somewhere.

Mariah's eyes widened. "I beg your pardon?"

"Sugar Joe."

"Oh." She reached down and smoothed her nightgown over her thighs. He found himself watching too closely, leaning infinitesimally to the side to see, and dragged his eyes back to her face. "In all the settlement, there are maybe ten surnames," she explained. "We're all descended from the same group of immigrants. There are many thousands of us, but we're all Fishers or Bylers, Lapps, Millers, Esslers. And our given names are generally either biblical or German. So we have a *lot* of Joseph Lapps, for instance."

"Sugar Joe is Joseph Lapp," Adam said hoarsely. *Noah Lapp.* Dear God. The hurt, the panic, the denial began churning in his gut all over again.

"One of many Joseph Lapps," Mariah was saying. "There's Sugar Joe Lapp and Joe Junior Lapp—there are many Joe Juniors, actually—and there's Boundary Joe Lapp." She began ticking names off on her fingers. "There's Chubby Joe and Chicken Joe and—"

"I get your drift," Adam interrupted shortly. "Okay, so where did the Sugar part come from?"

She heard all he didn't ask: *Who are they? What are they? How do they treat him?* "Joe is from Berks County, from one of the other *Gemeides* that I told you about. He visited ours with his family on one of their off-Sundays many years ago, and that was when he met his Sarah for the first time."

"Off-Sundays," he repeated.

"We only have services every other week. They're all-day affairs with a community dinner. Sometimes supper, too, depending on how many visitors there are from other *Gemeides*. On alternate weekends, we just spend time with—"

"Family," he supplied for her.

"Yes. Anyway, Joe Lapp was so besotted with Sarah Gehler when he met her that he barely had enough sense to bring his mama a cup of coffee. He was finally making it for her, staring at little Sarah, and he poured nearly the whole sugar bowl into the cup. So he's been Sugar Joe ever since."

"Sounds like an imbecile," Adam snapped.

"Oh, no, he was in love." Her eyes glowed.

"He'd never laid eyes on her before."

"You outsiders don't believe in thunderbolts?" she asked softly.

He opened his mouth to answer. And then he saw Jannel Payne

again, across a crowded room, and felt that old electricity, the jolt.

It hadn't been love. He knew that now. It had been pure...sex. Physical attraction, a tangible pull. Pheromones, maybe. Once he'd begun to know that there wasn't too much going on inside that perfect shell, that drive had begun to wane.

He hadn't understood it then. It was just another revelation of the many that had come tumbling in on him lately.

"It's never smart," he answered finally.

"I'm not sure smart has anything to do with it," she said wryly. "The Lapps—Bo's Lapps—are a good family, Adam. They have four children of their own, besides your Bo."

"Only four?" He was too troubled to be really curious. It was an idle question.

"Sarah bled badly when her youngest was born. She really shouldn't have more children. Birth control goes against the *Ordnung,* but..." She shrugged. What she didn't say was clear. Sarah had stopped having children, so something was afoot.

"So...what you're saying in a roundabout way is that she loves Bo like her own."

"Oh, yes."

His voice darkened, lowered. "And it would kill her to lose him."

"Kill is a strong word, Adam. It would certainly break her heart, as it broke yours."

Suddenly, without warning, he drove a fist against the table. Mariah jumped.

"Would you prefer that he wasn't cherished?" she chided. "First by you, then by the people who took him in? Would you prefer that he didn't know love?"

He looked at her, his eyes angry, then bleak. "I don't know. No. God, of course not. I just don't know what to do," he admitted hoarsely. "I don't know what to do about this. There's no easy way to break it to him. Not if he doesn't remember me."

"You don't have to do anything, Adam," she said softly. "Not now. Not right away."

He looked at her, his eyes tortured. He didn't answer.

"What do you have to rush home to?" she asked.

And the answer came easily, troubling him. "Nothing." ChildSearch, he thought. But ChildSearch had always been run admirably by Jake in his absences. He'd been out of town these past four years more often than he'd been in Dallas.

Mariah shook her head slowly. "You think you must make an unconscionable decision right away. That you must decide to leave Noah—Bo—where he is, in the life he's embraced, and turn your back on him, and that is intolerable. But to hurt him, to wrench him away, is unbearable, too."

He had come here because he had known she would understand. Yet hearing her speak the words aloud almost terrified him. "Yeah," he said.

"But that's simply not true."

"I've got to move one way or the other," he snapped. "There's a fork in the road, and I can't just stand here. I've got to go left or right."

"Why? Why not just stay put and contemplate it for a while?"

"I've got to make a decision."

"But not tonight, Adam. Not tomorrow. Not even next week, if it comes to it."

"What the hell—" He broke off at her expression. "What are you saying?" he corrected himself.

"That Bo isn't going anywhere, and you have nowhere to go."

He waited, his heart beating too hard, and a small part of him wondered at that unconscious reaction. As though he was on the brink. Of something. "Go on."

"You should stay for a while. You could enjoy Bo's company. You could watch him, see how he's grown up, get to know him all over again. You could love him. You don't have to tell him who you are to do any of those things."

No, he thought, he didn't. His heart both swelled with the possibility and ached that it was even necessary.

"You could give yourself some time, and when it's right the answer will probably just come to you. I don't think you'll have to search for it or torment yourself over it. Some day you'll just...wake up and it will simply be there, and you'll understand which way it is you should go."

His eyes narrowed on her, and he smiled mirthlessly. "How come you got to be so smart in college, when all I did was blunder through?"

Her smile became pained again. "If that's true, then I think it's probably because going to college was no big deal for you, while I had to give up everything for it. So I cherished it. I wrung everything out of the experience that was there for the taking. Besides, this isn't learned knowledge, Adam. It's faith."

"I never had any." And in that moment, he knew it was true.

She got up and took his plate. "Can you afford to stay in your motel for a while?"

"Yeah." He bit the word out, still watching her, still frowning.

"If you prefer, I could probably find you a family to stay with. Some of the *Gemeides* don't practice the *Meidung*. Some practice it, but only for the harshest of sins. This area is strict, maybe the most orthodox of all. But I have friends in Berks County who see me. They would take you in if I asked."

"No. I don't like...I've never been any good with strangers." Besides, he thought, it would increase his driving time back to this little hamlet, if he stayed in another county. And if Bo was here, this was where he needed to be.

"Another difference between us," Mariah murmured thoughtfully. "Solitude is only comfortable when it's an option."

Adam stood. "I should go. I've probably caused you a million problems already."

She half smiled at him. "Slicing off a few pieces of beef? That's hardly a problem."

"It's late."

"I don't sleep much anyway. Not anymore."

"I meant, you know, what I mentioned at the door."

"Ah." She smiled fully. "And I told you then that you didn't understand." Without even thinking, she reached out and zipped his coat for him. They were both startled, then embarrassed. She stepped back quickly, tucking her hands beneath her shawl.

"Nurturing again?" Adam asked hoarsely.

"I...yes, I imagine so."

"You should be somebody's mother." He said it impulsively and hated himself immediately because her face blanched.

"I would have liked that very much." She seemed to swallow carefully. "Come on, I'll walk you to the door."

How could she be so warm and yet so...removed? he wondered, following her, watching her dark head bow. But then, almost as soon as he wondered, he understood. Her pain was private. She would hold it close. Of course he understood that. Hadn't he been the same way for too many years to count?

She didn't walk. She glided. He was struck again by how beautiful she was, especially without the trappings of her Amish faith. He thought again that it was just as well if he left now.

"Sure I shouldn't sneak out through the window?" He tried for humor, but his voice was oddly raw again.

She glanced back at him. "Everyone's asleep, Adam. And if

someone is awake, they'll certainly look the other way when you leave my door. We're not puritans.''

He thought of the plain dress she wore to school, and the neat bonnet. And the fact that she was punished so severely for having gone to college. "You could have fooled me."

"You're thinking contradictions again." She opened the door. "*Family*, Adam. Remember family. And consider what one must do to make one."

His gaze glanced over her nightgown. He had seen a lot of women in a lot less over the years, and he was suddenly glad for the shawl she covered herself with.

"I'd rather not." It was out before he could stop himself. She seemed to flush, though in the dim light from the lamp and the stove he couldn't be sure.

Mariah rushed on, looking away from him now. "Yes, well, romance is encouraged. One can't marry and make babies without spending a little private time together first, hmm? Not that that's what we were doing..." She trailed off, and this time he was absolutely sure she blushed. He was mesmerized. She cleared her throat. "I only meant that that's what anyone watching will assume," she finished lamely.

"I see." They were the only words he trusted himself with. He pushed his hands a little deeper into his pockets.

"I mean..." Her voice faded again, then she laughed, a lilting, self-amused sound that reminded him of bells. "What *do* I mean? For instance, if you were to park somewhere in the rural settlement just before dawn on any Saturday or Sunday morning, and if you should listen carefully, you would hear the clop-clop of many horses traveling home."

"I would, huh?"

"Yes. The young people have been courting, you see. They wait until the girls' parents go to bed for the night, then the young men will shine flashlights on their bedroom windows. They'll sneak in. And of course everyone knows it, but no one speaks of it. In fact, if you saw that same young man and woman at church or at any public social, they probably wouldn't be caught speaking to each other at all."

"Why?"

Mariah shrugged one shoulder. "Courting is private, personal. Some things are just expected to be kept quiet. I—" This time she broke off abruptly.

"You what?"

She took a breath and continued, but her voice changed. "I left a tablecloth in a boy's buggy once, and I was teased mercilessly for weeks."

"A tablecloth," he repeated blankly.

"Yes."

"What's so scandalous about a tablecloth?"

"It was proof that he had given me a ride home."

"For shame."

And then she did it again. She looked back at him quickly and she laughed so clearly that it was like something silvery raining through the air. She leaned back against the open door and hugged her arms over her waist.

"Adam, you do have a way with words."

Suddenly, he wanted to have a way with many, many other things. Things he had not given any thought to in a very long time.

You need a woman, bro. But not this one. Definitely not this one.

"I have to go," he said abruptly.

"Good night, then."

He was halfway to the car before he stopped. He told himself he was asking because this was his son's world now. Because he wanted, needed, to understand the place where Bo had been living. "These kids...are you saying they're doing what I think you're saying they're doing? You know, when they...sneak around?"

"It's called *Rumspringa*. It means...sowing wild oats, I guess, experimenting a little before you settle down to a life of duty to the church. We probably don't experiment to the extent you're thinking, though. I think mostly our girls are virgins when they marry. But they get a decent head start. They know what they're getting into."

"I'll be damned."

She leaned a little more lazily against the open door. Her hair spilled and seemed to glisten in the moonlight. "We can only marry in October and November," she explained. "That's the only time the church allows it, when the fields are fallow and we don't have to ignore our work to host a wedding, before Thanksgiving and Christmas demand our attention. Sometimes the wait for nuptials is agonizingly long." And sometimes, she thought with a pang, it was long enough to allow you time to change your mind. Her smile faded. "We marry for life, Adam. There are no ex-wives here. So, you see, before you marry you must really be sure of your choice.''

He realized he couldn't even fathom that kind of surety. He realized that when he had married Jannel he had always figured that if it didn't work out it would just cost him a little bit of money. They would not live together forever, bitter and angry and drunk, as his parents had done.

How wrong he'd been. He'd certainly lived bitter and angry, although not together with her.

He finally got into his car. He went back to his room and returned Jake's calls.

Chapter 6

Mariah was crossing the Esslers' fields the next morning when she heard a furtive hissing sound. She immediately stopped and smiled. After a moment, Katya poked her head out of the barn, looking about warily.

Mariah pulled her shawl tighter when the wind would have snatched it. She hurried that way and Katya urged her inside, out of the wind. Mariah frowned as they both moved back from the drafty door. Katya was limping again.

Katya waved her hand as though it was nothing. "Frank got drunk last night," she explained in an undertone.

Mariah shook her head. They had been so close once, as girls. Then Katya had married Frank and Mariah had left the settlement, and now the best they could do was whisper in barns. There was nothing either of them could do to help the other. Mariah consoled herself with the fact that there would have been little she could have done for Katya even if she *wasn't* living under the *Meidung*.

"Did he bring the liquor out here?" she finally asked. "To the barn?"

"Of course. He's not stupid." There was more resignation in Katya's voice than anything else. "I wish he was."

Mariah understood. If Frank would only stumble, make a mistake, get caught, he would probably be shunned. Then Katya could at least separate from him. In fact, she would have to. But here was another of the contradictions that seemed to trouble Adam. If Frank Essler drank in a tavern, that would have brought the *Meidung* upon him for sure, at least until he confessed and repented. As it was, liquor was frowned upon by the church, but as long as it was consumed at home and out of sight the deacons looked the other way. Everyone suspected what he was doing to Katya, too, but no one had actually seen him strike her, so they couldn't say for sure.

Frank Essler was a snake, Mariah thought angrily. "Is there anything I can do?" she asked anyway, knowing again that there wasn't.

Katya smiled sadly. "They don't even see you." She changed the subject. "What happened with that man?"

Mariah's heart gave an odd little thump. "You mean Adam Wallace?"

"The one I sent to you. He was asking about Noah Lapp."

Mariah swallowed carefully. "Yes. I know."

Katya watched her. She had always known her so well, too well, Mariah thought.

"He looks like Noah," Katya ventured finally. "He said he was his father."

Mariah turned haunted eyes on her. She didn't answer.

"You called him, didn't you? How did you ever find him?" Katya cried.

Mariah put a hand to her friend's arm. "It's best that you don't know the details." What she didn't say was clear, too. If Katya didn't know, then her husband couldn't beat the information out of her. Then Mariah relented a little.

"He works with an *anner Satt Leit* company that looks for lost children," she explained vaguely. "I found the number on a milk carton."

Katya finally nodded, her eyes pained. "Did you take him to Noah, then?"

"Yes."

"What will he do?"

"I don't know yet. I don't think he knows himself. But he won't act rashly."

Katya nodded. "He's a good man, then?"

Mariah stared thoughtfully over her shoulder into the darkened barn. She could hear horses chewing and snorting from the shadows. "Yes," she said finally. "He's lost all his peace, Katya.

Someone took it from him. Maybe it was his wife, but I think it happened before that." She thought of the little he had told her about his family. "He needs to get back to himself. And I think, once he does that, he'll do the right thing by Noah."

"You think he'll *stay* here?"

Mariah looked back at her quickly. "No. Oh, no. I think our contradictions make him a little crazy. But he'll handle the situation...right."

Katya looked over her shoulder again. "When he came here to the farm, when he showed me those pictures, I didn't know what to do. And Frank was yelling. I couldn't think."

"You did just the right thing," Mariah assured her.

The door at the other end of the barn opened. A shaft of sunlight cut through the gloom, then disappeared again. Footsteps hurried. They both looked and saw Rachel coming, Katya's ten-year-old.

"This is about more than Noah, isn't it?" Katya blurted. "You're going to ask him to find little Lizzie and the others."

Mariah hesitated, then nodded.

"Oh, Mariah. The settlement will be so angry at you."

"They're already angry. But I owe it to the children." She simply could not bow her head in acceptance when she believed something was wrong. And the church was wrong in not looking for those little ones.

"Will he help, this Adam Wallace?" Katya asked breathlessly.

"I don't know yet."

"Why not?"

Because she couldn't trouble him with the problem now, Mariah thought, not until he had worked through his own pain and difficulties. That was the easiest answer, but maybe not the only one. She also knew that when he figured out that she herself had made that phone call and realized how long it had taken her to do it he was probably going to be angry with her. And suddenly she realized that that was going to be very hard to bear.

Her eyes widened a little at how very important Adam Wallace's opinion had already become to her, in so short a time. She knew why. Of course, she knew why. He'd eased her silence. He'd given her companionship. She enjoyed him and cherished their conversations. And oh, how she dreaded losing that.

Was *that* why she had told him last night to take his time, to remain in the settlement? So she could enjoy being with him a while longer? The possibility that she was that selfish shamed her and made her face go warm.

"What?" Katya whispered. "Mariah, what's wrong?"

She shook her head. "I'll talk to him soon enough," she promised, evading the question.

"He's coming, Mama!" Rachel interrupted.

The warning brought Mariah back to more immediate problems. "Would you like to walk to school with me?" she asked the girl. If Frank was angry and hungover, she wanted to get Rachel out of the line of fire. Even more than she bled for Katya, her heart broke for the Essler children, who had to witness their mother's torments. Unlike those domestic-abuse victims in the *anner Satt Leit* world, neither Katya nor her children had any means of escape. The *Ordnung* prohibited divorce. The idea of a woman leaving her husband was blasphemous. And unlike her husband, Katya could not clandestinely commit such a sin behind the barn.

Mariah wondered how the deacons thought Katya's children would possibly want to grow up to embrace a life where such abuse was sanctioned because escape was forbidden. It was just another traitorous opinion she never spoke aloud.

Mariah took Rachel's hand. "Come, we'll hurry out this way."

"I left my books."

Katya was already hurrying back to the other door. "I'll send them with Levi. Now go on." But then she stopped, looking back at them. "You care for him, the Wallace man," she said to her friend, as though they had not been interrupted.

Mariah felt a warmth spread across her chest. "Yes, I think I do." And oh, she thought, that was dangerous indeed.

Adam came back to the school exactly at three o'clock. He didn't knock.

Mariah was sweeping when the door swung open. She was too lost in her own thoughts to hear him coming this time. She looked up sharply and felt something good and soft fill her heart.

"Adam! How are you today?" Not good, she thought, when he stomped inside, closing the door hard behind him.

"Can I go watch the hockey game?" he demanded without preamble.

"Of course." She put the broom back in the closet. "Coffee?"

"Hockey," he snapped.

He was, she thought, a long, long way from peace right now.

Adam watched her. He could still see her hair as it had been the night before. And he thought again that she was still beautiful, even with it all tucked up. All he had to do was step into this room with her and he began feeling soothed, quiet...warm.

He wanted more. He wanted to reach out and touch her, the smooth curve of her jaw, the frown lines on her forehead.

"We could go stand out in that field," she explained, breaking his thoughts, "and we could wait there. But we'd get very cold, Adam. They won't be playing for a while yet."

He had to drag his mind back to what she was saying. "They were there at this time yesterday."

"No. They were there at three-*thirty* yesterday, and that was unusually early. I'm not sure why it happened. I think Paul Byler's milking machine broke down. The fathers were all off fixing it, so the boys got to postpone their after-school chores."

"And that won't happen two days in a row."

"Probably not."

"So what time do they usually get there?"

"Around four. They'll play for a quick hour, then go home for supper."

"I'll have a cup of coffee."

She smiled at him. "Good."

Today she had brought lemon sponge cake. Adam wondered when she had found time to bake it. He hadn't noticed it in her kitchen last night, nor had he smelled it baking in her wood stove. And with that simple thought, it all rushed back at him again, how feminine, how soft, how absurdly *alluring* she had looked with her feet bare, in that virginal white nightgown.

A dead-end street if ever he'd been faced with one.

He took a large gulp of coffee. It was scalding hot and he choked, his eyes tearing.

"Are you all right?" Mariah asked, alarmed.

"Yeah. Fine." He blew across the top of the mug. "Do you think I should just turn around and leave here and let Bo be? That I should leave well enough alone?" he asked abruptly. "Is that what you were leading up to last night?"

Mariah's heart spasmed, because she knew what it had cost him to even speak the words. She had been right. His heart was good, so very kind and caring, to be able to entertain such a heart-wrenching possibility for Bo's sake. She felt something swell inside her, something warm and even more fluttery than when she had been speaking to Katya. Was it respect? That was all she *dared* feel for him.

"No," she answered softly. "I don't think that's what you should do."

For a moment he doubted his own ears. He had been so sure she would say yes. "What?"

"No," she repeated. "He's your son. He belongs with you."

An odd sensation went through him. It started with a hard thump of his heart, then a vague tingling went through his limbs. He forgot to breathe, and when he did, it was in a harsh burst.

Gratitude, he thought. It was purely gratitude, sweet and strong. She was on his side. Despite her comfort, her help, until that moment he hadn't entirely been sure.

"The problem is how to separate him," Mariah went on. "How to do it most kindly." She stood again. "Come on."

"Where?"

"You wanted to go to the pond. If they're not there yet, we can always drive around a bit while we wait."

"Trust me, there's nothing left for me to see. I've covered every inch of this place six times in the last few days."

"Ah, but you didn't know then which one was Sugar Joe's farm, did you?"

His heart thumped again. No, he thought, he hadn't known which was Bo's home. He zipped his jacket—and suddenly remembered her doing it the night before.

"What did Bo say yesterday, when I took off?" he asked as they went to the door, and again his voice was strained. He'd meant to ask her the previous night, and had somehow forgotten as their conversation had wandered.

"Mikey Gehler asked, 'Who is that crazy *anner Satt Leit?*'" she replied.

"Huh?"

"Outsider. Technically, it's German for 'the other sort of people.'"

"Did it ever occur to you guys that you've got it backward? That there are more of us than there are of you, and that we got here first?"

"No. Never once." And he knew before he looked at her that she would be smiling.

He opened the car door for her. "So what did Bo do when Mikey said that?"

"He laughed, looked around and saw that no one was near the

puck. Then he raced back and scored a goal while everyone's
guard was down.''

Adam found he could still laugh. "That's my boy.''

They watched the hockey game until dark began to fall. They
stood at the edge of the field near Adam's car, and if any of the
kids wondered why the crazy *anner Satt Leit* had come to watch
them again, they didn't ask. In fact, they didn't pay any attention
at all.

Bo scored the game-winning goal.

Adam almost shouted. He could see it happening before it actually did, watched it all unfold in sort of split-second freeze
frames. Five or six boys were checking each other madly at one
edge of the pond. Adam knew that it was more for the sheer fun
of knocking each other down than to advance the game. He
grinned, glanced at Mariah, and found her doing the same. Something shifted and settled inside him.

Then the puck squirted out from all the feet and blades. Bo had
been at the far end of the ice, skating hard toward the commotion,
and Adam guessed he'd had every intention of piling on with the
others. But then he saw the puck come free and he braked, ice
spraying, and came around it. He slapped it squarely and it went
airborne.

Adam watched in slow motion as it seemed to hover, then it
dropped down neatly behind the goalie's shoulder. Pandemonium
erupted. Bo thrust his hands and his stick in the air. The knot of
wrestling kids broke up, and those who were apparently his teammates fell upon him instead.

"He's certainly quick," Mariah observed. "He doesn't let
much opportunity get past him.''

Adam opened his mouth to answer and realized his throat was
closed tight. He coughed. "It's in his genes.''

She cocked a brow at him.

"The athleticism." And then, because it sounded like he was
tooting his own horn, he added, "His uncle was a hell of a quar-
terback. He played football.''

"Like you played baseball? For money?''

Adam shook his head. "No. Jake knows just when and where
to draw the line, so he doesn't get too involved in anything he
might enjoy too much.''

As soon as he said it, he was shaken by his own observation.

But he thought about it as he turned back to the car, and it was true. It was even evident in the lecture his brother had given him before he'd flown up here.

If this one doesn't pan out, maybe you ought to think about shelving it. That was Jake. Give up, give out, before it gets too good...before it hurts.

Adam wondered if it had something to do with this almost magically peaceful land, that lately he seemed to be understanding things he'd never really thought about before. He wondered if it was the woman who walked beside him. He realized that he talked to her almost as if he was talking to himself aloud. And she was always listening.

"I'd buy you dinner," he heard himself say, "but I guess restaurants are on the blacklist, huh?"

"To eat in one, yes. To eat *from* one, no."

He gave her an exasperated look. "What's the difference this time?"

"Family, Adam."

"Cut me a break. There's no connection."

"There certainly is. If you're *in* a restaurant, there are interruptions. Waiters, other people at other tables. You can't focus on your own. Meals should be taken at one's own table or at the table of a friend. Besides, restaurants are worldly."

He stopped at the car and looked over it at her. "But if I go to a restaurant, buy takeout and bring it to your house, that's okay."

"Yes."

"Oh, man."

"Is that an invitation, Adam?"

"Yeah. I guess." He got behind the wheel. Why not? He'd eat a frozen dinner at his desk, alone. She'd eat a home-cooked meal in her pretty kitchen, alone. They might as well eat together, and he'd spare her the work.

He realized that he was trying just a little too hard to rationalize the decision. That image of her long hair and her nightgown still had a way of flashing before him at odd times, and it worried him.

Hell, it *panicked* him.

"Then I accept," she said quietly.

"I'll drop you off and go back out."

"That would be fine."

Neither one of them spoke again until he had stopped in front of her house. "There's something I don't understand here," he said finally.

"Just one thing?"

He looked at her sharply and realized she was teasing. He managed a small smile. "Okay, a lot of things, but this one stands out. If you're already being shunned, then why worry about all the other little fine points of the—what did you call it?"

"The *Ordnung*."

"Yeah. I mean, you went to school, so they shut you out. But you still avoid restaurants and you power your refrigerator with a battery. Isn't it a little late to be worrying about that stuff?"

"I power my refrigerator with a hydraulic motor."

He made a sound of exasperation. "Same difference."

Mariah sighed. "It's pride, I'd guess."

"I thought that was a sin among you folks."

"It is, but it's also human nature, so it's difficult to stomp out."

He thought about that and finally nodded.

"For instance, the *Ordnung* says a man should wear his hair to a length just about here." She touched a finger beneath her earlobe. "My father wears it even longer. Why? Because he takes pride in being well within the rules. Is the church going to chastise him for being overly devout? No, of course not. So his pride...flourishes. As for me, I really do believe in the *Ordnung*, Adam. I think that, for the most part, it is a right and good thing. I think family, children *should* be the focus of one's life. And I follow that dictate for my own gratification now. Just as my father wears his hair longer than he has to, I observe rules I am no longer technically bound by. Just...because."

"I thought maybe you were hoping they'll...I don't know, relent. That the church will change their minds about you if you're good enough for long enough."

Her violet eyes widened a little and pain shimmied briefly inside her. "You're wiser than you give yourself credit for," she said softly. "But it won't happen. I know that."

He was inordinately pleased that he was right. And that she admitted it. And he was angered that her people could be so rigid and stubborn.

"Why?" he demanded.

"They fought the government on the education issue, Adam, and fighting is not their policy. That's how strongly they feel about it. They think that everything we need to know is taught before high school. Taking more time than that for studies would just pull us away from our—''

"Families," he interrupted.

"Yes. And it would make us worldly, would make us want more."

"But you've proved that's not the case, damn it! You came back." He couldn't say why he was getting angry.

She sighed again. "It doesn't matter."

"So what are you going to do?" he demanded.

"Do?"

"Are you just going to live out the rest of your life here? On the boundaries?" And then his heart pounded, because he wondered what he was really asking. He wondered if her answer was so important, if maybe, just maybe he had been leading up to it all along.

"Probably," she answered softly.

"That's crazy." His anger was growing. "You're young. You could have a husband, children. You said you wanted children. And you sure as hell can't marry a man who can't see you, right? So you're just going to stay here and give all that up?"

"I can't marry," she agreed without answering. "Not within the church. No one can marry a shunned member. The deacons wouldn't approve it, wouldn't recognize the union."

"So you'll just...wither up and die here," he said cruelly. "Alone."

Her expression crumbled for a moment, and he felt like hell for hurting her. But damn it, *he* wasn't the one who had shunned her.

"I'm not all that unhappy, Adam," she said finally.

Her eyes said differently. "You have a lot more to give," he snapped.

She ducked her head. He thought she was blushing again.

"What about that other county you've talked about?" he demanded. "Berks? You said they can see you there."

"Yes. They're mostly New Order in Berks. We're Old Order."

"So go live there."

"My family is here."

"They don't even see you!" He swore. It was her choice, damn it. Her life. If she wanted to waste it, that was her business.

"I might be forced to move, sooner or later," she said finally, thoughtfully. "I have to support myself. The settlement can't—won't—help me, as they do others who fall upon hard times."

"You're running out of money?" he asked sharply. "I have plenty. I'll give you some."

She looked up at him, her jaw falling open. Then she gave that laugh again, the one that sounded like something silvery falling.

"Don't be silly, Adam. Why in the world would you want to give me money?"

He hadn't a clue. To let her go on leading this chastised, empty life he thought was wrong? And the fact was, he didn't have all that much money left, anyway; not if he was going to keep on funding ChildSearch to the extent he did, not if he had to keep paying rent plus two mortgages.

He looked away from her, glaring out his side window. "I haven't been all that...kind to you," he said finally, roughly. "I guess I just wanted to do something to thank you."

"No thanks are necessary, Adam. And you haven't been *unkind*. You've just been...you. Determined. In a hurry."

He made a noncommittal sound deep in his throat.

"Besides, I have very few needs, and as long as I can teach, I can pay my way," she went on. "I've even managed to save a little bit. And it would only become a problem if they find someone else to take my school. Then I would have to go to whatever *Gemeide* had an opening, whichever one would tolerate me, assuming I could find one here in Lancaster County. If not, I'd have to go to Berks."

He didn't answer.

"Adam?"

"What?" he growled.

"I'm starving."

He finally looked back at her again. "So get out and let me go find us something to eat."

She gave him a rare full smile, and left the car. He saw that smile for a long time after she had gone inside her little house and shut the door behind her.

Chapter 7

Adam drove down to Strasburg, the largest, nearest town. It didn't seem to be part of the "settlement," as Mariah called it. It was moving, alive with people like himself, though admittedly the business district was only five blocks long.

He hadn't realized how much he missed the real world. Even at his motel, he'd remained mostly isolated. All his contact lately had been with the Amish. With Mariah. Now he thirsted for the cacophony of civilization. He savored the smell of exhaust fumes and the ringing of telephones. For maybe the first time in his life, he wasn't impatient when a girl broke off from taking his order to glance up at the television affixed to a corner of the ceiling.

And nowhere, he thought, no matter where he looked, did he see any beautiful women in long white nightgowns with spilling hair. At least here he wasn't tempted into wanting something he couldn't possibly have.

He didn't know if she had any food taboos and decided to play it safe. He found an Italian place and bought a pizza. Then he went four doors down and picked up a quart of chow mein and some egg rolls. Finally he found a chicken place. He got a bucket of extra crispy, another of barbecue, some mashed potatoes and corn on the cob. Satisfied, he drove back to Divinity.

When Mariah opened her door, her eyes widened. "Adam, what have you done?"

He juggled his purchases. "Let me in so I can put some of this down, will you?"

She stepped back, then followed him, her hand clapped to her mouth. When everything was spread out on her kitchen table, she shook her head slowly. "I'm...amazed."

"I didn't know what you liked."

She pried open the carton of chow mein. "All of it." She grinned. "I'll get plates."

She ate with relish. It pleased him, that he had finally done something for her, something she seemed to appreciate. Her sheer enjoyment of the food warmed something inside him again.

"Oh, this is good," she said, swallowing a mouthful of egg roll, biting into a piece of pizza.

"You're going to be sick." The only thing she had barely touched was the corn, and he was in agreement with her there. He was pretty sure it had been frozen.

"Yes, probably. I have working plumbing."

"Not against the *Ordnung?*"

"I have a septic tank, not sewer. So—"

"You're not dependent on the outside world," he finished for her.

"Right." She finished the pizza and went for another slice. "Adam, I've been thinking."

"About what?"

"About your Bo."

She was almost sorry she had mentioned it. For whole periods of time, since he had come back with the food, he had seemed almost relaxed. Now his face hardened again.

"We need to speak to Sugar Joe," she rushed on. "He should be told what's happening, that you've come." Now that Katya knew, rumors would begin circulating, she thought. And she didn't want Joe to hear about this that way.

Adam didn't know what he'd expected her to say, but it wasn't that. "Yeah," he agreed cautiously. "I'm all for it." It had been killing him, he realized, knowing there was another man out there, a faceless man, presuming to be Bo's father. No matter how good, how kind that man might be, no matter how well he had taken care of Bo over the years, Adam hated him.

Pride, he thought. Ego. He watched Mariah reach for more chicken.

"Where the he—" He cleared his throat. "Where are you putting all that? You're eating like a truck driver."

She glanced up at him, chewing, and swallowed prettily. "I don't know when I'll have such bounty again. This is not something I ever do."

He thought of what she had said about college. *I wrung everything out of the experience that was there for the taking.* For all her prim femininity, there was a certain gusto lurking just beneath it, he realized, then he decided he didn't want to think about that too much. Because he found himself wondering just how that gusto might manifest itself in other areas.

He pushed the container of potatoes her way.

"Thank you." She dug in with a spoon for all she was worth. He gave a bark of laughter and she smiled again.

"Anyway, about this Sugar Joe," he went on finally. "I don't imagine I can simply go up and knock on his door and say, 'Excuse me, I'm your kid's father.'"

"Well, no. That's not what I would recommend. Oh, he'd certainly be polite. But think of the shock you'd give the poor man. Think of the effect such an announcement would have on Bo, if he happened to be within hearing distance at the time."

Adam sobered. "I do, Mariah. Trust me. I think about that every minute of every day." Except, he realized, on those numerous occasions when she somehow diverted him.

"I think *I* should approach him," she went on. "I could try to arrange for us to talk."

"How? How can you do that if he doesn't see you?"

"Ah. Well, Sugar Joe is from Berks County. Remember, I told you that?"

"So he sees you." Adam scowled. "Why do I feel another contradiction coming on here?"

A corner of her mouth lifted. "No contradiction. Technically, he can't see me, either."

"So what are you saying?"

"That he might if no one is looking." His expression warned her that he was running out of patience again. She rushed on. "The Berks County *Gemeides* don't practice the *Meidung*. Of course, Sugar Joe had to convert to our more strict church in order to marry Sarah, or else *she* would have been shunned by her own people." His expression darkened. "Never mind," she said quickly. "My point is that Sugar Joe was raised in a certain way, and I can personally attest to the fact that the heart seems to cling to whatever you were used to as a child, no matter how much your head tries to convince you otherwise. I honestly don't think he approves of the *Meidung* as much as he goes along with it for Sarah's sake. He might sneak aside to see me, to talk to me."

Adam's eyes narrowed. Already he wasn't liking the sounds of this, but it was an instinct more than anything else. He couldn't put his finger on why.

"This Sunday is *Gemeesunndaag,* our church Sunday. Everyone will be together. I'll get a message to Sugar Joe through one of his children, to meet me somewhere isolated and safe."

"I'm going with you." The instinct, the unease, was getting stronger. Maybe it was the way she was suddenly avoiding his eyes.

Mariah nodded. "Yes, I think you should."

She stood and began collecting their dishes. Adam got to his feet as well. He closed some of the various cartons and boxes. Then something she'd said jiggled another thought in his mind—that she would get a message to the man through one of his kids.

"Mariah."

She looked over her shoulder at him as she rinsed their plates. "Yes?"

"The children can talk to you. They must. You teach them. Do they see you?"

"Yes."

"What am I missing here?"

She turned around and took a dish towel from a hook on the wall. She dried her hands and still wouldn't look at him. He went to her, catching her chin with his finger, tilting it up, making her meet his eyes. "What's the catch?"

"It's silly, really."

He refrained from saying that he thought a lot of their *Ordnung* was—all of it that made her suffer, anyway. He waited.

"This explanation goes back a little way," she said evasively.

"I'm listening."

She sighed. "My people broke off from the church in Germany in the sixteenth century because of a disagreement regarding baptism," she said finally. "We don't believe in baptizing a child, forcing religion down his throat, so to speak, before he's old enough to decide for himself what he wants. Adherence to the *Ordnung* is...hard. Only an adult can voluntarily embrace it. A little one can't be expected to make a mature decision as to whether that's how he wants to live the rest of his life or not."

She was finally holding his eyes. He didn't like what he saw in hers. "Okay," he said warily.

"Since children haven't yet embraced the *Ordnung,* neither are they bound by it."

"Then why is everybody so fired up about you having gone to college?"

"I...made a mistake."

Her voice was so small, he barely heard it. "Come again?"

"I made a mistake. I was wrong. I...goofed."

"Goofed," he repeated, because it sounded almost incongruous coming out of her mouth.

"I thought I could do it," she rushed on. "I was just trying to be obedient, to do what everyone expected of me, to do what I was raised to do. I got my high-school diploma through that correspondence course and that was okay, that was forgiven and overlooked because I hadn't promised my life yet. I hadn't been baptized. I put that paper in my drawer and I thought it was enough. It was prideful, but it pleased me."

Her words were tumbling now, and that warned him. Adam felt his muscles stiffen. "But it wasn't enough."

She didn't answer, not directly. "Then Asher asked me to marry him. I said yes, and he asked the deacons and they said yes, but you can't marry unless you're baptized, so I did it. That was in the spring and we had to wait until October, and somewhere in there...sometime that summer, I just knew I couldn't go through with it. I...couldn't." Her eyes became pleading, and it hurt something inside him. "I didn't love him. I wanted...more."

He thought she whispered it as though it were some shameful treachery. He felt his rage starting.

"I didn't go to Penn State because I wanted to *be* anything. I just wanted to *know.* Things. Just...things. I just wanted to learn. And nobody can understand why I destroyed my life for the right to do that. But my life would have been miserable either way, do you see? At least if I went to college, I would have something to show for my misery. I would have learned a million things before I had to start suffering in this...this solitude."

His temper pounded inside his head. He didn't trust himself to speak. He cleared his throat with a great effort, and his own voice was as low, as tense as hers had been.

"Let me get this straight. If you had gone to college, come back, gotten baptized, everything would have been fine. Forgiven."

She nodded spasmodically.

"But because you *tried* to conform, because you did it the other way around, because you attempted to do as they wanted and ended up not being able to swallow it, they're going to make you suffer for it for the rest of your life?"

His low voice scared her. "That's too harsh, Adam," she said quickly, jolted out of her own misery. "I keep telling you. I'm not *un*happy. And it was my choice."

"They've robbed from you the right to marry, to have children of your own," he went on. "They've taken—"

"But—"

"They make you live in silence," he finished harshly.

He didn't know he was going to do it. Didn't mean to do it. But she was trembling with pain over a simple, understandable mistake that had gone drastically wrong. And he was furious, he was enraged, that they would punish her for it like this, so severely. Who in the hell did they think they were?

He touched her. He put his hands on her shoulders as though to steady her, and he fought to keep from clenching his fingers and hurting her.

"I had a choice," she said again, her voice a whisper now.

"No."

"I made it. I'll live with it."

"I'm sorry." It seemed the stupidest thing to say. But he was—terribly, bitterly sorry for her, though he knew she would resent pity. He thought it was a sacrilege that this woman, this beautiful woman who was so kind, so good with children, so alive with hidden gusto, should live her life as a ghost, should be doomed to stepping into rooms just to have the people there avert their eyes as if she were some kind of pariah.

He wanted to hurt somebody, those who had done this to her. He wanted to fight it, to do something about it. But like the day when he had understood the situation with Bo, he was helpless.

Maybe that was why he drew her slowly toward him—all he could offer was comfort. He wrapped his arms around her and rested his chin on top of her head and closed his eyes and he knew he was crazy. He didn't dare touch this woman, because she could never be more than a friend. He didn't dare inch across that line because he had the feeling that he wouldn't easily get back again. When she smoothed her nightgown over her thighs, when she padded around barefoot with her hair spilling, what he felt toward her left friendly far behind. But she kept trembling, and then she slid her hands beneath his jacket and took fistfuls of his shirt and held on. And she cried.

He didn't, couldn't, pull away again.

Her hair smelled like violets, he thought. It carried a hint of something that was the color of her eyes. So he just continued to hold her.

Chapter 8

Adam didn't see Mariah again for several days. He told himself he wasn't actually avoiding her. He just didn't really need her to go stand by the frozen pond in the afternoons. He didn't need her with him to drive past the Lapp farm and catch a glimpse of Bo chasing the cows into the barn for their afternoon milking. He didn't need her company in order to digest a meal. And he was busy, too busy to seek her out, anyway.

ChildSearch had problems. Rebecca, the day receptionist, had quit abruptly in favor of a better paying job. Diana, one of the night operators who manned the phones during the off-hours, was currently working sixteen-hour shifts so no potential tip would go unanswered. Jake reported that her energy was beginning to flag.

If Adam had been there, he would have manned the phones himself until he could hire someone else, someone with her heart in the right place, someone willing to work for minimum wage to save children snatched and taken against their will. As it was, the best he could do was hire an answering service for the nights at a whole lot more than what he had been paying Rebecca. He moved Diana from evenings to the eight-hour day shifts and promised her Sunday off. Jake would fill in the holes until Adam could get back to Dallas.

That wasn't going to happen any time soon.

He told himself the decision had nothing to do with Mariah's opinion that he had nothing particular to go home to, not even for a quick visit to set things straight. It had everything to do with the paralysis of indecision that continued to grip him. He didn't know what to do about Bo yet. He *couldn't* do anything, at least not until he had spoken to this Sugar Joe. And he would not leave this place until there was some resolution. The thought was preposterous.

That was why, on Sunday morning, he turned up at her door a little too early. Because he needed to *do* something, he told himself, to start setting things in motion. Because he couldn't just hang in limbo forever.

That was what he told himself.

The truth of the matter was that when she opened her door to him, his heart seemed to kick and flop over at her smile. And not a nightgown in sight. She was dressed as she always was, in her deep purple dress with the black apron, and it all fell demurely to a point just at her knees. The black tights, the plain shoes, the small white bonnet perched at the back of her head—it was all the same. And this time the purple seemed to bring out the violet of her eyes. This time all the black made her skin seem fair as porcelain, except for a faint blush that touched her cheeks when she saw him.

"Hey," he said awkwardly. "You...uh, said something about church."

"Yes. We have a little bit of time yet. Coffee?"

He thought that with all the coffee she urged on him, he was going to have a caffeine high that would stay with him long after he left this settlement behind. He looked at his watch.

"It's already past eight-thirty."

"Yes, they'll be starting soon. It takes a while to get the cows milked and the morning chores done and to get everyone piled into the buggy to go to whatever home the services are being held at this time."

"It changes?"

She smiled and ushered him inside. "Yes. Its—"

"Family," he interrupted. Somehow he found himself standing in her living room with his hands shoved in his jacket pockets again, though he'd thought he would just pick her up and...go.

"We believe in doing nearly everything in the home, even our church services. So we have no churches. We simply rotate from one family's barn or living room to the next."

"You don't go anymore." It wasn't a question.

"No. I can't." She hurried off to the kitchen. He followed her.

"Have you had breakfast?" she asked.

"Yeah. A fast food egg sandwich."

She wrinkled her nose. "That's awful."

He felt oddly chastised. "You did all right with that fast food the other night."

"That was entirely different."

"In what way?"

"It was real chicken, real vegetables, real cheese. They use egg substitutes in some of those sandwiches, Adam. I heard that when I was away at school."

She began dragging out frying pans. He moved to put a hand on her arm to stop her, then he snatched it back before he actually touched her.

"Mariah, you don't have to cook me anything."

"Of course I don't. I want to."

Why? He almost asked aloud and bit the word back.

Everything had changed between them, he realized. Somewhere along the line, somehow, things had changed. He wasn't even sure when it had happened. When he had held her in his arms and let her cry? As early as when she had come to the door in her nightgown? Or had it been somewhere in between? He honestly didn't know, but it panicked him all over again. Because there were no doors in this room of hers. He could get in, but it was pretty clear now that she wouldn't come out.

He didn't want to go in. He didn't like the world she subjected herself to. Oh, it had its own unique peace. It was quiet and a man could breathe the air here. It was a tolerable respite, but he didn't want to stay.

And if he didn't want to stay, if he could not offer her—or himself—more than a few moments of physical pleasure, then he had no business touching her, getting too close to her, at all. If that was all he could offer, then he doubted if she would entertain the possibility, anyway.

"Adam?"

"What?" He jolted.

"You look troubled. What is it?"

"I'm always troubled."

"*More* troubled, then."

"I'm fine. Put the pans away. We should get to the church— or the barn or wherever the hell we're going."

Her violet eyes searched his face. He realized it was the first time he had cursed in her presence for a while now. He wondered if it was just another little way of putting some distance between them or reminding himself of the gulf that was already there.

He was starting to hate understanding himself so well.

"It won't do us any good until noon or so," she answered.

"*Noon?*" He almost hollered. "Why? You said everyone would be getting there now."

"Getting there, and going right inside. Services last several hours. And I can't go in, and neither can you. So we should wait until the children come out again."

"Terrific." It was his own fault for having rushed over here. He raked a hand through his hair. He was not going to sit in this woman's kitchen for three hours.

"So...eggs?" she suggested. "Scrambled or fried?"

"Damn it—"

"Perhaps if you take your coffee and relax in front of the fire while I throw something together, you won't feel so wound up, Adam."

"I was born this way."

"But there's no need to be so tense here."

He gave a snort of disbelief. Did she honestly not feel it? Did she honestly not recognize the change? Didn't she feel the danger here?

That possibility shook him, that he was the only one suddenly imagining touching. That only he had been wondering what her skin would feel like, how heavy her hair would be when it finally filled his hands.

"Damn it," he muttered aloud. He took the mug of coffee she had poured for him and stalked into the other room.

The hell of it was, he did relax. One moment he was glaring into the flames in the open stove as they danced way too gently to give any appreciable warmth. Then her voice called him to the table, and he realized that at some point he had leaned his head back against the rocker and had closed his eyes.

He refused to admit that maybe—just *maybe*—he had dozed off for a moment or two.

She'd fried eggs and scrapple and potatoes. He ate for a long time, famished, before he looked at her. "How exactly are you going to do this?"

His mind was working again, Mariah realized. But that was okay. He'd slept in the rocker. She guessed he probably didn't

sleep any better than she did these days, and she always felt the
tension in him, knew how much he needed to rest.

"I've written a note." She patted her apron pocket and sat
across from him. "I'll give it to one of his boys. If he can, Joe
will meet me."

"Where?"

"I've suggested the schoolhouse. Today's service is at Katya
Essler's place, so the school is relatively nearby."

His eyes narrowed thoughtfully. "Why didn't you just give the
note to one of his kids on Friday? Don't you teach them?"

"I was afraid there'd be too much chance for it to get lost
between their hands and his in the meantime. Or that Sarah might
stumble upon it. It will be better if Joe tells her what's happening."

He felt an odd twist of something—anger, maybe, tangled with
regret and misplaced guilt—as he remembered what Mariah had
said about the woman not being able to have any more children.

"Makes sense." He pushed his plate away abruptly and kept
his tone inflectionless. "So...we wait."

"Not much longer now."

It was nearly eleven, he realized, startled.

Silence fell over the table. *Now,* a little voice inside Mariah
whispered. Tell him about the other children, tell him that you
didn't see Bo in the farmers' market, that it was *you* who called
his company in Dallas. Tell him, clear the slate now.

It was growing more important all the time, with every day,
with every moment that passed. It wasn't just that she suspected
that the more time that elapsed, the harder it was going to be to
find Lizzie and the others. Nor was it entirely her fear that the
children might be suffering while they were gone. Of course that
terrified her. She'd felt urgent from the time she'd first called
ChildSearch, from the moment she'd let herself take the first step.
But she'd deliberately tucked that urgency away so that Adam
wouldn't see it or sense it. She'd done it at first because she'd
been able to convince herself that she didn't want to burden him
with the settlement's troubles while he was busy with his own.

But she had known, all along she had known, that she was
afraid as well.

He'd given her dull gray world such light, a wonderful new
texture, when he'd come into it. He brought surprise and pleasure
and anticipation to her days. And it was purely selfish of her to
base her actions on the probability of losing that when he knew

the whole truth. Because she would certainly lose it anyway, sooner or later, when he took his Bo and went home.

But not, she prayed, not before he found the others.

She took a breath and clamped her hands together in front of her on the table. "Adam, there's something else we need to talk about."

"I can't deal with it right now," he said abruptly, and startled even himself. He had no idea where the words had come from.

Her eyes widened. "I beg your pardon?"

Instinct again, he realized. She was going to talk about...them. He was certain of it. She had read something in his eyes, some dawning desire. But there *was* no them and there couldn't be a them and every instinct was telling him to make her shut up.

"Can't we go?" He stood and glared down at her when she remained seated. "Look, if it's all the same to you, I'd really like to do something about getting my kid back so I can get the hell out of Dodge. Are you coming or not?"

He thought he saw her flinch, and he knew he was being rude. But panic was carrying him now. And her expression went smooth again almost immediately, anyway.

"Just let me get my coat and shawl," she said.

Just a little while longer, she thought. Would it hurt to enjoy his company just a little while longer? Besides, he really wasn't ready to help her yet. Wasn't the situation with Bo still unresolved?

She stood and hurried from the kitchen. Adam watched her go, and wondered suddenly where she kept her clothing, her personal things...where she slept.

He went back into the living room and realized he was getting a headache. He looked around pensively. As pretty and feminine as it was in its simplicity, there really wasn't anything personal about the space. There were no pictures of family or friends. No books beside the chair that might tell him what she liked to read— this woman who had craved knowledge enough to sacrifice her world for it.

When she came back, she seemed slightly out of breath. He looked at her and wondered if he was crazy or if her eyes looked even more sad than usual. As if she, too, had finally come to the conclusion that their friendship had reached a brick wall, and it was going to have to stop evolving right here, right now.

"Mariah, you don't have to do this. You don't have to go with me."

"Of course I do. How else will we let Joe know what's happening?"

"I could approach him."

"You don't even know what he looks like."

He took a deep breath and raked a hand through his hair. "So we'll drive by and you can point him out to me. I'll take it from there."

"This is better. I might be shunned, but at least he knows me. He knows my family. You're..."

"Anner Satt Leit," he finished for her, his mood lifting a little, absurdly pleased that he had remembered the phrase.

Mariah let out her breath. "Yes."

He didn't fight her. He knew he should and couldn't find the will or the energy.

They went out to his car. This time she stopped him on Ronks Road, heading south, before they turned onto Star Road toward the school and the Essler farm.

"Park here, Adam. I think that's best."

He pulled over, scowling. "Why?"

"In this *Gemeide,* it would be considered in poor taste to bring an automobile to *Gemeesunndaag,* to Church Sunday."

He thought about it. "Okay." He didn't want to offend anyone. He didn't want to make enemies right off the bat. He wanted to get his kid back, as simply and kindly and easily as possible.

They got out of the car and started up the road on foot. Mariah still seemed too quiet, too pensive. He, on the other hand, felt better, stronger, more charged with every step he took. He was finally *doing* something.

They reached the Essler farm just as the side door of the house shot open. He was boggled by the sheer number of buggies crammed into the front paddocks—easily a hundred of them. What seemed like an equal amount of children spilled outside, laughing, chasing each other like they did when they were released from school for the year. Then again, three hours was a long service, he thought, and he remembered that Mariah had mentioned they all did their milking and chores first. This would be their first taste of freedom since dawn.

A handful of men emerged from the house after the children. Like Katya's husband, they were all bearded. Like everyone else he had met here, they all wore black. But like men the world over, they moved off to the side of a barn by themselves, congregating for their own masculine talk and pleasures, patting pockets, looking for their pipes.

"Guess nobody told them that that's bad for their health," Adam muttered as one of them began puffing. He and Mariah had stopped at the foot of the drive.

"It doesn't matter," Mariah murmured, her eyes searching the burgeoning crowd. "Cancer, too, is God's will. I doubt most of them know or care what cholesterol is, either."

Adam snorted in disbelief.

"There's little Matthew," she said suddenly. "He'll do. Wait here, Adam."

He'd intended to. He stuck his hands into his pockets for warmth and watched as she hurried up the drive. The children had scattered, the girls going off in one direction, the boys in another, except for one group of teenagers. They stayed together but kept a good distance from each other, and Adam found himself wondering which of the boys had shone flashlights on the windows of which girls' homes the night before.

Rumspringa, he thought. All fine and dandy, as long as you were going to marry the lady. It made his gut tighten.

Then it happened. As Mariah passed the teenagers, they looked at her quickly, clearly shocked. Adam saw their surprise turn to discomfiture, then to disapproval before they quickly retreated from her path, almost stumbling into each other in their haste.

She had to pass the little girls, as well, to get to the boys who were playing tag in the field behind the barn. The girls started to call out to her, then they quickly looked at their fathers as though unsure if they were allowed to speak to her here or not. And no matter if they accepted her now, Adam knew they were all going to grow into women who disdained her.

The men at the barn all seemed to notice her at the same time. They turned their backs on her as one. Their faces were angry, full of censure, even disgust.

A heavy silence had fallen. Even the horses in a distant pasture seemed to have stopped chewing to watch the scene unfold. Adam saw Mariah miss a step and her face colored in shame. His pulse roared.

Not for me, don't do this for me. He was torn suddenly between guilt and fury at these holier-than-thou people, who acted as if they had never, not once, made a mistake.

A woman came out of the house in response to the unnatural

quiet. "What's going—" Then she saw Mariah and stopped in her tracks, as well. She turned quickly and went back inside.

Adam took a step without meaning to. Damn them. Damn them all. Why had Mariah done this to herself? She had to have known what she was walking into—hell, on some level so had he. But seeing it, watching it, was harder than he had known it would be.

He called out to her reflexively, his voice loud and raw. Gazes flicked to him, then, furtively and briefly, to her again. Mariah didn't answer, just kept hurrying toward the boys.

He waited, feeling sick, his head pounding now. He prayed to a God he had never really gotten in touch with. *Come on, come on, let her get it done and come back to me. As though I deserve her.*

He saw her tuck her note into a youngster's hand. He wondered if anyone else noticed. Probably not. They were all looking deliberately away. She knelt and talked to the boy quickly, then she got to her feet again and hurried back toward the drive.

Past the men. Past the teenagers. She kept her head high now, and her face had gone from red to pale. She did not look at any one of them.

He caught an arm around her shoulders when she reached him, pushing her down the drive to the street again. She was trembling hard, as she had on the night she had cried, and it tore his heart out.

"I shouldn't have let you do this." *For me.*

"You didn't let me," she gasped.

"Yeah, I did."

"No. Please, just...hurry, Adam. Just...let's get out of here."

They reached the street and turned. "How dare they?" he growled.

"Some of them didn't want to, but they had to."

That tipped him off. She wasn't trembling, wasn't on the verge of breaking, because her community had shunned her. Or at least, it wasn't only because of that.

"Your family was there," he said hoarsely. "God, were some of those people your *family?*"

"Adam, please. Don't use His name in vain."

She didn't answer his question, and that was answer enough. She moved a little closer to him, as though for strength and comfort, and that was when he realized that his arm was still around her shoulder. He held her as they walked, as though he could somehow shield her from everything back there on that farm with his own body. As though to keep those censuring eyes from watching her furtively, now that her back was turned. He knew without looking that they would all be staring now. Contemplating her shame, her defiance, wondering if she would break soon. Probably wondering who he was.

Suddenly her arm snaked around his waist. And as she had the other night, she grabbed a handful of his jacket and just...held on. And if that was all he could give her, then he would give her that much.

"I didn't think it would be that bad," he admitted as they reached the school. She finally let go of him to unlock the door. He released her, as well. The wind felt colder for it.

She laughed a little too harshly. "I always think I'm strong enough to handle anything. Another sin of pride. Anyway, it's over now."

"Will Sugar Joe come?"

"Maybe. Maybe not. We'll wait and see."

"He damned well better," he snapped.

Mariah looked at him, surprised.

"Was he one of those men outside?" he demanded.

"Yes, but—"

"Then he saw what you went through to get that note to his kid. And if he doesn't have the heart to find out what you need him for, then I'll be damned if I'm going to give him another five minutes with my Bo."

Mariah sighed tremulously and went to put some wood into the stove. The little schoolhouse was gripped with a chill.

His words still lingered in the air when the door behind them opened. Mariah came to her feet, looking around quickly, and relief flooded her face.

"Sugar Joe! Oh, thank you."

At first glance, Adam thought Joe Lapp was as unobtrusive as the rest of the men. He wore the same black hat. He sported the same black clothing and the same beard. But the beard was shorter than those Adam had noticed earlier, and the man's eyes were deep and dark and thoughtful.

Sugar Joe's gaze moved to Mariah, and Adam thought he saw regret there. Then they came around to him and they were measuring, assessing, hardly the eyes of an ignorant, uneducated man.

"So," Sugar Joe said finally. "I guess you'd be Noah's father."

Chapter 9

Adam tensed, and a spurt of irrational indignation hit him. "Bo," he corrected. "His name is Bo Wallace."

Sugar Joe only nodded. His face was one of jaded calm. Adam realized that that would have been a contradiction in terms anywhere but here, in this quiet, simple land. There were gentle lines at the corners of his eyes, and the skin that showed above his beard was tanned, even in January, and weathered from working in the elements. But his eyes remained steady, knowing and peaceful.

He took off his broad-brimmed hat and placed it on a desk, then he looked quickly at Mariah and picked it up again. "Sorry. Do you mind?"

She seemed shaken that he had even acknowledged her, much less with respect. "No. Of course not. Please, make yourself comfortable." She bent back to the hearth to stoke the fire. Adam thought she was shivering, but from the cold or from nerves, he couldn't be sure.

Joe finally put the hat down again. He leaned a hip against the desk. "So you've come for your boy."

"I have papers. Custody papers." Adam patted his pockets, then he realized that he hadn't been carrying them on him. Not this trip, this time when he had finally hit pay dirt and needed them most of all.

That realization made him scowl.

Sugar Joe waved a hand. "We have no use for that sort of thing. I've always imagined that was one of the reasons he was dropped off here. Besides, there's not a doubt in my mind that you are who you say you are. He looks like you."

Adam's heart swelled so suddenly, so completely, it caught him off guard. His eyes hurt and he had to look away. He heard Mariah's voice as though from a great distance, although she had finished with the fire and had come to join them.

"How did you know?" she asked.

Joe gave a laugh. "The deacons might consider me a Berks County heathen, but I'm not a stupid heathen. I've always expected this would happen sooner or later. I've kept warning Sarah. Matt and Noah said an outsider, a man, has been watching them play hockey. Then you turned up in the Essler drive."

Adam found himself liking the man. He extended his hand. "Adam Wallace."

Sugar Joe shook. "Joe Lapp. I'd appreciate it if you could ignore the nickname. It's been the bane of my existence for a while now."

Adam almost grinned, then he sobered again. "His mother?" he asked hoarsely. There was so much he needed to ask, to know. "Where *is* Jannel? Mariah thought she just...just gave him to you and...and took off again?"

"She turned up on our porch four years ago," Joe said slowly. "She said that she'd read about our people, our culture. She knew we might be generous enough to take care of her child for a while without asking questions."

Everything inside Adam began roaring again, as it had when the people at the Essler farm had shunned Mariah. He realized that it was the same sort of rage. If these people had only notified the authorities, he would have found Bo a long time ago.

But that, of course, was what Jannel had obviously counted on. Why? And where the hell *was* she?

"Why take him with her at all if she was just going to drop him off somewhere?" he demanded aloud.

"Maybe she didn't intend to, not at the start," Joe said levelly. "She said she'd come back for him, but she never did."

"She was blond?" Adam croaked, needing to be sure.

"Yes. Quite attractive, as I remember. She wasn't a woman you'd forget easily."

Mariah felt something odd and uncomfortable settle inside her.

"That's Jannel," Adam said bluntly. "That's her."

"Sometime later, perhaps as long as two years, a man came looking for her. He asked if we had seen her. He came right into services. It was a Church Sunday. The deacons said she had been here once but she had gone again. They asked the man to leave. He never questioned us about the boy, and of course we didn't volunteer anything, although Noah was sitting right there at the time. My Sarah took him outside, out the back, until the man had gone."

It was the hottest lead Adam had ever gotten, other than the milk-carton call that had led him here to the settlement. He told himself he didn't care where Jannel was. He'd located Bo. That was all that was important.

But he needed to know how it had all happened, where he'd been.

"What time of year was this?" he demanded. "When was it that Bo came here?"

Joe thought about it a moment. "We were busy with the first of the harvests. That would have made it early fall."

So she hadn't wandered first, Adam thought. She'd read about these people and had come to them directly, entrusting them with her—*his*—son.

"Who was the man who followed her?" Adam asked, and felt himself scowl as he realized how stupid the question was.

"He never gave us a name," Sugar Joe replied.

"I mean, what did he look like? Do you remember that?"

"None among us liked his eyes."

It wasn't much of a description. It wasn't a description at all. But it was something. A drug dealer? Adam rubbed his forehead and tried to think like Jake. "Could you draw a picture of him?"

"Why?"

Adam stared at him.

"Are you looking to find her, as well?" Joe went on. "Do you want her back or would you just like to see her punished for what she's done to you? I take it she took him against your will."

Adam let his breath out. "I don't particularly want her back," he admitted. It was enough of an understatement that even Joe smiled.

"Well, if I were a good Old Order Amishman, I'd tell you that you *must* take her back. But I'm an incorrigible Berks man at heart. So my advice to you, my friend, would be to forget it. It was painful. Let it pass. Rejoice in being reunited with your child." He picked his hat up again. "I'll go get him."

"No."

Adam's abrupt response startled all of them. He heard Mariah suck in her breath.

He looked at her quickly and thought her eyes were shining. With *what?* Tears? Relief? Pride in *him?* He had to look away.

"Not yet," he said hoarsely. "I've got time."

Joe waited.

"I don't want to hurt him," Adam explained. Inadequately, he thought. "I don't want to hurt your wife, your family."

"Thank you," Joe said simply.

"He'd be...he's part of you now." Then his voice tightened. "There's a lot about this place that I don't approve of. There's a certain lack of forgiveness about you folks that I find hard to swallow. But it's Bo's world. It's what he's lived for more than half his life. I'm aware of that. I won't pass judgment. For now. And I won't wrench him out of it so fast that it would cause him pain."

Joe nodded. "I don't think he remembers much of that other world he lived in. Going back there will be something of a jolt if you do it too abruptly."

Adam flinched at the truth of that. It felt as if something cold and sharp had gone into his chest. "I've considered that."

"At first, in the beginning, he asked for you—for his parents—quite often. There was nothing we could tell him. We didn't know, of course. And he was just a baby, really. I'm not sure how much he would have understood even if we *had* had answers."

"He was three," Adam said hoarsely.

"Yes, that was about what we guessed. Your wife never said. She didn't tell us his name or his birthday. That's why I've always believed that she didn't mean for him to stay here so long. And she was nervous, frightened, very much in a hurry. When she didn't come back, we made up a birthday for him and we gave him a name of our own. We had to call him something."

Adam's throat had tightened to the point of physical pain. "His birthday was...is...June twenty-fifth. But he wouldn't remember that."

"No."

"He just stopped asking?"

"After six months or so."

Adam looked at him closely. "Was it hard for him? Changing? Doing things your way?"

The man's smile was almost amused. "No. Our young children are not so very different from yours. They have no television, of course, and they work hard as soon as they are able. But the girls have their dolls and the boys have their toy tractors. And my home is more lenient than most in this *Gemeide*. I feel strongly that what we do within the privacy of our own walls is not particularly the church's business."

Adam remembered Mariah saying that he had moved to this *Gemeide* purely for his wife's sake, so she wouldn't be cut off from her own family. He nodded.

And then, without warning, the pain burst to the surface again. It wasn't an explosion, more like a little bubble coming up in a boiling pot, popping open.

"He doesn't remember me," he said, his voice strangled. "Dear God, he looked right at me and didn't know me at all."

"Oh, I think he does," Joe answered. "On some level."

Adam looked at him sharply.

"The crazy *anner Satt Leit* is all he's talked about for days, much more so than the other children. Something about you is touching him in a place too deep for him to recognize or understand."

Adam nodded. He didn't trust himself to speak.

Joe put his hat on again. "Could you give me a few days to talk to my Sarah? I need to break this to her gently. And then you should come to supper. You could meet him all over again. We could begin paving the way to telling him who you are. I think it will be far easier for him if you and Sarah and I put up a united front. Then we'll decide where to go from there. Wednesday?" he suggested.

He was, Adam thought, a wise man, education or no education. He looked at Mariah. Her hands were clasped together in front of her again.

"No," he heard himself say.

She looked up quickly, her breath catching. "Adam!" she cried, understanding. "I have no part in this!"

He shook his head. Maybe it was lingering anger over what he had witnessed at the church services. Or maybe it was something he simply could not look at too closely. But he wanted her there. Maybe he even needed her.

"What are you going to do?" he demanded, still looking at her. "Wait in disgrace outside the door? I won't be a part of that."

"I don't have to go with you!"

"Yeah," he said flatly. "You do." At her tortured expression, he added, "Please. And if they won't see you, then we'll find another way."

Mariah's lip trembled. She looked frantically between him and Sugar Joe. "You don't have to—" she began, but he interrupted.

"Actually, I'm not all that comfortable with a woman standing outside my door, either."

"The *Ordnung* says you can't eat with me," Mariah whispered. She looked at Adam. "And Sarah's father is a deacon. It's asking too much."

"The children can eat with you," Joe replied. "You can do your actual ingestion among their company."

Mariah shook her head. "But Sarah—" she tried again.

"My Sarah would slay dragons for the sake of her children." Mariah finally nodded, almost helplessly.

"Wednesday supper, then," Joe said, then he tipped his hat to them, put it on and left.

Adam looked at Mariah. "Is what I'm asking so hard? So much of a...I don't know, a taboo?"

She shook her head again. "It's just..." She trailed off and covered her face with her hands. So much, she thought. There were so many complications in all of this.

"What?" Adam prompted after a moment.

"It's a gift I never dared hope for." Mariah lowered her hands and smiled at him. He thought her mouth trembled. "Thank you, Adam."

Something about her smile or maybe her simple words hit him deeply. "I'll be right back," he said suddenly. He needed to get away from her, from her shimmering violet eyes, as desperately as he had ever needed anything in his life. He didn't trust what he might do, what he might say next if he stayed.

He went outside and shut the door carefully behind him. Sugar Joe had just reached his buggy. A single horse stomped its hooves impatiently in the snow.

"Hey, hold on a minute," Adam called out.

Sugar Joe turned back to him. He didn't seem surprised that

Adam had followed. Yet once Adam was standing beside the horse, the pungent steam of exertion wafting off the beast, he had no idea what to say.

"Did you tell the people at the services where you were going?" he asked finally.

Joe smiled and waved a hand at the enclosed buggy. Adam peered inside and saw a boy of about eighteen.

"That's Nathaniel, my oldest," Joe said. "He got taken with a sudden bout of the flu. Needs to go home and rest. Imagine that."

"So...he knows."

"Yes, I told him. He's old enough now to understand and to act as my accomplice on those occasions when I need him. I think, when all is said and done, he'll probably go back to Berks to take his baptism. He's strong and open-minded, my Nathaniel, and he's uncomfortable in this rigid *Gemeide*. He chafes a bit."

"I don't want to hurt any of you." He had said that earlier, but Adam felt as if he needed to repeat it.

"You can't help it," Joe said without rancor or anger.

Suddenly Adam was furious again. "How can you be so damned complacent about all this?"

"How can you not be?"

Adam narrowed his eyes. "It can't be that easy. Believing. Accepting."

The man leaned back against the buggy and crossed his arms over his broad chest. "It's all in the mind-set," he explained, "in how you decide you're going to feel about something. I live by their rules, Mr. Wallace, by what this *Gemeide* ordains. That doesn't mean I have to embrace all that down here—" he thumped a fist against his heart "—where no one else can see."

"That's more of a blasphemy than Mariah believing with all her heart and being shut out for something stupid," Adam argued, his temper burning.

"No. Not really. I've been married to Sarah for nineteen years now. We've lived here all that time. And the strangest thing happened, Mr. Wallace. Somewhere along the line nearly all of their *Ordnung* has come to be my own. It pervaded me, you see. Slowly. While I wasn't paying enough attention."

"You came here for her. For love of a woman." Adam almost snarled it and was immediately embarrassed. It was none of his business. He started to turn away. "Never mind."

"You don't understand," Joe said, as though he pitied him.

Adam looked back at him. "No. I really don't."

"Life is a tangle of compromises, my friend." Joe balanced his hands like two sides of a scale. "You come to a fork in the road. You didn't ask for that fork, never saw it coming, but there it is. And the road behind you is suddenly blocked. That's God's will."

Adam was a little jolted. He'd used the fork-in-the-road analogy himself not too long ago, talking to Mariah. And he'd thought a great deal about roadblocks lately.

"What you do with that fork ahead of you is your *own* will," Sugar Joe went on. "So you weigh it. Or at least I did. I could go left, join with my Sarah, and live by rules I didn't necessarily agree with at the time. Or I could go right and take her back to my own *Gemeide*. But I would cause her great pain by taking her from her family. They would have shunned her, you see, for...well, for marrying down. Perhaps she would even have come to hate me for that after a while." He finally dropped his hands. "I couldn't bear that and I couldn't hurt her, so I joined her world instead."

"The lesser of two evils," Adam said hoarsely.

"No. There was really no evil about it. As long as she's in my life and she's happy, everything else is secondary." He finally opened the buggy door. "And so, my friend, we all compromise when something is important enough to us. Will you come by on Wednesday, then?"

It was a simple question. Why, then, did Adam feel as if there were too many complex answers? "Yeah," he answered finally.

"Good. We'll look forward to seeing you. About five o'clock will be fine. We eat early, as soon as chores are done, because we need to get up well before dawn the following day."

Adam nodded absently. Sugar Joe's horse clop-clopped away. Adam watched it for a long time before he returned to the schoolhouse.

He found Mariah hunkered down by the stove. He shoved his hands into his pockets again. She didn't look up. Her hands just began to work faster.

"Why don't you wait here and keep warm?" he suggested. "I'll walk back for the car and bring it to you."

"It's always so cold here on Monday mornings," she fretted as if she hadn't heard him. "On school nights I always bank the fire so that it lasts into the night. It's never quite as frigid on those mornings. But Mondays are like a slap in the face. So I thought

I'd try the same thing as long as I'm here today. Although it's early. The coals probably won't last much past dusk. I—''

"Mariah," he interrupted.

She looked over her shoulder at him. "Yes?"

"You're babbling."

She flushed and looked back into the stove, scowling intently. Then she closed the door almost too carefully and got to her feet, wiping her hands on her apron.

"Any particular reason?" It was rare to see her this flustered.

"No, of course not. I..." She trailed off and smoothed back a wisp of her dark hair where it had come untucked above her ear. She heard Sugar Joe's voice again. *Blond and quite attractive.* One thing was for certain, she thought with angry frustration she rarely succumbed to. Jannel Wallace probably had not trudged through life in black hose and sensible shoes.

"Mariah?" Adam said again. When she looked at him her face took on a serene expression that seemed forced and deliberate this time.

"I'm very happy for you, Adam," she said stiffly.

"Thank you." He crossed the room to stand in front of her. "What *is* it?" he asked again. "What's wrong? Is it going to their house? Is that what's bothering you?"

"No. Yes. It's—I should be thanking you." She looked away from him. "For having a care about whether they'd leave me standing outside the door or not."

"Mariah, it's no big deal. I just don't approve of the way they treat you. Maybe I'm just a plain, old Catholic, but we've got this thing about forgiveness."

"Have you forgiven your wife?" she blurted. "This...Jannel?"

His heart kicked. He needed to move away from her now, but he stepped a little closer to her instead. "Maybe," he answered, and he realized, stunned, that it was suddenly true. "Yeah. I think someday I will, when all this is settled. I'm getting closer."

Then she touched him and shattered his thoughts. It was only a feather-light kiss of her fingertips along his cheek, but she seemed to be searching for something with the caress. "It's almost over, Adam," she said almost wonderingly. "Your pain. Your problem. I don't think it's going to take as long to set things straight as we thought." She paused to swallow. "If Bo remembers a little, as Sugar Joe seems to think, then perhaps it won't take long, at all. You could nearly be to the end of your road, Adam."

Roads again, he thought, and panic tried to flutter inside him. "Yeah."

She dropped her hand and looked away. There was something underneath there, he thought again, something in her eyes, hiding behind her calm expression, that he couldn't put his finger on and couldn't do a thing about.

"I'll get the car," he repeated hoarsely.

This time Mariah let him go.

She'd been wrong, she realized, hugging herself. She didn't have time. It was slipping through her fingers like sand.

Chapter 10

Adam called Dallas as soon as he got back to his room. His pulse danced. His head throbbed. If Mariah had been the only one to understand the impact of what had happened the first day he'd seen Bo again, then only Jake could understand the enormity of being this close to reclaiming him again.

He found his brother easily this time. Jake answered Child-Search's phone.

"What are you doing there?" Adam asked warily. "What's happened now?"

"You gave Diana the day off, remember? It's Sunday. Listen, it's no problem now, but I've got a paying job that's going to need my attention in about an hour or so."

"Put the answering service on."

He thought he could hear Jake shrugging. "Yeah, I already called them. I just wanted to make sure the expense would clear the coffers. Listen, speaking of money, you know that real honest-to-God paying case we have? Amber Calabrese? The girl from North Carolina?"

"Yeah, I remember her."

"The service took a call last night. Somebody thinks they saw her in Phoenix. Berry checked the school records there. No Amber Calabrese, but there's an Annie Perez who matches her description pretty closely. The kid was enrolled twelve days ago, right after Amber was snatched. According to the girl's file, her mother's supposed to be dead. No siblings.''

"That was easy." Sometimes it happened. "Sounds like the father took her. The mother was right.''

"Yeah," Jake answered. "So anyway, Berry contacted that guy we sometimes use with the LAPD. He's off on Thursday, so he says he'll drive over and see what he can see.''

"Tell him to fly and charge the company account.''

"Huh?''

"You heard me.'' Adam couldn't have explained why, but suddenly he had an urgent, immediate need to put that little girl back with her mother. Maybe it was just having his own Bo so close now, within reach but still not his.

Amber Calabrese, he thought, had been gone less than a month. She would still remember her mother.

"Sure. Okay," Jake said slowly.

"And while you're at it," Adam went on, "hop on a plane yourself.''

"What the hell is happening up there?" Jake burst out.

Adam finally said the words, the sweet, sweet words. "Looks like I'm going to have dinner with Bo Wednesday night.''

Jake's silence was long and appropriately awed, as Adam had known it would be. Then his brother swore softly.

"You know, this might be the first thing that's actually gone right in our whole wretched, rotten lives," he murmured.

Adam was surprised. Jake rarely spoke about their wretched, rotten lives.

"He remembers you after all, then?" Jake went on.

"The guy who's been taking care of him thinks he might, a little bit. Probably not consciously, though. We're going to start closing the gap. This guy's been...helpful. He's a good man. There's no bitterness there that I can see, and if there is it's buried so deep I don't even think he knows about it.''

"Well, that's good. That's great." Another silence. "So what do you need me for?''

Adam hesitated. "Jannel's *not* here. I need to find her. I need closure, Jake.''

A part of him wanted to do as Sugar Joe had suggested—let it go, let it die, rejoice in simply being reunited with Bo. But it just wasn't that easy.

Once he had wanted to shake her, to hurt and punish her for

what she'd done. Now he felt only a certain disgust when he thought of her, that she had failed him, their child, herself so miserably. It was why he had realized, talking to Mariah today, that he might finally be able to forgive her. He should have been able to close his mind to her now, but...

Something was nagging him. It was all so unfinished, a thread just dangling. Something didn't feel right. There was something else at play here, he thought, and though he couldn't put his finger on it, he needed to find out what it was.

He told Jake in quick, concise terms what Sugar Joe had told him, how Jannel had said she'd come back, but she hadn't. And how a man had turned up looking for her two years later.

"One of her drug friends," Jake muttered.

"Yeah, that was my first thought," Adam agreed.

"There's a 'but' in your voice, bro."

"I need to be sure."

"I'm off on Thursday and Saturday. I'll see what I can do about getting Friday, too, and coming up. Worst case, I'll have to trade off my Saturday for Friday, and I'll only be able to snoop around up there for a couple of days."

"I think that's all it'll take." Everything felt close now, he realized. "If you just ask around, you know, maybe you could get some physical pointers on this guy. *Something.* I have a gut feeling he's the key to all this."

"Yeah," Jake agreed. "Sounds like it."

"I ought to warn you, though. You were right. These people are a pretty private bunch. Most of them." In spite of himself, he thought of Mariah again, saw her in his mind's eye, though he'd promised himself he would put her out of his head until Wednesday.

"Hey, they'll talk to me," Jake answered, snagging his attention again. "I'm a nonthreatening guy."

"Right." At his best and most charming, there was still something vaguely menacing about his brother, a wildness just beneath the surface.

"Well, one way or the other," Jake answered, "I'll see you Wednesday night."

Adam's heart hitched. By then he would have had dinner— supper, they called it—with his son. "Perfect timing."

Mariah's hands trembled as she tied her apron into place late on Wednesday afternoon. She'd rushed home from school, her feet fairly flying over the snow. She'd bathed, and now she was doing something unconscionable. She was...primping.

That was what the deacons called it, and for the life of her she could not think of a better word. But the deacons weren't here to see.

She had no mirror. Mirrors were against the *Ordnung.* Her *Gemeide,* though not all of them, considered such a reflection to be a graven image. They also could see no good reason why a woman should have to look into one. Anyone worth her salt could manage her hair into a bun without looking.

Mariah smoothed her hands back over hers nervously, again and again. Then she looked down at herself and decided to change her dress. She'd first thought she'd wear the turquoise one, because it was her newest. But—her heart almost thundered with the treacherous thought—the purple one would match her eyes.

They'd had mirrors at Penn State, she thought, trembling harder, her teeth almost snicking together now. And she knew violet, lavender, purple were her best colors.

She had not felt this glorious, this excited, this *shivery,* in years, she realized, fumbling as she yanked the first dress back over her head. Then she corrected herself. In all honesty, she wasn't sure she had *ever* felt this good. She'd felt something like it on the day she'd left the settlement to go away, but then it had been heavily tinged with fear and regret and sorrow.

Tonight she felt no fear. There was no regret in her heart. Tonight she would *eat with a family again.* It didn't matter to her in the least if she would have to be seated with the children. She loved children. She craved their guileless bursts of laughter. And this was the closest she had come to community, to being a part of anything, in ten years, since the day she had left.

Sugar Joe would include her. Adam had seen to it.

Adam.

He was, of course, the other reason for her anticipation. Once, long ago with Asher, she had felt something like this, too. On evenings when she knew he would come and shine his flashlight on her window, a certain fluttery feeling had filled her. And it had lasted, too, until he'd actually arrived, until they'd sat together in her mother's parlor and had searched for things to say to each other. Then, with a reluctant ache, the fluttery feeling would die.

Somehow she knew that that would never happen with Adam.

Not if he stayed here a year. Almost everything that came out of his mouth was a surprise. Much of it made her think, if only to explain herself and her people. Sometimes he even made her smile, and she had forgotten how to do that so very long ago.

She stopped with her turquoise dress in her hands, her fingers tightening around it like claws. Adam wouldn't stay a year. Soon, very soon now, he would be gone. The best she could hope for was a few more weeks, if he agreed to help find the other children. And for that to happen, she would have to tell him about those little ones.

Her heart squeezed as she had her worst, most heinous thought yet. *What if she didn't?*

"Oh, Jesus, forgive me," she whispered aloud, sitting weakly on the edge of her narrow bed.

Of course, she would tell Adam about those babies. She would ask him to find them, because no matter what the deacons said, letting them disappear, not resisting the horror was wrong. Except once she allowed the treacherous thought into her head the first time, it wouldn't seem to go again. It giggled nastily, mocking her.

Don't ask him.

Adam was going to go. But maybe, if she was very good, very obedient, if she didn't do anything else wrong, the Lapps would invite her to supper again some time without him.

She began shaking with the possibility. This was the first visible crack in her *Meidung* since it had been thrown on her. Until Adam had protested, until Sugar Joe had told her they would arrange it somehow, she had not ever, not even once allowed herself to wish for it. But now, given this small chance, she began to ache, to yearn for more. If she kept being very good, perhaps this crack would widen.

If she didn't make waves again.

If she didn't try to find the missing babies and go against one of the most important rules of the *Ordnung: we shall not resist God's will.*

She didn't realize she was crying until a tear dropped down, staining the turquoise dress in her hands. How had this gotten so complicated?

She took a shaky breath and got to her feet. She found the purple dress and pulled it over her head, hanging the other one neatly in her closet with trembling hands. She would wear the one that would make her look prettiest. She would go to supper at the Lapps with Adam and savor this one, singular respite from her *Meidung*—almost like a date, she thought a little giddily. And she would ask him to find those other children, maybe even tonight. The deacons would be enraged and they would never let her back in. The Lapps' door would slam shut again. And she would live with that, too. She would do it because she had to.

She finished dressing, and it wasn't until yet another wet spot appeared on the bodice of the purple dress that she realized she was still crying.

Adam thought Mariah looked more beautiful than ever. She was a little flushed when she answered her door and her eyes sparkled. There was something different about her tonight. She was...radiant.

And he knew then that no matter how much this evening meant to him, it meant just as much, if not more, to her.

"Adam, come in," she said breathlessly. "Would you—"

"No."

"What?" She blinked in surprise. "You don't even know what I was going to suggest."

"Let me guess." But his voice was more wry than impatient this time. "Coffee?"

She flushed even deeper.

"Honey, if I drink one more cup, I'm going to be able to fly back to Dallas without the plane. And my nerves are wound up enough tonight, as it is."

Mariah's heart skipped. It hung in her chest for a moment without beating, then it thundered. *Honey.* A whole new ache swept through her, sweet and hungry and wanting at the endearment. *Back to Dallas.* The ache changed into something ugly and bloomed into physical pain.

Adam watched her face and realized what he had said a moment too late. He felt his own skin go warm. In a heartbeat, he was mired in panic and confusion again, when a moment ago he had felt purely good—as Jake had said, for one of the few times in his whole wretched life.

Honey. It had slid off his tongue effortlessly, right and sweet and oddly comfortable. As right and sweet and comfortable as the thought of flying back to Dallas with his boy at his side.

Mariah took a jerky step backward. She left him standing at

the door, to hurry down the hall she had disappeared into the other day. ''I'll get the blankets,'' she said breathlessly.

Blankets? ''What do we need blankets for?'' he called after her hoarsely.

She probably hadn't heard him. She didn't reply. When she came back into the living room, she was holding a pile of them. She had her coat on now. He barely noticed that. He was staring at the simple woolens she held clutched to her breast.

He wondered if there was something inherent in going to the Lapps for dinner together that he hadn't realized. There was so much about her culture that he didn't understand yet. Dear God, were they going to end up rolling around in a field together somewhere? Was this like shining flashlights on windows?

His blood roared suddenly, and in that moment he could *feel* her hair in his hands, could imagine her skin against his, and it would be warm and smooth as satin. And she would fit against him perfectly, and he would slide inside her the way a hand moved inside a velvet glove—

''For the buggy,'' she said, interrupting his thoughts. She stared at him, clearly confused.

''The...buggy.'' He coughed, clearing his throat. ''The buggy.''

''Yes.'' She took a step closer, looking into his face, all her own troubles suddenly forgotten. ''Adam, are you ill?'' He'd flushed, she thought, then his skin had gone a sickly shade of pale.

''I'm—'' His heart kept pounding. ''I'm fine. What...buggy?''

''I want to do this right,'' she said fervently. ''There are some occasions when we simply shouldn't take your automobile. This is one of them. So I've arranged for a buggy.''

''Okay. Good. Great.'' He turned for the door, then he stopped. ''I don't know how to drive a horse. You know, giddy-up and all that.''

She finally smiled again, but it didn't reach her eyes this time. She was no longer glowing, he thought.

When—how—had this gotten so damned complicated?

''That's okay,'' she answered. ''I do. At least, I used to. Come on, let's go. We're going to be late. We can take your car as far as Abe's.''

''Abe's.'' He followed her and watched her lock up.

''Abe Miller. He rents buggies and horses. Mostly to take tourists out in the summer, but he loans me one whenever I need one.''

''He's not Amish? He sees you?''

She flinched ever so slightly. ''He broke away from the *Gemeide* before he was baptized. It's not the same. Like I said, that's forgiven, though I'm sure it broke his parents' hearts. Anyway, we're friends. He's a dear man.''

A dear man? ''What, you date him?'' And his gut clenched all over again.

Mariah looked over at him, startled, as they got into the car. ''No, of course not.''

''Why, of course not?''

''Well, because he's not part of the settlement, for one thing. The deacons wouldn't sanction such a marriage.''

And that simply, that suddenly his temper erupted. It blazed helplessly out of control.

''Why the hell does it have to be *marriage,* Mariah? So what if you can't *marry* him, for God Almighty's sake?'' He jabbed the key into the ignition. He stomped his foot on the gas and jerked the wheel, turning back up the one-way street in the wrong direction. ''Just go have dinner with the guy, goddamn it! Get away from all this—this *Meidung* garbage. For once in your sorry life, take some pleasure for yourself!''

Mariah gasped. Her *sorry* life? Her eyes filled, in spite of the fact that she told herself crying was ridiculous. ''Why are you angry with me? Adam, why are you so upset about this?''

''I'm not,'' he ground out. He set his jaw. ''Sometimes I just don't like what I see, and I say so.''

''Please don't ruin it, Adam. *Please.*''

He looked over at her sharply. ''What?''

''Tonight. I've waited for something like this for *so long.* I never thought I'd ever be invited into anyone's home again. Please don't ruin it.'' She blinked hard.

He felt as if she had kicked him in the chest. Slowly, carefully, he pulled the car off the road. He closed his eyes, then rubbed them. ''I'm sorry.''

Mariah tried to breathe again. Surreptitiously, she wiped her eyes.

''I don't know what's wrong with me,'' he went on finally. And that was enough of a lie to make his face tighten all over again. He knew what was wrong. This *chasm* was wrong. The gulf of culture and upbringing that separated them was wrong, because it kept her on one side and him on the other, aching yet unable to join her.

He wasn't sure when the wanting had turned into an ache. But it was poignant now, bittersweet and consuming. Suddenly, tonight, he just couldn't seem to get past it. Her puritanical values enraged him. *Because the deacons wouldn't sanction such a marriage.* So she couldn't even have dinner with the guy, for God's sake, unless it headed them toward the damned altar! And she wasn't bound by those deacons in the first place!

She was only tied to them in her heart.

"Nerves," he said hoarsely, lying again because the first one had been easy enough. "Just...nerves. I've waited for tonight for a long time, too."

"Are you going to tell Bo?" she asked suddenly. "Tonight?"

Adam looked at her again almost angrily. "No, Mariah. I'm not going to tell him. I'm going to let him get to know me all over again. I'm going to speak with him, eat dinner with him, maybe I'll even have an opportunity to hold him again. I'm going to follow the original plan."

Her eyes filled again. Oh, she was far, far too emotional tonight for anyone's good.

"Turn on this street right up here," she told him quietly. "Abe's carriage house is four doors down on the right."

Abe, he thought, driving again. Just her friend. Only her friend, because she couldn't marry him.

Oh, God help him.

Chapter 11

The buggy was nothing like what he'd expected. Adam hadn't anticipated the teak dashboard with all its shiny silver knobs. He was caught off guard by the rich blue carpet. He thought the velour upholstery was a little much, but all in all, it was roomy, comfortable and warm. It wasn't necessarily wide, but it was deep.

"I feel like Cinderella," he muttered, joining Mariah inside.

Her eyes flashed to him, though she still didn't quite smile after their argument in the car. "Yes. So do I."

Probably in a more accurate respect than he did, Adam reflected. He'd been thinking of climbing into the pumpkin carriage. She was going to the ball.

She gathered up the reins where they came inside through silver-trimmed gaps in the dashboard. Even with that slight touch, the horse outside picked its head up and its ears pricked.

"Scootch over, Adam," she said quietly, frowning. "I need a little more room."

"I don't scootch." But he tried to shift his weight.

And only ended up settling more closely beside her. His thigh was flush against hers. He wore jeans, and she that purple dress. The blankets were still on the floor—she'd said they wouldn't need them until the ride home. He wanted to grab them and wad

them down between them, because he was too aware of the
warmth of her even through their various layers of clothing. And
his heart began picking up its pace because he didn't dare make
a big deal of moving again, especially since there really wasn't
anywhere for him to move *to*. He didn't want to focus both their
minds on body heat and flesh cozily nestling against flesh. His
own thoughts being there was trouble enough.

"Adios, Abe," he muttered, leaning an arm on the door just
below the glass. He was just as glad to be rid of the "dear" and
gallant Abe Miller. The man had hovered over her, helping her
into the coach before Adam could, resting a hand on her back
whenever he could manage it, grinning at her, laughing with her,
though her own laughter had seemed a bit forced. He'd given her
the nicest buggy on the lot, free of charge, and had eyed Adam
frequently and not entirely unobtrusively.

Mariah jiggled the reins and they began moving. In the close
space, he could smell her hair again. He found himself wondering
how she managed that. If the Amish women didn't wear makeup,
then he doubted if they used perfume, either. And the violets were
much more subtle than that, anyway. They were more an elusive
whiff now and again, when he moved his head just the right way.

"What?" he asked, jolting, realizing that she had spoken to
him.

"I said that I haven't done this for so long, I'm rusty."

"Driving the buggy, you mean?" He wasn't sure if she was
talking about that or going for supper.

"Driving the horse," she muttered, concentrating fiercely, her
jaw setting.

"Seems to me you're doing fine. I thought you said Abe loaned
you buggies before."

"He always drove."

He'd had to ask. "Well, we're moving," he muttered.

"But we keep drifting out onto the road. Get back there, Goliath," she murmured fiercely, tugging a little harder on the right
rein.

She kept mostly to the shoulder. A lot of the snow there had
melted by now. The roads had been gradually widening during
his stay here, which told him how long he had been idling in
neutral.

He tried to think about Bo, about what he might say to him
tonight, and he was still only aware of her warm leg pressed
against his. He realized that he was afraid to think of Bo too

much anyway. He was afraid to give any imagining to how this evening might turn out, for fear of being grossly disappointed.

It didn't take them long to get to the Lapp farm. Goliath's pace was steady and brisk. Sugar Joe's spread was different from many of the others Adam had seen. The paved road bisected the farm. A white two-story farmhouse stood off to the right of the macadam. Mariah went past it and turned onto a narrow drive to the left.

A small carriage house sat on this side, and close behind it was a horse barn. A few of the animals poked their heads out their stall windows when they heard Goliath's hoofbeats. One whinnied. The others looked bored and went back to their oats.

There was a small paddock in front of an aluminum-roofed building that Adam recognized, from his other trips past the farm, as the milking barn. The standard motor shed was affixed to that, sending hydraulic power to the milking machines. A silo sat flush against either side of the big barn. Far in the back was another small, neat shed, whose purpose Adam couldn't identify.

They were all white with gray roofs—even the aluminum was a dull silver. Against the lingering snow it should have looked stark, plain, bleak. Instead, as Mariah stopped the buggy, Adam saw a light flicker, then begin to fill one of the windows of the house. Someone had put a lantern on in there, and he felt like he was coming home after a long, hard, cold day.

Home to warmth and respite and family.

Before he could dwell on that, the front door opened. His breath snagged, but it was only the oldest boy, Nathaniel, a genuine Lapp. The teenager hurried across the road to join them as Mariah pushed open her door.

This time Adam moved fast enough to reach her before the boy could. She glanced at him. It seemed to him that her eyes merely brushed his now, almost warily, where they had always lingered before. She put a hand to his shoulder reluctantly and braced her other against the door. He caught her waist as she gave a little jump and he wondered if he imagined it or if she really did seem to stop breathing for a moment. Then her eyes finally touched his again, hesitant, aware, widening.

He wanted suddenly, desperately, to get them back where they'd been before he'd erupted in the car like some kind of fool. Before she'd mentioned blankets and made him imagine the things they could do with one. Before she'd talked of not dating a man because she couldn't marry him. Not only was it safer there in that old place they'd shared, but he found he missed the easy warmth of their uncomplicated friendship. He made a strangled sound in his throat. Had it actually ever been uncomplicated?

"Mariah—"

"I'll unhitch the horse for you, Miz Fisher," Nathaniel said.

She turned away from Adam to look at the boy. And Adam knew in that moment that the road behind him had been blocked. There was no turning around, no going back. All he could do was face the fork.

A sudden wind screamed across the nearest open pasture. It tugged at her hair, pulling a strand free. And he wanted to touch it, to tuck it back into place for her, and there was no use in pretending he didn't.

"What, Adam?" She looked at him again. "You were saying something?"

"Nothing," he said hoarsely. "Never mind."

A door on the milking barn slid open with a sharp squeak. Sugar Joe came out, stomping his feet a little on a mat outside the door. "Hello!" he called out. He eyed the carriage as he passed it, chuckling. "Abe's?"

"Yes," Mariah agreed softly.

"Must be sweet on you. He's outdone himself this time."

Mariah blushed to the roots of her hair. She looked quickly at Adam, as though pleading with him not to make another scene about it. He felt ashamed all over again.

"Come on," Joe said. "Sarah's waiting."

They started across the road. And then Adam felt Mariah's cold hand slide into his. She squeezed. Because, he thought, she was that kind of woman. No matter what had gone between them in the past hour, she knew and understood what he felt upon walking through that door.

Adam didn't trust himself to speak. He squeezed back.

They went inside, through a glass-enclosed porch to another, more solid door. Inside he saw large, sprawling rooms to both the right and left of the entry. But the house was surprisingly narrow. A door directly across from them led outside again. There was another off to the right of that, and the smells and sounds coming from there told him it was the kitchen.

His attention returned to the back door.

It was ajar, and three kids were gathered around a pump just outside in the yard. A girl of about eleven worked the handle vigorously. Two boys jostled each other, thrusting their hands quickly under the splashing icy water to make it spray. The girl shrieked when she got wet from their shenanigans.

One was the dark-haired boy Mariah had passed the note to on Sunday. The other was Bo.

Adam's heart simply stopped. He found himself holding on to Mariah's hand hard enough to crush her bones. Then his heart finally moved again. It crowded up into his throat and he could hear nothing over its roar. His every muscle hardened to granite as he steeled himself against going out there, against grabbing his son and holding him for his own.

He finally tore his eyes away and found Joe watching him. The man gave a slow, understanding nod and went to the back door. "Too cold to be swimming in it, boys," he called out. "Let Grace have a turn at it, will you?"

The boys backed up from the spigot, but when Bo turned away, the dark-haired boy slapped a hand through the tumbling water one last time, splashing his back. Bo veered about again and tumbled on top of him, fists pummeling.

"Matthew's eight," Mariah explained in a careful undertone. "They're close enough in age that they're generally in trouble together."

"What one doesn't think of, the other does," Joe muttered, stepping outside the door this time. "Enough!" he bellowed, and the fists went still. Two heads popped up to eye him warily. "We have company. Can you pretend to be civilized?"

"Yes, sir," Matthew muttered.

Bo nodded reluctantly.

Sugar Joe grabbed the back of each small jacket and pulled the boys to their feet. "You've each got two minutes to get to your room, change into dry shirts and get back to the table."

The boys pushed past him and bolted up the stairs. The girl— Grace, Joe had called her—came in behind her father and crowded close to his back. She smiled shyly at Mariah and tried hard not to stare at Adam.

Adam barely noticed. His heart was pounding too hard for sense now. The silence seemed to hang on interminably.

"It's the crazy *anner Satt Leit*," Matthew blurted. He had changed his shirt in record time and came back to stand on the stairs, a little out of breath. A moment later, Bo joined him.

Bo said nothing, nothing at all.

He didn't frown. He didn't smile. He seemed lost in deep, profound thought. A little wrinkle appeared between his eyes.

Adam wondered if they all would have stood like that indefinitely if a small, dark woman with chocolate eyes hadn't come bustling in from the kitchen.

"You're here!" She seemed nervous. "Take their coats, Joe. Where are your manners? Did you meet everyone, Mr. Wallace? Gracie and Matthew and Noah? Dinah—our oldest girl—is helping me with dinner. And Nathaniel—"

"He took our horse for us," Adam said quietly, trying to put her at ease. "He's a fine boy, Mrs. Lapp."

She seemed to relax a little. She gave a fleeting but genuine smile. "Yes, he is. Thank you. And he's growing up so quickly, too. He spends an awful lot of time in Berks now, with Joe's family." She broke off. "I'm babbling, aren't I? Well. I've got roast."

Mariah seemed to shiver a little deliberately. "I haven't had that in a very long time."

"It's difficult to make it right with only one chicken. That's what I've found. It just doesn't taste the same unless you make it for a crowd. This is some I saved from the last big batch I made for *Gemeesunndaag.*"

Adam noticed that Sarah answered without looking at Mariah, but her response was clearly to her comment. It was an ingenious compromise, and in that moment Adam thought the world of Sarah Lapp, too. Her father, the deacon, could have been planted in the keeping room, watching them, and he would not have been able to chastise her for breaking Mariah's *Meidung.* Yet already she had managed to make Mariah feel welcome and part of the gathering.

"It's chicken and stuffing," Mariah explained, glancing at Adam. He looked at her blankly. "Roast," she clarified. "It's chicken and stuffing in a casserole."

He didn't think it sounded extraordinarily appetizing, but he wasn't here for the food.

Her hand was still tucked in his. It was warm now.

"How come you were watching us play hockey?" Bo demanded suddenly.

Adam looked back at the stairs and searched for his voice. "Well, I like it." And then he wondered if he had ever come up with a more inane response in his life.

Bo, however, was satisfied. He nodded.

"He cheats," Matthew muttered.

"Do not." Bo elbowed him.

"Do, too."

Adam found his voice again. "I never saw him cheat."

"He shoots goals when nobody's looking," Matthew complained.

"You *oughta* be looking." Bo looked at Adam again. "Do you like to play, mister? Is that why you watch us so much?"

Adam shook his head. "Uh, no." He wasn't sure which question he was answering. The first seemed safer. "I never tried it."

"He likes baseball," Mariah said quietly.

Adam felt his heart kick and he looked at her. She had seen an opportunity to throw out a line, he realized, some unobtrusive, idle comment that might make Bo remember something. He was overwhelmingly grateful, because he couldn't seem to think clearly enough at the moment to manage such a thing himself. But he saw in her eyes that it pained her deeply, that she'd had to force herself.

In that moment he understood everything as clearly as he knew his own name—her strange behavior on the morning after Joe had come to the schoolhouse, some of her tension tonight. When this was over, when Bo remembered enough, they would go. And she didn't want that. She didn't want him to leave.

His heart staggered. The truth slammed into him. He wondered how much more he could be expected to deal with tonight. He felt swamped, overwhelmed, and touched in a place that scared him. Bo was saying something and his heart was trying to go that way and pay attention to him. But Mariah's eyes were haunted and he wanted to hold her, too, needed to tell her why he had to go before this could get any worse.

"Baseball?" Matthew repeated.

"What?" Adam asked vacantly.

"You play baseball? We do that in the summer. Noah's good at that, too. He's good at everything." This time Matthew elbowed Bo. But it seemed to Adam that there was a good bit of pride in his voice. His heart spasmed.

Bo would miss this boy when he took him away, he realized.

"Mama, I took everything out of the oven," another girl said, coming out of the kitchen.

"This is my Dinah," Sarah said quietly, watching every proceeding with sad, dark eyes.

Sugar Joe returned from the keeping room where he had put their coats. "Dinah, Matt, Gracie and Noah all go to school with

124

Loving Mariah

Miss Fisher,'' he explained for Adam's benefit. ''Nathaniel finished several years ago, so he never had her.''

''They're looking at another application,'' Sarah burst out suddenly.

This time she stared determinedly at a ceiling beam. At first Adam didn't understand, but he noticed Mariah lose some color. Then it came to him—the deacons were actively looking for another teacher.

Helpless anger washed over him.

''I overheard it at my parents' house,'' Sarah went on, her skin flaming. ''I think it's supposed to be a secret.''

''Why don't you just say you were wrong, Miz Fisher?'' Bo demanded suddenly. He looked near tears. ''Then they'll let you stay.''

Mariah moved to the banister. Her face was pale. ''Because that would be a lie.''

''You're *not* sorry?'' He scowled. ''But they make you so sad!''

''I'm not sorry for learning,'' she explained. ''No, not for that. For hurting people, for doing it too late, certainly.''

''Well, maybe you could just say that.''

''It wouldn't be enough, Noah. They'd want more.'' She looked at Sugar Joe again, then at Adam, trying to put on a brave front. ''It's always been inevitable. It was bound to happen sooner or later. I always knew that.''

''That doesn't make things like this easier,'' Sarah blurted, her eyes shining a little now, and they all knew she was talking about Bo this time.

''Mama, I'm hungry,'' Matthew complained, and the moment was broken.

''And I'm the queen of England,'' Sarah replied, finally smiling, running a trembling finger beneath her eye. ''Who stole those eggs I put on the table earlier?''

''But roast is special,'' Matthew confided in Adam as they went into the kitchen. ''Mostly we only get it on Church Sundays. I'm *always* hungry for that.''

So, Adam thought, Sarah had pulled out all the stops for this. He was touched and his heart hurt for her, that she had put on a special dinner in honor of giving up a child she'd come to love.

She caught him, coming up beside him just before they sat down. Her eyes were pleading. ''Mr. Wallace,'' she whispered.

''Adam. Just Adam.'' His voice was tight.

She whispered so no one else would hear. "I need to ask. Could you...would you bring him back to visit once in a while when this is...done?"

He couldn't answer.

Everything crammed in his throat, and if he had allowed himself to, he knew he could have unburdened himself to this woman with the deep brown compassionate eyes. He could have poured everything out to her, why he had to leave and why he had to stay away. He knew, once he told her, that she would understand. She had that kind of face. It possessed a weary kind of wisdom, an acceptance of life's oddest quirks.

"I'm not taking him tonight," he said instead, and tried hard to remember a time when this issue had been simple, a black-and-white matter of just finding his kid and taking him home.

The kitchen table was long enough to seat a small army. It was covered with a green-and-white checked cloth and a lantern hung from the ceiling above it. Sweeping butcher-block counters nearly encircled the room. Adam hadn't been aware of being cold before, but here, in this room, he was warm. A wood stove gave off ample heat. There was a fireplace, too, and broad windows let in the falling night. A teapot stood on the stove, bursting with steam.

The table was set with three places at one end. Then there was a small gap, and the remaining six plates sat a bit apart. But not, Adam noted, so far distant that conversation would be impossible. There were separate bowls of food.

The kids went to one side, and Mariah moved to go with them. Far from seeming disturbed, she was glowing again. But Adam was uncomfortable with the situation, even as he knew it was for the best. No one could ask Sarah Lapp, the deacon's daughter, to compromise more than she already had. And it was time, long past time, maybe even too late, to start putting some kind of distance between himself and Mariah Fisher.

Damn it, he wasn't her keeper, her champion, her guard dog, for God's sake.

Adam sat with Sarah at the other end of the table. Conversation billowed, burst, ebbed.

"Eyes down," Joe said, moving along the children's end of the table toward his own seat at the head. Matthew kept staring at the casserole dish at that end. Joe planted a big palm on his crown and tilted his face downward. Matthew sighed.

Joe sat and began a prayer. Something inside Adam stiffened in old habit and for a moment it was not Joe's voice he heard but

his own, old words he had prayed a long time ago, prayers that
he had never gotten any answers to.

Where were you when my mother was crying? Where were you
when Dad was drinking and ranting? When Kimmie cringed be-
hind the rocker to get away from him, so he picked it up and
crashed it against the wall and got her anyway? Where were you
when Jake sneaked into my bed, even though we were too old for
that stuff, and he held on, crying, while the shouting and banging
and the thud of flesh hitting flesh just kept on and on downstairs?
I was supposed to be the older one, the smart one, but you
wouldn't tell me what to do, what to say to make it livable. So
don't tell me you care. Don't tell me you love me. Because when
something good came into my life, when my own kid grinned at
me and laughed and I managed not to repeat the sins of my father,
you took him away, too. You took everything that ever mattered,
as though I was cursed from the moment I took my first breath,
as though every one of us, every single Wallace, was beneath
your attention.

And then he realized that there was quiet, that Joe had finished.
Adam looked up from his own sham of a prayer to realize that
everyone was staring at him. For a horrible moment he wondered
if he had spoken aloud.

But the expressions were all curious, probably because he had
taken so long to lift his head again. He glanced down the table,
right into Bo's eyes.

His boy was back in his life. And the angel who had brought
him was sitting beside him, and what did that say for unanswered
prayers?

For a moment Adam simply sat, unable to think. There was a
coiling tension in his head, right behind his eyes, and around his
heart. Then Sarah handed him one of the casseroles.

Joe nodded at Mariah, who was busy heaping food on the little
ones' plates. "She's the best teacher that school ever had," he
said quietly. "I hate to see this happen."

Sarah's eyes came up from her plate. "Noah's right, though,"
she whispered. "The church has given her two years." She shook
her head helplessly. "If only she would just go to the deacons
and beg their forgiveness, they'd give it. I know they would."

Joe smiled thinly. "But she's right, too. She would only be
committing another sin—one *she* can't live with. She'd be lying,
and she'd know it even if they didn't."

"I don't think they'd care if they did," Sarah muttered, and that made Adam's head hurt even more, that these anonymous deacons just wanted to make her crawl for defying their ways. They didn't seem to particularly care what was in her heart.

"You went to school, too, didn't you?" Adam asked suddenly, looking at Joe. There was something about him, some hint of worldliness and wisdom, or maybe it was his not entirely simple vocabulary. "Didn't you?" he repeated.

"Just high school," Joe admitted. "Where I come from, that's not frowned upon. And I did it before I was rebaptized here."

Contradictions. Rules. They infuriated Adam.

"They—the deacons—are starting to realize they're not going to break her," Joe added, turning the conversation back to Mariah.

"I could have told them that." Sarah sighed. "She's so stubborn. So strong."

"They're about ready to give up on her," Joe went on. "And that means returning to the fine line of their principles. They've edged over them a bit to let her teach." He paused. "Noah, if those potatoes leave your plate, you're cleaning them up and going to your room."

"Busted," Adam muttered under his breath, watching his son slowly lower the spoonful he had been about to catapult across the table at Matthew. And then, as though he had heard Adam, Bo looked at him and grinned.

"They splat good," he informed him.

"I know," Adam answered, his heart chugging again.

Bo's eyes widened then got suspicious. "How?"

"I've splatted a few of my own."

Something like respect touched his face. "Did your pa make you clean it up?"

Adam decided not to get into what Edward Wallace had done on the rare occasions when he had been present, at all. "He wasn't happy."

"Who'd you splat at?"

"My brother." Kimmie, he reflected, had been an infant at that point. There had been a good ten years between them.

"Is he bigger than you?" Bo asked. "Your brother?"

"He's taller, but I'm stronger. Maybe. A little."

"Me, too," Matthew announced. "I'm stronger than he is."

"No, you ain't," Bo argued.

"You're not," Mariah corrected automatically.

And suddenly, in that moment, Adam knew he was as close to

feeling happy as he had ever been in his life. Unfortunately, everything that made him feel that way was at the other end of the table.

He glanced at Sarah, shaking his head in apology. "I'm sorry," he said quietly. "I just...I can't do this."

Joe watched appraisingly. Sarah seemed briefly alarmed, then she nodded, understanding.

"I see her," Adam went on. She was nearly all he saw. "I've never promised my life to anyone other than myself, and I never will. So as near as I can tell, there's no reason why I can't eat with her."

"Nope," Joe said. "There's not. Although 'never' is a strong word, my friend. I've learned it can rear up and bite you on occasion."

Adam barely heard him. He stood and took his plate. There was a short spell of surprised quiet from the children. He met and held Mariah's eyes.

"Got room for another down here?"

Her smile was slow. Her lip trembled. And her eyes...ah, God, her eyes, he thought. Wide, nearly as deep and dark as her dress now, and shining. He saw himself in them.

"Guess I ought to go check on that sick calf, anyway," Nathaniel said, rising. "Here, Mr. Wallace, you can have my place."

"What sick calf?" Grace demanded.

"We don't have a sick calf," Matt objected.

"Reckon I gave it the flu," Nathaniel muttered, and at the other end of the table, Sugar Joe laughed. And then Adam chuckled, and Nathaniel grinned and even Sarah ducked her head to hide a smile.

"I don't get it," Matthew complained.

"'Cause you're a lamebrain," Bo charged.

"Am not."

"Are too."

"Do *you* get it?" Matt demanded.

"'Course I do."

"Then 'splain it. I dare ya."

Bo stuttered and blushed.

Then there was shouting and the clinking of glassware. And somewhere, threaded through all of it, Adam was excruciatingly aware of Mariah's soft laughter.

Chapter 12

The peace and pleasure of the evening lasted until they were back in the buggy and heading for home. Joe had invited them for Sunday supper, as well. It was the settlement's off-week from church. He and Mariah would go in the afternoon and just enjoy...family. And Mariah had smiled a little tremulously at being included again, and Adam had felt damned good at that, that he was somehow instrumental in giving her pleasure again, especially now that her job seemed in doubt.

That was one worm in the apple, he thought—her job. She'd told him this could happen, and she seemed accepting of the blow. And that left a rancid taste in his mouth.

"Adam, could you get the blankets?"

He looked over at her abruptly. She was shivering a little as the horse clop-clopped along. It was beginning to snow again, tiny, gentle flurries drifting down.

Adam reached to the floor and got one for her, opening it onto her lap. He ignored the urge to tuck it around her legs, even as the idea occurred to him.

"I wonder if he'd remember Jannel," he said suddenly, looking out his side window.

Mariah's silence was long. "A young child's memory is an

iffy thing, Adam,'' she said finally. ''I don't think there's any way to know that.''

''Jannel was with him all the time,'' he went on as though she hadn't spoken. ''She was a big part of his first three years.''

''So were you.''

''No.''

He fell quiet again, digesting the truth of that as it occurred to him. Then more words burst out of him, anguished and confused. ''Would he remember me if I had been there all the time? Every day? Would he remember me if I'd taken the time to tuck him in at night once in a while when I was home?''

''You had to work. You had to make a living.''

''I should have taken him with me more.'' There was that, always that.

''He'll remember, Adam. Sooner or later, he'll begin to remember. You can almost see it happening already, the way he was watching you, asking you questions.''

''Yeah,'' he said shortly, unsure why that made his heart ache. ''I'll do better this time.''

Mariah nodded. She doubted if he had ever been a bad father to begin with.

''He's going to miss Matt,'' Adam went on finally, hoarsely.

''Maybe you could bring him back to visit him.''

''That's what Sarah said.'' What he would probably do was promise to, he thought, then pray to God that Bo never took him up on the offer.

''But you won't,'' Mariah said quietly.

His heart slammed as she read his mind. ''I can't.''

He didn't know he had spoken aloud, and then he realized that he'd said more than he'd intended to. But maybe it was better to get it all out now. Before she could look at him again the way she had tonight, he thought, with her eyes both luminous and pained as she spoke words to close the gap between him and his son's memory. Because he had to go, and she had to know it, before either of them could pretend or dream or get in too deeply.

''Pull over,'' he said abruptly, but she was already doing it, easing back on the reins. Goliath trudged to a stop on the side of the road. The flurries began to turn to flakes.

''You just don't get it yet, do you?'' he demanded finally.

''I'm not sure what you're talking about, Adam.'' She put the reins down, carefully, he thought. She put her hands together in her lap again, hitching around a little to face him, and he wanted to shout at her not to, because for some reason this was impossible if he had to look at her, if he had to look into those eyes as he spoke.

He closed his own and rubbed his forehead against the headache there. The road behind him was blocked and he didn't want to go right, and he sure as hell didn't want to go left, so there was nowhere to go at all. He felt trapped.

"Do you know what I was thinking about tonight?" he asked finally.

"Well, Bo, of course."

He made a deprecating sound in his throat. "When I *should* have been thinking about Bo, when I *wanted* to be thinking about Bo, I was thinking about you. I was thinking about how you'd looked that night with your hair down. I was wondering what it might feel like, wondering what you might taste like...and I don't know what the hell your Amish boys do when they get together with your Amish girls after the lights go out, but I can pretty much guarantee you that my thoughts weren't running parallel."

She didn't answer, but he heard her breath quicken. He dropped his hand to look at her sharply.

"Don't *do* that," he snarled.

"Do *what?*"

"Breathe like you'd like nothing better in the world."

"But I wouldn't."

One minute he was rational, reasonably so. And then her words echoed around in his head, with promise he didn't dare entertain. He grabbed her shoulders. He looked into her eyes—*damn her eyes.* Sometimes it felt as if they could see right through him...and sometimes they missed the most important things of all.

He shook her a little, without meaning to. "Don't say that. You have no clue what you're saying."

She shook her head hard as hope thundered in her chest. "What I didn't know, didn't dream, was that you—you never said, never made me believe—"

"Because I don't play by your rules, damn it!" he shouted. "And I have *some* honor!"

Mariah flinched. And that was good, he thought, that was great, because maybe she was beginning to understand. He went on, brutally, just to make sure. "I'm not going to marry you. I don't want to stay here. I'm not going to settle down to a life in the country. Are you catching on? I don't like your *Ordnung.* I think it's ridiculous that people can't go to college. And I sure as hell don't want to spend the rest of my life pushing a plow without benefit of so much as a tractor! I like short skirts and I like your hair down. And I won't spend day after day stomping cow manure off my boots and watching you grovel to a lot of holier-than-thou men!''

"You're that unhappy here?" she whispered.

"*No*, damn it! I'm fine! I'm fine, because sooner or later I know I can go home. It's okay for the time being, and falling asleep in front of your wood stove has its merits. But I've got no intention of doing it forever and *I don't want my son raised this way.* I don't want him kowtowing to your damned deacons the way you do!''

She recoiled. Her eyes shone. He felt as if he had just taken a new spring flower and crushed it in his hands. But he wouldn't, *couldn't* apologize any more than she could beg the forgiveness of her church.

"I won't marry you," he said again, because that seemed like the most important part. His voice lowered dangerously, angrily. "And even I'm not so much of a bastard that I'd touch you anyway."

"I don't have to follow the *Ordnung.*"

"But you still do it. And that says it all, doesn't it?" He was suddenly weary to the bone. He let go of her.

Mariah opened her mouth, licked her lip, then closed it again. Somehow he made her feel ashamed. And that hurt, with a burning sensation deep inside her, more than his words ever could. She'd always known he felt this way. But hearing him say it, and the way he said it, made everything inside her cringe.

"Sugar Joe says you're a great teacher," he went on, talking to the side window now. "But you're going to waste that, aren't you?" Ah, yeah, he thought, now they were *really* getting into what bothered him. It started spewing out of him like poison. "You're going to let them kick you and you're just going to crawl away on your belly like you deserve it. And I *hate* that. You're going to leave your little schoolhouse and you're not going to take that skill, that talent to a public school, no matter how much they might need you there. No matter that you can juggle eight grades at once and you'd be a godsend to any second-grade glass." *No matter that you could do that and we could live like normal people so I could touch you.* "You'd stop teaching before you'd do that. Because *you believe.*" He spat the words. He hated her—and himself—because they were true. Because she believed, and he never would.

"I don't, Mariah," he went on hoarsely. "I don't even believe in God anymore, much less in a bunch of trumped-up rules and suffering to honor Him and be more like Him."

She gasped. "Adam, you don't mean—"

"Yeah." He cut her off. "I do."

He needed to get out of this buggy, he thought, away from the smell of violets. He needed it desperately. But when he made a move to go, she caught his arm.

"Adam, please. Wait! Where are you going?"

"I'm getting the hell out of this pumpkin." He wrenched away and reached for the door.

"*No!* Finish this!"

Maybe he stopped because it was the most temper he'd ever heard from her. Maybe he stopped because there was nowhere in particular he wanted to go and it was a long, cold walk back to Abe's and his car.

"Don't run now, Adam," Mariah went on breathlessly. "You're not that cruel, that unfair. You had your say. Now give me mine."

"You can't change my mind," he said, his voice rough.

"I wouldn't presume to. Not about the settlement."

Even the fact that she called it that burned the hell out of him, he realized. As if it was something reverent.

As if it was something a lot more important than anything he could give her.

The thought was sneaky, cold. It wormed its way into his heart and it tightened there, just painfully enough so that he knew it was true. It was why he was so angered by her adherence to rules she didn't have to adhere to. It was why he hated her faith, her pride in it, her steadfast morality. *Because it was all more important than he was.* He couldn't give her anything, couldn't even make love to her because of a God who broke promises and some men who were more into pious punishment than generosity of spirit.

"I know you're not going to stay," she went on, her voice shaking. "But at least leave me some memories to keep when you're gone."

"Haven't you heard a word I've said?" he growled.

"Yes," she whispered. "And a few you didn't. You don't want to hurt me. You're concerned because you can't live up to my

morals. We shouldn't run around because you can't marry me.''
She took a deep breath. ''And I'm saying I don't care.''

''Don't.'' His voice was ragged, a futile warning. ''You care.
What about Abe?''

She blinked. ''What about him?''

''You said you wouldn't date him because you couldn't marry
him!''

''No, Adam, *you* said that! If you had let me finish, I would
have told you that it wasn't worth bucking the rules for him! I
would have told you that he's kind and he's good, but he never
made me want anything!''

''Shut up, Mariah,'' he warned harshly. He had to make her
stop talking. Now.

''Remember what I told you about going to school?'' she
rushed on. ''That I was going to be miserable one way or the
other, so I thought I ought to have something to show for it?
That's how *this* is, Adam! I'm going to hurt when you're gone,
whether or not you…you do what…what you want to do or not,''
she finished lamely, the words tangling.

''Say it,'' he snarled, and the panic was wild now. ''You can't
even say it!''

''What?'' she gasped.

''What I want to do is make love to you.'' There, he thought
angrily. It was out. The air in the carriage seemed to go still with
waiting. She caught his arm again. He felt her fingers begin trembling. He could feel the tremors rock through her from that single
connection.

''Yes,'' she managed.

''Say it,'' he growled again and didn't know why he was doing
this to her, hated himself for it, but in that moment he hated her
more. Because she was so good, so perfect, and she was the
wrong woman for him. And that was her choice, purely her
choice, not his own.

Mariah's heart was pounding so hard she thought it would jump
out of her chest. It wasn't the words, she knew. She could say
them. It was the thought of stepping over the line.

And with that realization, she, too, grew furious. Not with him,
no, never with him. With herself and, God help her, with her
church. Because she had done everything right and she had been
so good, and now they would take her school away from her and
Adam would go, too. And she would be left with…nothing.

Adam was right. She would allow it because she had really

never learned how to resist. But there was that small burning ember inside her. It wasn't hurt, she realized now. It was fury. She would not, would *not* go quietly and meekly, without taking something for herself along the way.

There was no other route to happiness but the one right here in front of her. No other man in her limited world would dare dishonor her, would ever have the courage to cross the *Meidung*. And there was no other man she wanted, had ever wanted.

Adam tried to think about Bo. He needed to think about Bo now, about everything that had happened tonight, everything that had been said. It would put a mental barrier up between them, break off this treacherous conversation before it got any worse.

Then she spoke. "Make love to me, Adam," she whispered fiercely. "Please, *please* give me something to show for it all."

It stunned him. He hadn't expected it, and when she spoke the words something came undone inside him. A dam broke. "Oh, God," he said, strangled. "Oh, damn it."

He had expected a flood, but there was only an immense vibrating stillness inside him. It thrummed, waiting, poised. Not peace. It was something more tense and troubling than that. He thought it was like standing on a precipice, where the drop was so sheer you couldn't see the bottom of it.

He didn't leap. He inched over and let gravity take him.

She'd moved, somehow she'd moved while he'd been all caught up in his own turmoil. One leg was tucked beneath her now, and her palms were flush on the seat between them. She leaned toward him a little. And he moved toward her, as well, too slowly, too carefully, as though he knew he would need to damn himself later for not backing off when he had had all the opportunity in the world.

He touched his mouth to hers, their lips just meeting. A feeling almost like amazement hit him, that this was finally happening. In spite of his beliefs or the lack of them, he thought there was almost something reverent about this ultimate melding of their lips.

He didn't know how to be gentle, but somehow he was. He wanted to appreciate every nuance, because he didn't think he would dare do it again. He wasn't going to take her up on her offer—he really wasn't that much of a bastard. And he didn't think he could walk away if he sank all the way in over his head. But just one taste, he thought, just a moment, to say goodbye to all that could never be.

Her mouth was soft. He opened his. She opened hers. Her breath was a whisper. He touched her lips again, then again with his own, playing over them.

Her eyes stayed open, as though she wondered if there was more, as though she was watching him for some kind of clue. And then he saw a shiver course through her. It was visible and she sighed with it, as if she enjoyed every tremor.

That was when the flood finally came. Something exploded inside him. He felt control fall away from him in jagged pieces. He caught her head in his hands, and this time he slanted his own. He caught her lips with hard intent and swallowed her gasp. *Mariah.* He felt her hands move from the seat to his chest, felt her fingers tangling in his jacket in that way she had, as though she would hold on. But he was the one who was drowning.

Again. More. He used his tongue, and after a quick jolt she didn't seem surprised. For a wild moment, he could almost make himself believe that she was every woman, any woman, even when she was so different, so special it terrified him. He did it again, sweeping his tongue through her mouth, tasting her, hoping that maybe she'd meet its touch. Maybe she would, if he made this kiss good enough. Maybe if he made it sweet enough, she wouldn't regret it.

He didn't kiss like a man who would never come up for air, she thought, losing herself in swimming sensation. He didn't kiss as Asher had—the only man she had ever kissed. Asher had claimed her mouth sloppily and greedily, until she thought her chest would surely burst if she didn't breathe. Adam was relentless in his own way, as he was in everything. But his mouth claimed hers for only a brief moment, his tongue teasing before he eased back, nipping her lip, covering her own again. And again. And some more. Drawing back each time, as though to make her want more, as though he was nibbling some delicious delicacy and he wanted the experience to last, the taste to stay with him always.

Something hurt inside her. A sweet ache. Each time his mouth left hers, each time he took a breath so that he could keep doing this for eternity, she felt cold without him.

And she wanted more. She could feel his fingers, his hard fingers on her scalp, digging into her hair where it was tightly bound. And that was good, but she needed his warmth, too, the heat of his body, because there had been so very much cold and here was fire. She moved her hands suddenly to wrap her arms around his neck, tilting her own head to catch his mouth when he came back this time. And it was ridiculous, but her eyes began burning with tears again, this time from the sheer joy of it all.

When she held him like that, she had to arch her back, had to lean into him, and that brought her breasts flush with his chest. Adam heard himself groan into her mouth, knowing he had to pull away, had set her back away from him, but he was unable to find the will. Her breasts were small, nestling against him, and he found himself tightening his own arms around her to keep the contact. He thought again that her skin would be like satin, somewhere underneath that woolen jacket and all those clothes.

"Please, Adam," she whispered.

Dear God, what was she asking?

He couldn't have her skin. It was just like everything else in his life—there, so close, but so out of reach. But her hair, he thought. He could touch her hair. Maybe even her breasts.

He felt like a teenager on the brink of discovery, fumbling through his first encounter, afraid to dare and helpless against hope. His fingers tugged at the pins that held her bonnet on. His hands literally trembled. So with the same simplicity and generosity with which she did everything, Mariah hurried to help him.

She tugged out more of the pins until her hair tumbled down. He filled his hands with it even as he kissed her again, and it was thick and rich and cool in the frigid night air.

It tangled in his fingers and he let his mouth roam beneath it, finding her neck. That was when she cried out.

She felt him go still. She was afraid for a moment that he would stop, that her stupid, silly voice would change his mind, and she would have done anything, *anything* to have been able to swallow it back. When he swore, she was sure of it. But then she felt a tremor go through him as well.

He leaned back against the door and pulled her with him fast and hard, the movement unrestrained now. "I'm sorry." He dragged her body up over his until their legs tangled. Then his hands clenched in her hair again and his kiss deepened, and something started pounding inside her.

"So sorry. Didn't mean to do this," he said again, and then his hands were everywhere.

One slid to the side of her breast. Mariah held her breath until it came around to cup her completely, then she groaned. His other hand was at her thigh, moving, stroking, hard and demanding. And each time his hand slid up, her skirt moved with it. Her heart

began to pound, with daring and waiting and not a little bit of
fear. With wicked exhilaration. She craved his touch against her
bare skin, and if he would only move his hands higher, if he
would only *please* move his hand just a little bit higher, soon she
would have that to remember, too.

He meant to apologize again, because he'd never meant to let
himself go this far. He'd never meant to take what she could find
no peace in giving. But then his roving palm found skin.

It stunned him, then it inflamed him. Her stockings didn't go
all the way up. He swore to a God he no longer believed in and
knew he was damned. Because the soft cotton only went halfway
up her thighs, and he'd never anticipated that, couldn't *not* touch,
first the gentle grip of the elastic, then the satin of her flesh right
above and beneath it. His finger slid inside and traced around to
her inner thigh and she cried out again, softly, in wonder, moving
her legs apart, giving him access.

Then the night shattered.

He never heard it, not at first. It was only a gentle knock on
the glass over his head. But Mariah tensed and he felt her muscles
go hard beneath his hands. She let out something that might have
been a sob, maybe of frustration, probably of shame. She began
beating at his chest, frantically and ineffectually at first, then with
more force until she had managed to scramble upright, away from
him.

"Oh, no," she whispered aloud. "No, no, *no!*"

"What the—" And then he heard it himself this time, the rap-
ping on his window. He jerked into a sitting position, as well.

"Open the door Adam please hurry you've got to open the
door for him." Her words ran together over little gasps of panic.

"Who?" And he knew then that whatever she had just done
with him would not come without its price. No matter what she
had whispered she wanted, there was a very big part of her that
was cringing in shame. But hadn't he known that all along?

He swore a stream of invectives this time, knowing it would
surely make her hate him. He hit the door hard, making it swing
open. "What?" he demanded of the man standing outside. "What
the hell do you want?"

It was a cop. A *cop?* He'd only seen a face through the window, in the snow, and the upper part of it had been obscured by
a hat. He'd thought it was an Amishman, with one of those ever-
present broad-brimmed things they always wore on their heads.

He'd even thought, a little crazily and irrationally, that it was one of her all-knowing deacons.

But it was a cop.

The officer leaned down to look into the buggy. That was when Adam realized that there were lights flashing behind them. A squad car.

What the hell?

"Miss Fisher, you okay in there?" the cop asked.

"Fine," she squeaked.

"Well, there's a man on your porch. He wants to know what's happened to you."

"A man," she whispered and finally looked at the officer. "A *man?*"

The cop looked down at a small notebook he carried, as though wanting to make sure he got every detail right. "Officer Langston noticed a Caucasian male, mid to late thirties, loitering on your porch."

In that moment, Adam knew. He didn't need the man to continue. He wasn't sure if he wanted to kill Jake or kiss him.

"When Officer Langston approached to investigate, this Caucasian male identified himself as one Jacob Wallace," the cop went on. "He explained that he was looking for an Adam Wallace—would that be you, by any chance?" He glanced at Adam. "He said he had reason to believe that Miss Fisher would know your whereabouts and he was, uh, I quote, 'Cold as a bugger and freezing his butt off, and would someone please turn on the...uh, expletive heat around here.' Unquote. Officer Langston checked with Abe Miller to find out when and where you might have gone, if you'd rented a buggy. Mr. Miller said you had borrowed a horse and vehicle earlier and were going to the Lappses', whereupon the Lappses said you'd left the better part of an hour ago. So we...uh, thought there might have been trouble," he finished lamely. He gave a surreptitious glance at Adam again.

"No trouble," Mariah gasped.

Adam's pulse was still pounding. "You can tell Mr. Miller that we're on our way in with this contraption."

"Your—brother, is it?—is still at Miss Fisher's," the cop offered.

"Fine. I'll pick him up there."

The officer went back to his car. Mariah sat without moving, except to tremble.

"Welcome to Smalltown, U.S.A." she whispered finally, feebly. "I'm sorry, Adam. I'm so sorry. It's just that we're so rural here. I..." She trailed off.

"Drive, Mariah."

"But—"

"Drive the damned buggy."

She jumped and stared at him, her eyes stricken. "Yes. Okay. Of course."

She didn't say anything more, and Adam couldn't think of a thing to say, but he was panicked by how often "amen" came to mind.

Chapter 13

Jake was still on Mariah's small porch when they got there. He moved down the sidewalk as soon as Adam stopped the car. His stride managed to imply both laziness and anger. Adam read his irritation in his eyes—one more problem would send him over the edge into real temper.

He jerked open the door. "You said you were having dinner, not going for your damned doctorate—" He broke off. His jaw fell. Mariah inched out of the passenger seat and slipped past him.

She felt as if she had suddenly awakened from a bad dream to find herself made of glass. "Excuse me," she managed, then she scurried past him up the walk.

"Mariah!" Adam heard himself shout. It finally made her stop. She turned slowly. He got out of the car to look over the roof at her, then he couldn't think of a single thing to say. "I'll, uh, see you on Sunday, then. To go back to the Lappses'. Right?"

What was he asking? *Why* was he asking? Did he think they could pretend that nothing had just happened between them on that dark, deserted side road?

She nodded once, jerkily, and rushed away again.

She was dying inside, she realized, slowly and painfully, and her heart was going to go first. Mariah shut her door behind her and leaned back against it weakly. She was fiercely glad that she didn't have a telephone. She knew that if Adam could easily have gotten out of taking her with him on Sunday, if he could call and do it without actually having to face her, then he would do just that.

Maybe that would have been better.

Instead, he would probably take her with him, but he would never touch her again. Something had happened, something she didn't understand, and he had pulled back from her almost...almost *angrily* when that policeman had shown up, after giving her one of the most beautiful nights of her life.

For a heartbeat in time, she hated. She hated that police officer. She hated Jacob Wallace—what in heaven's name was he doing in the settlement, anyway? They had taken from her a chance for something wonderful and good, and she knew that she would never again have such an opportunity in her life.

She was thirty years old. A spinster. Her throat closed hard. It had taken thirty years for someone to make her feel as Adam had tonight. But he wouldn't do it again, and soon, very soon now, he would go. No one else would come along, no one else would make her heart sing and everything heat so sweetly inside her. No one else would make her laugh...and cry.

It was something she simply knew.

She slid her back down the door slowly until she was sitting, her knees drawn up. Then she lowered her forehead to them and cried for lost chances.

"Well," Jake said as Adam began to drive. "I take it that was the pretty Mariah. Seems you forgot to mention that your handy little contact here is a knockout."

"Shut up. Shut the hell up." He was ridiculously miffed that the first time Jake had seen her, her hair had been spilling. Jake, he thought, the most notorious and successful lady-killer in all of Dallas.

"I thought you said she wasn't Amish."

"She's not. Well, she is. What I said is that she doesn't actually belong to the church." He wasn't up to explaining the *Meidung* to him now, either.

"So then why was she wearing that stupid dress?"

Adam rounded on him, snarling. "It's not stupid."

Jake's eyes narrowed. "You're worrying me, bro."

"It's just that they all need to look like each other," he finished lamely, putting his eyes back on the road.

"Well, maybe you missed this, but she wouldn't blend in with the crowd if you dropped her down in the middle of the Miss America pageant. And I'm not talking sore thumbs sticking out here. More like a hothouse rose in a garden of weeds."

Adam grunted.

"I guess I interrupted something." Jake was fishing, and he did it unabashedly.

"No," Adam said shortly, then he added. "Nothing that didn't need to be interrupted."

Jake shot a brow up at that. "So how did dinner go?"

"It went."

"What am I missing here? Didn't you just have dinner with your son for the first time in four years?"

"He asked me a lot of questions." Adam quoted Mariah's impression without meaning to.

"Good." Jake nodded cautiously. "Well, I'm still having a hard time believing that you didn't remember I was flying in tonight."

"I remember. I just thought you'd be later." Adam pulled into the motel parking lot. He'd remembered and then he'd forgotten, in a blaze of need and the discovery of skin.

"I rented a car at the airport, dropped it off in the city of Lancaster. I took a cab back here and waited an hour or so. That pit bull of a desk clerk—the big guy—wouldn't let me into your room. So I had him dig up the address of one Mariah Fisher. I walked over there. That was one long, cold stroll." Jake watched for a reaction, any reaction. "Couldn't see why we'd need two cars, though, keeping your budget in mind, and all."

"We don't." Adam got out and slammed the door. Jake watched him go, then got out as well to holler after him.

"Your disposition has deteriorated drastically since I put you on that plane. This concerns me."

Jake had told him that day that he needed a woman. Well, he had found one, Adam thought. And he'd known from the start that she was all wrong for him. She couldn't even kiss him without having a nervous breakdown.

"I gave Gary Kanter your phone number here." Jake grabbed his duffel bag to give chase to the motel-room door.

Adam stopped, looking back. "Who the hell is Gary Kanter?"

Whoa, Jake thought. The man was losing it. "The LAPD cop,"

he answered slowly. "The guy who's flying to Phoenix tomorrow on your say-so. Amber Calabrese?"

"Oh, yeah. Right."

"If it pans out, are you gonna go down there?" Adam had always personally handled the ChildSearch reunions himself.

"We'll see how it goes," he said vaguely, thrusting his key into the door.

Jake finally nodded as though coming to a decision. "All right, bro. I think I've got just the thing for what ails you."

Adam gave him a jaundiced look. "Peace and quiet? You're going to shut up now?"

Jake grinned and dropped the duffel bag onto one of the beds, unzipping it. He held up a bottle of bourbon.

Adam's eyes went to slits. Yeah, he thought. Yeah. If he got drunk enough, he'd sleep tonight. If he got drunk enough, this gnawing pain in the pit of his stomach might go away. He might forget how she had scrambled away from him, beating on his chest in utter panic.

It had been a wake-up call, he told himself, just in the nick of time. Unfortunately, the dream had been a lot better, farfetched and brief as it had been.

"Give me that," he snapped, grabbing the bottle out of Jake's hand.

"Hey, wait a minute! That's *my* bourbon!"

Adam stalked into the bathroom and slammed the door hard. Jake stared after him, then he scratched his chin thoughtfully.

"I take it we're not going to get started on this project tonight?" he called.

"They all go to bed early," came Adam's muffled reply.

Jake heard the shower turn on. He picked up the car keys Adam had thrown on the desk.

"Guess I'll just have to get myself another bottle." Then again, sitting in a motel room alone while his brother sulked in the bathroom wasn't his idea of a resoundingly good time. He went outside, got back into the car and headed into Lancaster again.

Adam woke on Thursday morning with a splitting headache. It was a sharp yet throbbing feeling at the base of his skull, behind his ears. He sat up and glared at the bottle of bourbon sitting across the room on the desk. He was disgusted to realize that only a quarter, maybe a scant third of it was gone. So was Jake, but that was far less troubling.

He couldn't even drink with all his heart, Adam thought. He wondered if something was lacking within himself, because everything he started, everything he attempted, only got half done or fell apart. Even his stab at fatherhood had been aborted.

The door banged open and Jake cruised inside. He deposited two paper cups of coffee on the desk.

"Rise and shine," Jake greeted him.

Adam closed one eye to see him more clearly. "Where've you been?"

He began humming an old Beach Boys' tune. Something about northern girls keeping their boyfriends warm at night. Adam felt his heart kick his ribs. He was out of bed, standing, before he knew he did it.

"You went back to Mariah's." Every irrational male hormone he possessed reared up inside him. She had been ready enough, hungry enough, tired of her quiet, chaste world, and maybe after the panic of the cop had passed, she had erupted again.

"Get a grip, for God's sake," Jake muttered. He shot him an incredulous look and popped the lid off one of the coffees.

"I need one of those," Adam said weakly. He grabbed the other coffee.

"First of all, we've never shared women."

"There's nothing to share. I have no claim on her."

Jake gave a grunt of disgust. "And even more important, long, plain dresses and aprons just ain't my style."

You'd be surprised at what's underneath those dresses. Adam didn't answer.

"Little possessive, aren't you?" Jake prodded. "For someone without a claim."

Adam ignored that, too. "You're just getting back?"

Jake shrugged. Not that he was discreet. It was just that it went without saying. "I went back into the city. So give me some idea as to where I should start today."

Adam guzzled coffee, closing his eyes to rub the back of his head. "Got any aspirin?"

"There's a gift shop in the lobby. Never use the stuff, myself."

"Okay." He made himself think. "Joe Lapp. You should start with Sugar Joe Lapp. I'll drive you out there."

"Then make yourself scarce," Jake suggested.

"What are you going to do, strong-arm him?"

Jake stared at him. "What the hell is wrong with you these days? No, I'm not going to *strong-arm* him. I'm going to talk to the man. You always muddle things up when you come with me. You ask the wrong things at the wrong time."

Adam forced himself to relax. That was true enough. "Joe and his wife are good people. They're the ones who have Bo."

Jake scowled into his coffee. "What are the odds of Bo remembering *me,* do you think? Maybe my showing up might help."

Adam scowled. "He used to see even less of you than he did of me." Jannel had never liked Jake. She'd probably been afraid he would pick up on her cocaine habit. At the time she'd just acted as if his devil-may-care attitude was beneath her.

"Yeah, well, it was just a shot." Jake drained his coffee. "Anyway, tell me about the Lapps."

"They're the only ones who actually saw her."

"Jannel? I thought we were looking for the guy who came after her six months later."

"We are. They saw him, too. And they can probably tell you who else was in that church service, who else you should talk to. That's where the guy turned up."

"Good enough. Let's go."

"I need a shower," Adam muttered.

"You're big on showers all of a sudden, bro. Why don't you just jump in that creek I passed this morning? It's probably colder. Or better yet, do something to take off the edge. Judging by your tardiness last night, the pretty Mariah is willing."

Adam was on top of him with one quick move. Speed was usually Jake's style. Brute strength was his own. But this time he acted fast, without thought, and he had his brother pinned against the wall before either one of them could fully react.

"One thing," Adam said roughly. "We need to get one thing straight here."

Jake lifted a brow at him. Just as when they had fought in Dallas, he kept his hands at his sides. He wasn't a saint. He took great pride in sinning. But he had one small scrap of family left here, and the well-being of that scrap had been worrying him for a while now.

"Go ahead," he suggested. "Vent. Just try to spare the nose. It's my best feature."

Adam gritted his teeth. "This...this *thing* with Mariah—whatever the hell it is—is not a laughing matter. I don't want to joke

about it. She's off-limits insofar as discussion goes. You got it?''
He thought a moment. ''For that matter, she's off-limits to you,
period.''

''She's got you on your knees,'' Jake said quietly.

''No. Nor is she about to. Now let's find Jannel and get free
of this godforsaken place before everything gets even more
screwed up.''

''Fine by me, bro. I'd just as soon see you and Bo come home,
too. If you stay here much longer, you'll be getting religious
next.''

''Not a chance,'' Adam snapped, finally letting go of his shirt.
''God abandoned us Wallaces a long time ago.''

''Well...good. Just as long as you remember that.''

Adam rubbed at his headache again. ''We can cool our heels
long enough for you to grab a shower if you want.''

Jake grinned. ''Had mine no more than an hour ago.''

Adam knew better than to ask where.

Mariah couldn't function, couldn't concentrate. The children
were shouting and she had a headache. She knew she had to
restore order, and she couldn't find the will.

It was early Thursday afternoon. She hadn't heard from Adam
today. She hadn't expected to. Whatever his brother had come to
the settlement for, it obviously didn't concern her or require her
assistance.

She hugged herself and stared blankly out at the sea of small
faces. She knew that what had happened last night between them
wasn't the only thing that was bothering her. As a general rule,
she was always honest with herself. And she knew that she found
it very hard to teach right now because all this was going to be
snatched away from her very soon.

She was immensely grateful to Sarah Lapp for letting her know
what was going on. And she wished desperately that the woman
hadn't told her. Then she would have had just a little more time,
another few days, maybe a week or more of ignorant bliss.

''Noah, get down off that chair,'' she managed. ''Why are you
so wound up today?'' As if she didn't know. Subconsciously, at
least, he was in turmoil. Her heart hurt for him. ''Daniel, stop
pulling at Gracie's hair,'' she went on. ''What is *wrong* with you
children, all of a sudden?''

They went still, looking at her. She knew what was wrong with

them. They sensed the helplessness without her. Children had a
sixth sense that always told them when they could get away with
pushing the envelope. This was one of those times.

She forced herself to her feet, her legs feeling oddly hollow as
they had since she had gotten out of Adam's car the previous
night. *You're going to let them kick you and you're going to crawl
away on your belly like you deserve it.* She herded the first- and
second-graders to their art easels at the back of the room. *You're
not going to take that skill, that talent, to a public school, no
matter how much they might need you there.* She got the third-
and fourth-graders seated at their desks. *No matter that you can
juggle eight grades at once and you'd be a godsend.* She passed
tests out to her fifth-graders and got the sixth-graders to the black-
board. *You'd stop teaching first, because you believe.* She stared
at the seventh- and eighth-graders, wondering what it was she'd
meant to do with them this afternoon.

She *did* believe, she thought, going back to her desk to consult
her notes. And it was as simple and as complex as that.

Damn him, she thought angrily, throwing the notes down,
shocking herself. *Damn* him for making her think, making her
doubt, making her want, and then going away.

Adam arrived at Mariah's door at exactly noon on Sunday.
Sugar Joe had asked them to come at twelve-thirty. Adam wanted
to keep his time with her to a minimum. It shamed him a little
to admit that he'd actually tried to think of a way not to take her
with him, even knowing how much it meant to her to be included.

"Hey," he said when she opened the door. He talked fast and
abruptly. "I thought we'd skip the buggy routine this time. It's
occurred to Joe by now that I'm not Amish. He'll just have to
live with it." No way in hell was he going to allow himself to
be alone with her in those close confines again, he decided.

Mariah only nodded. She already wore her coat and shawl. She
swept past him and went outside to his car, opening the door
herself before he could do it for her. He was perversely irritated.

He was behaving exactly the way she had thought he'd behave,
Mariah realized. Distant. Polite, but with an edge. And her heart
was breaking.

She had determined to ask him about the other children today.
She wanted to do it now, before they got to the Lappses'. She
just wanted to get it over with. They were going to take her school

away from her, anyway. It didn't matter how good or how bad she was; her past sin, her only sin, would live forever. The deacons were not going to let her back into the community unless she confessed a guilt she did not feel. They were going to take her children from her, whether she tried to find Lizzie Stoltzfus and the others or not.

And Adam was already angry with her. He was already shutting her out. He couldn't possibly grow more distant once she asked him to do this for the settlement. He was already about as far away as he could get.

That being the case, there was no more reason to procrastinate. She would ask him, would do what she had to do to finally find those children, then she would get on with her life. Somewhere else, in some other *Gemeide* or county, where she knew virtually no one and would not even have Katya to whisper with in the mornings.

"Adam," she began. He didn't answer. She glanced over at him as he drove. His jaw was set like stone. She repeated his name. "We have to talk."

"No."

"But—"

A nerve or something twitched at his jaw. "I said no, Mariah. It's senseless. There's not a damned thing that either one of us can say. No matter what you tell me..." He trailed off. No matter what she *told* him, he thought, actions spoke louder than words.

If he lived to be ninety, he would remember her panic, her shame, when that cop had knocked on the glass of the buggy. Shame for wanting him. Shame for giving in to a perfectly healthy, relatively harmless human need.

He had only been kissing her.

And if he lived to be ninety, he would remember that skin at the top of her stockings. He knew it was there now. He couldn't even look at her without envisioning it, though he had "seen" it with only his touch, with his hands.

Mariah's heart slammed as she watched him and understood. He thought she wanted to talk about what had happened between them the other night.

"No, Adam," she protested. "I don't—it isn't—" But then, already, he was stopping the car in the Lapps' drive.

How had they gotten here so quickly? She'd been woolgathering, she thought helplessly, that was how. Procrastinating again, in some small measure. Mariah closed her eyes for a brief moment.

"Look," Adam said, turning the ignition off. He finally hitched around in the seat to face her, but he kept his hand on the door handle. "I can't apologize enough for what happened. I was sorry then. I said as much, didn't I? I should never have touched you. And now I'm doubly sorry that I did."

Pain, shame, embarrassment shimmied through her, taking her breath. Mariah brought her chin up with great effort. "Of all the things you might have said to me," she whispered, "I don't think any could hurt as much as that."

Chapter 14

"Damn it! *Damn* it!"

She was already out of the car. Adam pushed on his own door and jumped out as well. How could she twist this? How *dare* she twist it? He hadn't been the one hyperventilating when the cop had knocked on the buggy window.

By the time his feet hit the pavement, she was fairly running to the Lapps' porch. Sugar Joe came out. Mariah said something to him briefly and rushed past him, inside.

Joe intercepted Adam as he went after her. "Hold up there, friend."

"I have to—"

"I reckon there's a lot you have to do, but you're going to have to pick a few priorities first."

"What are you talking about?" Adam growled.

"There's been a slight change of plans."

Adam felt his heart kick. Painfully. This day was going to hell in a hand basket. "Like what?" he asked warily.

"Noah claims he's sick."

Claims? Adam settled down. "What are you saying?" But he thought he already knew.

"He told Sarah that he had the calf's flu," Joe explained.

"The calf's—" Adam made a choked sound. In that moment, all thoughts of Mariah fled from his mind.

"He won't come out of his room."

"He knows," Adam said finally. "He senses, suspects something. Maybe he even remembers me a little, from being around me again. And he's scared."

"That would be my guess," Joe agreed. "My opinion is that maybe you ought to go talk to him yourself. Maybe you ought to let him know that the road ahead isn't so scary or rocky as he might think." Joe finally moved to let him by. "Second door on the right, upstairs. I'll keep Matt down here, otherwise you'll never get a word in edgewise."

"Thanks," Adam managed, and went inside.

He climbed up the steps as though lead weighted his heels. Mariah was nowhere around. He needed her. Yet, he knew he couldn't drag her any more deeply into this than she already was. He was on his own.

He even wished, for one insane moment, that Jake hadn't gone home. Even his brother's dubious, irreverent company would be better than braving this alone. But Jake had talked to everyone he could talk to, had learned details about the strange man's appearance that Adam wouldn't even have thought to ask for, and last night he had taken his notes back home to the DPD. Their artist would draw up a composite of the man based on the information Jake had gotten, and they would give it to Berry to put on their website on the Internet.

So, Adam thought, he was very much under his own power on this one. He reached the top of the stairs. He thought his knees were knocking together.

He was a damned coward.

Second door on the right. He went to it and stood on the threshold, looking inside. Bo was laying on the bed, his back to the door. The room startled Adam because it wasn't so different from the one he and Jake had shared as boys. Except that they had had twin beds, he thought, and here there was a large double one. It was covered with beautiful quilting, something with royal-blue inserts that made the hem fuller where it brushed the floor. There was an oil lamp on each bedside table. Muddy rubber boots, a tennis racket, two hockey sticks and a baseball bat were crammed into a corner.

A rack of hunting rifles sat high and safely out of reach on one wall. Adam thought that dragging the desk chair over would give either Bo or Matt easy access to the guns. Then again, there was a certain discipline to these boys that had been lacking in him and Jake. Despite their high jinks, Bo and Matt really seemed to want to please. His and Jake's obedience—what little of it there had been—had been wrung out of them through fear.

Adam cleared his throat and his son twisted around to look at him. "Better not come in here," Bo said after a moment. "I got cow germs."

"I...uh, I'll take my chances. If it's okay with you, I mean."

Another long heartbeat passed. Bo finally shrugged. "I don't care."

Adam sat carefully on the edge of the bed, on the side Bo was facing. He had no idea where to start, what to say now. Maybe he hadn't learned so much by losing him, after all.

His heart was beating like a snare drum. This was the closest he'd been to his son physically in over four years. It made him ache. His hands burned to reach out and touch him.

"I used to be like you, didn't I?" Bo asked suddenly.

Adam's heart skipped. "What makes you say that?" he countered cautiously.

"Matt told me."

Adam cleared his throat. "Yeah?"

"A long time ago."

"What exactly did he tell you?"

"Just that he doesn't remember me being here when he was little. But he's not so much bigger than me. Older, I mean," he corrected quickly, not willing to give Matt any edge, even if the other boy wasn't here to hear it. "I figure we should have been together all along, you know? He should remember me when we were, like, pooping in diapers." He paused. "And I don't remember being real little with him, either."

"Yeah," Adam said with difficulty. "Well, I can see how you came to that conclusion."

"Plus I don't look like him. I don't look like any of them." Bo hugged something tighter to his chest. Adam looked closer, scowling, and realized it was a teddy bear. His heart spasmed. Bo saw him looking at it and he tucked it quickly under his ribs, out of sight.

"Do you remember where you came from?" Adam heard himself ask through the roar of blood in his ears.

"No," Bo said quickly. "Well, just...sort of. A little."

"What do you remember?"

"Riding in a car. A real fast red car. Sometimes I thought I dreamed it." Jannel's Corvette. Adam felt hope swell in his gut. "I didn't tell Matt," Bo went on. His chin thrust out. "Told him he was stupid."

"How come?"

"Because I don't want to be different. I don't want to be from anywhere else."

Adam's heart was cavorting now. "It's not so bad everywhere else. I kind of like it."

Bo sat up. He watched Adam suspiciously for a moment, realized the bear was in full view again and reached quickly to shove it under the pillow. "How come you came here?"

Oh, God, Adam thought. The fear. It was like something alive in his chest, something with claws, trying to wriggle up into his throat. He was excruciatingly aware of saying anything that would frighten him, hurt him, this child who was his reason for being. If he said the wrong thing now...

Don't even think about it. He followed his heart.

"To see if you might want to go back there," he said bluntly. Something spasmed visibly through the boy. "No."

"Okay," Adam said with a neutrality that killed him.

"Okay?"

"Yeah."

"You mean if I say no, you'll just go away and leave me alone?"

"I didn't say that. If you don't want to go, then I guess I'll just hang around here until you change your mind. There's no hurry...Noah."

Bo's eyes narrowed—and something raked through Adam's chest all over again. In that moment, despite the differences in their coloring, he looked exactly like Jake. *Family.*

"Is that my real name?" he asked after a moment. "Or is it just my name here?" He looked near tears. Adam nodded. "Do you know what my other name used to be?"

"Yeah."

"You *lied.*"

Adam flinched. "I did?"

"You pretended to just come here...you know, because. But you came to get me."

Adam took a careful breath. "I never once said I didn't come here to get you. I never said anything at all." *And is that what you want to teach him about lying? That half truths are all right?*

"Maybe that was wrong of me. Maybe I should have told you right from the start."

"Yeah. No. I don't know. It just seems kinda wrong."

"Maybe it was."

"I don't want to go back with you."

"Then I'll wait."

"I might *never* want to go."

"Well, just think about it."

Bo hesitated, then nodded. "I think I better sleep now. I'm real sick."

"That calf got you good, huh?" Adam's mouth nearly smiled.

"Yeah."

Adam got to his feet. His hand almost—*almost*—reached out to brush Bo's hair off his forehead. It had fallen forward, just as it had done all his life. Jannel had once gotten it styled to try to prevent it, but it hadn't worked.

He held back through sheer dint of will. He was at the door before his son, his child spoke again.

"So what was my name out there?" His small voice came muffled by the pillow.

"Bo," Adam said hoarsely. "Your name was Bo."

More silence. "That's a stupid name. It's not in the Bible."

"Not that I'm aware of."

"What's it short for?"

"Nothing. It's Irish, I think. It just sort of stands on its own." Adam's heart twisted hard this time.

"I was Irish?"

No, sport, you are *Irish.* He swallowed back on the words. "Partly."

"Matt and everybody are German."

"Yeah. I know."

"That's why I don't look like them."

"Probably, yeah. I guess that has something to do with it."

"Did I have a family?" Bo asked finally. "Like this one?"

This time he couldn't lie. There could be no half truths. Not for Bo, not for himself. This one was black-and-white.

"No," he said quietly. "Nothing like this one at all." Then, like the coward he was, he fled.

Mariah was in the kitchen, helping to peel potatoes. "We've got to go," he said shortly, rudely, stepping into the door.

Both she and Sarah turned to look at him. It took him a moment
longer to realize that Joe and Nathaniel were seated at the table.
They all watched him, waiting. It was Mariah who finally spoke.

"It went badly," she ventured.

"No. Yeah. I don't know what it did." He looked at Joe. *Help
me here.* Then it struck him that in that moment, Sugar Joe Lapp
probably needed his help more than he needed Joe's. He was
probably dying to know what had happened upstairs.

"He knows he wasn't always here," Adam went on, taking a
deep breath. "Matt told him."

Sarah gasped. "*Matt* did?"

"Children talk," Mariah said quietly. "They have whole secret
worlds we're not privy to. And Matt and Bo—Noah—are so
close."

"Yes," Sarah agreed faintly.

"He told Bo that he doesn't remember him being here when
he—Matt—was small. And Bo says he doesn't want to go anywhere else," Adam went on. Something flared in Sarah's eyes,
something like hope. He had to look away before he could continue. "So I'll give him more time."

"But then you'll go," the woman said flatly. "You'll take him
and go."

"Yeah."

Joe got up to put a hand on his wife's shoulder. "Does he
know you're his father?"

"No," Adam said shortly. "He didn't ask, and I didn't tell
him. Yet. Listen..." He trailed off, clearing his throat. "Thanks
for the offer of dinner, but I need to—I don't know, be on my
own to think about this."

"Of course," Sarah said softly.

Adam looked at Mariah again. "If you want to stay, I understand."

"No. I want to come with you."

And no matter that he knew it was wrong, that he knew it was
dangerous to keep spending too much time with her, Adam was
relieved. Because he needed her now, and, as always, she was
there.

"I'll be in the car," he said roughly. He turned away from
them and left the kitchen.

None of them noticed Matthew darting out the door, dashing
into the backyard before anyone realized that he had been listening.

* * *

Adam drove. He just...drove. When he got back to Ronks Road, when he should have gone right to take her back to her village, he turned left. Mariah said nothing. She waited.

The expression on his face hurt her. It was so tortured, she thought, so grim.

"He asked me..." he began finally, then he had to clear his throat. "He asked me if he had a family like the Lapps. And what the hell was I supposed to tell him?"

"He's got family," she said softly. "You. An uncle."

"His uncle is a *lunatic*," Adam snarled. "His uncle is as likely to snap handcuffs on a junkie's wrists as he is to brawl with one. His uncle goes through a woman a week."

"He didn't seem that bad," Mariah said helplessly. Actually, he seemed a little...scary, she thought. Adam was driven. The brief glimpse she had gotten of Jacob Wallace had been of a man possessed with an almost manic energy, deliberately disguised behind a forced laziness.

Adam shot her a look. "You said all of two words to him. 'Excuse me.' Trust me on this one. He's a lunatic."

"But—"

"But nothing, Mariah. I'm going to take Bo away from Matt, away from Sugar Joe and Sarah and Gracie and Dinah and Nathaniel. And you know what I'm going to give him? *Do you know?*" She shook her head mutely. "A big, slamming house in Dallas with six bedrooms and a family room with toys that suited him four years ago."

"I don't understand what's wrong with that. You can buy him new toys."

"The house is empty."

"It won't be when you get there."

"We'll rattle around in it," he went on as though she hadn't spoken. "Just the two of us. I can't take him back to the apartment. I can't raise a kid in that neighborhood. And every once in a while his Uncle Jake will flash through his life like some kind of damned wayward meteor. There won't be parents and there won't be siblings and, Jesus, how can I take all that away from him and give him back *nothing?*"

"Oh, Adam," she whispered. "The important thing is that he's with you. Then you can make any kind of world for him you choose."

The hell he could. All the roads were blocked or ugly.

"My mother's dead. So's my father—thank God for that," he added without remorse, without the slightest twinge of shame. He'd always hated the bastard with all his heart. "And Kimmie— God knows where Kimmie is. The best I can hope for is that she made something better of her life than Jake and I have. My mother was an alcoholic, Mariah. She drank herself to death, hiding from my father. He was a bully who beat up on folks for the sheer pleasure of it. I guess it made him feel like a big man. He always went after whoever was weakest at the time. Toward the end, when Jake and I were big enough to defend ourselves, it was always Mom or Kimmie he went for. So Mom drank and Kimmie ran away from home at seventeen with a black eye and a broken arm." He paused. "Now there's no one left."

"Adam, both you and Jake are good men," she insisted. Then, at his expression, she added, "*You're* a good man. And Jake must have a good streak, too, because he came here to help you."

"He came to help me find Jannel."

Her heart staggered a little. "I see."

"I thought I needed to close that door. I thought it was the last one. But it's not. Man, there are opened doors all over the place and I don't know what to do with any of them."

"Come inside," she suggested.

"Huh?" And only then did he realize that he had come full circle, all through the settlement, because somehow or other he found himself back on her street, parked in front of her house, though he'd known this wasn't a good place to go.

"Come inside," she repeated. "I won't offer you coffee. I won't offer myself." At his angry look, she flushed and hurried on. "You said once that falling asleep in front of my stove wasn't so bad. So come inside, Adam. Take a load off your feet and just...let things be for a little while."

"I can't," he said ridiculously. "I can't do that. Now I know that your stockings don't go all the way up."

Her skin flamed, but she held his eyes while her hand found the door handle. "It's your choice, Adam. Do what you like."

He waited a long time, until she had unlocked her front door and had gone inside. She left it ever so slightly ajar.

He got out of the car and followed her up the walk, not sure if he was heading straight for his own damnation or to a place where the fear might go away.

Chapter 15

He found her in the kitchen. No matter what she had promised, she was making coffee.

"Mariah."

She looked over her shoulder at him. She didn't seem surprised that he'd come in, after all, he realized.

"For myself," she explained quickly.

He waved off the little percolator she placed on top of the wood stove. "I don't know how to give him a family. I don't know how to *be* his family. I'm scared to death to try to be his father." That was the crux of it, he thought, the single thing that panicked him more than any other. And she was the only one he could say it to.

He heard her little indrawn breath. She turned back to him quickly, her expression soft and understanding. She crossed to him quickly and framed his face in her hands. His thoughts swerved as they did every time she got too close. He smelled violets again, and if she didn't stop touching him soon he wasn't going to be able to work this out at all.

"Adam, that's silly," she said quietly. "You've been a father, the best kind of father, for weeks now. Don't you even realize that?"

He stared at her disbelievingly. Then he shook his head. "I've had all of two conversations with him."

"And is that the measure of a father?"

He made an ugly sound in his throat. "I don't know. That's my point."

Her palms were warm, coaxing him to see. "Adam, for weeks now you've held back when you've longed to rush in, when rushing in is your style. Your every action, your every move, has been with Bo's best interest in mind. Since I've known you, you've spent nearly every moment protecting him from undue hurt in a situation where he can't protect himself."

It sounded so easy, so simple, when she said it. And it lulled him. It quieted some of the somersaulting panic in his belly. "You've been like some kind of wise angel through all this," he murmured.

Her eyes widened and she finally dropped her hands. "An *angel?*" She laughed nervously. "I can name a few deacons who might disagree with you."

"Then they're fools."

She looked up at him with a soft kind of yearning. "Thank you, Adam. I think, somewhere down the line, I'll often remember you saying that."

He thought of something else she'd wanted to remember, other memories she'd said she wanted to take with her when this was over. Something shifted inside him.

"I'm sorry," he said for what felt like the thousandth time. "For hurting you. For being rough on you. You don't deserve it."

She shook her head. "I'm hardly fragile, Adam. It doesn't matter."

"I made you cry," he went on doggedly. And *that* was something he thought *he'd* probably remember for an eternity.

She found his eyes. This time there was a certain plea there. "I've cried because I don't understand."

"What?" *Tell me, let me explain it and make everything right. Whatever it is.*

"Why you got so angry. Why you...shut me out after what happened the other night."

He stiffened. "I didn't shut you out. I took you with me today. I'm standing here in your kitchen, aren't I?" And he knew he was lying.

His sweater began to feel too tight. Too itchy and hot around his throat. But Bo had taught him something today. *Bo* had taught *him*. Evasions and half truths were for cowards. He shrugged out of his jacket, no matter that he hadn't intended to stay here that long. It was too hot. Her home had always seemed chilly before.

She let out a shaky breath. "What did I do *wrong*, Adam? Why were you so mad at me for what happened? I had no control over whether that policeman came or not."

"I was mad because you were so damned ashamed," he grated. *Honesty*. It had its own rewards. It felt like a weight lifting from his chest. "I was mad because you were ashamed for touching me. Maybe for wanting me. Whatever. I thought you were going to rattle right out of your skin." Another breath. More honesty. "It hurt. That the opinion of your damned deacons or your—your *settlement* mattered more than whatever it was we might have shared."

Her eyes widened. "I wanted what happened."

"You didn't act like it." His voice went short.

"I was melting inside."

And something hot and liquid sluiced through him. "You panicked."

"Adam, what kind of women have you known?" she cried. "What would you have had me do?"

He realized that she was genuinely angry. Hectic color bloomed in her cheeks. "React with a little pride!" he snapped, because that feeling like shame was rolling around in his gut again.

Mariah flinched, but she held his eyes. "Pride," she repeated slowly. "Please, Adam, please introduce me to the woman who could pull that off with her dress wrapped around her waist and a strange man peering in the window at her. I suppose I do have to apologize, because I've never been in that situation before in my life and I didn't know *how* to react, but I can assure you that I'll never be the kind of woman who could take that without embarrassment."

He stared at her. The kind of woman he wanted, the kind of woman he needed, would certainly be dismayed at having been caught with her dress around her waist by a strange man. He wondered if maybe he hadn't been angry with her for just that, for being everything he needed and so far out of reach.

The air went out of him.

"Can we try again?" she asked quietly. "Please? Here, where no one's likely to interrupt and steal it away from me again."

His knees turned to putty. "You don't want that. You really don't want that."

"Yes, Adam, I do. And I've already told you why."

"Because I'm leaving." Suddenly that seemed like a really bad reason. It was a reason that made him feel like hell.

"And they're going to take my school. And you're right. I'll let them." She smiled thinly. "Pride, Adam. It *is* all a matter of pride. Isn't it funny how many connotations that word can have? I wonder if my father, with his extra long hair, would have flinched at being caught like I was by a stranger?"

"Mariah—"

"You see, I don't know much about family, either, Adam. The only one I've ever known turned their back on me ten years ago. They're a family with *pride*. Do you know Katya Essler sneaks out to see me when I cross her fields in the morning? And Sara Lapp, the daughter of a *deacon*, made way for me at her table. But not my father. No, never my mother. Not my sisters or brothers. *They* are too good, too pure. And, God forbid, if they were caught glancing my way, meeting my eyes even once, people might talk about their lack of forbearance."

"Mariah—" he tried again.

"So maybe that's another reason why I want something for myself. Something precious and dear and...and, yes, a little wicked. Something I can hold in my heart when they all *really* turn their backs on me, as they surely will any time now. I'll be able to turn away, too. Maybe I'll even smile to myself a little, because I'll have a secret. They might *think* they're making my life unbearable, but I'll know that for a few brief, shining moments, it was not."

He was drowning.

"Do you still want me?" she asked almost fearfully. "Did you mean it?"

Half truths and lies. She had him backed into a corner. He had told her he wouldn't stay here. He had told her why, and he'd thought she understood. What the hell was a man supposed to do now, he wondered, when his blood was racing, when his body was already reacting with a will of its own? How virtuous was he expected to be?

Adam turned away blindly.

She cried out, a stricken sound. He spoke without looking back at her. "You've got thirty seconds," he said quietly. "A minute.

Maybe two. See if you feel the same way, then. Think about it. Be sure."

She thought that if she waited a lifetime, her answer, her wanting, would be the same. *Him,* she thought frantically. It had to be him, this man, and if he didn't come back, she would die. He went out the front door, slamming it behind him. She prayed hard, then laughed aloud, her skin feeling feverish, as she considered exactly what she was asking God for. But the God she believed in was one of love. And she loved the man who had just walked out that door.

The thought didn't shock her. It came into her heart quietly, almost as though it had always been there.

He was gone for a long time, longer than two minutes. *He wasn't coming back.* Her knees started feeling weak. When the door finally opened again, she almost cried out again. He had one arm behind his back.

"What?" she whispered. He stopped in front of her, and she felt herself getting lost in his blue-gray eyes.

His jaw worked. His eyes slid away, then came back, almost as though he was embarrassed. "If I can only give you this one thing, this one time, then I guess I want it to be pretty."

She laughed nervously. "You're pretty."

He scowled. "You come up with the damnedest things. Men aren't pretty."

"You are, Adam. You have a beautiful soul."

He made an odd sound and brought his hand from behind his back. He thrust a fistful of damp flowers at her. Snow-dampened flowers in full bloom. She stared at them uncomprehendingly, then touched a fingertip to one.

Plastic. Her eyes came back up to his face slowly, then she laughed, a sound that would haunt his dreams forever.

"They came from my neighbor's porch?"

"Yeah. I couldn't find any alternative."

"That's a *Grossdawdy* house, a grandfather's house. It belongs to that poultry farm behind us."

"So?" He wondered why she was telling him this now. And why she was still laughing.

"It's Old Mr. Miller's house," she went on. "He's a deacon."

Adam grinned slowly. She realized, then, how very rarely he grinned. It made that small dimple, the vague dent in his chin, go even deeper.

"Appropriate, then," he answered finally.

She took them, clutching them, holding them to her breast. "Thank you, Adam. They're perfect."

And then he finally kissed her.

It occurred to him that he had been playing with it a little, saving it, dancing around it with conversation, because at some point it had clearly become inevitable. And he thought it had happened long before tonight, before she'd asked him with that guileless innocence that was so uniquely her. It was sweet and it was fun to hold the possibility out there on a close horizon and allow its imminence to warm something inside.

His palms were damp. He felt sixteen again as he finally, finally put his arms around her and drew her closer. The cheap red flowers got caught between them.

She stood on tiptoe and wrapped her other arm around his neck to hold him. She was enervated and alive. She was so relieved it seemed to drain the breath out of her, and so excited she could barely draw in more. But he kissed her as he had the first time, over and over again, so she could taste him, could breathe in the scent of him, could revel in it.

"You're so good at this. I thought that the first time." She gave a long, shaky sigh and sank into him.

As before, his hands moved. He wasn't consciously aware of it this time. He needed, so he searched. He craved, so he sought. And somewhere, on some level, he remembered the delightful surprise he had found the first time. There was guilt. It still lingered in the very pit of his stomach. But there was far, far too much pleasure for him to heed it now.

She had always brought him pleasure. She had always *been* pleasure.

She felt his touch at the small of her back, up and down. To her shoulders, gripping. To her bottom, an intimacy that ignited her with that same longing for more that had come to her in the buggy. He caught her hips, holding her against him. She could feel him growing hard and her heart skipped, then thundered. *For her.* And then his hands went back to her hair. He pulled the pins out and took handfuls of it again as it tumbled down. He used it to pull her head back, making her mouth open wider. He kissed her harder, more hungrily, his tongue moving deeper, and she was afraid she would die. Here. Now. Too soon.

When his hands moved this time, he lifted her in his arms. She gave a gasp of surprise.

"Not the kitchen," he said, and looked around dumbly, like a man coming out of a dream. "Somewhere else."

"My room."

He went down the hallway and found it easily, the only other door beside the bathroom. And it was everything he'd thought, and a few things he hadn't.

Here there were personal things. A closet door stood ajar, and he could see lavender and purple and blue dresses. A tattered, faceless doll sat on a mirrorless dresser. And a stack of books, almost hidden beneath the nightstand next to the bed, as if they were something nasty she needed to keep from prying eyes.

Her bed was a twin.

He had a moment of near dumb indecision, because he was a big man. And now he was a big man with needs and wants he'd tried to ignore for too long. He was shaking with them. He looked at the floor, back at the hall, then he swiped the quilt off the bed without setting her down and turned back to the living room.

She said not a word. She watched him, her eyes huge, a little frown forming between them. He dropped the quilt in front of the wood stove and kicked the chair aside. He lowered her to the blanket, and he thought she was blushing. Because her schoolgirl bedroom was not made for a night of love? He laughed hoarsely and kissed her again.

"Wait," she whispered.

He drew back a little to look into her eyes. "What?" he murmured. "What's wrong?"

"The quilt. Adam, not this quilt."

So that was it, he thought. He didn't know if he wanted to laugh or weep with frustration. "It's fine," he said. "Here is just fine."

"That's not it."

Need clamored in him. Somehow, impossibly, he found patience. "What then?"

"It's two hundred years old. It's...famous," she said solemnly.

"Famous," he repeated.

"It's...a legend. And one of our traditions." She struggled to explain when speaking was the last thing she felt capable of. But he needed to know. It was so important that he know. "You might not want to use it. Before they married, my people did something called bundling." Now the words flew out of her. She wanted to get them over with. "It meant...well, sleeping together. *Just* sleeping together. Nothing more. This quilt...that's what it's al-

ways been used for. Oh, Adam, it's what I've been saving it for.
And it's fine, here, now, with us, but there's something you must
know.''

"Tell me." His voice was raw. He tried to chuckle. He kissed
her again. "Tell me and get it over with."

"Whoever bundles within it soon marries."

His heart kicked. "That's a...uh...rule? Like the *Ordnung?*"

"Oh, no!" she gasped. "That's the legend. That's its magic."

He looked at it again, where it peeked out from behind her
shoulder. Pale ivory. Blue stitching. Big, interlocking rings. And
this time when he laughed it was easy and warm.

"Are we bundling, Mariah?"

She nodded seriously. "In a manner of speaking."

"It's okay," he said, and his mouth found hers again. "It's
okay. I don't believe in magic."

This was exactly the way he'd wanted it to be, with the natural
warmth of a fire, in the place where he'd first seen her with her
long hair spilling, in that nightgown. When he'd first started wanting her.

Adam, what kind of women have you known? Not enough and
one too many, he thought, and none of them had kept faceless
dolls from their childhood or books that were a talisman against
everything that had left them lonely.

He leaned over her, smoothing her hair back with one hand. It
was trapped beneath her and she leaned up to pull it free, watching him, her eyes wide. Her hair spilled over the quilt then, liquid
and dark. He lowered himself carefully to feel her body against
his again.

She encircled him with her arms, almost shyly. And it occurred
to him that she probably had very little idea where to go from
here, but that was okay, too. He had ideas. He was full of them.

"Where were we?" he asked, his voice rumbling.

He rolled over, onto his back, taking her with him. It startled
her, but then she realized that they were almost in the same position they'd been in in the buggy. And then she understood what
he was doing, that he was picking up where they had left off, and
if there had been tears and shame and anger in between, they
were gone now, as if they had never been.

Once again, his hands began sliding over her clothing, drawing
her skirt up. And this time there were no surprises for either of
them. She anticipated the delicious heat that shot through her

when he found her skin. He was ready for the smooth warmth and what it did to him.

He realized she had a few ideas of her own. She was moving against him in a way that made him frown uncertainly, jogging one knee then the other, then he felt her stockinged foot slide over his calf. She'd been kicking her shoes off.

He didn't hesitate. He was too hungry, suddenly too desperate. He'd wanted to make this pretty. But there was nothing pretty about need, nothing soft about desperation. He slid his palm underneath one stocking and worked it down over her knee. He went to the other one and then he moved his hands upward with a determination that he'd been able to bring to only one other pursuit in his life—finding his son.

She felt as if she could read his mind. Or maybe she could only read his eyes. But she knew what he was thinking. She had helped to end one search for him, she thought, even if she'd had selfish reasons of her own. Now she would ease the other. She had no finesse, no experience. But he was a glory, so male, so perfect, and she loved him, so her hands moved with more instinct than thought.

She did to him all those things he had done to her, everything that had made her feel so good. She threaded her fingers into his hair. It was thicker, more tangled than she would have imagined, and that fascinated her. She remembered the way he had nibbled on her lip and she did it back, and felt elation and something unrestrained flash through her when he groaned.

And, of course, there were her stockings. He had slid them off her effortlessly, with a skill—and, she imagined, experience—that she simply did not possess. She did not think she could manage the same with his jeans. But she tried.

He was hard to the point of pain. It had started with the promise of what they would finally share. It had built to a throbbing urgency with each of her fleeting touches. Her hands were like something gossamer, like the breath of an angel. Each time his body reacted, his blood surging toward that point of contact. And each time it vanished before he could fully appreciate it. She moved on, leaving him straining and wanting more.

He wondered how he would stand it, how he would wait, knew only that he had to. Then her fingers found the zipper of his jeans, brushing over his hardness, and he had to catch her wrist.

"No," he said hoarsely.

"No?"

"Don't touch me there. I...won't be able to make it right. Make it perfect." And he needed to. Oh, how he needed to. Even now, caught in the throes of wanting her, he knew it would be his only salvation afterward.

"It's already perfect, Adam," she chided. "If it gets too much better, I'll die."

He was lost. He dragged her arm up, found her wrist with his mouth. Her pulse pounded there and he ran his tongue over it to soothe it, smiling when it only grew more erratic. He would have promised her a next time, a chance to explore when he wasn't this needy, this close to the edge. He felt something spasm inside him as he realized they probably would not have time for more.

This would have to be enough. This would have to be everything. He tumbled her beneath him again. He found the knot at the back of her waist and pulled the infuriating apron off her. But she wasn't a woman who could simply wait. For better or worse, through all her life, she had acted on what she wanted, what she needed, even if it cost her in tears. And if he wouldn't let her touch him, she thought, then she wanted to be free of these clothes so he could touch her.

Together, they finally got the simple cotton dress over her head. He had expected the pristine white bra. The high, daring cut of her panties stunned him as much as the stockings had. And he could feel everything inside him begin to churn with an urgency that wouldn't be denied much longer.

Her panties were white, too, but not cotton. They were almost silky, and the thighs were cut to the waist band. Her hips were smooth and sloping. he moved a hand along one as his mouth dove to her breast. He took her nipple through her bra, determined not to rush her, but needing, needing...

She cried out and arched into him. Her arms came hard around him, but when he would have expected her to dig her fingers into his sweater and hold onto him while sensation pummeled her, she grabbed the hem of it instead, dragging and tearing it upward.

"*Please,* Adam."

And that was when everything went crazy. He forgot about pretty. He forgot about giving her only sweetness to remember. He forgot to savor, because this would be the one and only time. He forgot not to scare her.

She got the sweater over his head at the same time he found the clasp of her bra. She tugged almost angrily, moving the offending wool away. He pushed cotton aside and found skin, and her breasts were perfect. Small enough that his hand covered her perfectly. He parted his fingers and went back for her nipple, and this time she raked her fingers down his back.

He had no memory of getting his jeans off or his briefs. But then his hands were beneath the waist of her panties, shearing them away, too. For a moment her hand fluttered and he thought she would try to cover herself, try to hide the soft black curls from his gaze. As if she were ashamed. But she held his eyes and her hand fell away, almost defiantly. Emotion burned in him and he kissed her again hard.

She wrapped her legs around him and held on, cleaving to him, and she fit as perfectly as he had always known she would. Her mouth went to his neck, below his ear. He moved his head enough to claim her lips again, shifting his weight, pulling her closer, and that easily, that simply he slid inside her as if it were ordained, meant, written in the stars all along.

And then he felt resistance.

For a moment he froze. But on some level, in some unconscious, murky place in his heart, he had known this would be, too. He had known. And it was why he had tried to protest, as best he knew how; why he had tried to be strong against what both his body and his heart had wanted.

"Mariah, I don't want to hurt you," he growled.

"You can't. Ever."

"You don't know." *How could he take her virginity from her and go?*

He was torn with regret, panic, with indecision between honor and need. But it was too late. It had been too late from the first time she had smiled at him with her hands clasped together in front of her, too late from the first time she had stood beside him in that field watching Bo. It had been too late when she had zipped his jacket for him, and far, far too late when he had found skin beneath her skirt. And now, now that he was already, finally, inside her, it would be agony to go. Such restraint was more than he possessed.

So he pushed. He tried to do it gently, but a growl of pain—his own pain—rolled in his chest, because he knew he was going to hate himself for this later. He felt her back arch a little and he thought he could feel something hot tear through him, as well.

"I'm sorry." *How stupid. How helpless.*

Mariah couldn't answer. Yes, there was pain, brief, hot but somehow galvanizing. For a moment there seemed to be friction,

where there had only been liquid fire before. But then something
new flooded her. It was still hot, but now it coiled in her muscles;
now it throbbed in low, secret parts of her. She moved against
him tentatively and heard him moan. She had started out wanting
to take something for herself. Now she knew, incredibly, that she
was giving something back, as well, and that was beautiful.

Mariah felt the most amazing thing. *Pride.* Again. And this
time it was fierce and strong and glorious.

She moved again, and this time he rocked against her, and then
all rational thought died. She was only vaguely aware of him
burying his face at her throat. Everything inside her was centered
low and exploding.

He said her name, in that gravelly way he had when he was
very emotional. And it was sweet enough to bring tears to her
eyes.

She had been right. It was her last clear thought. She would
remember this moment, this man, for a lifetime, and nothing could
ever, ever tarnish that. She clutched the single flower that remained in her hand, wound her arms around his neck and held
on.

Chapter 16

Sunlight speared through the living-room window and caught Adam squarely in the eyes. He rolled over on the hard floor, chilled and needing Mariah's warmth, subconsciously seeking just a few more moments of sleep and peace before the realities of the day sank in. Mariah snuggled backward into him, and his body woke up.

He knew he had to leave her alone. Not for any profound emotional reason—it was too late for that now—but because she would undoubtedly be sore this morning, tender in places she hadn't known she'd had. He steeled himself against the fresh need that twitched and the ever-present guilt. Then she gave a soft, groaning sound that sounded like, ''Cold,'' and sat up to reach for the wood stove.

It took her maybe thirty seconds to take two small logs from the pile of wood beside it, and less than a minute to push them inside. Another fifteen seconds passed while she settled them and irritated the lingering embers with a poker. Less than two minutes from the time she'd sat up, the fire was burning again and she'd closed the metal door.

It was plenty long enough.

He watched her with his breath hanging halfway in his chest, enjoying the bending curve of her spine and the way her skin pulled into gooseflesh, knowing she would welcome his body heat. Her bare bottom had been aimed in his direction as she kneeled and leaned forward. He caught her around the waist and pulled her back to him. She turned as he did and sprawled over his chest.

"How long do we have before you have to go to school?" he asked, his voice like sand with sleep and wanting.

Faint color touched her face, her beautiful face. "Time enough," she whispered.

"Good. Good." He caught her mouth again, forgetting whatever resolve and solicitude he had ever tried to possess.

She was amazed, thrilled, that he still seemed to want her this morning. That he would give her more memories to squirrel away. Briefly, with the thought, a cloud seemed to move and blot out the warmth of his touch. But, then, his hands moved to her breasts and there was only sensation again, and such a feeling of goodness inside, swelling to fill her.

This time, today, she would be able to touch him. The night before she had felt as if she were freefalling, tumbling faster and faster without knowing exactly what would greet her when she landed. Excitement still arced inside her now, but his touch was slower, less driven, allowing her more time to melt and explore.

She ran her hands over his chest, delighted with what she found. He was so big, so strong. A fine mat of golden hair covered his skin and she threaded her fingers through it, brushing a thumb over his nipple. She sucked in her breath in surprise when it puckered just as her own had. She did it again, then used her mouth, gasping when he caught her to stop her.

"You keep pushing me," he growled. "You make it so hard to keep control."

She smiled. "Good."

Her hands moved downward. And she was amazed all over again that he wanted her so much, so quickly, even though she wasn't blond and polished or dressed in the finest fashions. She allowed herself to think once, longingly, of a lifetime of this, of waking every single morning to find him hard and eager, of sharing this with him every dawn. Then she pushed the dream away angrily, because in her world after dawn came cows and milking and plowing pastures, things this man wanted no part of.

She touched his hardness, wrapping her hand around him, and then because her mouth had had such a reaction on him a moment before, she bent to touch her tongue to him there too, curious and wanting so desperately to give him the pleasure he had given her the night before. But after a few moments that passed much too quickly, his hands dove into her hair again, pulling her up.

"I don't...I can't..."

His voice was so low she could barely hear it. "What?"

"I have to make it better for you this time," he managed.

"You couldn't possibly."

He made a deep growling sound. His hands went to her hips, lifting her, moving her until she straddled him, and then she felt him fill her again and it was so much easier this time. There was no pain at all, only liquid fire, sudden and overwhelming. It poured through her, raining flames. She found his chest again with her hands and braced herself against him, struggling to move with him. And, then, with an instinct as old as time, she picked up the rhythm and they rocked together.

This time the flowers were scattered over the quilt, and Adam never felt the hard plastic edge of a single petal digging into his shoulder.

It was a long time before either of them stirred. Too much time had passed, and her heart twisted in frustration.

"I don't want to go to school," she complained.

Laughter rumbled through his chest. She could feel it where her ear was pressed to his heart. "You sound like a little kid on the first really nice spring day."

"I feel that way. I want to play."

"Me, too." He wanted it with enough urgency that he knew if he stayed there a moment longer, he'd be hard again, needy again, and a whole lot of kids would be milling aimlessly around that schoolhouse today on their own. And if her college education didn't get her fired, then that certainly would.

That sobered him. He swatted her bottom, but he felt his muscles tense. "Go on. Get yourself ready. I'll do something about coffee."

Her lower lip pouted. He steeled himself not to kiss it, did it anyway, then gave her a gentle shove. "You're going to be late. And I need to get to a phone, unless you've got one hidden away here somewhere."

She gave a little shake of her head. "The *Ordnung*—"

"I know, I know." Adam sat up, raked his hand through his

hair. "As much as I'd like to hang around here all day myself, I need to find out if Jake got anywhere with that picture."

"What picture?"

Something constricted in his gut as he remembered that he'd avoided her for several days over nothing that was her fault; that he hadn't told her exactly what Jake had been doing. "He was going to make a composite of the guy who followed Jannel here," he said neutrally.

"Ah." She wondered what that could possibly tell him, and why he wouldn't let the whole issue of Jannel just...go away. The question brought a tightness to her chest as she thought of the beautiful blond woman again, a woman he would marry. She scrambled to her feet and tugged at the quilt until he moved off it. Flowers scattered, suddenly looking like what they were— cheap plastic imitations.

She wrapped the quilt around herself and fled down the hall. Already the day was changing, she thought helplessly. She looked out the bathroom window and saw clouds scudding in on a strong wind, blotting out the sun, chilling her heart.

Adam dressed slowly, reluctantly, and went into the kitchen. The percolator she had put on the wood stove the night before was ruined. Neither of them had ever thought to remove it. Grounds were baked to a crust inside. He grabbed it, burned himself and swore. He found a towel and picked it up with that, dropping everything into the sink. He poured water over it and steam rose, hissing.

His body was craving caffeine now. He felt groggy. His limbs felt weighted. And he knew it had less to do with the conditions under which he'd slept than with the lethargic satisfaction of having loved her.

He scrubbed his hand over his unshaven jaw. He was in over his head, he thought. He hadn't meant for this to happen, yet that sense of inevitability still lingered, and he wondered how much choice he'd really had. He couldn't regret it. But there was an ache inside him now that it was over, a hard, tangled knot. And still that insidious thought...

What he had taken from her deserved so much more than the renewed silence he would leave in her life when he went home.

He cursed in self-defense. He had never lied to her. Never. He had given her the best of what he could. What she needed—okay, what she *deserved* now—was simply beyond him to give, and he had never pretended otherwise.

A stunning thought came to him. If she had been anyone else, if she had *lived* anywhere else, he might have taken the chance. No matter how horribly blind and foolish he'd been with Jannel, Mariah wore truth and honesty like a cloak. It was there, visible, the first thing anyone sensed about her. He didn't have to fear his own perceptions with her.

But he couldn't stay here with her because he simply couldn't reconcile himself to her pious deacons and the gleeful punishment of her church. The faith that made her what she was was the same thing he wanted no part of. He believed in her. He believed in himself. But he could not trust a God who would allow the nightmare of his childhood, who would allow innocent children to suffer a man's wrath without even a mother to guide them.

No, he couldn't stay. But he loved her.

It hit him hard, slamming into him almost physically. He actually took a few stumbling steps back from the sink, as though the coffeepot had reared up and struck him. But even then, the truth remained, simple and just...there. She was the kind of woman he hadn't known existed and certainly had never believed he would find.

And even loving her, he cursed her. *Goddammit, let them take your school. Leave these people who don't even want you. Come home with me.*

''Adam?''

''Huh?'' He jerked around to face her.

His skin was ashen. Mariah frowned. ''Did you make coffee?''

''No. We nearly burned your house down last night.''

''I know.'' She grinned smugly, almost seductively. And his breath left him all over again. *God, how was he supposed to live without her? How could he do anything else?*

He managed to thrust a thumb at the sink. ''You left the pot on. It's a goner.''

''Oh.'' She scowled and went to the sink to peer down at the percolator.

Adam grabbed his jacket as if it represented some sort of salvation. ''Come on. I'll give you a ride to school and we'll buy a couple cups along the way. Jake found someplace with a take-out window the other day.''

Mariah nodded. ''There's a drive-through place up on Route 30. We can go the long way to the school.''

''Well...good.'' He was already halfway to the door, and he had to toss the words behind him.

Mariah hurriedly gathered her coat and shawl. She was going to miss seeing Katya this morning. She hoped Frank hadn't hurt her badly overnight. Her morning visits were as much out of concern for Katya as they were for her own pleasure. Seeing her five days a week assured her that her friend was alive, if not well.

Outside, Adam honked his horn. She wouldn't see Katya, she thought, but she would have a few more precious moments with this man. It was a trade-off she could live with. She went out, smiling.

Adam found Jake at work, at the detectives' bureau. He gave his name to the dispatcher and barely had time to swallow a mouthful of coffee before his brother came on the line.

"Where the hell have you been?" Jake demanded. "I've been trying to reach you all night."

Adam didn't answer. He was doing his level best at the moment to forget where he had been, what he had done, what he was feeling.

"Like that, is it?" Jake muttered. "Should I applaud or worry? Best-case scenario is that at least the cold-water supply up there will last a little longer."

Since he couldn't threaten to hit him again, Adam ignored him. "What's with that guy who was following Jannel?"

Jake was quiet for a couple of heartbeats. "Okay. We'll talk about him."

"Have you found anything?"

"Sure. Well, Berry did. It's the wonders of cyberspace, bro. Nothing is the way it was when we were kids. Plug in and presto—information. Millions of people cruise the Net every day. A healthy few visited our site and felt compelled to leave e-mail trying to ID this week's composite."

People always did, Adam thought, but the pictures were usually of missing kids and the tips tended to be wild-goose chases. He felt his heart begin sliding. "Well? Did we get a hit this time?"

"Yeah. An anonymous somebody from Toms River, New Jersey, identified the guy as one Devon Mills. Berry hacked his way into a few places and put together a dossier on the dude. It works. At the moment, he's in custody."

Adam's heart hit bottom. "Berry or Devon Mills?"

"Mills," Jake said scornfully. "Come on, bro, Berry's too good to get caught. I had a friend in New Jersey arrange to have

Mills picked up late yesterday afternoon. Admittedly, he's being held on charges that fall into a gray area. Suspicion of kidnapping across state lines, both of an adult and a minor. We've got to be careful with that. The FBI will come barreling in if they get wind of it, and we don't want that."

"We don't," Adam repeated, his pulse rushing.

"Nope. All we're doing at the moment is bullying good ol' Devon with a few felony threats. When push comes to shove, there's nothing we can really charge him with. Jannel's not currently with him, and we know where Bo is. But he's just a small-time scam artist, real outclassed by the rest of our conniving, intelligent minds, and he's been singing like a bird, anyway."

"Scam artist," Adam echoed. That single word stuck in his mind.

"Of the minor variety," Jake clarified again. "He's got a rap sheet as long as the tails on those horses you've been playing giddy-up with up there, but it's all reasonably puny stuff. Possession of controlled substances, but not enough to get him into real trouble. Forgery and a few rubber checks, that kind of thing. We're using it all to lean on him. He's on probation, needs to keep his nose clean right now."

"What's he saying?" Adam asked hoarsely. "Where's Jannel? Goddammit, Jake, what did you find out?"

"Hold your horses, cowboy. I'm getting to it." Jake paused. "Are you sitting down?"

It was bad then. Adam stiffened. "Yeah."

Jake cleared his throat. For the first time in Adam's memory, his brother seemed awkward, uncomfortable. "Well," he said finally, "you were had big-time, bro."

"Had."

"If this guy is to be believed—and according to my friend in New Jersey, he's sweating bullets, so he probably can—then your happily-ever-after was all a grand scheme he cooked up with one Linda Porter."

His happily-ever-after? His *marriage?* Stealing Bo? *What?* "He's not a drug dealer? Not Jannel's supplier?"

"Oh, I'm sure he kept her happy in that respect, too, but—no. No, what he actually was was her accomplice."

Adam felt nausea begin to roll in his stomach. "Go on."

"There was no Jannel, Adam," Jake reminded him quietly. "That's why we could never find any bureaucratic record of her. Her name was Linda Porter, and she was an actress with the regional theater in Atlantic City, if Devon is to be believed. Guess she got tired of waiting for her big break and Devon concocted a scheme to rake in a windfall a lot sooner.'' He paused. ''They used to do the nightclub circuit in New York, New Jersey, and Philadelphia, upper-scale places, playing to the kind of rich guys they needed.''

''She was a *hooker?*''

Jake hesitated. ''Well, that's one way of looking at it. But it wasn't that simple.''

''Go on,'' Adam said again, his voice rough as sandpaper now.

''She didn't...you know, charge these guys. Exactly. She took 'gifts' from them—ain't that pretty? She'd keep one around for a few months, milk him dry, wreck his life, move on. Eventually, they outgrew the New Jersey tri-state, and one guy in New Orleans set her up in a real neat high-rise condo there. She talked him into putting that place in her name—there's one conversation I would liked to have heard—then she sold the place and took off again. Shared the money with Devon, of course.''

This wasn't the woman he'd known, Adam thought sickly. But she was. The hell of it was, she *could* be the cool, remote, perfect Jannel Payne he had married.

Adam swore aloud. ''You're wrong,'' he tried, a little desperate.

''No. I'm not, bro,'' Jake said levelly. ''Sorry. Anyway, the condo thing was such a success, Devon said they decided to play the same thing on a grander scale.''

''Me.''

Jake hesitated. ''Not you per se, bro. It could have been anybody with a high visible profile. They didn't go after you by name, but you were the fish who bit.''

''Me,'' he said again, his head pounding. His world was falling apart. Which was stupid—her betrayal was part of the past. It was four years old. He'd found his kid again. But he was sick with rage and his own sense of being played for a fool.

''You were in the right place at the right time,'' Jake reiterated. ''The idea was that she would stay married to you for a couple of years, funnel off what money she could whenever she could, and when they had a couple million collected they'd take off to an island somewhere.''

''She did that.''

''Yeah.''

''She took me for a couple of million.''

"Yeah."

He snarled a few choice invectives. "So what the hell is Devon Mills doing in Toms River, New Jersey instead of Montego Bay?"

"She took your money and left without him."

The motel room seemed to go very still. Adam had the wild feeling that the air was being sucked out of it. "Bo," he said hoarsely.

"Yeah, well, Bo was never really part of the plan," Jake said quietly. "She wasn't supposed to get pregnant while she was married to you."

His blood raged. "Then why the hell did she take him with her? Why didn't she just leave him with me?"

"Because Devon thought to grab him and hold him until she coughed up his half of the money. I'd think she had to have anticipated that. So she hid him somewhere safe, instead."

Suddenly, Adam understood it all. Her distance—the way she had never seemed interested in sharing anything with him. The way she'd always kept herself...apart. It had all been a game. Just a game. A role she was playing, and he was the male lead. She'd gone through the motions, but it had never been her real life or her real heart that she was putting into it.

Even Bo's conception had been a sham.

He almost wished he didn't know. He almost wished he'd never called Jake to the settlement. The first domino, he thought helplessly. It was the way it always happened. All it took was one little clue coming to the surface, then everything else fell down and into place. In this case it had been the milk-carton call placing Bo in Lancaster County. And that had led to Sugar Joe and to the strange man who had followed Jannel—information they probably would never have stumbled onto otherwise. Mills and Jannel had covered their tracks too well.

Sugar Joe's revelation had led to more clarity than he could stand.

"She didn't have to take him at all," Adam said, his voice flat and deadly now. "She didn't have to take Bo."

"Hey, you don't mean that, bro. Think about it. If she had left him, Devon would have grabbed him. Better that he was safe with the God-fearing folks of Lancaster County. At least she had one decent bone in her body."

"She didn't have to take him in the first place!" No matter

what Jake said, no matter how right his brother was, he just couldn't seem to get past that.

The words burned out of him, through him, a litany in his head, echoing over and over again. Adam slammed down the phone without waiting for a response he knew he wouldn't want to hear.

His head was pounding. *Fool.* He'd been a world-class sucker. But he'd known that from the start.

There was no peace to be found in this answer, he thought again. There was no closure in the shutting of this door. It made him feel worse, incredibly naive, infuriated.

Adam grabbed the bottle of bourbon from the desk and pressed it to the throbbing pulse in his temple. But he didn't want to drink. Suddenly he was drained. Exhausted. Hollow. He swore violently and hurled the bottle across the room. It shattered against the far wall, raining glass and spraying bourbon.

And still he didn't feel better. Still his head pounded.

"Oh, Bo. Damn it. *Damn* it. I'm so sorry." For what? he wondered. For not catching on to Jannel sooner? Or for stubbornly refusing to take him on the road again, giving Jannel the chance to take him? He was being irrational. He knew he was being irrational, but that did not soothe him.

He dropped down onto one of the beds, flopping onto his back, covering his eyes with one forearm because the dim light in the room was blinding. For a long while he counted his breaths, but the number that kept ricocheting through his mind was four. *Four years.* Four years! Long enough that Bo didn't even recognize him.

He would have given her the goddammed money, if only she had left the boy behind. She could have let him know what was going on so he could have protected Bo himself. He laughed bitterly aloud as he heard his own thought. *Darling, this was all a setup and I'm going to take you for all the cash you have on hand. Please take care of our baby, because my accomplice will probably try to kidnap him.*

He kept seeing his son's eyes as they had been yesterday, frightened yet somehow defiant. And that teddy bear he'd clung to for comfort in the face of changes too big for him to deal with. Adam swore. He could kill her for that alone.

He took a thick, steadying breath. After a long while he escaped from the rage and the pain into a place where his heart was numb. Somehow, mercifully, he slept.

The room was strangely dark when he woke again. Something—somewhere—was pounding. He sat up, feeling disoriented. He glanced at the bedside clock. It was five-fifteen. He'd slept all *day?* The gloominess of the room, the fall of daylight, left no doubt about it.

He stood without any idea of where he meant to go. Then the pounding began again, more frantic this time.

"Adam! Please, if you're in there, *open the door!*"

Mariah? He didn't think he had ever told her exactly where he was staying. But she could have found out, of course, in an emergency. She could have used a pay phone and called all the motels within a reasonable distance of the village.

In an emergency.

He stumbled to the door and wrenched it open. Mariah was on the other side, looking wild enough that if he had not loved her last night, if he had not only recently seen her in this state of disarray for thoroughly different reasons, it would have taken him a moment to recognize her. Her hair was windblown, tangles of it pulling free from her bonnet. Her face was flushed and her breasts rose and fell with exertion. She'd been running. Had she run all this way?

His heart stalled. "What? What is it?" he demanded, his voice still raspy from sleep.

"It's Bo," she gasped. She was shaking her head hard, then harder, as though in frantic denial. "He didn't come to school today. I thought he was still pretending to be sick, that Sarah was humoring him. But then *she* came to the school to find out why he hadn't come home." She struggled for breath and her tears spilled over. "Adam, Bo's gone!"

Chapter 17

Her words hit him like sledgehammers. Shock flew through him. *Not again.* Something hard and cold rushed up from the pit of his stomach, to each of his nerve endings, freezing them. He stared at her blankly.

"Did you hear me?" she cried. "Bo's *gone!*"

"No," he managed, strangled. Then the ice cracked. It shattered down inside him and rage came, blinding, killing, staining his vision red. *"No!"* he roared this time, then he veered for the phone.

Jake. He had to get Jake to come back here *now*. Because this time the trail wasn't three days' worth of cold. This time they knew who and what they were up against. This time—

And even as he gripped the phone, he realized dazedly that this nightmare was the same, but different. The odds of this having anything to do with Jannel and a scam artist named Devon Mills were simply too remote.

No, he thought. No. This time it had nothing to do with Jannel, and everything to do with him.

"Adam—"

He jerked around to find Mariah again. "I scared him," he realized aloud. "He ran." He had to wrestle the words to get them out, they were that bitter, that rancid. "He ran and hid so he wouldn't have to go away with me."

Mariah shook her head frantically. "We don't know that! Other children—"

"Let's go," he interrupted, grabbing his jacket from the desk chair.

"Where?" she gasped. "What do you want to do?"

"Look for him," he snarled. "What else?" And blessedly, some of the knowledge he had managed to glean from Jake over the years began settling, clicking into place in his brain. "The Lapps. We'll go to the Lapps first. We'll start there."

He pushed past her out the door. Mariah turned to watch him helplessly. *Please, God, let him be right, please don't let anyone have taken Bo, not this child! Not this one. Adam only just found him again. If someone took him with Lizzie and the others, I can't believe in you anymore, because that's just too cruel.* She pulled the door closed behind her and ran for him, scrambling into the passenger seat.

He drove like a madman, even more erratically, even faster than he had that first day when they had gone to the pond. And he talked to himself, scaring her, muttering helpless protests aloud again and again. Her heart bled for him, and she had to dash tears from her eyes with trembling hands. *God, don't do this to him, please,* she prayed again. *Tell the deacons I'll slink off into the sunset and they'll never hear another word from me again. Just please don't take this man's child.*

Her neck snapped a little when he braked hard in the Lapps' drive. He got out without waiting for her and ran across the road to the house without looking back.

He didn't knock. He didn't have to. Sarah and Sugar Joe were already on the porch. Joe was pale and his eyes looked too large and dark. Sarah's face was mottled and swollen from crying.

Mariah hurried to catch up with them all. "He probably ran away from all the changes that are happening," she volunteered, trying immediately to calm everyone—as if it were possible. "Come on, let's go inside where it's warm."

Sugar Joe seemed to nod. "Of course. We have to assume that first before we...before we consider other things."

"Where's Matt?" Mariah asked as they all stumbled dazedly inside. She took Sarah's hand, and the *Meidung* could be damned, she thought angrily. "If Bo was planning to run away, then Matt would almost certainly have known about it."

"But you said Matt was in school!" Sarah cried.

"He was. But that doesn't mean he doesn't know what's going on."

"Upstairs," Joe barked. "I sent all the kids to their rooms until we could make some sense of this. Gracie was..." He trailed off.

"They're all very upset," Sarah whispered. "Crying. We just couldn't... I couldn't deal with anything, with all the crying. We asked them to wait." Her eyes said she didn't know exactly what they were waiting for. Mariah thought sickly that if this was like the other children, there would be no quick resolution. She knew Sarah was thinking the same thing.

She took a deep breath and flashed a look at Adam. "I'll be right back. Matt might be more likely to talk to me. He might fear Sarah and Joe's anger, if he *did* have anything to do with this."

Adam was staring at her strangely, as if he didn't really see her. She turned away from him and hurried up the stairs, taking them two at a time.

Sarah turned into Joe's arms. "Maybe she's right. Maybe that's all this is," she moaned.

Adam finally snapped himself out of it. "It is. It's got to be. It *can't* be Jannel. Even if she finally came back to get him, she wouldn't just steal him, for God's sake." *Unless she knew he was here, too.* "Bo wouldn't have known her, either!" *But maybe he would have.*

He was going to throw up.

He turned away, his throat working, and raked a hand through his hair. He went on almost without taking a breath. "We need to get a search party together. He's around here somewhere. He's got to be. He couldn't have gone far." Jesus, he thought, looking out the back door. Full dark had fallen now. Bo was seven years old and he was out there in the dark somewhere alone, and if Adam had learned anything in the time he'd been here, it was that when it got dark in Lancaster County, it got damned cold, too.

He rounded on Sarah. "Call those deacons, or the church, or whoever."

She looked at him blankly. "We don't have a phone. The *Ordnung*—"

"Screw the *Ordnung!*" he roared. "My kid is gone!"

Sarah blanched. Joe squeezed her shoulder. "What do you

want them to do?'' he asked Adam. ''I'll find a way to get word to all of them. I'll send the other kids out to find them.''

''No!'' Sarah cried irrationally. ''Not the children! Please, Joe, don't send the children. If they've taken Noah, then who knows who's next? Maybe they were watching our house. Maybe—''

''Sarah,'' Joe interrupted. ''Mariah and Adam are probably right. He probably just got scared about all this and ran off.''

''They?'' Adam echoed Sarah, his voice grating. He was missing something here. ''Who the hell is *they?*''

''Whoever took the other children,'' Joe answered absently.

''*What* other children?''

''Lizzie Stoltzfus. Michael Miller. The little ones. There are four of them missing now.'' He refused to count Noah.

Adam sensed that he was on the brink of something again, and this time he wasn't going to like it. ''Missing?'' he repeated, enunciating too carefully.

Sarah looked confused. ''Everyone is saying that that was why Mariah finally contacted you about your Bo,'' she blurted. ''The rumor going around is that she brought you here so that you would look for the others. That's what Katya Essler told me. Mariah's the only one who could really do it. She's already been shunned. And she's one of the few of us who would ever have seen that milk carton that Katya said she found.''

His heart was beating slow and with a booming resonance against his chest. *Finally. She brought you here so you would look for the others.* He shook his head, but that one nasty phrase kept coming back. *Mariah finally contacted you.*

He opened his mouth to respond, and something unintelligible came out.

''It's been going on for, oh, five months now,'' Joe explained, ''and it's tearing the settlement apart. They were all just babies. Their mothers looked away for a moment—and they just vanished,'' Joe explained. ''The church ruled that—''

He broke off as Mariah's footsteps rushed down the stairs again. Then there were more, tumbling behind her, as the other children crowded down with her. She gripped the banister and Adam watched almost dispassionately as her knuckles turned white.

''Matthew's gone, too,'' she blurted.

Sarah cried out and swayed. Joe caught her.

''We looked everywhere for him,'' Gracie sobbed. ''In the closets, *everywhere.*''

"We thought maybe he was hiding," Nathaniel explained, in an almost calm voice of reason. "That maybe this was all just some stupid game. But the window in his room is open."

"He's gone," Dinah repeated, gnawing on a trembling lip.

Joe cradled Sarah against his chest and looked for Adam's eyes. "Maybe he's gone to Bo."

"Yeah," Adam managed. *Mariah finally contacted you.* He shook the words out of his head. "We need to get together a search party," he repeated. "Get the deacons to organize the men as quickly as possible."

"They won't do it," Sarah wept.

Adam's eyes slashed to her. "Why not?"

"It's what Joe was just saying. They won't look for the others, either. They say we shouldn't resist what's happening, because it's God's will. It's God's wish that the children are gone."

Adam was stupefied. Then rage swallowed him. It was an immense pressure against his chest. He stared at Sarah for a long time before words would come to him, then he ground them out. "The...hell...it...is."

Mariah gasped, feeling his rage and disbelief like a palpable thing. Adam shot a furious look at Joe.

"Don't ask them, then. *Tell* them. Because if they refuse to help, I'll bring every court in the land down upon their pious, pompous heads. *Children are missing.* And the last I heard, they generally can't take care of themselves, no matter how religious they are."

Dinah gasped. Joe's face twisted, but he nodded. "I'll go talk to people myself. Nathaniel, come with me. Dinah, take care of your mother."

Adam headed for the back door.

"Where are you going?" Mariah called after him.

Something about his face was frightening her now. It was different from the rage and pain that had been there when she had gone upstairs. Something had changed. He turned to look at her and his face was closed.

Mariah finally contacted you... Finally...finally...finally...

He turned away without answering her. He couldn't deal with her now. He needed to find Bo.

Adam circled the house, trying to think. He had to calm down, had to function. Bo's life could very possibly depend on it.

Damn, it was getting cold.

He pulled his gloves out of his jacket pockets and looked up at the windows on the second floor, wondering if anyone had closed the one Matt had escaped through. He hoped they hadn't, because then he would have to go back inside to pinpoint exactly which window was his. He could guess from having been in the room yesterday, but he didn't want to guess. He had to be sure.

And he didn't want to go inside. He didn't want to see her face, her lying-angel eyes.

Pain bloomed. Emotion rolled. He pushed down on it, down, then ignored it when it fought back. But he couldn't ignore the taunting voice in his head, the one that insisted that he'd known *something* was off about all this. He had just never guessed, had never believed, that that something involved her.

He should have guessed, known, suspected, not because it was all too easy but because she had just seemed too...good.

Truth and honesty, he thought bitterly. The first things he'd sensed about her. But again, all over again, his perceptions had only gone as far as his own mind. He was a damned fool and he'd never learned. That sweet, generous kindness was all a sham.

He'd thought of the way she'd weighed his motives in the beginning. Of the way, once her internal decisions were made, she'd taken him directly to Bo. And she'd told him in a round-about way. *When they all really turn their backs on me, as they surely will any time now...*

Somewhere in his heart he had suspected strings left dangling, something unfinished. But he had pushed for answers in the wrong direction, had gone after the man who had followed Jannel, because the truth was simply too disappointing, too crushing to tolerate.

Don't think about her. She doesn't matter. Bo matters.

He forced his attention back to the house and saw that the window was still open. It was easy enough to see how Matthew had made his escape. The drainpipe restraints were broken so that the upper half of it swung wide. He was going to catch hell, Adam thought, when they found him. He crossed to the ground beneath it and realized that the little hellion had fallen. One side of a bush there was almost flattened, its limbs spreading out unnaturally. A few were broken. The ground was churned up, snow and rich, dark loam.

But Matt was all right, Adam thought, realizing he cared strongly about that boy's welfare, as well. He had scrambled to his feet and had taken off again. He was unhurt enough to have run.

Adam hunkered down to look at the ground, trying to think like Jake, wondering what his brother would look for. Then he saw the cookie. He picked it up and broke it absently in half. Oatmeal, he thought inanely. Matthew had taken a stash of food to his brother, a determined, misguided accomplice. Adam's mouth widened into a grim parody of a smile. He pushed to his feet again and went back inside.

Sarah was in the kitchen now. Dinah had made her tea. Gracie was pressing against her shoulder, needing to be held, but Sarah was beyond giving solace. She sat with her shoulders hunched and shaking, her face in her hands.

"It's going to be all right," Adam heard himself say, holding out the cookie.

"What is it?" Dinah asked, coming to look. "Oh, gosh."

"What?" Sarah cried, dropping her hands and coming to her feet.

Dinah took the cookie and showed it to her. Sarah looked at it blankly, then she choked back a cry. "I made them yesterday. For company dinner. Before..."

She trailed off. A less kind woman would have looked at him accusingly, Adam thought. A less kind woman would have said *before you came and talked to my Noah and my family fell apart.*

"Yeah, well, I think Matt raided the cookie jar," he managed.

Sarah went to it like a woman sleepwalking. She lifted the lid and peered inside. "No," she said finally. "I think he saved the ones from his school lunch." Her eyes widened. "I think he saved his *whole* lunch. As soon as he got home from school, he came to the refrigerator and wolfed down half of what I'd started getting together for supper. I never thought...I didn't..."

Adam thought she was going to cry again. Dinah hugged her. "It's all right, Ma. Don't you see? It's just Matt and Noah being up to something again. We'll find them."

"I'm sorry," Adam heard himself say. God, but he used those words a lot lately. "I'm sorry for what I said...earlier. Your beliefs are your own. I was wrong to criticize them just because I don't share them."

Sarah finally met his eyes. "You're entitled to your opinions, Mr. Wallace."

"Yeah, I am. And so are you. It doesn't mean that I have the right to rip yours.'' He looked around, finally wondering where Mariah had gone. Finally allowing himself to wonder.

"She went to get people to look, too,'' Dinah said as though reading his mind.

"They don't see her. How can she ask them to help?''

"I don't think she cares right now,'' Sarah said softly. "I think she'll just rush into their kitchens and say her piece. What are they going to do? Hold their hands over their ears? Ignore her? They have to hear her because they can't physically help it. And maybe her words will reach them. Many of them are unhappy about the church's stand on this...this issue. But no one has dared do anything, no one but her.''

This issue. Those other kids. Adam started to answer, when they heard the front door burst open.

He went back to the entry. A man he didn't know came in, his jaw set under his dark beard, the ever-present hat throwing his eyes into shadow.

"Nathaniel said you needed help over here,'' he said.

"Yeah. Yeah, we do. Matt and...and Noah have taken off.''

"Well, point me in the right direction. I know this land as well as anyone.'' He thrust a hand at Adam. "I'm Chicken Joe Lapp from up the road a ways.''

Adam shook his hand bemusedly. "Right.'' The door banged again. Another man came in, trailed by a teenage boy. The boy was grumbling.

"I don't care what they say, Pa. It's time we did something about this.''

"I ain't been all that comfortable with the situation, either,'' his father agreed, "but the church fathers—'' Then he saw Adam. He, too, held out a hand. "Isaiah Miller. This here's my boy Dan. We came to help. Can't see that there's any harm in looking about a bit, no matter what they say.''

Adam shook his hand, nodded, and moved to the door. He felt as if he were caught in a bad dream. He wanted to dislike these people for their naive and stubborn faith, for their cruel laws, but they were here. They had come.

Buggy after buggy streamed into the small paddock across the road. It was already too full to accommodate any more. People began parking on the drive, on the macadam, pulling in behind the barnyard.

If any of them was angry about his ultimatum to help, it didn't show. He wondered if any of them, or which of them, were the exalted deacons. He thought Sugar Joe had probably been too polite to repeat his threat verbatim.

Mariah got out of one of the buggies and rushed toward the house. He turned his back hard and fast.

"All right," he said to the men who'd begun gathering in the entry and the kitchen door. "Here's what we're going to do. Matt went out the back way, through his window."

Nathaniel rushed in the back door. "I've been back there," he interrupted. "There's still a lot of snow over on the other side of the creek, where the sun doesn't hit it because of that shade tree. His footprints go straight through there." He shook his head in disbelief. "Some sneak he is." Then his voice cracked. "Anyway, from there he turned south."

"All right," Adam said, hope swelling hard inside him for the first time since Mariah had come to his motel-room door. She had squeezed her way through the crowd and was standing at the back of the kitchen now. There was a little circle of space around her as people gave her a wide berth and pretended she wasn't there.

Adam ignored her, as well, even as she tried to catch his eye.

"All right," he said again. "We'll split into four groups and we'll fan out from the creek like spokes from a wheel." He wished to God for handguns or flares. "Anybody know how to do a catcall?" he asked. They needed a distinct and out-of-place sound for an alarm.

One of the teenagers in the back of the room whistled, then flushed. A few other boys laughed. A couple of the fathers shook their heads.

"That's it," Adam said, unable to grin. "If anyone sees anything—anything at all—that might tell us where they've gone, make that whistle. Joe—Sugar Joe, I mean," he corrected himself, glancing at Chicken Joe. "Sugar Joe and Nathaniel and I will bring up the rear, and whenever we hear that sound we'll come running to see what you've found. Then we'll all meet at that point and use it as a home base to fan out again." He looked around. "Okay?"

There were nods everywhere.

"You think it's just some tomfoolery on their part?" one man asked, and the fear in his voice made a lot of faces blanche. "That it's not like the others?"

"I don't know enough about the others to say for sure." He couldn't help himself. He shot a hard, angry look at Mariah. "Let's just pray that their disappearance is exactly what it looks like—two boys with a boy-type idea that got them into a sticky mess. All right, then. Are we all set?''

"Soon's Sugar Joe comes back," someone pointed out.

"I'm here." Joe came in through the front door. "What are we doing?"

Adam told him as everyone began spilling out the back way. Then Mariah's voice sneaked up on him. "I'll come, too."

"No," he snapped. "Stay here with the women. The kids'll be cold, maybe wet, probably hungry when we find them."

Sarah gave an irritated little sigh and a watery smile. "Probably not hungry. Noah had both Matt's lunch and his own, and Matt ate most of tonight's sauerkraut and rolls. I'm going to strangle those boys when I get my hands on them." She paused, then her legs seemed to give out on her and she stumbled back to the table to sit down again.

Mariah went to her to offer what comfort she could, but her eyes followed Adam. He knew about the others now. And he was angry.

No, she thought helplessly, what had been on his face had gone deeper than that. He felt...betrayed.

It wasn't anything she hadn't expected, but it had happened too soon, before she could brace herself. And it had happened too late, after she'd gotten in so deeply she couldn't bear it.

Chapter 18

They walked for half an hour without finding anything. The silence of the four search groups grew until it was deafening. Adam could no longer even see them as they disappeared behind hillocks, around the curves of creek beds and into night-blackened fields. At first the steady murmur of their disjointed conversations was comforting, but then he lost even that.

A solid tree line was looming in front of them now. It seemed to rise straight up on a hill that rolled all the way into the sky. And for the first time in his life Adam found himself praying, *really* praying. Not bitter accusations but a plea.

Don't let him have gone in there. Not into the woods. We'll never find him in there in all this darkness.

God didn't answer him, but Joe Lapp did.

"Best thing that could happen is that they went in there," he said, his breath almost crystallizing in the icy air.

Adam looked at him sharply, a little shaken that the man had so easily read his mind.

"It's true," Nathaniel agreed. "It's not as thick as it looks."

Crunch, trudge. Their footsteps put up an almost sweet sort of background music. The sound meant that they were going somewhere, doing something, no matter how helplessly dismal it was beginning to look to Adam.

"There's about a hundred yards of forest," Joe said, speaking over the sound. "Then there's a big break. Several more farms. The Bylers' place and Simon Stoltzfus's farm, among others. The tree line is deceiving, because the land rises again right on the other side of those spreads. The naked eye really can't see the break in the woods, but it's there."

"A hundred yards," Adam repeated. Not comforting, he thought, feeling a little sick. He'd hit home runs little farther than that, and it had taken a sweet angle on the ball and all the strength he possessed. It was a long way across a baseball diamond. He couldn't even comprehend it filled with trees and undergrowth.

He swore again.

"The good part is that if they went through, the Bylers' farm and the Stoltzfus place are both tucked against the shady side of the hill. There's still a whole lot of snow over there," Nathaniel pointed out.

That Adam understood. "Footprints," he said.

"Footprints," Joe repeated. "And if they *didn't* go through, there's only so many places they can hide in the woods."

Adam felt faint, thready hope stir in his blood again.

They walked on in silence. And in spite of himself, Adam thought of lies. Jannel had been a scam artist and Mariah Fisher wasn't an angel. He'd had enough of women springing secret identities on him today to last a lifetime, he thought, rage rising in his blood again. But that fury was aimed mostly at himself, for believing again, for being a world-class chump.

Twenty minutes later, they reached the tree line. Adam stopped and stared grimly into the trees, not quite convinced by Nathaniel and Joe's assurances. Sugar Joe took over without question, letting out a long, undulating catcall. His son blinked at him in surprise, then grinned slowly. But Nathaniel's smile faded as the other groups converged on them.

"What is it?" someone shouted.

"What'd you find?"

"Nothing," Adam bit out.

"We're going to have to change the plan here," Joe shouted. "Everyone listening? Is everyone here?" There were murmurs and nods. "Okay, from here on in we need to stretch out in one long line and enter the trees that way. Each man is responsible for the area directly ahead of him and a foot or so on either side."

"It's going to be dark as pitch in there," someone complained. And only a few of the men had had the foresight to bring lanterns.

"Once we get through, we can gather more lights from Simon's and Gabe's places," Joe answered. "If we don't see any foot-prints over there, we'll know they're probably still in the woods, so we'll turn around and go right back in."

"I'll set the gol-darned barn on fire if I have to," a voice shouted angrily. "Then we'll see everything there is to find."

Adam felt a surge of gratitude for the unseen man who had spoken, then the search party began to form into a line.

"That was Simon Stoltzfus," Joe said as they trudged on again. "He has the farm directly across the woods from here. His little girl—Lizzie—disappeared a couple of months ago."

Don't say it, I don't want to know. The protest was instinctive. But even as it reared up inside Adam, he knew it was too late. Until that point, Mariah's betrayal had been a personal thing, something just between the two of them. He hadn't allowed him-self to think of anything more than that. It was selfish, it was ugly, but Bo's disappearance was all he could deal with at the moment. The other children Sarah and Joe had spoken of had been faceless, anonymous.

Now one of them had a name. One of them had a father. And that man was helping him find Bo.

"Goddammit," he growled aloud.

Joe glanced at him appraisingly. "For now," he went on, "let's just find our boys, before we get too fired up about the others. One thing at a time. Mostly that's all God expects us to handle. We just have to have the wisdom to acknowledge it."

Adam didn't believe him. He walked on in silence.

It happened almost too easily. So easily, in fact, that when Adam heard the sneeze he simply kept walking. He thought it was one of the younger men to the right of him in the line. But, then, other furtive sounds followed—"Shh!", then a grunt, then soft thuds.

Small fists. Pummeling. Adam's heart stopped.

Sugar Joe reached out to grab his arm, to hold him back. He inclined his head to his right and waved his son on ahead, then he laid a finger to his lips. Adam broke off from the line and followed him as the others trooped onward. Nathaniel would tell them what had happened once they all got out of the woods.

The thudding, rustling noises stopped and silence fell again.

Briefly, too suddenly to be believed, the clouds over their heads shifted. And for a moment that left Adam's skin pebbled with gooseflesh, the moon beamed down. It shot light through a gap in the tree cover, and for a crazy, impossible moment it seemed to Adam that the deadfall in front of them was illuminated by a ghostly, heavenly glow. Two pairs of eyes peered out from beneath the chaotic pile of wood and branches. Then, as quickly as it had happened, the moonlight was gone again. They were left in darkness.

"Hope we can find them before too long," Joe said loudly. "What with it going down below zero tonight."

Adam caught on. "I'm not so worried about the temperature as I am about that..." He thought fast. "That bear."

"The grizzly, you mean? Well, I do believe he's way up on the other side of the Stoltzfus place. That was where he was last spotted."

"Yeah, but those suckers are big, Joe. They can cover a lot of ground real fast. I've heard they can run as fast as any train."

They were rewarded with a muffled squeak.

"As long as it's not too hungry, I think the boys'll be all right," Sugar Joe answered.

"Yeah, probably," Adam agreed. "But..."

"But what?" Joe forced a good shot of feigned alarm into his voice.

"Well, you just said it's supposed to go down below zero tonight, right?"

"So?"

"So bears need a lot of food when it gets cold like that, to keep their body heat up. I read that somewhere. Seems to me that the lower it gets below freezing, the hungrier they get. I've heard they'll eat anything, then."

There was another faint squeal, then a thump. Joe went in for the kill.

"I never thought about that. Poor Sarah. She hasn't stopped crying since Noah didn't come home from school. Just think how she's going to feel if all we find is, say, a scrap of Matt's coat."

"Or maybe just one of Noah's fingers. I've heard grizzlies don't eat fingers."

"Nah, too bony, no meat on 'em. They spit them out."

"Then all we might find is a pile of fingers."

"Well, toes, too, I'd think."

The men waited. Nothing. Then there was a harsh sniff.

"Hey, Joe, did you just hear something?"

"Like this, you mean?" Sugar Joe drew breath in through his nose.

"Just like that."

"Could be the bear."

"No," came a small voice. "It ain't the bear."

Adam's heart dropped down to his toes, then it bounced up again and filled his throat. "Who is it, then?"

"Me." It was Matt's voice. Bo was silent.

"Come on out, son," Joe said. "Game's over."

"I can't." Another long silence. "I broke the drainpipe."

"I saw that." Joe paused. "One way or the other, you're going to be up late and cold as the dickens tonight. Either you'll stay out here or you'll be home fixing that pipe. Guess if I were you, I'd rather be working at the house. That bear won't be as likely to come there, and your ma will have some hot cider waiting for you when you're done."

Matt scrambled out from beneath the deadfall. Adam scowled. There was barely enough room in there for two bodies. Bo remained silent. *Was* he in there?

Yeah, he thought, yeah. He had distinctly seen two pair of eyes. "Noah?" he called.

"I ain't coming. I'll take my chances with the bear. Heard they sleep all winter, anyway. I think you're wrong."

Adam felt a choked laugh catch in his throat and something hot touch his eyes. Pride swelled. *Smart kid.* He took a deep, careful breath. He looked at Joe, ready to motion him to go on. He needed to talk to his kid. Then he realized that Sugar Joe and Matt had already left.

He looked at the deadfall. "So you're that scared, huh?"

"I ain't scared."

"Maybe not." But Adam was reasonably sure the teddy bear was beneath that pile of wood with him. "Maybe you just really, really don't want to go back to Texas with me. I mean, if you'd rather freeze to death or get eaten by a bear, I guess you think Texas will be really bad."

The quiet was broken by a hiccup this time. Adam's heart clenched. Oh, God, was he crying?

"Texas?" the boy muttered finally. "You never said nothing about Texas."

"Well, that's where I came here from."

"Miz Fisher told us about that place."

Adam's heart should have been all for Bo at the moment, but it spasmed at the mention of her name. "Yeah?" he prompted, and his voice changed.

"Are there still Indians there?"

"Uh, no. I mean, not wild ones. Not anymore."

"Shoot."

Adam's face hurt from the biting cold, from the need to grin and frown all at once.

"Anyway, I don't care about Texas," Bo said finally. "I don't care if there's a *million* Indians there. I don't want a new pa. The one I got is fine."

One minute Adam was breathing reasonably fine, simply grappling with a few wayward emotions, and then there was nothing in his lungs at all. It hurt. God help him, it hurt badly. Who had told him he was his father?

"You still out there?" Bo asked when he didn't answer.

"Yeah," Adam managed. "Who told you anything about having a new pa?"

"Matt. He heard you. Yesterday."

What the hell had he said? Adam couldn't remember exactly, but he couldn't believe it had been anything all that threatening. He'd said he'd stay here until Bo was ready for the change. He'd said he'd wait. Hadn't he?

"Matt said you lied again," Bo charged. "That you weren't no stranger just come from the place I used to live. He said that you were my *pa.*"

"Well, I am," Adam said hoarsely. "But I'm not...new. I mean, I was your dad a long time ago, when you were little, before Sugar Joe. You know, when Matt didn't remember you being around."

"That's what he said." Bo's voice trembled. It broke Adam's heart.

"I'm not so bad."

"You shoulda told me yesterday. When I was asking you questions."

Adam started to agree with him. He opened his mouth, and heard himself say the exact opposite. "No."

"*No?* How come?" Bo demanded.

And God help him, but Mariah's voice, her words came back to him when he needed them most. "Sometimes a father can't be entirely honest. Sometimes he wants to tell you more than anything in the world who you are, who he is, and he can't, he's got to hold back, because he loves you and he knows it'll hurt you. Sometimes he wants to rush in because rushing is his style. And

sometimes he holds back, because other things are more important.''

This time the silence was longer. Then there was a rustling
sound stitched with cracks and snaps. Bo crawled out of the deadfall.

For a moment Adam thought his legs might fold in utter relief.
But while Bo had come out, it quickly became clear that he wasn't
easily going to give another inch. He's such a tough kid, Adam
thought. *I love him so.* The years hadn't changed that, would
never even make a dent in it.

"So did you lie about the other, too?" Bo demanded, crossing
his arms over his chest in a challenge.

"About what?" Adam felt his heart skid, because somehow he
knew what was coming.

"About if I didn't want to go with you. You said you'd hang
around and wait 'til I *did* want to go.''

Unbidden, unwelcome, an image of Mariah's face hung before
his mind's eye. He blinked hard and scrubbed a hand over his
eyes to banish it. "I didn't lie," he managed. "I meant it. Then.''

"Oh, man! Figures." Bo looked like he was going to cry. "I
knew it.''

That was it for his legs. Adam sat hard on one of the fallen
trees. "Well, you're a true Wallace, anyway.''

"What do you mean?" Bo asked suspiciously.

"You don't trust the ground you're standing on." And maybe
that was good, he thought. At least he wouldn't fall blindly for a
Mariah Fisher.

Still, it hurt. It hurt more than anything that had happened yet.
Because he'd given his best to this kid since he had found him
again, and even, for the most part, before he'd lost him. He'd
been a little impatient back then, often too busy, but he had tried
his damnedest not to let the Wallace genes take hold. A lot of
times he'd done it self-consciously, and sometimes he'd faltered,
but damn it, he'd *tried.* But neither Jannel nor Sugar Joe, not
Sarah nor Mariah's influence at school could change the facts. Bo
had Wallace genes through and through. Maybe he'd just been
born knowing that everything good in life had its price, and that
the things that looked good at first glance usually weren't when
you stared at them a little longer.

Bo waited. When Adam didn't go on, he came slowly, in fitful
starts and stops, to the log. He sat gingerly, keeping good space
between them.

"Well, you know, it just seemed too good to be true," he complained.

Adam flinched. "It was." But suddenly, he wasn't thinking of the promise he'd made Bo any longer. He was thinking of Mariah again.

For once in his sorry life, he *had* believed. He'd believed in her. For a brief moment in time, his own Wallace genes *hadn't* shone through. He'd let himself believe she was exactly what she seemed to be. So good. So perfect. So right for him.

Sucker. Fool.

"So what happens now?" Bo asked, dragging his attention back to him, and Adam realized that the boy's voice quavered. "Are you gonna just take me away, anyway, whether I like it or not?"

He had to think, couldn't think. He needed desperately to say the right thing, but no words would come. Then he heard his own voice and he was shaken, because the words came on their own, good ones, right ones. "How about a compromise?"

"I don't get it," Bo muttered warily. "What's a compromise?"

Honesty, Adam thought. And sometimes it required half truths. "I can't stay here anymore, pal." *It's not the same place. It's not the place I thought it was.* He'd never thought he'd be able to stay indefinitely, but he'd believed it had been a good, patient spot for a respite. Now he could no longer tolerate the smells, the sights, the sounds.

"It would be really hard for me to do that," he went on hoarsely. "So how about this? Why don't you come back to Texas with me for a certain period of time? Like two weeks or maybe a month. Why don't you come back with me and just see what it's like?"

"Then what?" Bo asked, his eyes narrowing in a suspicious Jake look.

"Then you can come back here and visit."

"You'll bring me back?"

Half truths. "I'll make damned sure you get here." He'd get Jake to bring him, if he had to.

Bo's jaw dropped. "That's a bad word."

Get used to it. I'm going to be a bastard at times. I've lost things I didn't even know I wanted. "Sorry."

"S'okay, I guess. You just surprised me." Bo paused. "Just two weeks? That's all I have to do?"

"If that's all you think you can handle."

"What about school?"

And that brought another flashing image of his teacher. Adam's gut clenched and twisted. "We'll decide after you come back here for a visit. After we see how you feel about everything. I don't think there's any law that says a kid can't take a couple weeks off."

"Ma's going to cry."

"Ma—oh." Sarah, he thought. He still wasn't used to that, but he knew better than to correct him. "Maybe," he said finally, cautiously. "But I think she'll feel better if she knows you'll come back pretty soon."

"So what if I stay there two weeks and I *hate* it? What if I don't want to go back a second time?"

Adam raked a gloved hand through his hair. The kid was good. "I don't know," he answered honestly. "I don't have an answer for that yet. I guess we'll just have to see when we get to that point. *If* we get to that point. You could really like it there, you know." He wished suddenly he hadn't given him the two-week option. A month would be better. Maybe in a month Bo would forget everything he had left behind. Maybe, then, Dallas wouldn't seem so bad.

Who the hell am I kidding? Bo was leaving a family, a real family, and he wasn't gaining much at all.

Bo dragged a toe through a small mound of snow. Something was still bothering him.

"What?" Adam prompted.

"Do I have another ma there, too?"

Adam lost his breath. "No."

"I *don't?* Where'd she go?"

"I don't know."

Bo was staring at him, stricken and confused. Adam searched for more words, and once again they came like gifts placed kindly and generously in his throat. "Bo...Noah, I mean...you did have one. That's how you got here, to Pennsylvania. She decided she didn't want to live with me anymore, and she left and she took you with her. She came here. But then she probably had some kind of trouble, because she asked Sarah and Sugar Joe to take care of you for a little while. And they did. They did a real good job, too. They took care of you until your mom could come back or I could find you. I just got here first, that's all."

"How come it took you so long?"

"Huh?" That one left him dizzy.

"How come it took you so long to come? I must have been here *forever*."

"There were a lot of places to look for you." Adam forced himself to breathe. "And I had to go through every one. I looked every day. Every single day. It was all I ever did. The most important thing in the world was finding you again."

Bo digested that. "It's that big out there, huh?" There was fear and false bravado in his voice now. It still stumped Adam to think that the world he knew, the one he had lived in every day for thirty-eight years, was so alien to his own child now.

"Well, yeah," he said softly. "I guess it is."

"Do you have a fast red car?"

His heart thumped. "No. That was your mother's. But your uncle has a fast yellow one." *If he hasn't self-destructed again and totaled it in the weeks I've been gone.* That was always a possibility.

"Can I bring Bear?"

Adam jolted back from his own hellish thoughts. His eyes burned again. And this time he couldn't quite blink back the tears. "Sure."

"Okay. Then, I guess I'll go on the compmise. You know, just to see how big it really is out there."

"Of course."

Bo got to his feet and trudged out of the woods. After a moment, Adam got up to follow him.

Chapter 19

Mariah was gone when they got back to the house. Matt was sitting in the kitchen, shoveling down a bowl of hot soup. Both boys' cheeks were apple red. Adam wondered how much of it was from the cold and how much was guilt.

Sarah hovered over Matt, touching him again and again, brushing his hair back, plucking a piece of unseen lint off his shoulder. She brought Bo some soup, as well, almost visibly trying to restrain herself, but then she cried out softly and hugged him, holding him so tightly and for so long that the boy finally began to wriggle.

Her eyes brimmed with tears as she looked up at Adam. "Thank you. Thank you for bringing them back, for...insisting."

Thank you? He was tearing her life up six ways to Sunday, he thought, and there wasn't a thing he could do any differently. Adam shook his head, unable to answer.

"Would you like something warm to drink, Mr. Wallace?" she went on. "Cider? Coffee?"

He shook his head. He'd already turned down the soup. He had a hunch that nothing was going to thaw the strange cold inside him.

"Well," Joe said finally. "What's the plan now?"

"Are you gonna make me leave tonight?" Bo piped up, and his voice trembled.

Everything inside Adam, every instinct and all his love needed desperately to take Bo back to the motel with him. He wanted to sit in the chair there watching over him all night, needed to stare at him steadily and relentlessly while he slept, so that he could not possibly slip away again. Even if he didn't run, someone in the settlement was stealing kids.

And then he thought of those wretched, jaded, distrustful Wallace genes. "Are you planning on running anywhere again?" he heard himself ask Bo.

The boy's face colored even brighter. "Uh-uh."

"Promise? Here's the thing...Bo." It was getting past time to straighten out this name business, he realized. He glanced quickly at Sugar Joe and saw the man nod silently, slightly. "If I let you stay here tonight, it means I'm trusting you. I'm trusting you to be here tomorrow when I come back. You'd have to give me your word."

Matt muttered something like, "Two cold out there, anyway." Joe gave him a gentle warning shot to the back of the head.

"Yeah," Bo mumbled.

"What?"

"I said, yeah. I'll be here."

"Do you want me to keep him home from school, then?" Sarah blurted, understanding finally settling in on her. Tomorrow would be the day.

"Please," Adam said shortly. "I'll be back around eight o'clock." And it would kill him to wait even that long. He had virtually nothing to pack, nothing to keep him busy at the motel. He needed to get on a plane and go. Now. The need practically screamed through his blood, but he had never been of the mind that yanking a bandage off all at once hurt any less.

He ruffled Bo's hair and hunkered down until he was eye level with him. "Eat your soup and get warm, then grab yourself a good night's sleep. You've got quite an adventure waiting for you tomorrow."

For a brief moment, something avid, a kind of universal boyish excitement, touched his eyes. Then they slid away from Adam's. "Yeah."

Adam stood again, nodding at Joe. "Thanks for everything."

"We'll see you in the morning, then."

As he let himself out, Adam thought that Sugar Joe's voice had sounded thick and pained, also.

This should have been the happiest night of his life, or at least the last four years of it. Instead Adam felt like weeping.

He was halfway up Ronks Road, on his way back to the motel, before the insidious little voice in his head started whispering again. *Lizzie Stoltzfus. Michael Miller.*

He made a growling sound under his breath. It didn't matter. Those kids weren't his problem. He'd solved his own problem, would pick his son up tomorrow and go home. His heartache, his terror, was over. *Simon Stoltzfus,* the voice murmured. Simon's wasn't. *I'll set the gol-darned barn on fire if I have to.*

Adam slammed a fist against the steering wheel and pulled off the road.

Ah, what a day it had been. He needed to leave this place. He wanted desperately to get back to everything that was familiar, and he hoped to the settlement's God that he'd find some peace in that. He needed to get away from all the betrayals, both old and new, and make the best of a world that was never going to be perfect.

But Lizzie Stoltzfus and the others were still missing.

It *wasn't* his responsibility. Mariah had never actually laid that whole mess upon his shoulders, no matter that she had obviously planned to do so. His stomach twisted. He turned the wheel of the car hard and headed back the other way.

It wasn't his responsibility. And he sure as hell wasn't going to look for those kids. His plate was full right now, and he had more to handle than he honestly thought he was capable of. A nightmare was over, but a new one was blooming, because somehow he was going to have to get Bo to embrace an alien world that had once been his. He couldn't give Lizzie Stoltzfus anything, because he had nothing left to give.

But he knew who could, and he knew how to get it done.

For Simon, he told himself. And for the other fathers who didn't know that their kids were safe and sound tonight, but who had found it in their hearts to buck their deacons and help him, anyway. He told himself he was doing this because he, of all people, knew that fathomless ache, that hole in the soul that came from losing a child.

He, at least, had known that Jannel had taken Bo. He hadn't

really feared for Bo's life, hadn't worried that physical harm would come to him, that he might be cold and wounded, frightened and alone...at least not until tonight. And tonight had been hell.

He stopped the car in front of Mariah's house and got out. He made his way up the sidewalk slowly at first, then he found himself jogging. He reached the door and hit his fist upon it like a battering ram. And at the last possible moment terror struck him, that he would find her in that nightgown again. And he thought that if he did he would turn tail and run, and Simon Stoltzfus could be damned.

But then the door cracked open and her face peered out at him, her eyes red and swollen. And though her hair spilled, though she stood in stockinged feet, she still wore her dress, her apron. Adam opened his mouth and was stunned when he heard his own voice, because the words weren't what he'd meant to say.

"You know, I think I could live with your ulterior motives for bringing me here. I don't give a damn *why* you called me. You did it. That's all that matters. But why did you *wait?*" He heard Sarah's voice again, pounding in his head, echoing. *Finally... finally...finally.* "How long, Mariah? How long did you have that milk carton before you actually contacted me?" It had been her, he realized anew, but with full impact now that he was addressing it. *She* had called ChildSearch. And she'd hadn't seen Bo in any godforsaken farmers' market. She was his teacher.

Lies, he thought. All lies, right from the start. And he'd been too blind to see the almost obvious glare of them because she had captivated him with her sad violet eyes and rare smiles.

Mariah didn't answer. Her eyes were wide and grief filled now. She seemed to be gasping, but no breath came out.

"How long?" he roared.

She jumped back from his voice, trembling. "Five weeks."

He stared at her, stunned. *"Five?"*

"Ab-b-bout that. More than a month."

"How could you do that to me?"

"I didn't even know you, then!" she cried.

"How could you do that to *anyone?*" he shouted.

She cried out in panic when he reached out and grabbed her by the shoulders. He lifted her bodily and set her back from the door, stepping inside and slamming it hard behind him again. He thrust a finger in her face and realized almost distantly that it shook. He was as enraged as he had ever been in his life.

"You sit here in your ivory tower, so sweet, so precious and pure, and the whole time you're dishing out pain!"

She blanched. "No."

"It doesn't matter that it was me. ChildSearch puts a lot of pictures on a lot of milk cartons. They weren't just of my own kid. And I know every one of those parents. Damn you, they've cried in my office. They've wept into my phone. And *you knew*. Whoever it was, whether it was my kid or someone else's, you arbitrarily decided those parents should suffer for five more weeks! *Who gave you that right, lady?* Through all this Amish hogwash you've fed me, I guess you just plain forgot to mention that someone appointed you to be *God!*"

A tear spilled over. He watched, enraged, as it tracked down her cheek. And he realized almost distantly that Jannel's perfidy had been bad, but somehow this was worse. This was a nightmare on so many levels.

"How dare you?" he breathed again.

Her heart was hammering so hard she thought she might faint. She opened her mouth, needing to make him understand. Because she had never dreamed, hadn't even dared to pray that he would come here one last time, that she might have the *chance* to explain. But now that he had, now that she did, his words, his accusations echoed in her head and she couldn't say a word.

Because he was right. She gave a small pained cry.

"Cut it out," he growled ruthlessly. "Don't act all heartbroken and try to guilt me out. *You* did this! You brought this upon yourself and a whole lot of other people besides!"

Say something, she pleaded with herself. "N-noah. I waited b-because I wanted to be sure I was doing the right thing for Noah. For B-Bo."

"It wasn't your decision to make! *You had no right!*" His voice crashed into the quiet, pretty room.

No, Mariah thought helplessly. She hadn't. And at least a part of her had known that all along. Still... "It wasn't as though he was in California!" she protested. "It wasn't as though your wife had just taken him to some other part of the country! She'd changed his whole life, Adam! He'd become *Amish!* I couldn't see him wrenched cruelly away!"

She knew immediately that it was the wrong thing to say. His face mottled. For a wild moment, she thought he might even strike her. But of course he wouldn't do that, not Adam. He was too inherently honorable, and in the end he was too strong to let anger completely take him.

He jerked himself away from her, stepping back, turning around so he wouldn't have to look at her. When his voice came back again, it was deathly quiet. "I've got a news flash for you, Miss Fisher, and for the rest of your *settlement*. Your way isn't the only way. And a whole lot of us don't even believe it's a *good* way. Some of us think it's a sick, obsessed way. And some of us think the best thing that could happen to a kid would be to get free of it as quickly as possible."

Mariah swayed. "I—"

He didn't let her finish. Now that he had come inside, he realized that he couldn't tolerate being in her company even one more moment. *The betrayal.* He couldn't stand looking at the floor in front of the hearth, where he had made love to a woman who didn't even really exist. *Another* woman who didn't exist. He felt bile push up in his throat.

Simon Stoltzfus.

"As for the other," he interrupted, his voice flat now, "as far as those other kids are concerned, it's not my help you need. I suggest you call your local authorities. Or NCMEC—the National Center for Missing and Exploited Children. That's who you need, not ChildSearch. Or you need the FBI. This isn't a case of non-custodial parents taking off with their kids. It's not a simple kidnapping, if it's happened four times. You've got a big problem and you need the law." He opened the door.

"They won't do that!" she cried. "That's why I asked *you!*"

He shot a deadly look back over his shoulder. "Wrong, Mariah. You never asked me, at all. If you had, maybe we wouldn't be having this conversation now." Then he realized that he was wrong. Because if she had told him all this at the beginning, if she had admitted then that she'd waited five whole weeks to contact him while she decided if she wanted to tell him where his child was, he would have disliked her from the very start.

That was what got to him most of all. Jannel had taken four years and Mariah Fisher had only taken five weeks. But Mariah had done it and then she'd held a hand out to him in friendship, chastising him gently when he got off the beaten path, somehow making him measure up to each sticky challenge...hiding something all along. Pulling his strings. Making him dance.

"Damn you," he bit out and started outside again.

"Adam, *wait!*"

This time when he glanced at her, she gasped at the look of
loathing in his eyes. *Dear God, he hates me.*

She could live with that. On some level, in some measure,
maybe she even believed she deserved it. But if he went away
without helping to find the other children, then it was all for
naught. And always, forever, she was strong enough to deal with
that which she had brought upon herself—as long as she came
away with one small morsel of goodness, one thing of light.

He had to help them find the others.

She clasped her hands together to keep them from shaking.
"They won't do that," she repeated. "The deacons will *not* go
to the authorities or to the FBI or—or to any national center. They
say it's God's will, that we must not resist, and even the parents—
dear God, even the *parents*—won't go against them. So I tried to
think of a way, some way that I could get help for those little
ones...surreptitiously. All I ever wanted was a way to get them
back that wasn't too far beyond the *Ordnung,* a way the deacons
might be able to forgive!" she cried suddenly. "And then I
bought that milk. And it was like God was showing me the way.
Because no one else—*hardly* anyone else around here—buys cartons of milk. Why should they? They live on dairy farms!"

She laughed giddily, almost hysterically. "No one else would
ever have known that you were looking for Bo, but I did, and I
thought about it and thought about it and then I realized that *here*
was the way. I'd get those people—ChildSearch—to come for
Noah, and when they got here, I'd ask them to please put those
composite pictures on milk cartons for the other babies, as well.
Maybe the church wouldn't even have to know about it! But,
then, ChildSearch didn't just send...people. The woman said you
were Noah's father. And you came here yourself and everything
got complicated, because Noah—Bo—didn't know you, so I decided to wait until you'd resolved your own problems before I
asked you about...about the others."

He was staring at her. His face was expressionless, like stone.
"Playing God again, Mariah?"

"*No!* I—"

"Sure you were. Deciding those other kids could wait a
while—God knows where, with God knows who. You decided
they could wait until you found the optimum time and way to
string me along!"

It was true enough that something cracked inside her. She drew
in a breath and it was thick with tears. "It was...wrong," she

whispered, her voice suddenly so quiet he could barely hear her. "Yes, yes, it was. But what you don't see—'' what even she had not admitted herself until this very moment, she realized, blanching "—is that this wasn't even really about you, at all.''

If she had had only one truly honest thought over the past few weeks, she admitted, then it had been that night when she had been dressing for the first supper at the Lapps. *What if I don't?* What if she didn't ask Adam to help? What if she did as the deacons ordained and let the children remain lost?

Adam watched with a vaguely curious feeling, a detached sort of halfhearted interest, as the color drained from her face. "What?'' he prompted flatly.

"It wasn't even about Bo or Lizzie or Michael,'' she went on, her voice tightening. "In the end, it was just about me.''

"You,'' he repeated.

"I was thinking of myself. Only myself. And I was a...coward.''

He'd had every intention of leaving. He stood staring at her instead, though God help him, he couldn't find a voice to ask her what she meant again. He couldn't find it in his heart to sift through her own pain. There was too much of his own and he couldn't battle his way through it.

"The deacons are wrong,'' she said, her voice a monotone now. "The church is wrong. While we sit back, not resisting this horror, children are being hurt.'' She shuddered. "And I started out thinking that I *hated* the men who would allow that to happen. Men who would not protect the little ones God's given us. I started out thinking that they were so caught up in their precious *Ordnung,* in self-righteous pride like my father's, that somewhere along the line they'd lost their hearts.

"So I determined to do something. I called you. I didn't do it lightly. Even believing as I did that I was doing the right thing, it tore me up inside. That's why it took me five weeks. I had to find the courage. But I did it, and then everything...changed. The Lapps included me in dinner. And I thought...*what if?*''

She sank down in the rocker. She was crying visibly now, her tears streaming, but she made no move to wipe them away. She would no longer even look at him. She stared into the fire in the stove.

"I thought...of going along with the deacons so I could maybe...so I could...have my life back,'' she finished wretchedly. "Even though I knew it was wrong. That *they* were wrong. I

forgot for a little while that I didn't want to be like them, that I
didn't want to be anything like people who would allow children
to suffer. I forgot because it was so good, so very, very *good,* to
be included at the Lapps', to share dinner with others again.''

"The people agree with you,'' Adam heard himself say.
"About looking for the kids. They came tonight to help.''

She gave a shudder that he thought he could feel even on the
other side of the room. "It won't be enough. And I...failed them.
In the end, I failed the children. Because I got you here, then I
was too afraid, too *selfish* to take that second plunge, to see it
through. Once I did that, my *Meidung* really would be hopeless.
Irrevocable. Complete. There'd never be any way out of it. I just
couldn't bear to do that to myself. And now you're leaving.'' She
finally looked at him. "Aren't you?'' she whispered.

He cleared his throat, couldn't find his voice. He nodded.

He thought about telling her she was only one woman. That
there was a whole community out there that could have done
something, as well, that there was no need for her to take this
whole thing upon her own shoulders. He still couldn't find the
words.

"I tried to tell you, you know,'' she went on softly. "At least
twice before today. And then you interrupted me, misunderstood
me, and I let it drop.''

"I've got to go,'' he said hoarsely.

"I'm sorry,'' she whispered wretchedly, "so very sorry. For
all of it.''

"You lied to me.'' The words nearly stuck in his throat.

"No.'' She shook her head a little. "I didn't *lie.*''

Half truths, then, he thought. Omissions. In the end, they were
still the same thing. "You lied,'' he repeated. "And I'd thought
you were the only good, honest thing I'd ever found.''

He pulled the door shut behind him with a solid crack. Mariah
winced. Then she fumbled blindly behind her for the afghan
draped over the back of the chair. She pulled it over herself without hope.

This cold was never going to go away. It didn't matter if Adam
Wallace never forgave her, because she was never going to forgive herself.

Chapter 20

Bo sat frozen on the plane. Every muscle was locked in place, as though he expected the aircraft to launch up to the moon instead of leveling out at thirty thousand feet. Bear was clutched so tightly against his chest that Adam was glad the thing didn't actually need to breathe.

He watched his son, feeling vaguely irritated, which shamed him, and more than a little frightened, which made his head hurt with a steady, throbbing pain right behind his eyes. Then again, he'd had an unrelenting headache since he'd left Mariah the night before.

"Want to change places?" he suggested.

Bo looked at him, moving only his eyes. "Why?" he croaked.

"Well, it's not quite as scary if you don't look at the ground."

"Can't see the ground," he squeaked. "There's clouds out there. We're on *top* of 'em."

"You know, you *could* just look at this as an adventure, like I said last night," he snapped, and remorse grabbed his throat and squeezed. "Bo, nobody's telling you that you have to immediately love everything I show you," he went on more quietly. "And, yeah, some things are going to be scary. But you could at least consider it like a lesson at school." He didn't want to think about his school. Adam's stomach shifted. "What I mean is, it's

all just something new and different. Like going to the zoo. Hell,
Just pretend everyone's in cages. Half of us belong there anyway.''

"You said a bad word again.''

Adam closed his eyes.

"Could we trade seats?'' he asked in a small voice. "I think
that might be a good idea, after all.''

Adam looked at him again, his heart rolling over. "Sure. Any
minute now.''

"Why do we have to wait?''

"Just until the pilot turns off that seat-belt sign. It's just...it's
a rule.''

"Like the *Ordnung?*''

Adam winced. He'd known that was coming. "Yeah. Only in
this case it's the FAA.''

"What's that mean?''

"Federal Aviation Administration. They make the rules of the
sky.''

"Well, if it's okay with them, and all, I guess I'd feel better if
I didn't have to look down on clouds.''

Adam nodded helplessly. And felt angry again. *What had they
done to his kid?* Where was the boy who'd run hell bent for
leather down the concourse in Houston?

"You've flown before,'' he heard himself say.

"I *did?*''

"Yeah. I took you with me once.'' And then he started talking.
And like before, the words appeared magically, easily, and Bo
finally turned a little bit in his seat to watch him, rapt, as he told
him about baseball games and the Houston Astros and about moving sidewalks in airports that could take a kid into eternity before
his father could blink.

By the time the stewardess brought lunch, both of them had
forgotten to change seats.

Supper at the Lapps' was a subdued affair. Conversation ebbed
and flowed stiltedly. There were no bursts of laughter. Matthew
was as good as gold.

Of course, it could well be that the boy was just exhausted. It
had taken him until nearly midnight to fix the drainpipe the previous night. At that point, Joe had told him it looked fine, and

when the boy had gone to bed, he'd worked off his own tension by finishing it himself.

It had been a long, bad day, and with all the confusion of Bo leaving and Sarah's heart breaking, the farm chores were only half-done. He had a long night ahead of him to catch things up.

He probably wouldn't have slept anyway.

"It's not right," he said suddenly.

Sarah looked at him, her deep brown eyes widening in alarm. "But we agreed—"

"I'm not talking about Bo," he went on. Everyone had been inching around his name all afternoon.

"He was never ours," he pointed out more quietly. "God loaned him to us. We got to make him happy for a little while. But his place is with his pa, with his true family."

Nathaniel nodded, then Dinah did, too. But the little ones still looked confused and hurting over their loss. Gracie was almost too young to remember a life without Noah, and Matt had been Bo's sidekick for an eternity.

"What I'm talking about is this other thing," he went on. He heard his wife suck in her breath. "I'm sorry, honey. I am. I know your own pa is going to bust a gut, but I can't go along with not looking for those other kids any longer. Last night...all this with Bo...it just drove it home. Losing Matt for that little while did it. Simon and the Millers and the others aren't likely to get their boys and girls back so easily, if at all. It's not right, and it's the first thing I've come up against since I came to this *Gemeide* that I just can't live with. Not even for you. Not if I hope to maintain any self-respect."

"What do you want to do?" she breathed.

"What would the church do if the whole settlement rose up against their decision?" Nathaniel asked suddenly.

Sarah and Joe looked down the table at him. Sarah let out her breath. Joe nodded.

"Good point," Joe said slowly.

"It's impossible for them to throw the *Meidung* on a whole group of us, isn't it?" Nathaniel went on hurriedly. "I mean, what would be the point? Those of us who were shunned could still see each other, so there *couldn't* be a *Meidung* among us."

"It's happened before," Joe agreed.

"It has?" Dinah was fascinated.

"That's how your grandparents—my family—ended up in

Berks. Something happened here that they felt strongly against, so a whole group of people broke off and migrated."

"Joe, please!" Sarah cried. "My *parents!*"

Joe looked at her. "Can you honestly, in your heart, inflict upon other mothers what you went through last night?" He didn't have to wait for an answer. He knew her too well. She would not. He looked down the table at his son again. "The last of the chores can wait, I think. We'll do double work tomorrow, skip lunch. What do you say?" Nathaniel nodded hard. "Tonight we'll pay a few visits around the *Gemeide.* Let's find out how many other people really agree with us."

Nathaniel pushed his plate away without hesitation. "I'll hitch up the buggy."

"If the church gets wind of what you're doing, they'll shun *you,*" Sarah gasped. "They'll turn you out for trying to organize a...a rebellion."

Sugar Joe met his wife's eyes and nodded.

"Wow." It was scarcely a breath. Bo's eyes were the size of saucers as he inspected Jake's car. "Matt should see this."

Hope soared in Adam. And then, in a heartbeat, it died again. Color seized Bo's cheeks. He looked quickly away from the Thunderbird, grabbed his bear from its seat atop Adam's suitcase and clamped it to his chest again.

"I can...uh...put the top down," Jake suggested, at a loss over Bo's change of mood.

"No," Adam snapped. "It won't do a damned bit of good. Look, Bo, you can tell Matt all about this in a couple of weeks. It's not like you're never going to see him again."

"Forever," Bo mumbled. "That's *forever.*"

"Half that long," Adam corrected, then he gave a gusty sigh.

Whatever rapport they'd reached on the plane had shattered into a million pieces when Bo had been confronted with the Dallas-Fort Worth airport. The fear and panic in his eyes had been intense. Jake had met them at the gate and rushed them through to his car, but things still weren't right.

It had only been one day—a long, *aggravating* day full of traveling—but Adam was already beginning to wonder if the situation would ever improve.

"Come on. Load up," he went on, gripping the suitcase, tossing it in his brother's direction. Jake caught it and stashed it in the trunk.

Bo looked torn. Adam guessed that half of him wanted desperately to ride in the yellow car. The other half of him probably thought a lightning bolt was going to come down from the sky and zap him. *Damn those people.*

"Bo," he said tightly, holding back on his temper when the boy refused to budge. "I happen to know for a fact that riding *in* an automobile isn't against the *Ordnung.*"

"The what?" Jake asked.

Adam waved a hand at him to shut him up and waited.

"Yeah?" Bo said belligerently. "So?"

"I also happen to know that as a seven-year-old kid, you're not affected by the *Ordnung,* anyway. You don't *have* to follow it."

"I can if I wanna."

Adam took a deep breath. "Yeah. If you want to." *And I don't want you to.* "But there's no *Ordnung* here other than the rules I make as your father. Sorry."

Bo's eyes filled. "I bet *not!* I bet you're *not* sorry! Matt said you *hated* us, that you think we're *stupid* the way we do things!" He turned on his heel and began running, legs pumping. Hell, he was flying. Straight for the nearest concourse.

"What a picnic," Jake muttered. "Now what?"

"I'm going to catch him. And if I ever see Matthew Lapp again, I'm going to strangle him." Adam began jogging, then broke into a run when Bo neared the moving sidewalk. Depending upon how stymied and shook up he was by all this technology, he might or might not jump on it.

At least, Adam thought, this was something he had a little experience with.

Mariah muddled through.

It was the only word she could think of to describe her days during the week after Adam and Bo left. She taught. She baked. She read. And she did it all as though watching her own actions from behind a drab, filmy curtain. Often she set about accomplishing some chore only to discover she'd already done it, though she didn't remember.

She wished desperately that the ache inside her was only that of loss. But it was worse than that, a bitter, choking guilt at how far out of control things had spun—even her own treacherous heart.

She knew what she ought to do now. There was only one course of action that would set things right. Not with Adam. He was gone to her, and each time she admitted that to herself her heart twisted hard enough to make her gasp aloud. But the other issue still dangled. She had to finish what she had started.

She had to call those people—what had Adam called them? Something about missing and exploited children. She could find out with a few calls from the pay phone in the village. In any event, it was the only thing she could do, if she was going to be able to continue living within her own skin.

And yet...she did nothing. She *planned* to call those people, she really did, but she simply couldn't find the energy. She muddled through—until Katya didn't peek out of her barn on Friday morning.

For a long time Mariah only stood in the snow, confused. More had fallen, and bitter flurries were beginning to sting her cheeks again. She dragged her shawl closer about her shoulders and wondered if she was early. Or late. She honestly didn't know, and had no clue what to do now. For two years she had been checking on Katya nearly every weekday morning, for fear that her friend wouldn't be able to show up. Now that it had happened, she was lost.

Then an angry male voice cracked into the quiet morning.

"You there! You! Get out of here!" She pivoted a little in place. She saw Frank Essler coming at her from across the nearest paddock. "You've caused my family enough trouble! Now *go!*"

"*I* have?" Mariah stared at him. Of all the people she had caused hurt to, she did not think Katya or her children had been among them.

Frank didn't answer. He picked up a muddy bullwhip as he came across the paddock. He had never been especially neat or orderly with his equipment, she thought absently. It was one of the things people didn't care for about him. He bore down on her, lifting the thing high, as though to strike her with it.

And she still couldn't move.

"What are you, dense or deaf? I told you! Go! You're trespassing!"

It was true. She was. "Where's Katya? What have you done to her?"

The bullwhip came down hard and fast, slicing the air just

inches from her right shoulder. A warning. Mariah couldn't find the will to wince, even reflexively. She barely heard its crack.

Then, suddenly, the muddy curtain lifted. Rage filled her.

This man could not hurt her. He could do nothing to her that would inflict more pain than she had already perpetrated upon herself. She pushed brazenly past him. For a moment he was so stunned he didn't follow her.

It didn't last. She heard his footsteps and began running. "If you've killed her, Frank, I'll call the police!" she called back to him. "What will the deacons do? Shun me?" She laughed hysterically with the rush of new emotion, emotion that had been gone for so many days now. She reached the back door of the house just ahead of him and dragged it open, rushing inside.

Katya's children were still seated at the kitchen table, eating breakfast. Rachel had a swollen red cheek. The bruise was going purple-yellow around the edges. Mariah gasped.

"You?" she cried. "You too, how?" Her head swam with the horror of it.

Rachel's eyes slid away.

"Where is she?" Mariah pleaded. "One of you, please—" But then Frank came in behind her and she fled again.

She hit the entryway, skidding, and grabbed the banister to stop her momentum. Then she raced up the stairs. She had no clue which was Katya's bedroom—she had never been permitted to enter this house. It didn't matter. She glanced in each door she passed until she found her friend.

Katya was in bed. Her left eye was swollen shut.

"Oh, dear God," Mariah whispered.

"What are you doing here?" Katya struggled to sit up, stunned.

By way of an answer, Mariah slammed the door closed and shoved a shoulder against a dresser to push it in front of it.

"Are you crazy?" Katya demanded. "He'll kill both of us!"

Mariah leaned back against the dresser, out of breath. Then the confusion began settling on her again. "You've alive. Why didn't you come to the barn?"

She began crying harder. "I think I broke my leg. I went down and made breakfast, but then I just needed...I had to rest it."

"Oh, dear God," Mariah said again, moving to the bed. Frank's fists began pummeling the door. That was when she realized what she had done. They were trapped in here. If Katya's leg was broken, they couldn't even climb out the window. *She* could, but she would have to leave Katya behind to face her husband's wrath.

That was something she would not do.

She bit her lip hard. She had wreaked havoc on so many lives lately, and what she had done to Adam—making him wait to find Bo, deluding him as to her motives—was the most bitter pill to swallow of all. Now she had brought the fury of Frank Essler down on Katya's head all over again. But this time, God help her, this time she wouldn't cower, wouldn't quit halfway.

"*You* didn't break your leg!" she snapped.

Katya looked away. "No. He pushed me down the stairs. He was angry because Sugar Joe Lapp visited. Sugar Joe has been trying to organize the *Gemeide* into going up against the deacons to find those children."

Mariah's heart leaped. *Thank you, Joe Lapp.* She had never expected anyone to help her on that issue, and was not in the least surprised that that particular man had.

Frank started pounding on the door again. Mariah spun that way to shout at him. "Stop it, Frank! *Stop it!* I'm not going to let you get away with this anymore!"

Katya gaped at her. "You've lost your mind."

"What can they do to me?" Mariah asked with a smile that was only bitter around the edges.

"They can do a lot to *me,*" Katya answered simply. "Frank can."

The truth of that overwhelmed her, if only for a moment. Then Mariah recovered and rushed to the window. It was one of those that faced the road. That was good. She turned back to the bed and began ripping off the blankets.

"He won't kill you. He won't hurt you again. I won't let him. Anyway, what does this have to do with Sugar Joe?"

"Rachel slipped," Katya explained absently, watching her friend, little furrows deepening between her eyes. "She blurted out that she thought *you* were going to do something about finding those children. Which would have been fine—everyone has thought that since Adam came here and I told them about his company. But Rachel said something about hearing you say so in the barn."

Mariah closed her eyes briefly. "I'm so sorry."

Katya smiled thinly. "It's not your fault. You never dragged me out there to meet you. I did it because it's the only sanity, the only respite I have." She eyed the blankets and sheets Mariah was knotting together. "I can do this," she decided suddenly, her eyes widening, then narrowing with determination. "I have one good leg."

"Yes," Mariah agreed. "You do. And we'll manage."

Color was coming to Katya's cheeks now, healthy color this time, but then it faded abruptly.

"What?" Mariah demanded, tying furiously now, dumping the linked portions out the window as Frank pounded harder. "Don't you come in here, Frank!" she screamed, hoping to keep him at the door so he wouldn't realize what they were up to on the other side of the house. "I'll...I'll shoot you! I'll do it with your own hunting rifle!"

"It's not loaded!" He threw his shoulder into the effort.

"Oh, sweet Jesus, help me," Katya whispered, then she rallied again. "I know where your ammo is, Frank! Stay out!" She slid off the bed in her nightgown and hopped toward Mariah on her good leg. The bad one was a mottled purple color at her ankle.

"If nothing else, we've got to get you to a doctor," Mariah muttered grimly.

"But—"

"You'll go to my house," she decided. "He'd never be caught dead going in there because of my *Meidung*. When the kids come to school—he'll have to let them attend because you know how the deacons get about that—I'll bring them home with me after class."

"Yes." Katya's voice was breathy, terrified. But Frank *would* have to let the children go to school. The government watched the Amish education system closely, just waiting for them to make a mistake. The settlement's agreement stipulated that if the youngsters missed school to work in the fields, then the community would lose the right to educate them themselves. The deacons got upset when children skipped for anything other than genuine illness.

If Frank kept them all home today, then the deacons would certainly know why, and he wouldn't invite their inspection of his life. And yet...

"This is worse than what you did!" Katya blurted.

Mariah shot her a quick look as she worked their ladder to the ground. "Yes."

"The church won't let me leave him!" She was overwhelmed with committing a sin of such magnitude. The ban against divorce and separation was so carved in granite it wasn't even mentioned in the *Ordnung*. It went without saying.

"And if you stay, you'll die. Or worse, your children will," Mariah bit out ruthlessly. "He hit Rachel, didn't he?"

"Yes," Katya whispered miserably.

"Oh, Katya, I *told* you! I told you it was just going to get worse and worse, the longer it went on without him getting caught!"

"He wasn't even drunk last night," Katya said helplessly. "He just...went off. It only ever happened before when he was drinking, but last night he just snapped. But what can I do about it?" she wailed.

"You can stay with me. I have some money saved. I can support us for a while."

"They'll shun me! I don't think I can...I couldn't bear living the way they've made you live." She began weeping.

"You won't have to, Katya," Mariah said quietly. "You'll have me. I've had no one." There was a particularly terrifying cracking sound as the door began to give. "We've got to go now," she warned in an undertone. "The wood is going to crack."

Katya took a deep breath. "Okay. Let's do it." She looked down at herself, at her nightgown, then up at Mariah again. "Oh, gosh. I've got to change first!"

"No." Mariah managed to crack a smile. "Look at it this way—no sane woman would run from her house in her nightgown unless she left some unspeakable horror behind. Even if the deacons won't believe you about Frank, the *Gemeide* women will have to after you do this."

Katya managed a trembling smile of her own. She scrubbed her hands over her cheeks. She peered out at the ground through the open window. It looked like an awfully long way to the ground.

"Geronimo," she said weakly.

Chapter 21

"Your first tactical error was the two-week bit." Jake took a bottle of beer from the refrigerator, popped the top and aimed it for the trash can with a quick overhand flick of his wrist. Then he pulled a chair out from the kitchen table, turned it around and straddled it backward.

Adam didn't answer. He continued to glare at the kitchen table as if it somehow offended him.

Actually, it did. He'd opened the Dallas house, but while some of the furniture had still been in place, he'd sold and given away a lot of pieces over the years. So he'd bought a new kitchen table and a few other assorted pieces, but the table was the pièce de résistance. It was a big, slamming butcher-block thing with faux marble inserts on the top. The salesman had said it would seat fourteen easily. Adam knew that so many people would never sit at it, not in this lifetime, but he'd hoped it would at least *look* right to Bo, like the kind of table he was used to.

Another tactical error, he thought grimly. They'd felt small and lost sitting there, like specks in a vacuum. They'd both been overwhelmed by the empty enormity of the thing, even on the many occasions when Jake had joined them for meals.

"I mean, I've caught him forgetting to act mad and grumpy

more than once these last couple days,'' Jake went on. ''If you
only had a couple more weeks—''

''Yeah, well, I don't,'' Adam snapped. Tomorrow was Tues-
day. The two weeks were up. And though he hadn't actually
asked Bo yet, he knew as well as he knew his own name that his
son didn't want to hang around in Texas any longer.

Their time here hadn't been all bad. Jake was right—sometimes, especially in the past week, some boyish wonder at this
surprise or that burst through Bo's gloom. Sometimes he relaxed.
The first couple of nights he'd had nightmares, but Adam had
figured out easily enough that he was just scared sleeping in his
big double bed all by himself, so he'd brought him into his own
room.

Things were coming along. It was happening slowly and pains-
takingly, but it was happening. With another couple of weeks at
his disposal, Adam might even have been able to shake Bo loose
from some of the tentacles of that settlement.

''They're like some kind of *cult!*'' he exploded suddenly, angrily.

Jake shrugged one shoulder. ''They *are* a cult, bro, in the purest
sense of the word. Hell, they were a 'cult' before anyone else
ever heard of one, before the things started getting nasty and
twisted connotations.''

''They tell kids they have a choice,'' Adam ranted on, ''but
do they? They don't make them get baptized or whatever until
they're ready to get married, but by that point they don't *know*
anything else! They say they wait until the kids are old enough
to make an educated decision about committing themselves, but
they can't make an educated decision if they don't know what
the hell else is out there, if they've been brainwashed from the
cradle to believe it's all wicked and evil! Jake, that boy won't
even watch TV!''

''Yeah, actually he did,'' Jake answered mildly. ''I caught him
at it yesterday when you were at the office. Those superhero
dudes. His jaw was hanging open enough that I could have driven
my car through it.''

''And I bet as soon as you went in the room, he snapped it off,
right?''

Jake swigged from his beer. ''Yeah, sure. But, hey, at least he
turned it on in the first place.''

Adam got up to get his own bottle. ''God forbid he should turn
on the Nintendo. He used to *love* that thing, remember? He could

do that helicopter game when he was two, like some kind of genius. Up, down, pick up fuel, blow the hell out of the bad guy.''

"Yeah," Jake said. "I remember. I bought him that one."

"Now he won't even look at it. He won't let me cut his hair and he looks like a scarecrow."

"Hey," Jake said. "Watch it there." His own dark locks went a fair bit beyond his collar.

"Yours is long because you like it that way. Or because you're too lazy to get it cut. I never could figure out which."

"A little of both," Jake admitted, drinking again. "Anyway, that ain't no crew cut you're sporting there, bro."

"The point is," Adam growled, "he's clinging to that hair for all the wrong reasons."

"Wrong to you," Jake pointed out.

"Wrong to *Dallas!* Wrong to the United damned States of America!"

"Chill out. You're going to wake him up."

But Adam was on a roll. For the first time in two weeks, he was venting. And damn it, it felt good. Up until now, this very moment, everything had been tangled inside, like some fishing wire they'd found wrapped around a duck once when they were kids.

Sometimes he couldn't even breathe for the tightness of it. Sometimes thoughts and memories snapped in his head like rubber bands. *Mariah. Lizzie Stoltzfus. Sugar Joe Lapp. Can't eat out in a restaurant because it disrupts family.* And then always, always, Mariah again.

"And that's another thing," he ranted on, pulling his mind off her again. "When we went to McDonald's, I thought he was going to have a nervous breakdown."

"He probably was," Jake answered. "But I got him to go outside onto that sliding board, didn't I?"

They hell of it was, Adam thought, the *mind-boggling* part of it was, that Jake was dealing with this mess better than he was. Jake...who had once fed Bo cheese when he was baby-sitting him, hoping to constipate him so he wouldn't have to change a diaper.

But Jake wasn't quite as personally involved. Jake wasn't wrapped up with fishing wire.

"So what are you going to do?" Jake asked.

Adam sat again, the air going out of him. "I don't know."

"Well, you better come up with something before about six o'clock tomorrow morning, 'cause I can almost guarantee you that that's going to be the first question out of his mouth when he wakes up. *Are we going home today?*''

Adam stiffened. "*This* is home."

Jake grunted noncommittally.

"I don't know what to do," Adam said yet again.

"Shouldn't be too hard. You've only got two choices. Take him yourself, or wait until I get back next Friday. Then, I'll take him." Jake was heading out to Virginia on a morning flight. Periodically—every six months to a year—he went back to the FBI academy at Quantico for continuing-education courses. Like the first time he had enrolled there, sixteen years ago after college, nothing would come of it. They'd offer him a position. Jake Wallace would say thanks but no thanks, and he would come back to working long hours for relatively lousy pay with the Dallas PD.

Never *ever* get too caught up in anything that makes you too happy, Adam thought bitterly. That was Jake's motto. And maybe it was sane.

"I promised him tomorrow," Adam muttered.

"Yours won't be the first promise broken, bro."

"There's a point." But it wasn't comforting. In fact, it made his gut roll with something thick and cold.

"You know, at the risk of having my head taken off, I fail to see what the big deal is here," Jake went on. "Go back. Hang around a week. Start all over again and this time talk him into staying here for a month."

The big deal is Mariah Fisher. Adam didn't say it, because this time he was grappling with his own fair bit of guilt. He just didn't want to get into that whole mess with Jake. Mostly because she was the biggest cause of the fishing wire, but also because he'd told his brother only that she had had that milk carton for five weeks. He had *not* filled him in on the other missing children. Not Jake the bloodhound. It would be like waving a red flag in front of a bull. Next thing Adam knew, the three of them would be back in the settlement while Jake grilled everyone and everything on two feet and four.

No, he thought, Jake would never be able to leave such an intriguing mystery alone. His brother's caution and restricting mottoes didn't extend to investigations. Jake could always throw himself freely and completely into them, because investigations had resolutions one way or the other. They ended. And then Jake moved happily on.

So he hadn't told Jake, but he *had* called NCMEC, not entirely willing to trust Mariah to do it. They'd promised to send someone up there to nose around. He'd called a cop he knew in Philly, too, to tip off the law. Even if the guy wasn't in the right jurisdiction, Adam figured he might know someone who was.

The fishing wire pulled tighter. His mind went back to Mariah. *Would* she do it? Would she have called anyone herself by now? As of last Wednesday, NCMEC hadn't heard from her.

The woman he'd thought he knew would have made the call, he thought. The woman he'd thought he knew had been brave, gutsy, stubborn, even while she had been soft. But what about the woman who had deceived him?

"I'd rather steep myself in boiling water than go back there," he ground out, surprising himself by speaking aloud.

Jake raised a brow. "Do tell."

"There's nothing to say."

"Apparently not even her name."

Adam got up and leaned across the table at him menacingly. "What's your point, Jake?"

"Don't have one, bro." He got up to toss his bottle in the trash. "Just seems odd to me that for a man who was stuck to her like glue for several weeks, now you can't even say her name without changing color and choking."

"I told you why."

Jake put on a mock expression of horror. "*Five* weeks! Unforgivable! Man, she's *human.* Calling you about your kid was going to bring the wrath of her God down on her head, right?"

"Back off," Adam snarled. "You don't have a clue what you're talking about, not to mention the fact that it's none of your business."

"When has that ever stopped me? Seems to me you ought to take Bo back up there tomorrow and get down on your knees and kiss her feet."

Adam's eyes narrowed. He didn't want to hear why. "Why?"

"Because she gave you just the excuse you needed, right? Where would you be without those missing five weeks, bro? I'll tell you where, much as I hate to say it. You'd be in Divinity, P-A. You would have been tempted to hang around."

His heart was banging hard. "When did you become a shrink?"

Jake shrugged. "I've learned a few things with my studying over the years."

"Yeah, well, I don't want to be psychoanalyzed."

"Can't help it. You're too easy. Too transparent."

Adam grabbed his shirt front again. Jake looked down at his brother's fist slowly. "We've been here before," he muttered. "And it's getting old. *We're* too old."

"I'll never be too old to enjoy feeling your face flatten when you're obnoxious."

"Or when I'm saying something you're afraid to hear."

Adam's fist tightened. "Don't talk to me about fear. You're as screwed up as they come."

"Sure I am. And I admit it. You, on the other hand, have to hide behind excuses."

"You wanted me to come home. Now you want to send me *back* there?"

"No. I want you to be honest with yourself."

"Me? *Me? I'm* honest! Every word I spoke to her was the truth! She *lied* to me, Jake. She pretended to be something she wasn't. And damn it, I can't take that again. I could live with a lot, but not that. God, not another impostor."

Jake clamped a hand on his brother's wrist and pulled it from his shirt. It was difficult. His brother's muscles were locked in place by rage.

"Let's be honest here," Jake said evenly. "What you can't live with is the same thing I can't live with—believing. Trusting in things that are too good. So either let go of hope and be done with it—it has its merits—or take a stab at grabbing it. But don't make everybody miserable by straddling the fence and complaining about how other people don't play fair."

"I'm not inflicting this on anybody else."

"The hell you're not. There's that little boy upstairs, not to mention what you've done to my own delicate psyche. Now if you'll excuse me, I'm expected at the Roadhouse by a good-looking blonde who would like to wish me a safe trip tomorrow." He reached for the back door with its big brass knob and wiggled his brows. "My favorite flavor."

Adam sat down again slowly when he was gone, just staring at the door.

Mariah had gone outside to sweep the latest snow off the porch. Katya had volunteered to do it, but she was on crutches, her fractured ankle in a cast. Now she was just as glad she hadn't been able to manage it, because something had happened out there. Mariah came bolting inside, then she stood pressed against the glass, watching out the window.

"What is it?" Katya cried. "What's wrong?"

"I don't...I'm not sure," Mariah answered, frowning.

She had just been finishing up, when the first of the buggies had turned onto her street. Fear had been her immediate reaction, a drenching, numbing coldness. Not for herself, but for Katya. It had been a little over a week since they had run from Frank. That first Sunday had been *Gelassenheit,* but the deacons had not chosen that service to publicly and officially shun her. She'd only been gone from home a few days at that point. Mariah knew from her own experience that the deacons used every advantage they possessed to pressure people back into the fold. They gave a little...like a school to teach. And then they waited.

They were waiting for Katya now. They thought she would come to her senses, get tired of being an outcast even before it became official, and return to her husband. Her brief days of insanity would never be spoken of again, at least not by the deacons. But Frank would never let her forget them. She had fled with the understanding that she *couldn't* go back. Frank would kill her for the shame she'd dragged him through. He'd spent the past week and a half lamenting his loss at every opportunity, crying to anyone who would listen about how wronged he'd been.

No one but the deacons seemed to believe him. But, then, no one but the deacons had to.

Katya came to look out the window, as well, then she saw the buggies and gasped. "They're coming for me!" she cried. "Oh, no! *No!*"

She turned blindly, frantically, away from the window. Rachel, her oldest daughter, caught her arm and clung helplessly, starting to cry.

"I can't go back there," Rachel wailed. "Please, Ma, *do* something!"

"Wait," Mariah interrupted. "Just...wait. Let me think."

She pressed her fingers to her temples. *Think,* she repeated silently. Easier said than done. Her life had been one explosion of rebellion after another these past two weeks, and it had left her reeling. First she'd helped Katya escape, then she'd called the FBI about the children. *The FBI!* Even now she could scarcely believe she'd done that, but when she'd called that missing children's place that Adam had mentioned, she'd been passed from one extension to another until her change had run out and the pay phone had disconnected. Rather than try that again, she'd taken another avenue.

Then, to top it all off, she had sneaked into church services the previous Sunday to hear what the deacons might say or do about Katya. Mariah was an old hand at living with the church's slow, grinding decision making. But unlike Katya, she had not been battered and beaten into submission for ten years. Katya simply could not bear such uncertainty right now. So...Mariah had crept into her uncle's home, where the most recent services had been held, and she had just listened.

"No," she said finally. "They wouldn't come here to drag you back. Not the whole community. And the deacons wouldn't do something that radical. They haven't even put the *Meidung* on you yet."

"But *look!*" Katya cried.

Mariah peered out the window again and her jaw dropped. There were close to fifty buggies on the narrow street now, crowded in every which way, horses whinnying and nudging each other. Men climbed out and stood congregating, waiting, and many women were present, too.

That made her even more certain. "No," she said again. "For heaven's sake, there's Sarah Lapp. She'd never want you to go back. And there's your sister! She knows what you've been going through, too. Besides, it would be against the *Ordnung* to force you into anything. No, Katya, I can't believe that they'd drag you back to Frank against your will. It's got to be something else."

A *hundred* buggies now, she thought dazedly. And then she knew.

"It's the children," she breathed. "It *must* be the children." It was the only issue she could think of that could make so many people feel so strongly.

"The children? *My* children? I knew I shouldn't have let Levi play hockey! They'll take him right from the ice!"

"No, no! It's the *missing* children. Joe did it! Sugar Joe did it!"

Before Katya could answer, Mariah grabbed her shawl again and shot out the door. They could see her or look away. She didn't care. But she would hear what was said, no matter who tried to chase her away.

"Mariah, wait!" Katya cried. When her friend didn't even hesitate, she turned back to her daughter. "Get our coats! I'll get

Delilah and Sam." Her youngest children were around some-place. "Hurry!"

"But what if Pa—"

Katya put a comforting hand to the crown of her daughter's head, stroking her hair despite the fact that her hand shook. "When have you ever known your father to involve himself in a worthwhile cause?"

"Whenever he thinks it'll make him look good."

Her answer hurt Katya down to her very soul. She hugged her daughter close. "Which is why he won't hurt us in front of every-one, even if he does come here. But you do what you feel best with."

Rachel hesitated. Her own bruise was only now fading. "I'll stay here, Ma, with the little ones. Please, *please* be careful. Maybe this is all a trick. Maybe—"

"No," Katya interrupted, her chin coming up. "This is Sugar Joe's doing, bless his heart. And Miss Fisher started it. I want to be there to see it end."

And with that, she went outside, facing the community, shut-ting the door smartly behind her. And though it took everything she had, when everyone turned to look at her, she kept her chin just where it was.

Chapter 22

The *Grossdawdy* house next door was, by definition, very small. The Amish did not send their old and infirm to nursing homes for strangers to care for. Neither did they rob them of their dignity. Their offspring simply took over their homes and their farms with all the grueling work and chores both entailed, then they built their parents new homes of their own. They were either attached to the original dwelling or a stone's throw away on the same property. The grandparents took meals with the family and contributed whatever minor work they were able.

Ethan Miller's home was a little larger than most. In addition to the usual living room and kitchen, bedroom and bath, there was a large keeping room built onto the back. He was a deacon, after all, and while services were held in the big farmhouse his daughter and her husband now lived in, Ethan played host to other church elders and gatherings from time to time.

Mariah thought that not once in his eighty-six years had Ethan ever greeted a crowd such as this.

She saw confusion in his pale eyes, and even though he had hurt her with his decisions over the years, she felt a pang of pity for him. His beard was long, frizzy and gray, and he stroked it repeatedly and nervously as he watched more and more people stream into his living room. They all nodded at him respectfully as they trooped into the keeping room. After a while, even that area couldn't hold them anymore.

No one had the choice of giving Mariah a wide berth. She was pressed back against the kitchen wall by a crush of bodies, just barely able to see the proceedings in the other room. After a moment, Katya squeezed through the crowd and joined her.

"Did I miss anything?" she whispered.

Mariah shook her head. "Not yet."

Sugar Joe and Nathaniel Lapp were still outside, greeting people, thanking them for coming. Just as the conversation of the crowd began rising impatiently with the wait, just as the heat of so many bodies became claustrophobic, Mariah heard a disturbance by the front door. She stood on tiptoe to see Sugar Joe come inside.

She didn't know where Nathaniel had gotten to, but Sarah held onto Joe's arm now with two white-knuckled hands. Her face was bleached white, but she managed to nod to friends and relatives as she passed them, even if her smile was thin.

They stopped at the front of the keeping room. A lot of the benches for Sunday services were kept here—to be loaded into a wagon and taken to whatever farm was hosting the *Gemeesunndaag* this Sunday. Someone had pulled them away from the walls and had unstacked them, but no one sat. People stood up on them instead, so they could see over the heads of the rest of the crowd.

The church fathers waited at the front—three deacons, the minister who conducted the *Gemeesunndaag* every other Sunday and Abner Fisher, the bishop. His extra-long gray hair swept his shoulders.

Mariah's throat closed painfully, as it always did on the few occasions she ran into him anymore. She doubted if he even realized she was here. He would certainly never expect it, and he seemed far too preoccupied with this alarming turn of events to glance around and take stock of who had come.

Joe and Sarah Lapp reached the men. Sarah stepped aside and Sugar Joe cleared his throat and jumped in, never one to mince words.

"There was a stranger here this week. An *anner Satt Leit* in a suit, with a briefcase. He came to my home. Perhaps you noticed him."

"It was a matter of curiosity," Ethan Miller acknowledged, "but we have no problem with opening our homes to visitors. That's permitted."

"He was from the FBI," Joe said flatly. "He came to look for the missing children. And I intend to help him."

Mariah shivered as silence crashed down among the deacons and elders. The people seemed to hold their breath in waiting. Then the quiet exploded as they all shouted that they intended to help, as well.

Sugar Joe held up a hand to quiet them. "I know it's against the *Ordnung* as this *Gemeide* perceives it. I know you honestly believe that God took those children away from us for some higher purpose. But I can't for the life of me imagine what that purpose might be. What I fear so deeply that I can barely sleep at night is that some madman did it. Some spawn of the devil. And I have to fight that."

"You dare speak of the devil in this house?" Abner Fisher roared.

"Yes."

"Even knowing the punishment, you'd go against our wishes on this?" Ethan demanded.

One corner of Sugar Joe's mouth crooked upward. "With all due respect, brother, if you implement it, you won't have a congregation left."

Mariah gasped. Voices rose again, but this time it was only those of the church elders.

"Are you threatening us?" one of the other deacons asked finally. His voice was reasonably calm under the circumstances. It was Paul Gehler, Sarah Lapp's father.

"Yes," Joe agreed again. "I imagine we are. And I say we, because everyone in this room is of one mind on this. It must be done. But I confess I instigated the movement. And I'll also tell you that I haven't done it without regret—regret because it's even necessary.

"I believe in our way. I believe it's a good way, and I hold strongly to all our *Ordnung*'s principles, however strict they are in this *Gemeide*. But we are one small island. An almost minuscule island. And the world out there is not always a good and kind place."

"It's not our world," Abner Fisher said caustically. "It's not our concern."

"Well, it affects us. It surrounds us. And now, lately, it's begun to infiltrate us. We can't ignore it. It won't go away."

"What are you telling me? That we should become *like* them?" Abener shouted angrily. "Of all the blasphemous—"

"No," Joe said sharply, cutting him off. "I'm saying that if we don't resist in this, if we don't fight back when it touches us, that outside world could very well destroy us. It's literally tearing our families apart."

"Resistance isn't—" Ethan began.

"It's not our way," Sugar Joe interrupted him as well. "But it's been done. Centuries ago, when our adversaries imprisoned us and tortured us for our differences, we resisted."

"No!" Abner bellowed, sensing a soapbox for his favorite topic. "We died at their hands to prove our faith!"

"We migrated," Joe said flatly. "The only ones who were killed were those slow enough to be caught, and I daresay they wished they'd been faster."

Someone chuckled nervously. Mariah caught her breath.

"We left Germany, Switzerland, and came to America for the right to worship as we chose," Joe went on. "And once we got here, we adapted. Because change in itself is not our enemy. Change in itself is not a sin. This is the strictest *Gemeide* in the county, maybe even in the country, but even we've adapted and you've allowed it. You—" he motioned at old Ethan "—you've been a deacon for forty-five years now. In that time you voted to allow this congregation to ride in automobiles in the event of emergency or to visit kin in other states. That's adapting. You've voted to allow us to go into the villages and put quarters into a pay phone, when the situation warrants it. That's adapting. It's small scale compared to some of the New Order *Gemeides,* but that's okay. We're all here because, for the most part, we agree with it. But we won't be governed by fear or threat. You've made mothers forsake their children, for the sake of your *Ordnung!*" His voice rose. "And that's not compassionate. That's not kind. That's not family and it's not our way!"

A shout went up. Then another. They were strong, joyous sounds. Mariah felt her eyes burn. They were finally *doing* something.

"With all due respect," Sugar Joe said again, "this church has become so preoccupied with sticking to the rules that you've forgotten everything else. You've forgotten the underlying reasons for the rules, and made them so lofty none of us can possibly adhere to them perfectly. Certainly not this time and not on this issue. Rules are not the point. Obedience is not the purpose. Our families are."

This time applause went up. Joe's voice finally softened.

"Whether you like it or not, whether you *approve* and want to recognize it or not, someone is stealing our children. Our own men are using brutal force against their wives and sons and daughters. Ignoring it won't make it go away. No matter how much you worship your *Ordnung,* it's going to keep happening until you can find the flexibility in your hearts to save our children, to protect our women. And our children and women are the reason most of us follow this path." He finally turned away.

"Wait," one of the deacons said. Sugar Joe looked back. It was his father-in-law. "We'll discuss this among ourselves and give you our decision when the *Ordnung* is read at the next services," Paul Gehler went on.

"I'm sorry," Joe said quietly, "but your opinion is irrelevant. We will do this. If you wait until next services, no one will be there. By then we'll have a *Gemeide* and services of our own."

Adam and Bo reached the front door of the *Grossdawdy* house just as Sugar Joe began speaking. It wasn't until the man was well underway that Adam's heart stopped racing and his palms stopped sweating.

He found her in the crowd.

For the first time in two weeks, he breathed. The fishing wire seemed to melt. An invisible weight lifted off his chest. *She was alive.*

He didn't know what he'd honestly expected, but when he'd driven down Ronks Road, past her street, and saw buggy after buggy turning in here, he'd panicked. No, he thought, panic was too weak a word. Every emotion he'd ever possessed had crashed in on him. He'd thought something had happened to her. Or, inanely, that she'd finally repented, maybe had agreed to marry that Asher character after all, despite all these years.

He had to stop it. She was his.

He'd left his rental car on the main road; the buggies had left no room for anything but pedestrian traffic. He'd abandoned it, jogging down the street, dragging a confused and curious Bo by the hand. And then, finally, he'd understood that it wasn't Mariah's house that all the people were going to. It was that grandfather's house next door, the one with the denuded flower box.

No one paid him much attention when he'd pushed his way inside. And then, listening to Joe talk, he'd understood why.

"Damn, I like that man," he muttered under his breath. "Ouch," he snapped as a small elbow dug into his thigh.

"That's a bad word," Bo said.

"Sorry."

"That's all right. You're doing better."

Oh, yeah, he thought. He was. He'd kept his promise. He'd brought Bo back here. And that was when things had started going right.

He'd struggled with himself for hours the previous night, after Jake had left. But in the end there was really no choice to make. Jake couldn't bring Bo to the settlement, not today, not at the time Adam had promised, so he had to do it. And this decision, this visit, was only one single stumbling block in their future, after all. He wasn't going to let Bo go. He was his son, his child, his everything. So one way or another they would work through this culture shock, and they would go on together for a long, long time.

Adam could not allow that long time to begin with a broken promise.

On the flight east, he had determined a million ways to handle the situation once he got here. They could go straight to the Lappses and confine their visit to Matt and the family. Or they could stay at the motel, spend most of their time together, with only occasional trips to the farm to ease the bandage off gently. He could see Mariah, or he could stay away from her.

A million scenarios, and all the choices were his own. Until he saw the buggies streaming into her street. Until he heard Sugar Joe talk.

The man finally finished and started to head back for the door. Both his brows shot up when he saw Adam and Bo. Under different circumstances, Adam knew he would have smiled. As it was, he confined himself to a nod.

"Wait," Adam heard himself say.

Joe stopped cold. One of the deacons had started to sit, then he shot to his feet again.

"Who are you?" the man demanded.

"He's my old pa," Bo told him, hugging Bear for all he was worth. "Sugar Joe was just my latest one."

"I beg your pardon?" He was a tall guy with very long hair. Something about that hair gave Adam pause.

"It doesn't matter," he answered, recovering. "I've got something to say, too."

"This I've got to hear," Joe muttered in an undertone, coming to stand beside him.

Mariah was close to fainting. She felt Katya brace her weight from behind. It was a godsend. Her blood was rushing, *swooshing,* and a laugh bubbled up in her throat even as tears tried to crowd there. "Adam?" she managed. *"Adam."* And Bo.

They had returned.

She watched him step a little deeper into the throng.

"I guess technically I don't have a place here," he went on, "and I sure don't have a voice in all this. For all I know, you don't even see me, either. Maybe there's some rule to that effect because I'm *anner Satt Leit.*"

"There's not," Bo informed him.

"Well, good. Because given the fact that you guys have tied my life up in knots for weeks now, I think we need to straighten a few things out here."

Belatedly, he was aware of the silence in the room. It had weight. He became aware of the stares, some wide-eyed, some openmouthed. But more than anything he was aware of Bo's delighted grin and the transparent love in Mariah Fisher's eyes. He looked at her and his heart stumbled and hurt. But this time it hurt with wanting.

"Anyway," he began again, then he had to pause to clear his throat. "What happened here is that I fell in love with that lady over there. And what *she* loves is all of you. And your children. I know you don't see her, but I also know that she's kept to all the rules of your *Ordnung* anyway. Because she believes in them. And she *knows* she believes in them because she left here, and whatever she found out there wasn't enough to sustain her, so she came back. And even though she doesn't really have to, she cooks on a wood stove and runs her refrigerator with a...with a..."

"Hydraulic motor," she whispered, but in the silence it was heard.

"Yeah." His eyes met hers again, held for a moment, and what she saw there nearly made her sway.

He loved her. He did! They hadn't been just words.

"I didn't think I could have her," Adam went on. "I thought I had to leave her, thought I had to drag my son away from this world he's known, a world he wants and he's thrived on, because in all honesty, a couple of your rules uh...need some work." His eyes moved to Joe. "It's not like what you told me. I can't just disagree down here—" he thumped his chest "—and live with it because I love her. The things I disagree with are just too big. And they hurt her.

"I have a real hard time trusting happiness," he explained, to the crowd and the deacons this time. "Maybe it's my upbringing. It wasn't quite as good as what all you folks have enjoyed. But I can tell you this—I've found happiness here. I found it, and it's been held just out of my reach by you deacons. I couldn't trust it because what you're doing to that woman is just proof that goodness can be twisted. How can I believe in a faith that destroys a woman's life for a single mistake? How can I trust that?"

"She could repent," the long-haired deacon said stonily. "It's her own choice, not ours."

Adam ignored him. He found her eyes again and this time he spoke only to her. "I tried to tell myself I couldn't trust you. But that's not it. It's God I can't quite trust. Maybe I can learn. Maybe you can teach me. Maybe enough years with you and Bo and...and just goodness can prove me wrong. I'm willing to give it a shot. But my vote goes with Sugar Joe. I'll never trust a God who would advocate children being abandoned to some unknown fate. And I won't trust one who looks the other way while a man beats up on a woman he's professed to love. And I sure as hell— *ouch!*" He glanced down at Bo. "Sorry. I sure as heck can't trust one who thinks its a good and righteous thing to destroy a woman's life because she...goofed."

He pinned the deacons—especially the one with the long gray hair—with a steel-blue gaze. "Correct me if I'm wrong, but the way I understand it is that if she had gone to college and come home to be baptized, then everything would have been hunky-dory with you guys. But because she rebelled a month or so too late, you'd prefer to love your rules more than you love her. Nope, I can't live with that. And I'll tell you something else. If my kid rebels, I'll even pray to your God that he does it by getting an education, because Sugar Joe is right. It's a big, bad, nasty place out there, and there are a whole lot of things he could do that are worse, that could break my heart."

The people stared. Mariah pressed a trembling hand to her mouth. Katya was the first to laugh a little breathlessly, then someone else joined in. And Adam wondered if he had ever said so many words at one time in his life.

"Uh...I'm done," he finished, embarrassed.

"Good." Sugar Joe clapped a hand on his shoulder. "I'm hungry. Let's go home."

Adam nodded, but waited. He looked at the far wall again, but she was gone now. His heart stopped. He wondered if she hated him for what he'd said, if he'd broken some horrible taboo, if he'd lost her after all.

Then the crowd parted. Mariah pushed her way through. For a moment he thought of angels again, of women who could float, because her feet barely seemed to touch the floor. She hurled herself at him and he caught her, and she was real and warm, all the good things he'd thought he'd never find.

"Yeah," he said quietly, against her hair. "Let's go home. Wherever that is."

They went back to Sugar Joe's farm, because his house was the largest. In Adam's absence, the adopted family seemed to have grown.

He recognized the woman Joe had been talking about in the meeting—Katya Essler. She was the same one who had directed him to Mariah's schoolhouse at the start, the one with hair that looked the color of buckwheat caught in the sun. The one who's husband had bellowed at her the whole while to come back inside.

Adam urged her and her ankle cast into his car. "Medical emergency," he explained, but it was hard to look at her, hard to keep his eyes off Mariah. "You'd probably have a hell—*don't do it!*" He broke off and looked down at his son. "You'd probably have the dickens of a time trying to get into Joe's buggy."

He realized then that it wouldn't matter if he *could* have taken his eyes off Mariah. A quick glance told him that Katya Essler wouldn't have met his gaze anyway. Her eyes were haunted and skittish with panic, and Adam thought with a pang that this woman had a long way to go to freedom.

Bo yelped when they reached the farm. He tumbled out of the car with another shriek when he saw Matt. He started to run to meet him, then he skidded to a stop and hurried back to the car.

"What?" Adam asked, concerned, getting out as well. "Is something wrong?"

"Don't curse."

"I didn't," he answered, indignant. "I've got enough bruises."

"Promise?" Bo searched his face. "Promise you won't?"

"Okay." Adam's heart rolled over, because he felt something important happening here.

"I just need to make sure, because Bear don't like it, either."

"Doesn't," Mariah corrected, getting out of the car to join them. "Bear *doesn't* like it."

Bo's gaze flashed to her. *"Shh!"*

"Oh," Mariah murmured, confused. "Sorry."

Bo's eyes came back to Adam. He thrust the bear at him and shot a quick look back over his shoulder to gauge Matt's approach. "So anyway, if you don't say bad words, maybe he could sort of hang out with you for a while," he whispered. "Don't let Matt see him. He teases me."

Adam took the bear and wondered if he was ever going to feel calm inside ever again. Then Matt tackled Bo from behind.

It seemed a lifetime, or maybe only a heartbeat, until the boys raced away. Katya limped off toward the house, a harrowing journey with all the new snow that had fallen. Mariah and Adam were finally alone. There were a million things he had to say, but he didn't know where to begin.

"It's a start," she said quietly, touching a finger to the bear's nose. "He's beginning to trust you with the precious things in his life."

"Yeah," Adam said hoarsely.

"But it's going to take a while, I think." She finally looked up into his eyes. God, he thought, hers were lovely.

"Yeah," he managed again. "He lived with the Lapps longer than he lived with me. And they got all his years with a memory." But it was said without rancor, without bitterness now. "We'll work it out."

"How? Where?" she blurted. Oh, there was so much she needed to know. "Did he like Dallas?"

"Which part?" Adam grimaced. "I think he's decided that moving sidewalks aren't going to be a part of his own personal *Ordnung* taboos. Other than that, going downtown threw him for a loop."

She smiled a little. "I'm sure."

"Listen." He changed course abruptly. "I'm sorry about everything I said."

Her eyes got warm. She blinked. "It was...wonderful."

"No, I mean...before. The night before I left."

Her eyes slid away. "It was justified."

"No. It wasn't." He thought of what Jake had said, and somehow he got the words out. He said them himself. "I was just latching on to an excuse to leave, rather than risk too much by staying. Now I've changed my mind."

Her heart stumbled. "For Bo? You're going to stay *here?* For Bo?"

"And for me. Marry me."

Mariah wondered if she was dreaming, but finally, this time, everything felt clear, focused, real again.

He caught her chin with his hand. "I wasn't just grandstanding back there for the cause. I meant it. I love you."

"Oh." For a moment it was all she could manage. She caught the front of his shirt and held on. "Yes! Yes, I love you, too." Her heart seemed to explode.

He hadn't known relief could be this sweet. It wasn't even the same as the night they had found Bo in the woods. That had been staggering. This was almost...debilitating. "But this business about waiting until November—"

Her own smile faded. "Oh, Adam, they'd never marry us."

"The deacons again?"

She nodded helplessly. "You're divorced and not even baptized, and I'm—"

"That's okay," he interrupted. "I won't wait for their blessing, anyway. Bo needs a home. I need a home. And we both need a family."

Her fingers tightened in his shirt. He was offering her the world. "Yes," she whispered.

"So we'll make one together."

"A big one," she breathed.

He grinned again. "I guess so, given that you folks don't believe in birth control."

"No, I meant...instantly. Katya and her children are staying with me. Frank was... abusing her. He's a drunkard. I promised she could stay with me until she can resolve this somehow, but I don't know how long it will be until they can get on their feet."

"Katya and her children," he said slowly. He remembered that most families had up to ten kids. "Uh, how many children? Exactly?"

"Four."

He breathed again. He could live with that. And he certainly had the kitchen table for the job.

"We'll get married now," he went on, "by a justice of the peace, and again later, with the church's blessing. If we can ever get the church's blessing. There seem to be a lot of changes afoot."

She was reduced to nodding. Then he kissed her. She sank into him, although she felt truly strong and whole and good for maybe the first time in her life.

"Hey, you're supposed to wait until after dark for that stuff," Sugar Joe called out from the house.

"Can I tell him to go to hell?" Adam murmured against her mouth.

"The bear would mutiny."

He groaned and stepped away from her.

They started to go inside.

Halfway to the door, she giggled suddenly. Adam looked down at her. "What?" he said curiously.

"I was thinking about that quilt."

He laughed, too, remembering her warning, one that had sounded so dire only a short time ago. So much had changed. "Powerful stuff there."

"Who do you suppose we should pass it on to?"

"Do we have to? Pass it on, I mean?"

She smiled. "Its job is done with us."

He grinned. "We could send it to Dallas, to my brother. Does it work outside the settlement?"

She thought about it seriously. "I don't know. It's never been tried."

Adam sobered, too. "Maybe it's done enough for one year. Maybe we should just tuck it away and keep it safe for awhile."

"Katya," she decided. "Or her babies. She's already married—" her beautiful face turned pained at that "—and her children are far, far too young to wed. That's perfect, Adam. It can provide them warmth and comfort while they stay with us. But—"

"But it can't do its thing," he interrupted.

"Exactly."

He stopped her before they stepped inside and kissed her again. "I do believe that was our first decision as man and wife."

Mariah laughed. "Close enough, I think."

Sarah was bustling around the kitchen. Katya was trying to help, but her cast slowed her down. Mariah pushed her friend into a chair and offered her a bowl of bread dough to knead. Joe caught Adam at the door.

"So," he prompted. "You're staying?"

"Yeah, if you'll stop sticking your nose out the door when it's least appreciated. And I don't want any nicknames."

Joe laughed. "I think you're safe from that. You must be the only.Wallace within a hundred-mile radius, so there's no need for one. What exactly are you going to do?''

"Do?"

"Sarah says she can't see you pushing a plow."

"Oh. That. Hel-ck if I know.'' He glanced down at the bear. "You were right, though. I'll do whatever I have to to be with her, to keep her happy.'' He rubbed his forehead, and finally said the words, something he'd started to realize a long time ago. "I've got ChildSearch, but it doesn't need me. It was designed to find my boy. I don't have an investigative bone in my body. Lately it's been as much my brother's baby as my own.''

"You'll fold it?"

"No.'' That was easy. "Too many people need it. I'll let Jake run it, if I can talk him into it. He might even get it to turn a profit—he's not a bleeding heart. In the meantime, I've got some money left. We won't starve. Not in the immediate future. We've got time.''

Joe nodded, watching the women.

"What's going to happen?'' Adam asked suddenly. "With what went on today, I mean?''

"The truth?'' Joe shrugged, but his eyes were shadowed. "Abner Fisher won't change. He'll go to his grave preaching the *Ordnung* in its strictest, most restrictive and suffocating sense. And Ethan Miller won't, either.''

Adam swore, and the bear be damned. "That long-haired guy was her father, then.''

"Yes. The bishop. The holiest of the holies, so to speak.''

"The bastard,'' Adam growled.

"Truth to tell, I've never liked him much myself,'' Joe admitted. "You hit the nail right on the head. He *does* love his rules more than he loves any human being, himself included. He won't relax them. He's a fanatic.'' He grinned sheepishly. "They pop up among the best of us.''

"So...''

"So Paul—Sarah's father—and maybe one or two of the others will probably show up at my door next Sunday. They've never seemed especially comfortable with the decision not to look for the children. I think I've been appointed ringleader for the time being, so they'll hold the first new *Gemeesunndaag* here. We'll draw lots for the other deacons, appoint one of the existing ones to bishop. We'll vote to search for the missing kids. We'll vote to allow Katya special circumstances to separate from Frank, although divorce would never pass anywhere, not even with the New Order folks. And we'll vote for Mariah to keep her school. Though we'll probably have to build her a new one. We'll have to build a lot of new ones, actually.''

Adam smiled again. *That* was something he could do to keep busy for the time being, something he could handle. And they would need a house of their own, as well. Mariah's was so small it would barely get the three of them through the night, much less accommodate Katya and her brood, as well.

''That wasn't the whole settlement there today,'' Joe went on. ''There are probably fifteen or twenty other families who wouldn't join us. Needless to say, they haven't lost any kids themselves. And they sure as the dickens won't cough up any of the old school buildings for pagans the likes of us.'' He paused. ''This shakes the *Gemeide* right down to its foundations, Adam. We won't migrate as my folks did—there are just too many of us. But we'll start over. And we'll go on.''

''Yeah,'' Adam said. And he found a certain peace in that, in the continuity. It was new to him and needed exploration.

''Will you look for the other kids?'' Joe asked. ''Or was it you who sent the FBI?''

''The *FBI?* No. I called NCMEC.'' They both looked at Mariah at the same time, and Adam's heart swelled. But then, he really had known all along that she would call someone.

''We won't need either one of them,'' he murmured.

''We won't? What do you know that I don't?''

''Not what. Who.''

Jake would find them, he thought, if they could be found. Then again, the *Gemeide* wouldn't know what shaken up was until his brother started hanging around.

In the meantime, he would marry Mariah. He would get to know his son all over again, in a place where there was nothing to scare him. Katya would live with them for a while, until she could restructure her life. They would have dinner with the Lapps and the Lapps would have dinner with them, and maybe the new deacons would finally let Mariah back into the fold. Maybe, he thought, he would even join them himself.

Then Mariah looked across the room at him and smiled. It was a radiant look, one that could have brightened heaven. And he knew again that Sugar Joe Lapp had been right.

None of the maybes mattered, at all. He could deal with them, as long as he had her in his life.

Epilogue

If Adam hadn't been watching it with his own eyes, he would never have believed it.

The house was two stories, with a gray shingled roof. Its fresh plywood sides seemed to glow golden-brown in the sun, probably because another foot of snow had fallen the previous day and the contrast was enough to hurt the eyes. There were two dark brick chimneys already in place. Mariah's few pieces of furniture were inside. All that remained to be done was the siding—white, of course—and the digging of a well and a septic tank.

They had only started constructing the place that morning. He and Bo had been back in the settlement less than a week.

Adam left the workers—every able-bodied man of Sugar Joe's new *Gemeide*—and headed for the refreshment table for a quick breather. It was well below freezing, and even the sun felt cold. He thought he'd probably get used to that, too, sooner or later. In the meantime, he needed a very hot cup of coffee.

He pulled off his gloves and poured himself a cup. Mariah appeared magically by his side.

"Is everything all right?" she asked worriedly.

He looked at her. There was a small furrow between her eyes, and that made him frown. "Sure. Why wouldn't it be?"

She flushed a little. Because she couldn't quite take all this sudden good fortune for granted, she realized. She wondered if she would ever be able to.

"I keep expecting the bottom to fall out again," she admitted a little sheepishly.

His face softened. He tucked a strand of her hair behind her ear again. The wind had pulled it free. "It won't," he said quietly. "I promise."

She met his eyes, and she believed it. She let out a shaky breath. "You might have to remind me from time to time. For a while."

"My pleasure." Then he grinned. "Hey, I'm the one with all the distrustful Wallace genes."

She smiled faintly. "Oh, Adam, there's nothing wrong with your genes. But speaking of them, where is Bo?"

"Hopefully anywhere else but up in that elm." He looked at it again to be certain. No branches rustled. No childish faces peered out.

He closed his hands around the mug and held on, the warmth radiating through him. Or maybe it was her smile. It was growing as she looked around.

"This is so wonderful," she breathed.

"Damn if that Sugar Joe didn't turn out to be a hell of a guy," he murmured.

"Adam!"

He winced. "Sorry." Watching his language was another thing he was gradually getting used to. He'd had it pretty much down pat until he'd returned to Texas for two weeks, then he had fallen out of the habit. "I just meant it was good of him to give us these five acres."

Mariah shook her head quickly. "He gave us fair market price and he wasn't using them."

Adam remained quiet for a moment, unwilling to disabuse her of the notion. It was his opinion that Sugar Joe had given the land over for a song. Then, again, he was from Texas. He had a lot to learn about this place yet. Still, he knew that Joe was worried about how he would earn a living here, seeing as how farming was so obviously not his forte.

That too, would work out, Adam thought. In time. Someday,

he would wake up, and the answer would just be there, the way Mariah had once promised with Bo.

"We'll be in by tonight," he murmured, looking at the house, still amazed by that.

Her lips quirked into a smile. "It helps that we don't have to worry about a heating system or electricity."

"Yeah, it simplifies things. A phone would be handy right about now, though."

"Oh, Adam, you're still worried about Jacob."

He hesitated. "Not yet." Jake had vanished for brief periods before. "But I'm frustrated." He'd left innumerable messages for him in Virginia, trekking in to the village to use the pay phone each time. The problem was compounded by the fact that his brother couldn't simply return his call. Adam's messages had all been urgent pleas to get on a plane and come to the settlement. Jake didn't even know about the missing children yet. The messages said only that Adam needed him.

Worse, the FBI was royally botching the investigation. The values and ways of the Amish settlement stymied them, and they seemed incapable of working around them. Adam remembered grimly that Jake had always said that if something wasn't in the bureau's rule book, their agents were lost.

Adam's gaze found Simon Stoltzfus in the crowd, as well as Michael Miller's father. *I'm trying, guys.* Then he spotted Katya Essler, who was scurrying—or trying to scurry—here and there, being helpful. She was still on crutches. "How long do you think she'll be with us?"

Mariah frowned again. "Oh, Adam, I just don't know. Her situation is so...unprecedented."

He caught her hand. "Hey, I'm not complaining."

"She is."

"She *is?*"

"She feels useless. Like she's taking advantage of us."

"That's ridiculous! I thought you folks were so big on helping each other out."

"We are. But God helps those who help themselves, and Katya can't. Even if she could, even if her ankle were healed, she doesn't know *what* to do to make herself useful. She has no family, no husband. We have no farm. It chafes, I think."

"Well, we'll just have to find something for her to do."

Mariah smiled at him beatifically and tucked her hand into his. "Thank you, Adam."

"I've got to get back to work," he said reluctantly. "I can't stand here ogling you while three hundred other guys build our house in a single day."

She nodded. "No, that wouldn't be good."

"But I'd rather send everyone home and inaugurate that new master bedroom."

She flushed again. Her smile held. She was beautiful. "I'd like that, too."

"Later," he promised.

"Yes," she agreed breathlessly. "Later."

He kissed her lightly. "See you then, Mrs. Wallace."

Her color heightened and she beamed.

It was all working out, he thought again, going back to the house. It would all fix itself slowly, almost without conscious thought, in this land where time seemed to have stalled. The loose ends already seemed to be reaching for each other and tying together of their own volition.

Sugar Joe's new *Gemeide* had come together more or less as he had predicted it would. Sarah's father had joined them, and he would be their bishop. And Joe himself had drawn the lot pronouncing him to be one of the new deacons.

Adam hammered up siding, and thought about that little process, still with a good deal of bemusement. He hadn't been able to go to the church service to see it done, but Mariah had explained it to him. Being a deacon was an immense responsibility. Only the most power-hungry men would voluntarily embrace such a thing, and the concept of power didn't exist here. Aspiring for office was considered arrogant and haughty. So the people allowed God to make the choice.

The congregation of the *Gemeide* had nominated twelve married men for the positions. They needed three deacons, so three pieces of paper were then hidden in three hymnbooks. As the twelve men entered the service, they each chose one book at random from the table bearing them. At a time chosen by the officiating bishop, the books were opened and the fateful slips of paper appeared. The lot fell on the men as the Lord decreed.

Mariah had told him that the service would swell with emotion, then. Like a bolt of lightning, the stunning realization hit the three men that they would serve the congregation for the rest of their lives.

Sugar Joe already wore the burden well, Adam thought. He'd immediately initiated a vote to remove from their new *Ordnung* the ban against education. Learning in itself was not a sin—only using that knowledge to better oneself in society, to accumulate monetary things, to branch out into the *anner Satt Leit* world, would be an offense worth shunning. The new rule had freed Mariah from her *Meidung.*

For that alone, Adam figured he owed Sugar Joe Lapp his life. Mariah could—and probably would—continue teaching until they had too many children of their own to allow it.

His heart swelled at that possibility. He was not, after all, like his father.

As for Katya, Joe and the other new deacons had voted to throw the *Meidung* on Frank for crimes against his family, though it was a lost gesture because Frank chose to stay with the old *Gemeide.* And why not? Adam thought angrily. There he could bluster self-righteously every time Abner Fisher and Ethan Miller lamented the blasphemous behavior of his heathen wife.

The only thing Joe hadn't been able to fix was a recognized Amish marriage between him and Mariah. Their new *Gemeide* was nestled comfortably somewhere between Old Order and New, but in no settlement was a marriage recognized when the husband had not been baptized. As far as the congregation was concerned, though they had married legally several days ago in front of a justice of the peace, Mariah was living in sin. But just as when the teenagers enjoyed their *Rumspringa,* the people were, for the most part, ignoring that little detail.

For now. And the old *Gemeide,* headed by Mariah's father, certainly didn't agree. They were fairly apoplectic over what she was doing now.

Adam knew that eventually their situation would begin to raise eyebrows and bring censure upon them here, as well. But he needed more time. He had to be sure. He needed to be exactly sure what he was getting into, and at the moment, he didn't particularly want to ever find any of those little slips of paper in his hymnbook. He searched Mariah's eyes daily for any anger, for any resentment, but he never found it. She gave him time gladly. As she had calmly pointed out, children were given at least twenty years to determine whether or not they wanted to embrace the church. He, too, should have all the leisure he needed. In the meantime, they would "run around."

It would work out, he thought again. Slowly, surely, it would all come together. As Sugar Joe had said, the details weren't important, so long as he had her in his life.

If Jake would just turn up, he thought, then he would, all in all, be a very happy man.

He was thinking that, nailing away blindly, when there was a cracking sound and a scream from behind him. Adam swung around, his heart leaping, and watched Bo land at the foot of the elm.

He ran for him, bellowing. This time, Mariah got there first. This time, over three hundred other people converged on them as they knelt over his son.

"Oh, man, oh, man, I can't believe you did this *again!*" Then Adam choked his own voice off, acutely aware of the others.

He knew immediately that Bo's other arm was broken, the opposite one from that he had fractured four years earlier. Bo bawled and Adam gave in to rampant emotion—the guilt for not watching him, the disbelief that he would make the same mistake twice, the anger at him for disobeying, the sweet, sweet relief that it was only his arm, not his neck.

Then his eyes met Mariah's.

"You can yell at him," she whispered. "Adam, your face is purple. If you don't, you'll explode."

He said nothing. He felt a million eyes on him.

"Just, for heaven's sake, don't *swear*," she warned in an undertone.

He wanted to. Needed to. He smoothed Bo's hair back off his forehead with a trembling hand, as panicked as he had ever been in his life. Worse.

He wanted to run to the nearest hospital. But he'd given up his rental car. He looked around bleakly and all he saw were buggies and slow-plodding horses.

"Okay, sport. Okay. Let me think," he said hoarsely. Then the crowd around them parted.

Katya Essler limped through. "I...I can help," she said tentatively. "Please. My grandmother was a healer. She taught me a lot.'' She looked down at Bo's arm. ''At least I can set bones. I did my own Sam's just last year.''

Adam let out a quavering breath. It was just another answer landing in his lap, he realized, another thread tying itself up. He felt Mariah's hand in his. He finally nodded.

''Please, Katya,'' he said quietly. ''Help.''

She almost beamed as she bent over Bo.

This time, Adam realized, he wasn't alone.

* * * * *

Watch for MARRYING JAKE, the next instalment of the WEDDING RING trilogy, which is coming in August 1998, only from Silhouette Sensation®.

SILHOUETTE

Sensation

COMING NEXT MONTH

HIDDEN STAR Nora Roberts

The Stars of Mithra

She didn't know who she was, but she had a loaded gun, a diamond and more than a million dollars in her bag. Private investigator Cade Parris had to unravel this mystery fast. He needed to know just what sort of trouble she was in, because she was the woman he'd been waiting for.

THE BACHELOR PARTY Paula Detmer Riggs

Always a Bridesmaid

Sheriff Ford Maguire was curious about and attracted to single mum Sophie Reynolds. But she clearly had no intention of getting romantically involved with him. He wondered why... Ford wasn't the kind of man a woman could resist for long.

MACNAMARA'S WOMAN Alicia Scott

Maximillian's Children

Tamara Allistair was trying to find out what had really happened ten years ago, but someone clearly didn't like it. Her car had been sabotaged and all that saved her was her own skill and handsome renegade CJ MacNamara. CJ became her self-appointed protector; with him on her side, Tamara might be able to give love a try after all—if she lived long enough!

THE TAMING OF REID DONOVAN
Marilyn Pappano

Southern Knights

Reid Donovan was the original bad boy, but Cassie Wade didn't see him that way. Everything he wanted was suddenly within his reach. And then he was asked to walk away from it all. And when the FBI asked, he wasn't sure he had a choice. Would Cassie wait for him?

On sale from July, 1998

COMING NEXT MONTH FROM

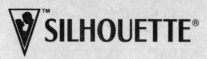 **SILHOUETTE**®

Intrigue
Danger, deception and desire

HER DESTINY Aimée Thurlo
RIDE THE THUNDER Patricia Werner
BEFORE THE FALL Patricia Rosemoor
BEN'S WIFE Charlotte Douglas

Special Edition
Satisfying romances packed with emotion

WHITE WOLF Lindsay McKenna
A COWBOY'S TEARS Anne McAllister
THE RANGER AND THE SCHOOLMARM Penny Richards
HUSBAND: BOUGHT AND PAID FOR Laurie Paige
WHO'S THE DADDY? Judy Christenberry
MOUNTAIN MAN Doris Rangel

Desire
*Provocative, sensual love stories for the
woman of today*

THE GROOM CANDIDATE Cait London
THE OFFICER AND THE RENEGADE Helen R. Myers
THE WOMEN IN JOE SULLIVAN'S LIFE Marie Ferrarella
BOSS LADY AND THE HIRED HAND Barbara McMahon
DR HOLT AND THE TEXAN Suzannah Davis
THE BACHELOR NEXT DOOR Katherine Garbera

On sale from July, 1998

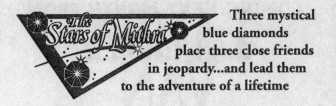

Three mystical blue diamonds place three close friends in jeopardy...and lead them to the adventure of a lifetime

SILHOUETTE SENSATION® brings you a thrilling new series by *New York Times* bestselling author

In JULY: HIDDEN STAR
Bailey James can't remember a thing, but she knows she's in big trouble. And she desperately needs the help of private investigator Cade Parris.

In SEPTEMBER: CAPTIVE STAR
Cynical bounty hunter Jack Dakota and spitfire M.J. O'Leary are handcuffed together and on the run from a pair of hired killers.

In NOVEMBER: SECRET STAR
Lieutenant Seth Buchanan's murder investigation takes a strange turn when Grace Fontaine turns up alive. But the notorious heiress is the biggest mystery of all.

LAURA VAN WORMER

⤝✦⤞

Just for the Summer

Nothing prepares Mary Liz for the summer she spends in
the moneyed town of East Hampton, Long Island. From
the death of one of their own, Mary Liz realises that these
stunningly beautiful people have some of the ugliest
agendas in the world.

*"Van Wormer,...has the glamorama Hampton's scene down to
a T. (Just for the Summer is) as voyeuristic as it is fun."*
—Kirkus Reviews

1-55166-439-9
AVAILABLE FROM JUNE 1998

4 FREE

books and a surprise gift!

We would like to take this opportunity to thank you for reading this Silhouette® book by offering you the chance to take FOUR more specially selected titles from the Sensation™ series absolutely FREE! We're also making this offer to introduce you to the benefits of the Reader Service™—

- ★ FREE home delivery
- ★ FREE gifts and competitions
- ★ FREE monthly newsletter
- ★ Books available before they're in the shops
- ★ Exclusive Reader Service discounts

Accepting these FREE books and gift places you under no obligation to buy; you may cancel at any time, even after receiving your free shipment. Simply complete your details below and return the entire page to the address below. *You don't even need a stamp!*

YES! Please send me 4 free Sensation books and a surprise gift. I understand that unless you hear from me, I will receive 4 superb new titles every month for just £2.50 each, postage and packing free. I am under no obligation to purchase any books and may cancel my subscription at any time. The free books and gift will be mine to keep in any case.

S8XE

Ms/Mrs/Miss/Mr ....Initials ....
BLOCK CAPITALS PLEASE

Surname ....

Address ....

....

....Postcode................................

Send this whole page to:
THE READER SERVICE, FREEPOST, CROYDON, CR9 3WZ
(Eire readers please send coupon to: P.O. BOX 4546, DUBLIN 24.)

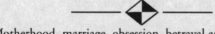